“YOU MUST WONDER WHY I HAVE COME,” SHE BEGAN . . .

“You see, I am here because I need someone to hold me. I—”

She got no further. He was there in an instant, and his arms closed around her with an eagerness that matched her own. He buried his face in the knotted hair on her crown. He whispered her name over and over, his voice sending a shiver down her spine, “I’ve scarce thought of anything else.” He stood there, holding her closely, savoring the feel of her.

“I don’t want you to let me go, Lucien,” she choked, clinging to him as though he were life itself.

“Do you know what you are wanting?”

She nodded. “More than anything in my life, Luce.” She raised her head and parted her lips. . . .

Autumn Rain

by

Anita Mills

AN ONYX BOOK

ONYX
Published by the Penguin Group
Penguin Books USA Inc., 375 Hudson Street,
New York, New York 10014, U.S.A.
Penguin Books Ltd, 27 Wrights Lane,
London W8 5TZ, England
Penguin Books Australia Ltd, Ringwood,
Victoria, Australia
Penguin Books Canada Ltd, 10 Alcorn Avenue,
Toronto, Ontario, Canada M4V 3B2
Penguin Books (N.Z.) Ltd, 182–190 Wairau Road,
Auckland 10, New Zealand

Penguin Books Ltd, Registered Offices:
Harmondsworth, Middlesex, England

First published by Onyx, an imprint of New American Library,
a divison of Penguin Books USA Inc.

First Printing, February, 1993
10 9 8 7 6 5 4 3 2 1

This book is dedicated

to

Martin L. Lovin

1935–1961

He was my Charley.

October 10, 1807

THE SOUND OF WATER thrown by the wheels mingled with the steady beat of the rain on the hard-packed road. Outside the carriage, the wind-strewn autumn leaves along the roadside provided the only brightness in an otherwise dreary day. From time to time, Thomas Ashton sighed heavily and wiped a trickle of water from the cracked window before it could seep onto the faded upholstery.

Elinor Ashton's head lay back against the worn squabs as she feigned sleep rather than speak with her father. Never ever would she forget the humiliation she'd endured earlier, the indignity of having full half the other girls hear him quibble over the paltry sum of five guineas, six shillings—her tuition for another year at Miss Roberts's Select Academy for Females in Upper Tilton.

The quarrel had been a loud one, with the usually reserved Miss Roberts insisting that she did not run a charitable institution, and if he would not make at least a token payment, he would have to take "dear Nell" with him. After a great deal of blustering, he'd done just that. And under the pretense of great affection, the other girls had lined the hallway watching her meager belongings carried down in a single trunk. Oh, they had kissed her and murmured fond farewells, but she knew that beneath the display there was a certain smugness.

She crossed her arms against the damp chill, pulling the braided frogs that closed her too-small brown merino pelisse even tauter over her breasts. At least at home, she consoled herself, it would be scarce noted that none of her clothes still fit her. She'd grown two full inches in the last year, but all her pleas for new gowns had apparently wound up in the fire with the tradesmen's bills. If her papa paid anything at all, and she was not at all certain he did, it must have been his gambling vouchers.

"Hungry, Nell?" he finally asked her.

She would have liked to ignore him, but the grumbling in her stomach made her sit up. "Yes," she said simply.

There was no mistaking her disappointment in him, but he could not help it. If she only knew how terrible things were, that only one hundred pounds stood between him and utter ruin, she'd feel differently. She'd know he'd had no choice. He cleared his throat.

"Send you back next year," he promised. "A man's luck cannot be forever bad."

"No," she answered noncommittally, leaving it to him to decide which she meant.

He'd wanted her to tell him that she did not blame him for it, but she was different from her usually complaisant mother and from his other daughters. The eldest of his brood, she could still remember when times had been better, when Thomas, Baron Ashton of Edgehill, had been held in higher esteem, when there had been money to spare. But that was before . . . Guilt washed over him, followed by a need to justify himself.

"If it hadn't been for the Corsican upstart—" he began.

"Yes, Papa," she said wearily, hoping he did not mean to launch into another tirade against the evil Napoleon had wrought. "It does not signify. You could not help that."

Her tone was flat and utterly unconvincing. "You don't understand, puss—had too much of m'money in the 'Change, and with the French blockading everything—dash it, there ain't any way to keep it!"

She sighed. "Perhaps if you had not gamed so much—"

Stung, he bristled. "I got to play if I am to come about, Nell—much you know of the matter."

She knew more than he thought she did, she told herself, turning to stare out into the steady rain. How could she help but know?—the last time she'd been home on holiday, she'd heard her mother plead with him to stop casting good money after bad, to try to keep what little he still had.

"I'll come about," he declared, scarce believing it himself. "It ain't your business to talk to your papa like this. If that's the manners the Roberts woman was teaching you, it's time you was coming home, anyways."

"Are you ever going to pay her?" she asked, cutting to the heart of the matter.

"For what? The woman insulted me, puss!" He wiped at the window again, then peered outside. "Blue Boar ahead," he muttered. "Won't stay—just eat. Got to press on to Edgehill tonight, lest your mama was to worry over you."

She knew that for a hum also. No doubt he did not want to spend the money to engage bedchambers for the both of them.

But the collection of carriages in the courtyard drew his attention. "Damme if it ain't young Townsend," he murmured. "Fellow plays deep. And Leighton! Well, now—ain't this something?" he added softly.

"Papa, I am not hungry," she lied, alarmed by his sudden interest.

"Thought you said you was."

"No."

"Well, I am." He rubbed his hands together and hunched his shoulders in anticipation. "Townsend," he repeated softly. "Luck's changing, Nell—I can feel it. Come on—got to get some food in you! Aye, and a warm bed for you also!"

* * *

The chamber was cold, the air damp, and she shivered beneath the bedcovers. She could do without a fire, her papa had insisted, but she knew it was because he would not pay for one. Her stomach still growled, for he'd ordered but bread and cheese for the both of them. Yet as she lay there, she could not help smelling the tantalizing aroma of onions and roasted meat wafting up the narrow stairs from the inn's kitchen. If only once he would think of food above his gaming . . .

Below, in one of the private parlors, she knew her papa played cards with a zeal born of desperation. It was folly, utter folly, on his part, for if he lost, she knew he could not redeem his vouchers. But "Bell Townsend is a plum ready to fall into my hands," he'd told her gleefully. "It's divine Providence, it is, Nell! A plum ready to fall into my hands!'' he'd repeated. ''Drinks too much—won't even know I'm fleecing him!''

Elinor pulled the covers more tightly beneath her chin and thought of her mother, wondering if she would worry when they did not arrive at home—or if she had already guessed what delayed them. Poor Mama. How disappointed she must be in her husband. Yet despite the quarrel Elinor had overheard, her mother never could be brought to criticize him before their daughters. All men gambled to excess, she maintained loyally, and Thomas Ashton was no different from the others. But Elinor knew that was not quite the truth—not all men wagered as much or lost as often as her papa. But someday it would not matter what he did, she told herself resolutely. Someday, she would make a brilliant marriage and take her mama and the girls away from Edgehill. And instead of scrimping for everything, she would give them pretty gowns and see her sisters properly launched. Someday she would be a great lady, surrounded by maids and footmen, with a grand carriage at her disposal. As farfetched as she knew the possibility to be, it was nonetheless a dream to be cherished.

For a time, she lay there, listening to the steady beat of rain on the roof, and tried to dwell on happier things, on times when everything did not depend on money. Finally, the chill ebbed from her body and she slipped into sleep to dream of a fairy world where she had exquisite, pretty things, where she was the Reigning Toast of the *ton*. In this netherworld, there were no other girls snickering behind her back because her gowns had been let out and still did not entirely cover her ankles.

The stairs creaked beneath heavy, unsteady footsteps, then there was a furious banging at the door. ''Nell!'' her father called out thickly, ''Let me in!''

She came awake with a start, and her heart sank. Judging by his voice, his news was not good—he'd probably begun losing as soon as he'd sat down to play. Rising with an effort, she stumbled to draw back the bolt. He lurched past her, muttering something about ''Thieves all—the pack of 'em, d'you hear me? Drew me in and fleeced me!''

''Oh, Papa! No!''

''And you—you'll hold your tongue, missy!'' Casting

about wildly, he sought the means to vent his fury. Taking the porcelain ewer from the washstand, he threw it against the brick-faced hearth, where it shattered into pieces. "I am cheated again—again!" he shouted, kicking a chair leg, sending it sliding across the floor. "Had Townsend down—ready to take it all! Leighton had already thrown in his cards, and Longford outwagered me—wouldn't take m'vouchers even! He had no right—no right at all! It was mine, I tell you—mine!"

She could see he was beside himself, and despite her own earlier anger with him, she sought to soothe him. "You'll come about, Papa—you will. Here—sit you down, and—"

"The devil take him—aye, and his money also! Got no right—earl or no, he's got no right—" His voice dropped into little more than a moan, and the wildness faded from his eyes as he seemed to shrink before her. "It's over, puss—I am done up," he said hollowly. "Might as well end it now. Got nothing."

"End it—end *what,* Papa?" she demanded, alarmed.

"Put a period to my existence, puss. I am done up now—done up, I tell you."

"But perhaps not all is lost—Mama's jewels—"

"Paste!" he snorted. "Paste—every one."

"Surely there must be something—"

"Edgehill is entailed for m'heirs—all else is gone. No, I am done! Done! And now there is Longford to pay also! Two thousand pounds he has stolen from me!"

"Two—two *thousand* pounds?" She gulped at the enormity of the sum. "Oh, Papa! How—"

"Told you—Townsend plays deep," he muttered, looking away. "Had to give 'em my vouchers to stay in the game. Then in the end, Longford refused to take any more of 'em." He ran his fingers over his face as though he could wake himself from a bad dream. "Me, puss—me as holds a peer's patent from the Tudors! And he refused to let me play further! Thing is—can't pay him—cannot pay any of 'em." His shoulders sagged with the realization of what he'd done.

"Well, perhaps if we went home—if we left now—you could stall—and . . ." Her voice trailed off. "Well, I am not tired, you know," she lied, "and if you cannot pay—we could go home before he collects—"

"Go?" he fairly howled, turning to her. "Go where? I tell you there's nothing! They'll be coming for m'furniture before you know it—and taking me off to prison!"

"Papa, there is my portion from Mama's mama."

"It's gone also," he retorted harshly. "No, I had the young fool where I wanted him—let him win a bit to get him there—and Longford—Longford—" Words failed him for a moment, then he seemed to regain his composure. His voice dropped. "Townsend was so disguised he could not count the spots on the cards, Nell, and Longford took the money," he recalled with disgust. "As if the de Clares need so much as a farthing—born rich, every one of 'em. You want to know the way of it, missy?" he demanded truculently. "Well, I'll tell you—them that has gets, and them that needs goes to jail!"

"Maybe if you went to this Longford and explained—that is, surely he would not expect to be paid before quarter day, and—"

"Surely," he mimicked her sarcastically. "Much you know of it, girl—bad fellow—blood's bad! Mad Jack de Clare's son! Much pity I could expect there. No, I got to pay him, else he'll take it out of my flesh. Devilish nasty fellow when he wants to be—got to think," he mumbled distractedly, running his fingers through his thinning hair.

"Maybe before we left—maybe I could speak with him for you," she offered. "If he saw what is happening to us—to Mama and the girls—"

"No. D'you think a man like Longford cares, puss?" But his gaze rested on her nightgown as though he were seeing her for the first time. "How old are you?" he demanded. "Sixteen?"

"You know I am fifteen," she reminded him. "I had my birth anniversary last month—September the seventeenth, to be precise. Mama made you sign the letter she sent." There was that in his eyes that disconcerted her, for there was nothing paternal in the way he regarded her. "I was born in '92."

"Pretty puss—say that for you," he mused slowly, his mind already racing. He walked around her speculatively. "Daresay the age could even be a help in the matter. Be the devil to pay if a fellow wasn't to do the right thing by an innocent," he murmured more to himself than to her. "Besides, some of 'em like a female as is green and biddable.'' He paused, his eyes on the front of her gown. His little Nell was no longer little at all.

''A woman grown, ain't you?'' he said softly, making her acutely conscious of the thinness of the lawn nightgown. His hand reached to smooth her coppery hair where it spilled over her shoulder. ''You've become a beauty, Nell, and I did not note it.''

The change in him frightened her, making her step back. ''As I am neither blond nor small, Miss Roberts quite despaired of me, Papa,'' she said, trying to speak lightly. ''She rather thought I ought to be a bluestocking, for she was positive I would never take. 'Carrot-tops are not the fashion,' she said.''

''The woman was blind, puss.'' This time, he caught her chin, forcing her to look up at him. For a long moment, he stared into brown eyes lightened with gold flecks around the pupils, making them seem to match the copper in her hair. Aye, there was no denying that with a little expense she could be an exquisitely lovely woman. As it was, she was going to keep him out of prison. ''Would you fancy yourself a viscountess, Nell?'' he asked, betraying his excitement.

''I am as like to be a royal princess, Papa—and well you know it,'' she retorted, pulling away. ''You have just told me I have no expectations.''

He could almost see the money in his hands. At best, Townsend would wed her, and at worst, the viscount would pay to scotch the scandal, for he could ill afford any more unpleasant gossip after that not quite hushed affair with Berkeley's wife. No, either way, Elinor was going to be her papa's salvation. He caught her shoulder, this time more roughly, and leaned into her face. ''Townsend's so gone with drink that Longford had to have help carrying him up to bed. He's in no state to harm you.''

She blinked blankly, trying to follow him. ''Harm me? Papa, whatever—?''

''You can save me, Nell—you can save your papa—and Edgehill also.'' He spoke urgently, intensely, hoping to persuade her. ''Aye, and you can provide for your sisters in the bargain.''

''Me?'' Her voice rose incredulously. ''Papa, I think it's you who are disguised!''

''Listen to me! Townsend's rich, Nell—richer than the

Ashtons has ever been—and he can make you a viscountess overnight."

"I don't want—"

His grip tightened painfully. "You'll do as I say in this, puss. All you got to do is go to his room, and I'll tend to the rest."

"Go to his *room*? Papa, I cannot!"

"Aye, you can. I told you—he's as out as if Gentleman Jackson had drawn his cork. And if he wasn't, I'd see as he didn't touch you until the ring was on your finger—I promise you that." Even as he spoke, he pushed her toward the door. "No time for faint hearts, puss—you got to do it."

"Papa!" she fairly screeched, "I am not even dressed!"

"All the better for the purpose." He reached for the doorknob, leaning to murmur against her ear, "When you are inside, sit down and wait. Better even if you was to lie down beside him." He spoke quickly, intensely. "Wait until you hear me pounding on this door. Then scream for me—do you hear? Your papa is going to take care of the rest for you."

"Oh, Papa—I cannot! No!"

"When I am done with the business, neither of us is going to want for anything—"

"It's madness! I'd not do it—Papa, I'd not! What if—?"

"Hush. It's for all of us—for your mama and the girls, too, Nell."

"Papa, there must be some other way," she whispered desperately. "I cannot—I cannot!"

"You've got to!"

As he thrust her into the darkened hallway, she struggled to free herself, but he held her arm tightly. Tears of humiliation welled in her eyes. If she cried out now, she would rouse the inn, they'd be thrown out into the night, and the whole *ton* would amuse themselves with the tale. If she did not, her father would accuse a stranger of the basest act, and unless this Lord Townsend wedded her, she would be utterly ruined. "Papa!" she wailed, only to have him clamp his other hand over her face, muffling her voice.

He half-dragged, half-pushed her toward a room at the end of the hall. Still holding her mouth, he released her arm to wrench the doorknob, muttering, ''Good—it's not locked—won't have to bribe the maid for the key.''

''Papa, don't—I beg of you, do not do this to me! If you love me at all, you will not—''

He shoved her inside and closed the door between them. She rattled the knob frantically, but apparently he held it from the other side. With no means of escape, she stood in the dark room, hearing now only the beating of her own heart in her ears. Her stomach knotted, making her totally, utterly sick, and for a moment, she feared the bread and cheese would come up.

Her eyes huge, she looked about the room apprehensively, seeing only faint outlines, shadows cast by the fire. Somewhere within, Viscount Townsend lay in a stupor, unaware of the awful trick about to be played on him. Perhaps if she tried to waken him, to warn him . . . then what? For one reason or another, her papa would go to prison. But if she said nothing until he came back, it was more like that it would be she who paid. As her eyes adjusted again to the darkness, she could see the bed.

Better even if you was to lie down beside him.

The image of an eternally angry husband sprang to mind, and she knew that, whatever the consequence, she could not do it. Very gingerly, she edged again to the door, hoping her papa had gone. She'd rather run.

''Don't move, else I'll shoot.''

She froze at the sound of the male voice, then spun around to see a man, his body bare where the covers fell away from it, sparking a candle in a reflector holder. The wick glowed as the spark took hold, then the orange flame grew, casting an eerie glow onto his face—and onto the barrel of an evil-looking pistol. To Nell, it was as though she faced the Prince of Darkness himself. An audible gasp escaped her.

''And I thought it was a respectable inn,'' he murmured, rising, revealing a decidedly masculine build clad in nothing more than rumpled breeches and stockings. ''I collect I forgot to lock the door. Deuced careless of me, but I was more than a trifle foxed myself.''

He spoke with a soft slur, but to her he appeared alarmingly awake. And he was big, considerably taller than her father. She stood rooted to the floor, now too afraid to flee, and yet even more afraid to stay. While her heart rose in her throat, he laid the pistol on a side table, then moved closer to peer through the shadows at her.

"Well, are you a thief—or Venus come calling *en deshabille*?" he asked softly. "I'd hear the answer." She turned and grasped the doorknob, only to have his hand close over hers. "No, you don't—not yet. If you are Leighton's notion of a gift—" He jerked her around roughly, forcing her to face him, and she could hear his sharp intake of breath. "Egad!"

"Please, sir—oh, please!"

Even in the faint light, he could see the girl was a beauty, and his irritation faded. "Well, well—he has taste, at least." His gaze raked over her, his glittering black eyes taking in her nightgown, and a faint smile curved his mouth. "Did he pay you—or do I?"

He was so close that she could smell the wine and feel the warmth of his breath against her cheek. But it was his physical size, the strength of the hand that held her that frightened her the most.

"It's a mistake!" she babbled. "I am in the wrong room! It's a mistake, I tell you!"

"I'll warrant it is," he agreed softly. "It always is." As he spoke, his other hand moved over her shoulder, his fingertips tracing the bone through the thin lawn.

"Please—"

"Please what?" His voice was little more than a husky whisper against her ear. "I always try to please."

"You do not understand—I—" To her horror, she realized he meant to kiss her. "Oh—no—I'm not—" But his lips silenced her, brushing lightly, then as his arms closed around her, his mouth was insistent, possessing hers, stifling her protest. His tongue teased, then plunged inside, shocking her utterly.

Her eyes were huge, luminous in the semidarkness, widening, then closing tightly as though somehow she could hide. She was going to play the innocent, but it didn't matter—she was also going to slake his rising desire. As his hands moved over her, feeling the warmth of her body through the thin cloth, she trembled against him. She ought to have been an actress, for she was good.

Despite her fright, she was somehow intrigued by the feel of him, and she could not help wondering what he meant to do to her. It was not until his mouth left hers, until his lips began tracing kisses along her jaw to her ear, that she dared to struggle, pushing at him, crying out breathlessly, "You don't understand! It's a mistake, I tell you! Let me go! Oh, please—let me go!"

Surprised, he released her and stepped back. His own breath was hot, uneven. "What the devil—? Is this a trap?" he demanded.

"It's nothing," she said quickly. "Please—I'd go, sir. There is no time to explain."

He was still between her and the door. "Who are you?"

"Who—who are you?" she countered nervously.

"Lucien de Clare. Lucifer. Longford. It doesn't matter."

"Oh."

"Come on—no faradiddles, if you please," he snapped impatiently. "I've half a mind to summon the constable, anyway." As he spoke, his hand caught her chin, cupping it, holding it with strong, warm fingers. "You appear a trifle young for this, you know."

"I—I—" Words failed her as she looked from his bare chest to the most striking countenance she'd ever seen. "I got lost," she managed to say finally, knowing it was a lame explanation. "I—I could not find my room."

One black eyebrow lifted. "In that?" he asked, disbelieving. Nonetheless, he let her go again. A faint smile played at the corners of his mouth. "In most assignations, it's the gentleman who goes to the lady's room, my dear," he added pointedly, his eyes once again on her nightgown. "It's more discreet."

"You think that I—oh, no!" Her chin came up. "You are mistaken, sir, I assure you. I am—or I was until now—in the schoolroom." As she spoke, she crossed her arms over her breasts. "I ask your pardon for the unseemly intrusion." She tried again, hoping to regain a semblance of dignity.

"No."

"But—but I've got to go before Papa comes looking for me," she said desperately. "Please—you do not understand! If he finds me here—"

The smile flattened, then one corner went down wryly. "I have faced angry parents before, my dear—angry husbands also." His black eyes seemed to bore into hers.

"You'll have to do better than that, you know. I'm not as green as Townsend. Who are you?" he repeated.

"Uh—Wilson—Miss Wilson—and I—"

"You lie badly, my dear."

Already she could hear her father calling loudly for her. "I—uh—I've got to go, sir. Good night."

She was too late. "Nell! Nell!" When she did not answer, her papa banged on the bedchamber door. "Nell!"

"Well, if you are lost, it would seem your parent knows where to find you, does it not?" Longford observed sardonically. Moving past her, he threw open the door.

"See here, sir—if one hair has been harmed, I shall demand satisfaction! My daughter is but fifteen, and an utter innocent—" Thomas Ashton stopped shouting suddenly and paled when he perceived the man before him. "Egad—Longford!"

The earl inclined his head slightly. "Ashton."

"It was the wrong chamber, Papa," Elinor tried to explain.

"Hold your tongue, Nell! Don't say anything!" he snapped at her, his color rising. "As for you, sir, I must admit I am surprised at your conduct. Despite all I have ever heard of you, debauching young girls is scarce—" He turned again to Elinor and demanded dramatically, "Did he touch you?" Before she could answer, he went on hastily, "Sir, I hope you mean to do the right thing in the matter. Nasty business, if this was to get out. But I ain't saying it ain't all a mistake, my lord. A little money to hush everything—"

She wanted to sink into the floor. "Papa!"

"You leave this to me, Elinor. You are too green to know what could have happened, but—"

"Cut line, Ashton!" Longford interrupted curtly. "I never pay where I have not played."

"Now see here—"

"Not a farthing."

"We are speaking of a young girl's honor," the baron responded stiffly. "She is but a child, sir—a child—a fifteen-year-old child too young to know what you are about! And I shall not stand idly by while my daughter's name is sullied!"

"Papa!" Elinor choked. *"Please!"* Her face hot, she

could not even look at Lord Longford. "I have already told him it was a mistake."

"The only sullying seems to be yours, Ashton. But if you wish to meet me over her—er—*honor,* I suppose I must oblige." There was no mistaking the derisive inflection he gave his words.

Thomas Ashton turned a pasty gray. *"No!"* he yelped. "No, of course not! Want to resolve the matter amicably, you understand. Both gentlemen, after all."

Although the mocking smile played again upon his lips, Longford shrugged. "Alas, but as you will recall, I have already wed my requisite widgeon. Rather publicly, too, and as this is England, I'm afraid I am not allowed two of them."

Seeing the Debtors' Door of Newgate opening before him, the baron could not help grasping at one last hope. "But your rep—if this was to be known—if this was to get out—"

"It would be said it was all of a piece with the rest," Longford snapped. "But for now, you bore me, Ashton."

"Bore you! Now, see here—"

"Bore me," the earl repeated. "So I suggest you get yourself off and take the chit with you before my oft regretted temper gets the best of both of us." He inclined his head slightly toward Elinor, and once again the faint, almost indiscernible smile curved the corners of his mouth.

"Good night, Miss Ashton. You can count yourself fortunate you are saved by Diana, my dear—she would tell you I am a damnable husband."

Mortified, she caught at her parent's sleeve. "Come on, Papa—*now.*"

As they passed Longford, her father muttered under his breath, "I could have sworn it was Townsend's room."

"It was, but there was a draft in mine, and I did not think poor Bell in any condition to know the difference," the earl answered. He waited until they were nearly out of earshot, then he added rather loudly, "Take the girl home and sell her on the Marriage Mart. She's a trifle young, but with her looks, you ought to get a good price for her."

The mockery in his voice seemed to follow them down the hall, and it was not until they reached her bedchamber that Elinor was able to speak. Turning to her father, she demanded, "Papa, how could you? I am your daughter! Have you no care for me at all? What if he'd ravished me?"

For a moment, hope seemed to flare in his eyes. "Did he take liberties? Tell your papa, Nell."

"No, of course not," she lied. "But he could have."

"Thought it was Townsend. I did it for you, puss."

"I am your flesh and blood, Papa!"

"Don't look at me like that! Do you think I wanted to do it? Thing is, if I was to go to prison for my debts, you and your mama and the other girls'd have to go on the rolls."

"I should rather earn my bread, I think."

"Come quarter day, I am done up," he went on morosely. "I got to do something, Nell—ain't any choice in the matter." A heavy sigh escaped him. "But we ain't done yet—I still got you."

After he left her, she burrowed beneath the covers and tried not to think about what had befallen her, but she could not help it. That her father's preposterous scheme had failed was small comfort now, for there was a chill within her that was as cold as the rain that beat against the roof. With sinking heart, she realized he would take the earl's advice, and he would do so quickly.

She lay awake for a long time, reliving the awful scene over and over, seeing the earl standing there, his body bared to the waist. She could still hear the contempt in his voice. She'd been wrong earlier—the humiliation of being turned out of school paled against this. Even in the safe darkness of her room, she wanted to hide, to run from ever encountering Longford again. In truth, she wanted to run away forever, but she knew she could not. For one thing, she had no place to go, and for another, she could not do that to her mother.

Finally, she forced herself to listen to the steady, calming rhythm of the rain, thinking wistfully of the safety of Miss Roberts's academy. But when at last she drifted toward sleep, it was the Earl of Longford's face she saw—and the black eyes and twisted smile of a man called Lucifer still mocked her. As she crossed her arms over her breasts, she could still feel the strength of his body against hers, and she could not help wondering what he would have done to her had she not broken away from his embrace.

Edgehill: October 31, 1807

HER HEART SANK when she saw him. For a moment, she clutched the doorknob for support and tried not to feel sick.

"Come in—come in," her father prompted impatiently. "Lord Kingsley wishes to gain your acquaintance." He turned to the thin, elderly man who stood by the fireplace, and he smiled proudly. "Is she not as I told you, my lord?"

The old gentleman leaned on his ebony cane, then moved rather deliberately to face her. He'd thought that Thomas Ashton in his eagerness for money had exaggerated, but he hadn't. He studied her silently, his face closed to his thoughts, lest he be taken in the bargain.

The girl before him was exceptionally pretty—slender but full-breasted, with the fine facial bones that gave promise of true beauty. And those eyes. He would have taken her for them alone, for he could not remember ever seeing the color before. They were, he reflected, a light, almost golden brown that reminded him of topazes. And that glorious red hair. But for all that she was precisely what he required, he continued to regard her shrewdly, wondering what Ashton would demand for her. Finally, he asked abruptly, "How old did you say she was?"

"Fifteen, but as you can see, she has grown beyond her years."

"Does she have any accomplishments other than her looks?"

"Tell him what you can do, Nell," her father urged. "Tell him what I paid for at the young ladies' seminary."

She did not want to meet the old man's eyes. Looking downward, she mumbled, "I was adequate in Latin and fair in Greek, my lord. But I excelled in literature and geometry."

Fearing Kingsley would think her a bluestocking, Thomas Ashton hastened to correct the impression. "Not that, puss—tell him how you can do the fashionable things!"

Elinor cast about in her mind for the means to discourage Lord Kingsley's interest. "Well, my watercolors were indifferent, and my music uninspired, but—"

"She's overmodest, my lord." Favoring his eldest with baleful eye, her father snapped, "I'd have you tell the truth, missy! None of this deprecation, you hear? Tell him how I have paid extra for a dancing master! Aye, and how you have excelled in your needlework! And how—"

"I am not interested in needlework," Kingsley interrupted him. His gaze still on the young girl before him, the old man reached to lift a lock of her hair from her shoulder. His fingers massaged it as though he studied the texture, then he let it slip through his fingers. "Does she use henna?" he wondered.

Thinking that perhaps Kingsley did not favor his daughter's red hair, her father hastened to answer, "No, but no doubt the color will change when she is older."

"It would be a pity if it did." The elderly baron leaned closer, peering intently into her averted face. When she would not look at him, he lifted her chin with one slender, bony finger. "Does she ever throw spots?"

"She is not given to freckles," Ashton assured him.

"I can see that," the other man remarked dryly. "But sometimes young girls get blemishes on otherwise impeccable skin."

"Never."

"I broke out last year," Elinor reminded him.

"It was the measles, my lord. Indeed, but her childhood complaints are behind her."

The finger dropped from her chin to her arm, tracing her arm through the muslin sleeve to her elbow, sending a shiver of revulsion through her. "She appears in good health."

"She is not given to megrims—are you, Nell?" Her father's manner indicated that even if she were consumptive, she had best not dare admit it. "Tell him how you have never had the headache."

"I had one last year," she remembered.

"It was with the measles," he growled at her through

clenched teeth. Turning again to Baron Kingsley, his manner changed. "Well, now that you have seen her, shall we speak frankly on the matter?" He waited, his breath seemingly abated, hoping against hope that the old man found her pleasing.

Kingsley continued to ignore him. His bony hand moved from her arm to her breast, and when she recoiled, he squeezed it. As blood rushed to her face, she pulled away, and before either of them could stop her, she ran from the room.

"Nell!" her father shouted angrily after her.

"Let her go," she heard Lord Kingsley tell him. "The child will get over her modesty. For now, I should rather have her meek than bold."

"I can assure you she has been sheltered, my lord," her father said. "Though I cannot think what you were about," he added a trifle stiffly. "It's beyond the bounds, sir. You'll give her a distaste of you."

The old man looked toward the open door, then dropped into a chair, sighing regretfully. "I did not mean to frighten the child, but there are young girls who resort to padding there, I am told."

"Well, you can see she is whole," Ashton insisted, trying to press him. "And if you do not want her, there is Langworthy . . ." He let his voice trail off, hoping he'd hooked Kingsley with the bait.

But the old man had not climbed from the trades by being outwitted. He sat there, mentally reviewing the girl, deciding what he would offer. She was young, lovely, malleable, and she would give him the consequence that his money alone could not buy him. Moreover, she could be made into the perfect display of his wealth. His only regret was that she was merely a baron's daughter, but he would not repine overlong on that.

"Well, my lord—?" Ashton persisted.

Tears of anger and humiliation stung Elinor's eyes, nearly blinding her. At the bottom of the stairs, she caught at the newel post, and too heartsick to go farther, she sank to sit on one of the treads. Waves of nausea swept over her as she listened while her father bargained her future away. Every fiber of her being seemed to revolt—it wasn't right—it wasn't fair! Surely God would not let him do it.

But in the salon, Thomas Ashton faced Arthur Kingsley, hating what he did, but knowing it had to be done. "I'd have twenty-five thousand in settlements, my lord."

"Preposterous!" the old man snorted. "I could get a duke's daughter for that, sir!"

"I offer you that rarest of gems," she heard her papa declare stiffly. "She will grow into a remarkable beauty—indeed, but she already shows promise of it."

"I should rather count her an uncut stone," Kingsley countered. "Each facet must be carefully done and polished before she shows to advantage."

"Still—"

"Ten thousand."

"I cannot allow it. I have need of more than that."

"And I had hoped for higher birth," the old man snapped.

"There have been Ashtons at Edgehill for four centuries, sir! Can you say the same for your family?" her father demanded angrily. "Of course you cannot! And naught's wrong with her birth—her mother is a Conniston!" Then, perceiving that perhaps the other baron was sensitive about the lateness of his title, Thomas Ashton backed off to try another tack. "There's not a man breathing as will not envy you for my Nell, Kingsley. And if she were to bear a child for you—"

The elderly baron cut him short. "I have an heir. My late son left a boy."

"Still—"

The old man's eyes narrowed shrewdly as he regarded Ashton. Very deliberately, he took out an enameled snuffbox, opened it, and held it out. "Would you take a pinch? It's excellent sort—East Indian, in fact."

"Thank you—no."

Kingsley snapped the box shut and returned it to his coat pocket. "A pity. Like everything else I have, it's the best I can obtain." For a moment, his blue eyes met Thomas Ashton's. "Tell me, my lord—and I shall expect you to be quite straightforward about it—how much do you owe?"

"What are you doing eavesdropping on Papa, Nell?" the girl whispered behind her.

"Shhh."

"I'll tell him."

"Be still. I am praying." Elinor leaned forward, closing her eyes tightly, and her lips moved fervently, silently, beseeching the Almighty to deliver her from the old man. Twelve-year-old Charlotte Ashton plopped down on the stairs next to Elinor.

"Whatever for?"

"Papa is trying to sell me to Baron Kingsley," the elder girl answered through clenched teeth. "I'd not do it. Now *will* you cease prattling?"

"How diverting," Charlotte murmured. "Is he rich and handsome?"

"He's *old*!" Nell retorted. "Be quiet."

Thomas Ashton appeared to be considering the question still, then he finally cleared his throat. "That, sir, is none of your affair."

"Then the ten thousand is my last offer," Kingsley told him coldly. "We are wasting our time."

"Dash it, sir—ten thousand will not do it!"

"Your debts, Ashton."

Again there was a pregnant silence, then the girls heard their father admit, "It will take sixteen thousand in the least, and I should like to have enough beyond that I may settle something on my other daughters. And of course I should expect—"

"It's never wise to expect another man's money. How do I know you will not come to this pass again?"

"I assure you—"

"A gamester's word is no better than that of an opium eater—both will lie to satisfy their habits," Kingsley responded acidly. "And I'd have my wife's family do me credit."

Hope rose in Elinor's breast, then was dashed almost immediately when the old man added, "But I am not adverse to extending you an allowance, Ashton—shall we say something in the area of two thousand per year?—and the clearance of your current debts, of course. The latter I will settle once and once only, you understand."

The younger baron had hoped for more, and he stalled, thinking perhaps to gain a little more. But Kingsley was impatient. "It will not support further gaming, but it's all I mean to pay, so you may accept it or we are done. A little economy and you can live quite comfortably on that, Thomas."

"The other girls—"

"I should not expect my wife's relations to come to London as paupers, but"—the old man paused, fixing Ashton with his gaze—"but I shall merely frank their entry into society when the time comes."

"Dash it, but—they cannot make matches without money!"

"You may give it out that I mean to settle decent sums on them—upon their marriages, of course."

"How much?"

"Shall we say five thousand? That ought to gain them respectable offers."

"The money—"

"The money goes to their husbands."

It was an utterly demeaning arrangement, but knowing that he faced complete disgrace without Kingsley's money, Ashton exhaled heavily and capitulated. "I would like the matter expedited. I'd have my creditors know they are to be paid."

"Send them announcements of the wedding." The old man leaned forward and favored Thomas Ashton with a thin smile. "I shall apply directly to the archbishop for a special license. Shall we say the sixteenth of December at Stoneleigh? It will allow me to have the house put in order for her by then."

"Stoneleigh? I'd thought Edgehill—"

"I do not travel much in winter, sir."

"It's soon. I'd thought to give her more time—she is but fifteen, and—well, once my creditors are told, there is no need for unseemly haste in the matter. Perhaps when she is sixteen—"

"I do not mind that she is young, Ashton—quite the contrary," the elderly baron countered. "Lady Kingsley will be precisely what I choose to make her."

"Still—"

"The sixteenth," Kingsley declared flatly. "I shall be giving a country party for her directly after the first of the year, where I may observe how she goes on in company." His gaze met Thomas Ashton's as he added meaningfully, "You are welcome to extend invitations to those who hold your most pressing vouchers, of course." He smiled thinly. "That should delay any foreclosures, I believe."

"I should not expect many to travel to Cornwall."

"The weather is milder there than here." Kingsley rose and leaned on the narrow ebony cane. "But I leave it to you to determine whom to tell. I shall, however, expect a rather complete accounting of your indebtedness for my solicitor before the settlements are drawn."

"Of course. And the allowance?"

"The allowance will commence upon the marriage, Ashton. Not one day sooner."

"You will frank the wedding?"

"As it's to be a small affair—I do not think any but her family would wish to be present—I cannot expect the expense to be great, but yes, I will." Balancing his weight on one hand, the old man reached into his coat and drew out a slim leather folder. Using his thumb, he counted out a number of crisp banknotes. "Here is five hundred pounds for the girl. See that you use it to purchase her some decent gowns before she comes to Stoneleigh."

"You are most generous, my lord."

"No insipid colors, mind you—and no stinting. And, as in the case of the other, I shall expect an accounting of every farthing. I'd see it expended on the girl and nothing else."

Trying not to betray his chagrin, Thomas Ashton bowed slightly. "It will, of course, be as you wish."

"See that it is. I did not gain my wealth by consorting with fools, sir."

"He's coming out!" Charlotte hissed excitedly. But as the black-coated figure moved slowly into the hall, and she could see his narrow, stooped shoulders, she gasped, "Lud—is that Kingsley, Nell?"

"Yes."

Instinctively, the younger girl clasped her sister's hand for comfort. The old man looked up, seeing them, and his thin mouth curved into another smile. He raised his cane to Nell. "You must not fear me, my dear, for I mean to treat you well. Indeed, but once you are at Stoneleigh, you shall want for nothing."

Elinor pulled away from her sister, and, covering her mouth, ran up the stairs. She did not stop until she reached the safety of her room, and then she was heartily sick in the washbasin. She retched violently, bringing up the contents of her nuncheon, until there was nothing left. Finally, she flung herself facedown onto her bed and cried.

"Here now, missy—what's this?" her papa asked from the door.

"I won't wed him," came the muffled reply. "I won't!"

He deeply regretted what he had done, and he felt for her, but he had to make her understand. "Aye, you will, Nell."

"I'd rather die!"

He moved closer, reaching out to her, then he sighed. "I had to do it, puss—I had to." When she said nothing, he dropped to sit beside her. "I did it for you, Nell. And for the other girls. Would you see them on the street? Would you have them begging for parish alms?"

"Papa, I cannot!" she wailed.

"Aye, you can." With uncharacteristic gentleness, he smoothed the copper hair against the back of her muslin gown. "Nell—"

"How could you?" she demanded miserably, her face buried in the covers. "He's old! And—and you let him touch me!"

"He is sixty-one, puss." He leaned over her. "Think on it—the man's rich as Croesus, Nell, and he cannot live forever. You'll be a rich widow before long," he reasoned softly. "You'll want for nothing—nothing. You'll have jewels, fancy gowns—a hundred servants to do your bidding—and you will be in a position to help your sisters."

"I am but fifteen, Papa! I have my own life yet to live!"

"I know, puss. I would that we could wait, but we cannot. As it is, I know not if I can fob off my creditors another month even. I had a note of Longford the other day—and that is not to mention the dozens of tradesmen—well, I have to count it a stroke of fortune that Kingsley wants you." When she did not move or speak again, he rose and stood awkwardly over her. "Someday you will understand, Nell—someday you will believe I do this for you." Her shoulders shook silently, shaming him. "Aye—one day you will remember and thank me for this."

"No."

"Nell—" It was useless. There were no words to ease what he did to her. Sighing heavily, he turned away.

As he left, she bit her knuckles to stifle an awful urge to scream. Thank him? she cried in silent anguish. For what? For selling her into an old man's arms? For denying her the love of a younger, stronger man? For a time, she wept pitifully into the bedcover, telling herself she would remember this day forever—it was the day her girlish dreams died.

She knew not how long she lay there, only that everything seemed to hurt from the hollowness in her chest to the ache in her throat. Beneath her, the covers were soaked with her tears until it seemed there could be no more, but there were.

The bed creaked beside her, and she felt her mother's hands upon her shoulders. "Dearest Nell," she crooned softly, smoothing the tangled hair.

For answer, Elinor turned into her mother's arms and sobbed. "Don't let him do this to me, Mama—I beg of you—" She choked, unable to go on as she was drawn into the comfort of her mother's lap.

For a time, they rocked together, a woman and a girl of nearly equal size, and the bed creaked against its posts. All the while Mary Ashton stroked her daughter's hair. Finally, against the comfort of her mother's breasts, Elinor ceased sobbing.

"You won't let him sell me, will you, Mama?"

Mary felt as though her own heart was breaking, and she had to wipe her own streaming eyes before she answered. "Nell—oh, Nell, I would that things were different," she whispered, betraying her anguish.

It was then that Elinor *knew*. There was no one to help her, no one to save her.

"I'm sorry, love." Even as she spoke, Mary's chin quivered and the tears spilled onto her cheeks. "But you will survive, Nell," she added fiercely. *"You will survive."*

"Oh, Mama—I cannot!"

"Yes, you can. Look at me, Nell—look at me! Do you think I wanted to wed a gamester? Do you think I wanted to live like this?" Her slender fingers brushed the tangled strands back from Elinor's face. "But I have survived, dearest—I *have* survived! And you will also."

"Mama—"

"No. Listen to me, Nell. At least Lord Kingsley is old. You will not have to suffer a lifetime before you are freed. Thomas says he is over sixty, you know—and how many live much longer than that? Next year—or the year after—or the year after that, you will find yourself alone and well fixed."

"I don't want—"

"Hush, dearest. Neither do I. But when he is gone, there will be someone else to cherish you. You will still be young, Nell."

"And Papa will sell me again," the girl reminded her bitterly.

"No. I have wrung from Thomas the promise that the next choice is yours."

"How?"

"I have told him that I will leave him before I let this happen twice." Mary Ashton's mouth twisted as she met her daughter's startled gaze. "I would have this time, but for you and the girls. Don't you see, Nell?" she pleaded. "This is the only way we have. But there will be no next time—not like this—again. Even if I have nowhere to go, I will leave him."

"Oh, Mama." Elinor's arms closed around her mother's neck. "When Lord Kingsley dies, you can live with me."

"Nonsense. You will have a far different life than that we live here, dearest." Very gently, she disengaged her daughter's arms, and forced a watery smile. "Your papa really believes he does this for you."

"It's because he could not leave the cards and dice alone," Elinor retorted, rubbing at her swollen eyes.

"It's a weakness he cannot help, I'm afraid. And weak men make excuses that they come to believe." Mary Ashton rose from the bed and turned away. "I did try, you know."

To Elinor, it was as though the last gate had closed, trapping her. "I know," she managed miserably. "But I shall hate Lord Kingsley—I know it."

Later, when all tears were spent, when she could do naught but stare into the faded canopy over her bed, Elinor heard her father's words again. *You'll want for nothing—nothing. You'll have jewels, fancy gowns—a hundred servants to do your bidding—and you will be in a position to help your sisters.* What had the vicar once preached? *Be careful what you seek.* Well, even God was against her, she decided bitterly, for He'd fulfilled her dreams in the cruelest way. She'd dared to hope for someone young and handsome like Longford. Instead, she faced a life with an old man.

Stoneleigh, Cornwall: December 16, 1807

IT DID NOT SEEM possible that this was happening to her, but after six weeks of tears interspersed between frenetic shopping and fittings, Elinor Elizabeth Anne Ashton faced her unwanted bridegroom in the elegantly appointed saloon and said the words that bound her to him, while her mother wept silently behind her. To her credit, the girl did not even flinch when he slipped the ring onto her finger. Telling herself that she no longer cared, she allowed Arthur Charles William Kingsley to lead her to the parish book, and there, on the carefully lined and numbered vellum page, she signed her name.

It was over. At fifteen, she was married. She now belonged to a man more than twenty years older than her own father. She stepped back, and her parents signed for witness. Behind her, her husband's grandson, a boy her own age, murmured his good wishes.

It was over. There would be but the elegant, intimate supper, an hour or so of quiet conversation, and then . . . her thoughts stopped there. She was not at all certain what to expect later. Whatever it would be, it would not matter either, she told herself. She cast a sidewise glance at her elderly bridegroom, wondering if he knew how much she wished him dead. Not dead precisely, she corrected herself guiltily. Just gone. Anywhere.

"Tired, my dear?" Arthur Kingsley asked her solicitously.

"No."

"Nonetheless, I should insist that you rest before we dine. I'd not have you out of looks tonight."

"Really, I—"

"Lord Kingsley is quite right, dearest," her mother

declared a trifle too brightly. "I shall be happy to go up with you."

"Go on, puss—plain to see your husband has business with me," Thomas Ashton said. "Got to be obedient—no time to argue with the man."

"Papa—"

"Not to look at me, Nell—got to learn to look to him."

"I want to go with Nell," Charlotte announced.

"Me, too," a six-year-old Frances chimed in.

The elderly baron exchanged a significant glance with Elinor's mother, making her color uncomfortably. "Yes, well—really, but I think Lord Kingsley has ordered entertainment for you, my dears," she murmured. "And I should like a few moments alone with Nell."

Dismissed, Elinor trod the stairs slowly, reluctantly, to the elegant bedchamber above. Behind her, her mother sucked in her breath. "Well, you cannot say he does not value you," she murmured. "I vow I have never seen the like."

"Yes," the girl answered without enthusiasm. "I shall be like a bird in a golden cage."

"It's not forever, dearest."

"I doubt he will die today, Mama."

"No—no, of course not. Indeed, you should not wish it—the settlements—"

"Hang the settlements, Mama!" Elinor cried. "Is that all any can think on? What about me? I am your daughter!" Looking around her, she sighed. "Your pardon, Mama—I do not blame you for this. But Papa—"

"There was nothing he could do—the situation was quite desperate."

"I know. It's done, in any event, isn't it?"

The girl studied the rose silk-covered walls, the ornately painted ceiling, the marble-faced fireplace, the elegant, polished mahogany furniture—and the high, four-poster bed with its floral damask hangings. Her mother followed her gaze, then cleared her throat.

"You are a married lady now."

"I don't feel it—I don't feel any different at all, Mama."

"Yes—well, no doubt you will." Her mother hesitated, then blurted out, "Do you have any notion, Nell—about tonight, I mean?"

Elinor started to say that Miss Roberts did not teach about that at the academy, then forebore. It was childish to lash out now, and whether she wished it or not, she was no longer a child. "No," she answered finally.

It was the first time she could remember her mother ever blushing. The older woman sank into one of the French chairs and looked away, her face reddening uncomfortably. "Well," she began, "I did not think so, of course." For the briefest moment, her brown eyes met Nell's, then she hastily averted them again. "I cannot know precisely what Lord Kingsley will wish, but—" Words failed her, then she collected herself. "You must not struggle when he lifts up your nightgown, dearest."

"Lifts up my *nightgown*, Mama?" the girl demanded incredulously. "Surely he would not!"

"Yes, well—he will do a great deal more than that, I'm afraid. He might even prefer that you take it off entirely."

Elinor regarded her mother suspiciously. "Why?"

"Well, he is your husband—and—and"—she floundered a bit, then blurted out—"and it gets in the way."

"In the way of what?" the girl asked bluntly. "Mama, what are you trying to say?"

By now, the woman's face was a deep red. Nonetheless, she drew in a deep breath, then persevered. "Well, you know the Bible does say that the two shall become one flesh, you know. And once you are wed, your body becomes your husband's property, so to speak." She fixed her gaze on one of the roses woven into the thick carpet. "He has the right to touch you anywhere he pleases, Nell. Even—even down there. There—I have said it."

"Down where? Mama—*where*?"

"In your most private places."

Revulsion washed over her. "I think I should rather die," Elinor declared flatly.

"It's the way of things between a man and a woman." Her mother rose quickly. "Yes—well, you ought to rest, dearest—truly you should. I know it's a trying day for you."

"Mama—"

"And you must not think I do not feel for you. However, I know that you will survive—we all do. You have but to lie there and let him have his way."

"Mama!"

"It will soon be over, anyway. Men are selfish creatures, you know." She leaned over to brush a kiss against her daughter's cheek, then embraced her, squeezing the girl's stiff shoulders. "On the morrow, you will think you worried for naught, I assure you."

After she left, Elinor lay wide-awake upon the high bed, staring up into the rich canopy, trying to imagine what Arthur Kingsley would do to her. But every time she thought of him touching her *there*, she felt sick in the pit of her stomach. Surely he would not expect anything like that. But she knew he would.

* * *

The wedding supper was a sumptuous, elegant repast served for only five, with Elinor's sisters taking their meal elsewhere in the house. As it was, a footman had placed Lord Kingsley at one end of the table and her at the other, with her parents on one side and young Charles across from them. Aside from murmurs of approval as each new dish was presented, there was little conversation beyond her father's forced attempts to engage Kingsley. For her part, Elinor could scarcely taste any of it, her mind dwelling gloomily instead on what would befall her later.

Finally, her father noted her, and his voice boomed out, "Here now, puss—don't look so pulled! You got Christmas coming, and after, Kingsley's giving you a party! Ain't that so, my lord?"

"Indeed." The older baron nodded. "We are accustomed here to having tenants and neighbors call after the holidays, of course, but this year I should like to have a somewhat larger affair to introduce Elinor to Cornish society."

"Be a bang-up affair, from all I have heard of it." Charles Kingsley spoke up. "Wish I was to be here, but I got to go back to school—unless Grandpapa relents."

"I am sure Elinor will write you about it, won't you, my dear?" the old man said smoothly. "I have hopes you will be friends, after all." He turned his attention to Thomas Ashford. "If you are meaning to invite any," he added meaningfully, "you'd best give over your list to Pemberly, that the cards may be posted forthwith."

"I doubt any would wish to travel this far, but I'd thought Longford—and perhaps Collinson—and Carstairs. They are among the more pressing ones."

"Longford?" Elinor looked up, surprised. Then, recalling her encounter with the earl, she dropped her head, reddening. "Oh."

Arthur Kingsley's eyebrows rose, and he frowned. "I shouldn't think—"

"Oh, she don't know him—do you, puss?" her father hastened to warn her. "But you yourself said—" He looked to his aging son-in-law. "That is, I thought—"

"Man's a devil!" Charles Kingsley snorted.

"That will be enough, Charles," his grandfather said sternly.

The boy lapsed into silence, piquing Elinor's curiosity. "What has he done?" she inquired cautiously.

"A sordid affair, I'm afraid," the old man murmured. Looking again to her father, he explained, "No doubt you cannot have heard it yet, but it will be a dreadful scandal when it's known."

Her father shook his head. "His damnable temper, I should suppose. Fellow can be deuced unpleasant when he wants. Still—"

"It wasn't a duel," Charles piped up again. Then, perceiving the old man's frown, he dropped his eyes and stabbed at the meat on his plate.

"I'm afraid he's done it this time. Wilcox, carry the peas to Lady Kingsley, if you please."

"Thank you, Wilcox, but I have had enough," Elinor told the footman, shaking her head. "But what has this Longford done?"

"It's not a fit matter for your ears, my dear," Lord Kingsley told her.

"Yes, well—if you do not wish it, I shall not ask him," his father decided. "Any objection to the others, my lord?"

"I have no objection to any of them, not even Longford, my dear Thomas. I merely meant that I doubt he will wish to show his face anywhere."

"He don't care," Charles declared. "Had it of m'friend Fenton that he don't."

"Fenton?" Elinor's father asked. "Ain't he married to a Fenton?"

"Yes. Next time, dear boy, you may dine with the children in the nursery," the old man said, glowering. "When I say enough, I mean enough."

"Yes, sir."

The brief diversion thus ended, the meal again became an ordeal of silence for Elinor. She found it rather irritating that she was somehow old enough to wed, yet too innocent to hear the tale of Longford's scandal. Briefly, she considered cornering the hapless Charles after dinner, then realized she probably would not get the chance. Yet as she pushed her food around her plate, she could not help wondering about the black-haired, black-eyed earl who'd told her he was a damnable husband.

Mercifully, no one was inclined to linger over dessert, a confection of sponge cake soaked in rum-laced, sweetened cream, and thus supper came to an end. As the last covers were removed, Lord Kingsley raised his half-empty wineglass to her.

"To Elinor—my lovely, lovely little bride." As her father joined him in the toast, her husband added, "No doubt you would wish to retire, my dear. I shall join you directly."

She'd expected to withdraw with her mother, to share a glass of ratafia or punch with her. Casting about helplessly for the means to delay, she directed a mute appeal to her mother, who merely looked away. Finding no ally, she rose, trying not to betray her nervousness. "Of course, my lord," she managed, dry-mouthed.

"Good night, puss," her father told her.

"In the future, you will address her as Elinor," Lord Kingsley declared coldly. "I had meant to mention that to you earlier, Thomas. She is my baroness now, and as such must command the dignity of her station."

Holding her back straight, she left the room, hearing her father change the subject once again to the Earl of Longford, wondering aloud what the "young devil" had done. She lingered as long as she dared, wanting to know also.

"It's scarcely fit for Lady Ashford's ears, either," Kingsley protested. Then, lowering his voice, he continued, "It will out anyway, I suppose, but Charles had it of young Fenton, the girl's brother, a schoolmate at Harrow."

"Yes—yes," her father interrupted impatiently. "Had what?"

"My dear Thomas, Longford's wife has made him the laughingstock—cuckolded him with Bellamy Townsend."

"Cannot say I blame her," her father admitted. "Fellow's cold. But I thought Townsend was his friend."

"Ah, but she played him false before he got his heir," Lord Kingsley reminded him. "The odd thing was that he didn't call Townsend out."

"I should have thought he'd have killed him anyway. Man's got pride, you know."

"Well, Townsend ain't a complete fool!" Charles snorted. "He wouldn't have gone anyway—denied everything even when caught! Said he was in his cups! Said he wasn't the only one, too. Named a couple of others."

"How very loyal of him," Lady Ashton murmured sarcastically.

"Yes, well, the short of it is that Longford has sued for a separation from his wife, claiming adultery," Kingsley explained.

"Case of the proverbial pot, ain't it?" the boy insisted. "Like there ain't any as knows of his bits of fluff."

"My dear Charles"—the baron's voice was pained—"adultery is not an offense for a man."

"Is he going to sue young Townsend?" Lady Ashton wondered.

"Aye, but it's worse than that—when he was collected of Townsend, he has told the Fentons he means to seek a divorce."

"A divorce!" she gasped. "But the scandal—he will not be received!"

"Precisely," Kingsley agreed. "There is enough dirty linen there to send 'em both into exile for life. And even if he were, which he will not be, a man of his pride will need time to lick his wounds before he comes about. But we tarry needlessly—do you join me for a bit of brandy before you retire?"

Afraid that her mother would come out and catch her eavesdropping, Elinor hurried on up the stairs. But as she reached the top, she fought the urge to flee, to hide from her aged bridegroom. For a moment, she considered it, then thought of her father going to debtor's prison, of her mother struggling to provide for the girls on a pittance from the poor roll, and she knew she had to stay.

Despite the warmth of the fresh-laid fire or the beauty of the room, she wished fervently for her small chamber at Edgehill. When a maid came up behind her, she jumped, panicked.

"Would your ladyship be wishful of assistance?" the girl asked her. The girl. The maid was actually older than she was. When Elinor did not answer, she went into the room and began laying out a new embroidered lawn nightgown and a silk wrapper. "Ohhh—how lovely," she crooned, fingering the delicate stitching at the neck.

"I—I should like something to drink, I think," Elinor managed to say.

"I could bring ye a pot o' tea—or a bit of ratafia," the girl offered. "Name's Mary, by the by."

"Actually, I should prefer something a bit stronger. Mary," she mused half to herself, "it's my mother's name also."

The girl laid aside the nightgown and surveyed Elinor sympathetically. "Never liked the name myself, ye know—always thought it plain. But aye, I'd wager ye'd take the stronger stuff. If ye was to want me to, I suppose I could get something outer his lordship's cabinet—if that hateful Daggett ain't in his room, you understand."

"Daggett?"

"His valet. Would ye have a finger or two of brandy—or a bit of port?"

"Brandy would be fine."

"Ever drink any?"

"No."

"Well, ye'd best drink it slow-like, else ye'll choke yerself on it."

"Thank you, Mary."

"Ye don't have to thank me. If it was me, I'd be a-drinking it also."

The maid brought the decanter and a glass. Dismissing her, Elinor undressed quickly, donned the nightgown and wrapper, poured herself a full glass of the liqueur, and carried it to a chair before the fire. Outside, the wind came up, and a burst of rain sprayed the windowpane beside her. The thought crossed her mind that it might sleet as she sank down and began to drink of the potent, fiery liquid. The maid had been right—as the first of it burned her throat, Elinor choked, and tears welled in her eyes. When she finished coughing, she resolved to sip it slowly, to let it warm her mouth before she swallowed. She sat there drinking, listening to the storm, watching the licking flames, trying not to think of Lord Kingsley.

She was on her third glass when he came up. As the door opened and closed behind her, she dropped it, spilling the liquid onto the hearth. A splash ignited, flashing outward, and the old man hastened to beat out the trail of fire on the marble before it reached the expensive rug. "What the devil are you doing?"

"I—I was having some brandy." She took a deep breath, then blurted out, "It was to help me sleep."

"I cannot abide a sotted female, Elinor," he told her coldly. "In the future, you will not partake of wine when you are not in my presence." Abruptly, his manner changed. To her horror, he moved closer and lifted her hair from her shoulder. "Lovely. It's like copper-colored silk. Fashion or no, I'd not see you cut it." He let the hair fall, and his hand slid to her shoulder, tracing the bony line to her neck, then upward to her jaw. "Has anyone told you what an exquisite creature you are?" he asked, his voice raspy.

"No—no." Disconcerted, she pulled away and tightened the sash on her wrapper.

The gesture was not lost on him. "You must not be missish before me, Elinor. Take it off."

"Uh—"

"The wrapper, Elinor. Take it off," he repeated.

"No."

"I'd see what I have paid for."

"I—I cannot."

"If I have to ask again, I'll take my cane to you."

She wanted to scream for aid, but knew none would be forthcoming. For a long moment, she met his glittering gaze, then she took a deep breath. With shaking hands, she untied the sash and let it fall at her feet. Turning away, she removed the silk wrapper, folded it, and lay it over the back of a chair. When she turned around, she realized that he had taken off his coat and cravat and was unbuttoning his vest.

"Curst buttons," he muttered. "I need your help."

"Your valet—Mr. Daggett—"

"I'd have you do it."

Her whole body trembling now, she held out her hands. "I—I cannot!"

He stared at her hard for a moment, then seemed to relent. "That fool did not tell you anything, did she?"

"I beg your pardon?"

"Your mama."

Heat flooded her face. "No," she lied.

"Take off the gown and get into bed."

"Please—could I not leave it on—just tonight, I mean? I—uh—"

"Get into bed."

"My lord—"

"My name is Arthur," he cut in abruptly. "You will use that when we are alone and Kingsley when we are in company. The title came dear to me, and I'd have none forget it." He finished with the vest and removed it. "I'd hear you say it."

"Kingsley?"

"Arthur." His thin, bony fingers worked at his shirt. When she said nothing, he again moved toward her. "Well?"

"I am getting into bed—Arthur," she mumbled, scrambling for the covers.

"Good."

She pulled the bedcoverings up to her chin and did not look at him as he finished undressing. But as each garment came off, her heart seemed to rise higher in her throat. By the time he blew out the candles, she was nearly rigid with terror. She could hear the rustle of the bedhangings, then feel the slight dip in the mattress as he crawled in beside her. For a long moment, there was no sound beyond the reverberation of her heartbeat in her ears and the high, reedy pitch of his breathing. She lay very still until she felt his fingers gather the cloth of her nightgown, pulling it upward, then she flinched.

"Oh, please—no. Not yet."

"Lie still."

She froze when his hand slid up her thigh to touch her, and then a cry of revulsion rose in her throat as his finger poked her *there*. She stiffened, then clutched at his arm.

"No!"

To her utter horror, his finger pushed inside her, hurting her, finding a place she did not even know she had. She tried to push him away, and would have screamed, but he rolled over onto her, pinning her beneath him, separating her legs with a bony knee. His breath wheezed in her face before his mouth came down hard on hers, stifling any sound beyond a frantic "No-mmmmph." She gagged and fought wildly, feeling his hands groping between her thighs, feeling the wet, limp softness of his flesh against hers. Before she could buck free of him, he suddenly rolled off, cursing. She felt an overwhelming relief.

"Is it—is it *over*?" she dared to ask.

He hit her then. "Hold your tongue—do you hear me? Hold your tongue!" He staggered from the bed to retrieve his cane and came back brandishing it over her. "Little witch!"

"Wha—what did I do?" The cane came down hard on her shoulders, and she raised her hands to cover her face as he hit her again and again. "I am innocent!" she cried, not knowing even what she protested. "Please—no! Arthur—my lord—," she babbled, "Arthur—*no*!"

He stopped suddenly, but she would never forget the awful expression of loathing on his face. Rolling into a ball on the bed, she began to sob loudly. She heard the cane hit the floor somewhere across the room, and then she felt his hands on her shoulders.

"Are you hurt?"

Thinking it some sort of a trick, or some form of punishment like that meted out at school, where if one admitted one was not, one got hit again, she was afraid to say anything. Instead, she clutched her knees to her breast and rocked. He rose, pulled on his nightshirt, and padded to the washstand, where he poured water into the basin. Carrying it back, he sat beside her and pulled her head onto his knees. Her teeth chattered, making speech impossible. Leaning across her, he managed to spark a candle wick, and then he began to wash her face.

"You are my wife, Elinor," he said finally. "You will obey me in all things. Do you understand that?"

She gulped for air and tried to control the tremors that shook her body. "You hurt me!" she cried.

"I'd not have you speak of this—not now—not ever,"

he went on as though she'd not spoken. "Do you understand me? Not to anyone—*not ever,*" he repeated.

She didn't understand at all, but she managed to nod her head. "Yes, b-but—"

A bony finger stilled her mouth as though she were a small child. "No. There will be no buts between us." His hands smoothed her hair much as her old nurse had done when she had been sick. "There—you are better, aren't you?"

She choked back tears and turned her face away from him. He laid the basin on the bedside table, blew out the candle, and lay down beside her. For a time, he was silent, and the only sounds seemed to be the rain against the window, the popping of dying embers in the fireplace, and his thin, reedy breath behind her ear. When she perceived finally that he did not mean to touch her again, she dared to exhale fully.

"Go on to sleep."

"I cannot." She could scarce speak for the awful ache in her throat.

"I did not intend to beat you, Elinor."

She had no answer for that. Once again the silence between them was nearly overwhelming. Surely he did not expect her to forgive him.

"On the morrow, I mean to give you your wedding gift," he murmured. When she still said nothing, he continued talking to her. His hand stroked her hair again. "It's emeralds—they will become you."

She did not want them. She did not want anything from him. Not now. Not ever.

"I have engaged a woman from the village to sew for you. While she cannot match the work of a London modiste, she is quite good. If you would like, I shall send for her in the morning. Later, in London—"

"Papa bought me dresses."

"Paltry, my dear. Paltry. When I take you to London, you will be gowned by the best." His hand moved to smooth her nightgown over her hip. "You will gain me the envy of every man in town, Elinor." He felt her stiffen anew, and he drew away. "You think you hate me, don't you?"

"Yes."

"You won't. You will come to realize what I can give

you, my dear. When I am done, there will be none to think you are not beautiful. You will attend routs and parties, royal presentations even, and you will be the reigning Toast,'' he predicted almost smugly.

She didn't care—all she wished was to be rid of him. ''I should like that,'' she responded finally, her voice betraying a decided lack of enthusiasm.

''Your task will not be onerous, my dear. You have but to appear devoted to your husband. And I shall not be demanding, I promise you.'' He coughed to clear his throat. ''I shall not be demanding,'' he repeated, ''but I intend to seek your bed twice each week—shall we say Wednesday and Saturday—to avert unpleasant gossip. I'd not be the butt of servants' jests, do you understand?''

''No.''

''You will speak of nothing that has passed here,'' he said again.

''Do I have to—that is, you will not—?'' She could not bring herself to say it.

''No. As long as you are obedient, you need not fear me again, child. I would do nothing to mar your looks.''

She breathed an audible sigh of relief that he would not touch her again, not like her mother had told her. For a moment, she dared to hope he would leave her this night. But his next words dashed that.

''Come—let us sleep. I'd have your hand, my dear.''

She did not want to touch him either, but neither did she wish to anger him again. Very gingerly, she extended her hand at her side, and his cold fingers curved over hers.

''Why did you wed me?'' she managed to ask.

There was a long silence, and for a time, she thought he'd not heard her. Finally, he spoke. ''Vanity, my dear. It flatters me to know I am envied. I came into the world but plain Arthur Kingsley, and now there's none as can ignore me. When I had but money, it was not enough. And when I was able to gain a title, it was still the same. But I have had the last jest of all, have I not? Now I shall be envied for you.''

''But there were others—''

''Think you I did not look? For years I have surveyed the daughters of the *ton*, but they were all too good to spend my money—and not a one of them above the common style, mind you." For the briefest moment, his fingers squeezed hers. "You, my dear, are not common at all."

"But—"

"And when I am done, you will be not an Incomparable, but rather *the* Incomparable. When I am done, we will give each other consequence, my dear. Wealth for beauty—it's a fair exchange, is it not?" When she said nothing, he predicted, "One day you will thank me for what I give you, Elinor."

It was as though her father spoke the words. But it would do no good to tell the old man it was a lie. Instead, she merely murmured, "Good night, sir."

"Arthur. It's 'good night, *Arthur,*' " he corrected her.

Long after his breathing evened out, long after he began to snore, she lay beside him, her hand in his. Was this marriage? Was this what every girl was supposed to want? To be touched like that? A new shudder of revulsion coursed through her, and for a moment, nausea rose again, forcing her to swallow the awful lump in her throat. No, it could not be. She was surely living a nightmare from which she would waken. Tomorrow, she would find this had not happened to her. But in her heart, she knew it was not a nightmare at all, but rather a dismal, lonely life she'd discover when she wakened. Very gingerly, she eased her fingers from his, and turned to stare into the glowing coals.

Outside, the wind seemed to have died, but the rain still pelted the tiled roof. Still, she could not sleep, thinking of the old man beside her, wondering if one night he would die in her bed. The only thing worse, she knew, would be if he should live until she were no longer young. And as they had so often done in the two months past, her thoughts turned once again to the notorious Earl of Longford—remembering the strength of his arms, the passion of his kiss, she wondered how on earth his wife could have preferred another man. Scoundrel, rake, or whatever, he would have been infinitely preferable to Arthur Kingsley. But she supposed Longford's wife to be quite beautiful, and no doubt she'd had scores of young bucks at her feet. She, on the other hand, had only Arthur.

SHE WAS ONE of the loveliest women he'd ever seen, he admitted that. She was also the biggest mistake of his life, and he was ready to put her behind him. He leaned back in his chair, facing her across the length of the bishop's meeting table, and took stock of the woman who had been his wife for two years.

She was in her best looks, her pale, wheat-blond hair curling delicately beneath the wide brim of a blue velvet bonnet, her porcelain skin infused with the barest tint of rose, her wide blue eyes reflecting an innocence totally at variance with the woman within. Even the prim, braid-edged blue velvet pelisse, unbuttoned to show a demure, lace-trimmed blue muslin gown, had been worn to elicit sympathy from the clergy present, he decided cynically. Blue was her color, and she knew it. It was also a color that was cool, delicate, and devoid of passion, the sort of thing one ought to wear to church.

"Harumph!" The bishop, Lord Quentin Harwell, cleared his throat, shuffled through an untidy stack of papers, and looked to Lucien. "You are unrepresented, my lord?"

"Yes."

He turned to Diana. "Are you, my lady?"

"I have brought my parents, Lord and Lady Fenton, and my solicitor, Mr. Tate," she answered softly.

"Is Lord Townsend present?" he inquired of one of the priests beside him.

"No, he is not. But as you know, he has changed his mind and decided to admit to the charges."

"A pity, for he must surely provide enlightenment."

"You have his deposition," Lucien reminded him curtly. "And I'd get on with this—with your permission, of course."

Harwell flashed him a look of disapproval. "Yes—well—" He cleared his throat again. "Highly irregular, I admit it, but I thought perhaps we could attempt a reconciliation."

"No." Lucien appeared absorbed in a nub of lint on the sleeve of his blue superfine coat for a moment, then he shook his head. "No, I don't think so."

Mr. Tate rose. "My lord bishop, Lady Longford does not desire a separation from her husband."

"What Lady Longford desires is immaterial at this point, Lucien declared coldly. "I intend to press for the divorce." He indicated the stack of papers. "You have more than enough evidence before you to support the charge I have brought against her."

"My lord bishop, if I may speak—" Lord Fenton rose to stand behind his daughter. "There has never been the slightest taint of scandal in this family, and naturally we should not wish to embroil ourselves in a public airing of grievances. Surely Longford himself is not blameless in the matter." He looked down, and resting his hand on Diana's shoulder, he went on, "There is the unfortunate circumstance of a number of"—he covered his mouth and coughed discreetly—"Forgive me for having to say this before the ladies, but it's well known that Longford has engaged in a number of alliances with other females."

"Inadmissable," Lucien retorted.

"Unfortunately, adultery, reprehensible though it is, is not a crime for a male," Bishop Harwell reminded Diana's father.

"But it was nonetheless devastating to a young wife eager to please her husband," Fenton argued. "Can she be blamed for falling prey to the attentions of an acknowledged rake like Bellamy Townsend when she has been all but deserted by Longford?"

"She does not deny the charge?" Harwell asked, leaning forward.

Diana lowered her head and stared at the table, but not before she summoned a couple of tears to her eyes. "No," she whispered almost inaudibly. "I did but wish to show Lucien the pain he has inflicted on me."

She should have been an actress, Lucien reflected bitterly, for had he not known better, he could almost have believed her himself. But he knew better. He knew if he told the whole truth, the lie that wounded his vanity still, every man in the room must surely feel the revulsion he felt. But for all that he wanted rid of her, he could not bring himself to touch upon that. Two years had not dimmed the bitterness he still felt toward her and Mad Jack. No, he would not tell them that Bell Townsend had been a godsend.

"Her motives are also immaterial," he stated abruptly.

The bishop had hoped to avoid a hearing of record, but he could see that the earl had not the least intention of being amenable to saving anyone's face, not even his own. Succumbing to a certain curiosity, he turned to the young countess.

"Perhaps you can explain yourself to your husband, Lady Longford. Perhaps that would alter—"

"Think you I have not tried?" she cried, dabbing at her welling eyes. "He is but determined to be rid of me!"

"Here now, Diana—" Her father patted her shoulder.

"Most irregular," Mr. Tate protested. "My lord bishop—"

"If it will end the matter, I am prepared to listen now," Lucien said. Taking out his watch, he flicked open the case and checked the time. "But whatever is said, I'd see it said quickly. I am promised to Leighton for the holidays, and I mean to leave within the hour." He favored his wife with a sardonic smile. "You behold me all ears, my dear."

She did not look at him. Instead, she focused on the bishop and the local vicar, who was regarding her kindly. "I did not mean to do it—it—it just happened. Lucien was gone so much, and—and I believed he did not care for me—" Her shoulders shook slightly, and she stopped, looking up through wet lashes. "Lord Townsend seemed so kind—so attentive—and Lucien was never there." Turning finally to Lucien, she cried, "You know it's true! You never cared for me, did you?"

"No," he admitted baldly. "But I paid your bills."

"That was not enough! You found me a crushing bore! And Bell—" Her voice dropped. "Bell did not."

Seizing the advantage her tears gave him, Tate rose

again. "My lord bishop, Lady Longford is desirous of a reconciliation. Is that not true, my lady?"

"Yes," she whispered.

"Very affecting, my dear," Lucien murmured, "but I am not thrice the fool."

"Surely there must have been some measure of affection when you wed her," the parish vicar reminded him.

"No."

"Then why in heaven's name did you offer for her?" the bishop demanded.

"Folly."

It was no use, and they all knew it. Finally, the Fentons' solicitor sighed. "Very well, my lord. If we concede that a reconciliation cannot be effected, my client is prepared to return discreetly to her family. She will, however, require a suitable allowance."

"Not a legal separation, of course," Lord Fenton hastily inserted. "Appearances—"

"Appearances be damned," Lucien interrupted coldly. "I shall be satisfied with nothing less than a divorce."

"It will be disastrous for both of you!" Fenton shouted at him. "Speak of folly, will you? *This* is utter folly!"

The bishop pursed his lips in disapproval, then addressed Lucien heavily, "I beg you will think on this, my lord. There will be unfortunate consequences—it's possible that neither of you will be received in society after the scandal."

"Possible!" Fenton snorted. "It's certain!"

"Perhaps Lord Longford has not considered—" Lady Fenton ventured timidly.

"It's ruination!" her husband insisted. "Ruination!"

Lucien rose and reached for his beaver hat. Turning to face the censure of the others, he shrugged. "It is a risk I am prepared to take. Good day, Diana. Lady Fenton." He bowed slightly toward the three clergymen. "Gentlemen."

Mr. Tate licked his lips nervously. "Wait—what of the settlements? You cannot merely abandon Lady Longford, sir."

"Lucien!" For a moment, Diana's mask slipped. "I shall be destitute! You cannot do this to me! Your father would not have wanted this!" Then, realizing what she'd said, she looked away.

For a moment, he felt betrayed again, and he had to force himself to hold his tongue. For all that Mad Jack was dead, he still hated him.

"The criminal court will assess damages on Townsend, and Longford will be compelled to settle an allowance on his wife before the matter can go before Parliament," the bishop reminded them. "But I cannot say you are being very civil in the matter, my lord," he added, addressing Lucien.

"Bell's solicitor assures me he does not intend to dispute the facts of my suit, and we have agreed to a sum of five thousand pounds."

"I object!" Tate protested. "We were not party to this, sir!"

"Unfortunately, we do not have jurisdiction over that portion of the matter," Bishop Harwell reminded him. "We can but decide if there are grounds for the separation. And," he continued, sighing, "the evidence does support the action Longford has brought against Lady Longford."

"Thank you." Lucien adjusted his hat to a rakish angle and turned to leave.

"I cannot live on five thousand pounds!" Then, perceiving how she must sound, Diana lowered her head and her voice. "That is, I should require an allowance."

"Before the Lords will hear the case, that must be agreed upon," the bishop murmured soothingly.

Lucien swung around. "I am willing to return what she brought to me upon the marriage."

"Paltry, sir!" Fenton howled, outraged.

Lucien's smile deepened. "You did not think so at the time," he murmured.

Knowing that Townsend's guilty plea would make his client's position untenable, Mr. Tate cleared his throat and prepared to sound reasonable. "My lord," he appealed to Lucien, "a small allowance in addition to the lump-sum distribution—" As the earl's smile faded, he went on hastily, "You are a wealthy man, and you would not have it perceived that you are unprepared to do the right thing—" He stopped, aware that Lucien's eyebrows had raised incredulously. "Yes, well—I should think that we could accept two thousand per annum," he finished lamely.

"Two thousand? I shall be in rags!" Diana screeched.

"I have no intention of providing an allowance, gentlemen. When the matter is settled, I mean to cut the connection completely."

"Dash it, but how's she to live?" Fenton demanded angrily.

"I will settle the five thousand from Townsend and the two thousand agreed upon at the marriage. Beyond that, I do not mean to give her a farthing."

"Seven thousand pounds?" The vicar, whose living was not one-tenth that nodded his head. "Most generous, my lord."

"Generous?" Diana wailed. "I shall have to practice the most shocking economies!"

"You can dispute it, of course, but in the process of a lengthy hearing, there is no telling what might come out," Lucien murmured meaningfully. "And neither of us would wish that, would we?" he added silkily.

Her father glanced uneasily to the solicitor, then exhaled heavily. It was all she was going to get, and he knew it. Under the circumstances, he had to admit to himself that it was more than Diana deserved. "Here now—no need to rake old coals, is there? If we accept—if we do not dispute the divorce—"

Lucien nodded. "There will be no need to bring more than the one charge against her."

"Papa!"

But Fenton was watching Lucien. "You will see the matter expedited as quickly and quietly as possible?"

"I cannot see any delay. As I shall be leaving the country after the holidays, and as Bell is prepared to plead guilty, Leighton has assured me he will offer the bill in Lords before spring."

"You do not mean to be there?"

"If it is undisputed, I see no necessity of it."

"We can sue for more," Tate reminded Fenton.

"I should not advise it," Lucien said shortly, his eyes on Diana's father.

"No, of course not. I had hoped for more, but I am prepared to agree."

"I thought you would. You may deal with Leighton in my absence, and George will see the papers are forwarded. Good day."

As he entered the foyer where the viscount awaited him, he could hear the low murmur of dissatisfaction behind him. It didn't matter—he meant to put that portion of his life behind him.

"How'd it go?" Leighton asked soberly.

"As well as could be expected."

"Bad business."

"Yes."

It was not until they were in the viscount's carriage that either spoke again. Leighton wiped the steam from his window and peered outside. "Looks as though it might snow."

Lucien did not answer. Instead, he leaned back, resting his head against the button-tufted velvet squabs. For a long time, he stared absently toward the ceiling. Finally, his friend could stand it no longer.

"Are you going through with the divorce?"

Lucien nodded. "I told them you would tend to everything for me."

"Well, I will, but I still cannot believe you mean to sign up. You are as mad as Mad Jack!"

"I've already done it."

"War's a nasty, uncivilized business. Liable to come home in a box," Leighton declared glumly.

"I doubt many would count it a loss."

"Ain't no reason for you to go! Dash it, but let Diana flee the country! It ain't as if you was the guilty party, is it?"

"I'd not talk about the divorce, George. Let us proceed with the holidays. Besides, it's to be expected that Mad Jack's son would want to go, don't you think? After all, everyone expects me to be like him," he added bitterly.

"Before your uncle died, Jack was the younger son. Ain't the same—you got the money and the title. You know, sometimes I think I don't know you at all," Leighton grumbled.

"How far is Stoneleigh from your place?" Lucien asked abruptly. "Or more to the point, how far is it from Langston Park? I bought the Park, you know."

"Neighbors then. Six or so miles from my house, depending on the road taken. Park's even closer. Why?"

"I have a bit of business there—a country party, I believe." He reached into his coat pocket and drew out Ashton's letter. "On the seventh of January."

"At Stoneleigh? Didn't know you knew Kingsley, and cannot think why you would want to pursue the acquaintance, anyway. Deuced encroaching fellow, if you was to ask me. Bought the title, you know."

"The old mushroom has wed."

"Wed! At his age?" For a moment, Leighton was diverted. "Got him a dowager, eh?"

"An infant."

"Thought he was too old to have one in the oven."

"My dear George, as far as I know the girl is not increasing—it's the infant he's wed." Lucien recalled his brief encounter with Elinor Ashton and her father. "A fifteen-year-old beauty."

"Egad! Why'd he want one so young? Fellow must be sixty—maybe older."

Lucien shrugged. "I expect for the usual reason."

"You've seen her?"

"Ashton's daughter. She was there the night he tried to fleece Bell."

"I didn't see her."

"Your loss," Lucien murmured. "You could have been a hasty bridegroom."

"I beg your pardon?" Leighton recoiled visibly. "Not me, I can tell you. I'm not ready to wed, and if I was I'd not take a poor girl—Ashton's damn near run off his legs."

"It doesn't signify. But you can look her over at Stoneleigh."

"Never knew you to frequent country parties. Deuced boring, if you was to ask me."

"In this case, I have business. I'd collect from Ashton before I go, else I'll never see the money."

"As if you needed it," Leighton snorted.

"I'll be hanged before I give Diana any of my own gold, George. I'd much rather give her Townsend's and Ashton's." He leaned back and pulled his hat forward so that the brim shadowed his eyes. "Call it principle, if you wish."

"If you won it, it's yours."

"Suffice it to say that somehow it seems different."

For a time, Leighton left him alone, choosing to stare

out at the spitting snow. He'd argued against the divorce, for he knew what it would do to Longford, but every point he'd raised had fallen on deaf ears, and he could not understand it. Had Diana been his, he'd have called Bell out on another pretext, and when it was done, he'd see to it that she lived more discreetly until he got his heir of her. After that, he'd not give a damn what she did. But Lucien was different. Whether out of wounded pride or bitter disappointment, he'd seized upon her indiscretion. He must've cared more about her than was thought, Leighton decided finally.

"The country is a good place to mend a bruised heart," he said softly.

Lucien roused and pushed back the beaver hat to fix his friend with his black eyes. "My dear George, after all these years, you must surely know there is no heart to bruise."

"She must have touched something within you."

Lucien was silent for a moment, and this time he could think of nothing witty or cutting to say. "No," he said finally, "I place the blame for that on Mad Jack."

January 7, 1808

HER FATHER LOOKED UP approvingly when she entered the saloon. ''Look as fine as fivepence, you do, my dear.'' His gaze traveled over the fine green lustring gown, then up to the perfectly matched pearls at her throat. ''You cannot say I did not do right by you, damme if I didn't.'' He laid aside the paper he had been reading and rose to inspect her more closely. ''Arthur must be besotted.''

''I should scarce call it that, Papa.''

''Here now—mustn't appear long-faced. He don't like that, you know. Likes to see you smiling.'' He looked around the elegantly appointed room, nodding his satisfaction. ''Giving you the best of everything, puss—you got no reason to mope.''

'' 'He don't like that, you know,' '' she mimicked. ''Papa, what about what *I* like? Have you no care for me?''

''Now, puss—you are but overset at parting with your mama,'' he soothed her.

''But do you and Mama have to go?'' she blurted out.

''Overstayed our welcome as it is, Nell. And after your party, we ain't got reason to stay.''

''Then I shall have no one.'' The very thought of being left there constricted her throat painfully. ''Please, Papa—I'd at least keep one of the girls.''

''Don't think Arthur likes 'em,'' he admitted bluntly. ''And you got Charles—boy's nearly of an age with you.''

''All he can speak of is the war,'' she retorted. ''Besides, he returns to Harrow tomorrow. No—when you and Mama and the girls are gone, I shall die.'' Her eyes swept the room, seeing not the exquisite things her husband had collected, but rather the walls, and she sought to explain. ''It will be naught but a prison here, Papa.''

"How can you say so?" he demanded. "Look at you! That gown must've cost Kingsley more'n I spend on your mama in a year! The man's besotted, I tell you! Twelve days of Christmas, and damme if he did not give you something for every one of them! I'd say he means to keep you like a royal princess!"

"Keep me, Papa?—those are the very words for the situation," she muttered. "I shall be like one of the animals in the Tower of London."

"The man dotes on you," he insisted. "And I'd not have you make the parting difficult for your mama," he added defensively. "It would not hurt anything if you was to make her believe you happy, you know."

"Happy? Is this what you would call happy? I would have more than things—indeed, but I do not want them! Look about you," she begged passionately. "See what you leave me!"

"I see an ingrate!" he retorted angrily.

"Look at this house—it's *huge*! There are so many servants I cannot learn their names, Papa! And the housekeeper—Mrs. Peake—answers only to my—my—" She could not bring herself to say it. "To Kingsley," she finished finally. "When I try to direct her, she tells me not to worry my pretty head, and when I ask for things, she discovers from him whether I am to have them before they are given."

"You will learn, puss—you will learn! It's but new to you, Nell. Already Kingsley is more than pleased with you."

"He would be as pleased with a trained dog, if he could say it cost him enough." She held out her hands, palms up. "Do you not see, Papa?—I am to be a cosseted pet!"

"All you got to do is bide your time, Nell."

It was no use, and she knew it. He would never understand what she feared. It was easier for him to believe he'd done his best for her. She dropped her hands and turned away. "For all that his leg is bad, he does not appear in poor health otherwise," she responded dryly. "I shall be here years."

"Man's sixty-one," he reminded her.

"And how many wives has he buried already?"

"Two, but they wasn't young."

"I doubt you even know what happened to them," she declared bitterly.

"What's to know? They died."

"From being overmanaged, no doubt."

"That's enough of this, Nell!" Nonetheless, he unbent enough to tell her, "It wasn't that way at all—had the tale from his solicitor. The first did not survive childbirth. The second was a common sort he wed to care for his boy. Fever took her off some years back, and he's been too busy gaining his wealth to be in the petticoat line since."

"But why me, Papa?"

"A pretty, well-bred creature gives a man consequence, and—"

"There you are, Elinor," Charles Kingsley interrupted them, coming into the room. "Your pardon, sir," he addressed her father, "but Grandpapa would see her before the company arrives."

"Is it that late?" Thomas Ashton took out his watch and flipped open the cover. "Egad. Yes—well, best run along, Nell. I've got to see what keeps your mother."

At the stairs, Charles stepped back to let her go up first. As she passed him, he blurted out, "The dress becomes you." And when she turned around, he flushed to the roots of his fair hair. "Ought not to have said that, I suppose, but you look smashing—truly. Bang up to the mark, in fact. Be a credit to the Kingsleys, I'll be bound."

"Thank you."

"Meant it." He ducked his head and lowered his voice. "When I heard he was to wed, I nearly howled at the thought, I can tell you."

"I cannot say I was overjoyed either," she admitted sourly.

"But it ain't so bad, is it? I mean, now when I am down from school I got somebody to talk with besides him." He looked toward the hall above. "He don't bend much, you know—had a devil of a time getting him to let me stay until tomorrow. But the term at Harrow don't start until Monday, anyways."

"At least you know the people who are coming."

"Ain't nobody of note, I'd say—not in Cornwall this time of year, unless they are rusticating. Guess that's why he wants to do it—to see how you fadge in company before he tosses you among the London tabbies.''

She started to admit that she had not the least notion of how to go on, then stopped herself for fear he would laugh at her. ''No doubt,'' she murmured instead.

''Hope you ain't cowhanded on the pianoforte.''

''I beg your pardon?''

He grinned. ''He'll make you play. Sing, too.''

''In company?'' she gasped. ''Oh, but I could not!''

''You'd best do what he asks. He don't like to be denied, I can tell you.'' He stopped in front of her bedchamber door. ''Ruthless,'' he declared succinctly. ''Make you do what you don't want to prove he can do it.''

''You do not seem to hold him in high regard,'' she chided.

His grin faded. ''The highest. Got to—can't help admiring a man as has done what he has done. Afraid of him, that's all. But he ain't going to want to be kept waiting—I can tell you that also. See you downstairs before the company arrives.''

She pushed open the door to see Arthur Kingsley sitting in a chair pulled before the fire. His long, thin legs were crossed above his polished highlows.

''Come give me a kiss, my dear,'' he ordered. But his brow creased and his lips pursed as he watched her walk toward him. He waited until she bent to place an obedient peck on his cheek. There was no mistaking that she did not like to do it.

''You look like an infant,'' he decided sourly.

''You chose the dress, my lord.''

''It's the hair. Mary''—he waved a bony hand toward the hovering maid—''I have changed my mind—Lady Kingsley will wear it pinned up.''

''Aye, my lord.''

''And the pearls are wrong also. I'd thought perhaps they denoted innocence, but now I merely think them plain. Daggett!''

''Aye, my lord?''

''Fetch the cases. I cannot abide insipidity, and she looks insipid, don't you think?''

The valet did not even look at her. ''Your taste is always impeccable, sir.''

''Just so.'' The old man leaned back, pressing his fingertips together as he continued to survey Elinor. ''Had I to do it over, I should have chosen a darker shade for the gown, I think, but you look presentable enough for tonight. Should it be emeralds—or is that too much green, I wonder?'' he mused more to himself than to anyone. ''Or perhaps the topazes.''

''The diamonds—?'' Daggett dared to suggest.

''No. No—not yet. It's a country party. I'd save the diamonds for London.''

She felt like a thing standing before him. ''I like the pearls,'' she declared stubbornly. ''I think them lovely.''

He favored her with a look usually reserved for fools. ''You are a schoolgirl no longer, Elinor,'' he told her coldly. ''Every gown or jewel you wear, every word you speak—your merest misstep—will reflect on me. I should not wish to be pitied for elevating you.''

She stiffened. Elevating her? She was daughter to a baron whose title was far less dubious than his own. For a moment, she wanted to tell him so, then bit back the words.

''You are quite wise, my dear,'' he murmured. ''I require obedience in all things.'' He looked up at his valet. ''The emeralds would favor her hair, but the topazes would show her eyes to advantage. What do you think—which will it be?''

''The topazes do not set off the green gown.''

''Quite right. Perhaps the bronze taffeta . . .'' His voice trailed off speculatively.

''I like the green, my lord,'' she managed through clenched teeth.

''Mary, fetch the bronze, if you please,'' Kingsley ordered, ignoring Elinor.

Sensing that he played some sort of game, one where only he knew the rules, she was at a loss. ''Please, my lord—this is the loveliest gown I have ever owned.''

''Please what?''

She blinked, unable to follow him. ''What?''

He sighed expressively. ''My dear, you will make me think I have wed an imbecile.'' With an effort, he heaved himself up from the chair, and leaning on his cane, he walked toward her. ''Do you always stand like that?''

''Like what?''

"Mary, on the morrow you will put her into a corset board."

"*What?* Naught's wrong with my posture!"

"Only for the days," he decided. "Just a precaution, my dear. I'd not have it said that Lady Kingsley's shoulders are rounded." Turning to the maid, he told her, "See that she wears the bronze—and pin up her hair. Daggett will ready the topazes for you."

"Aye, my lord," the valet answered promptly.

"Arthur," Elinor tried one last time. "I don't want to wear the bronze! The green—"

"I cannot abide tantrums, my dear." Favoring his left leg, the old man walked to the door. Without looking back, he added, "And when you are made presentable, Elinor, you will come to my chamber that we may go down together."

"We ain't got much time, my lady," Mary murmured, reaching for the hooks on the green gown.

"I wanted to wear this!"

The maid clucked sympathetically. "If ye was wanting to do that, mebbe ye oughta said it was the bronze ye favored. He allus has his way, ye know. It's the master as decides everything," she declared.

Elinor wanted to scream her vexation, but it would serve nothing to take out her anger on the maid. And certainly her papa would not understand. As Mary pulled her dress over her head, the girl's temper faded in the face of defeat. On the morrow, her whole family would be going, and she would be left in Kingsley's house with Kingsley's servants, at the mercy of her elderly husband. An almost terrifying chill seemed to encircle her heart. She would be *alone*.

TO ELINOR, if Cornwall were thin of company after Christmas, the crowd belied it. Whether from custom or curiosity, every member of the neighboring gentry came, pressing into the grand reception room and spilling over into the glittering, chandelier-lit saloons. It was, she overheard one richly gowned woman declare, "as fine an affair as any I have attended in London. But for all that one can say of him, Kingsley does not spare expense, after all."

"In this instance, I cannot say I blame him," another responded. "She is a pretty little thing, is she not?"

"Stunning," the first woman agreed.

"I own I had expected a mere child."

"Well, she is not that."

"My dear, our footman had it of one of his maids that she is but fifteen."

"How obscene."

"Well, I cannot pity her, of course, for she can say she has done exceedingly well for herself, given that I am told her father is quite run off his legs."

Elinor's face flushed, and she turned away. Despite the glittering topazes that blazed warmly against her neck, despite the bronze taffeta's shimmering iridescence, she felt like an object, nothing more than a display of an old man's wealth. And already she hated what she would become.

As she stood in the receiving line, trying to fix the names with the faces that passed her, Elinor was acutely conscious that her husband watched over her every word and gesture. Her face ached from the forced smiles until she longed for the evening to end. From time to time, Arthur Kingsley's hand rested proprietarily on her arm, directing her attention to one guest or another in particular. As the last of the latecomers passed by, she felt his fingers stiffen, and she looked up quickly. But his face remained blandly amiable.

"Lucien de Clare, Earl of Longford," he murmured. To the other man, he added, "You surprise me, my lord—I did not expect you. Indeed, but I had heard you were leaving the country." He smiled thinly. "My wife—Lady Kingsley."

"Let us just say I am rusticating until a few matters are attended," the earl answered smoothly. His black head bowed over Elinor's hand, and his fingers possessed hers. "My felicitations, my dear—Arthur is to be congratulated on his good fortune." When he looked up, his black eyes still seemed to mock her. "How is your fond parent, by the by? I had hopes of encountering him here."

"He is well, my lord."

"I'll wager he is—now."

"Yes—well—" Coloring, she pulled her hand away. "He is about somewhere."

"Then the luck is mine as well as his."

"I did not know you had property here," Kingsley said, his voice suddenly curt.

"Actually, I have acquired Langston Park recently, so I suppose we must be accounted neighbors. You recall George, do you not? Impeccable *ton*, I believe."

"Leighton," Arthur Kingsley acknowledged. "My dear," he murmured, turning to Elinor, "may I present George Maxwell, Viscount Leighton?" As he spoke, his hand possessed her elbow again. "Leighton Hall lies but a few miles from here."

Tall, slender, possessed of an open, friendly face, the viscount took her hand gracefully and lifted it to his lips, brushing it lightly. "Charming, my dear," he pronounced. "Utterly charming. You are all that Longford said."

Her husband's grip tightened. "I was unaware either of you were acquainted with my wife."

She felt her face grow hot. "Uh—not precisely."

Longford came to her rescue. "Actually, we have never been presented. It was my good fortune to glimpse Lady Kingsley when her father brought her home from school."

"Told me of it," Leighton corroborated quickly. "Said Ashton's chit was a beauty. And she is."

"Beware the northern charmer, my dear," Longford warned her. "It's the ones who do not look dangerous that are."

For a moment, Leighton looked pained. "It ain't me as—" He stopped, then addressed Elinor. "I collect he is disparaging my Scots ancestry again, Lady Kingsley. Got land up there, but it's too cold for my blood. Like Cornwall better. Reminds me of the lay of the land with the rocks and the coast, but the climate's more pleasant." He smiled again. "Have you ever been to Scotland, Lady Kingsley?"

"I'm afraid I haven't been anywhere," she admitted, warming to his easy manner. "But I should like—"

"When that Corsican upstart is gone, we'll tour the Continent," Arthur cut in abruptly. "Your pardon, sirs, but we tarry overlong, and it appears the musicians have started playing."

With one hand on his cane and the other on her elbow, he propelled her past the two men. When they were nearly out of earshot, she heard the earl tell the viscount, "There is none quite as vigilant as an old man with a young wife, I'd say."

"Feel. for the chit, though," Leighton responded. "Almost indecent. Ought to be a law."

"She's fifteen, I am told."

"Still—"

"I didn't come to ogle the infantry, George—I've business with Ashton before I leave the country."

Instinctively, Elinor looked for her father, but he seemed to have disappeared. Beside her, her husband motioned to Charles Kingsley, and the boy gulped the last of his punch before coming over.

"It's the custom for the host to lead the first country dance, my dear, but my leg pains me tonight. I'd watch Charles take you out."

"Oh, but I—"

His eyes narrowed. "I am told you have been taught to dance—did Ashton misinform me on that head also?"

"Also?" she echoed, trying to follow him.

"He promised you would be a credit to me."

Stung, she retorted, "I danced as well as any at Miss Roberts's academy, my lord."

"So I expect to see."

Not wanting him to know that she'd eavesdropped before, she asked casually, "Why were you surprised to see Lord Longford if Papa invited him?"

"The man's pride makes him a fool, Elinor. Suffice it to say that he's brought a scandal down on himself, and when it's out, he'll suffer for it. He'll be given the cut direct."

"What sort of scandal?"

"It's too sordid for your ears," he said dampeningly. "There you are, Charles—when the first set forms, you are to lead Elinor out."

"Me, sir?" The boy reddened. "Uh—don't know m'left foot from m'right. Be better if—" He cast about wildly for someone to take his place. "Uh—Crawford—or Pennington—or—Dash it, sir, but I don't dance with females!"

"Charles—" There was no mistaking the pained tone.

"Yes, sir."

"That's better."

The old man released Elinor's arm and sought one of the chairs that lined the wall. Charles looked helplessly at her. "Hope you don't mind if I count," he muttered. "I ain't no hand at this."

"Miss Roberts said if one showed spirit, no one would notice the style." Then, perceiving that her husband was beyond hearing, she asked, "How old do you think the earl is?"

"What earl?"

"Longford."

"Don't think—I know. Fellow's five and twenty. Had that from Fenton," he added importantly. "Connected to him—or was." He squinted toward where Longford lounged, a glass held absently in his hand, his mien one of utter boredom, then Charles frowned. "Shocking bad *ton*." He lowered his voice and leaned closer to speak for her ears alone. "What I know would keep everyone in this room from talking to him."

"Papa said he was rich."

"Rich!" he snorted. "Fellow's deuced lucky at the tables! And it don't hurt that he came into this world with a silver spoon stuck in his mouth, I can tell you! Mad Jack's son,'' he added succinctly, as though that ought to explain everything.

''Who's Mad Jack?''

''Was,'' he corrected her. ''He's dead.''

''Then who *was* he?'' she snapped, betraying her irritation.

''Longford's father.''

''Sometimes, Charles,'' she told him severely, ''I think you are a slowtop.''

''As you are even younger than I, I shall choose to excuse that remark,'' he retorted. Nonetheless, he explained, ''Mad Jack distinguished himself in the American thing—would have been lionized if we had won. Fought under Burgoyne—a colonel, I think. Don't know the whole tale, mind you—before my time, you know. But he was a rich rounder, too, from all I ever heard. Had a real eye for the beauties. And they had an eye for him. I think he fought a duel or two, maybe more, over 'em. Thing was, he never settled on any one of 'em.''

''But he must've married. There is Longford, after all,'' she pointed out reasonably.

''Not a love match. He was as inconstant as his son, I'm told.'' He looked toward Longford again. ''Word to the wise—don't pursue that acquaintance. Grandpapa will not like it.''

''Why? He allowed Papa to invite him.''

''Didn't think he'd come. Devil of a scandal brewing, I can tell you. It ain't going to do nobody any credit to know him. The time is coming when he ain't going to be received anywhere.''

''If he is rich, no doubt he will be forgiven,'' she observed acidly.

''Not for this.''

''For what?''

He looked both ways, then led her to a corner of the room. ''Can you hold your tongue?'' he asked earnestly. When she nodded, he turned his back to the crowd and whispered, ''He is divorcing his countess. For adultery.'' He'd expected her to recoil in horror, and when she did not, he hissed, ''Dash it, but it ain't done!''

''But if she—''

"And it ain't like his own slate was clean." His face betrayed his disgust with her lack of reaction. "You *are* green, ain't you?"

"I don't see—"

"A man don't drag his dirty linen in the gutter for the world to see, goose! The Fentons have begged him not to do it—said they'd take her back quietly—but he would not hear of it. Upshot is the both of 'em 'll have to leave the country." He twisted his head to look once more where Longford had stood, but the man was gone. "Dangerous fellow—got a devil of a temper."

Her curiosity thoroughly piqued, she longed to know more, but the musicians had changed their tune abruptly, striking up the beginning bars to a country dance. Charles grasped her hand and squared his shoulders manfully.

"Come on—got to get this over and done with," he muttered.

"Just remember—spirit disguises style," she advised him.

"It ain't easy to show spirit and count," he shot back.

As he led her out to join the first set, she could see Arthur Kingsley watching her critically, as though he assessed everything she did. Her chin came up. She'd show him she was not an awkward child.

"At least it's not one of those formal dances," Charles whispered. "Spirit don't do a thing for them."

Having failed to discover Thomas Ashton, Lucien de Clare stood watching the dancers, his expression distant and enigmatic. Beside him, Lord Leighton watched also.

"Girl's a beauty."

"If you like them that young." Abruptly, the earl straightened and sipped from his glass, his eyes on Elinor Kingsley. "But you are right—she is a beauty—and not in the ordinary style at all, George. Not in the ordinary style at all."

"I'll wager old Arthur don't remember what to do with her," Leighton observed. "A waste."

Lucien's eyes narrowed. "Don't squander your pity, George. She'll lead him a merry dance to the grave, and when it's done, she'll be a wealthy widow," he said cynically. "She knows what she is about—or if she does not, that father of hers does."

"For God's sake, Luce—the chit's a child!" Leighton protested. "Blame Ashton—not her."

"Poor George. Ever the romantic, aren't you? Well, you are wrong. Females are born with wiles—even that one."

"Don't see Ashton. If he saw you come in, I'd say he's determined to play least in sight."

"Yes."

"Cannot think why he sent you the card if he wasn't—"

"My dear George, he had not the least expectation I would come," Lucien declared. "It was but a ploy to keep me from pressing him." The music hit the final refrain, and he moved forward to intercept Elinor before she left the floor. Coming between her and the startled boy, he glanced at her wrist. "What—no card? Then I collect you are not promised for the next set, are you?" he murmured.

"I was getting her some punch," Charles said stiffly. "And my grandfather—"

"By all means do so."

It was a curt dismissal, and for a moment, the boy considered making an issue of it, but the earl was already bowing over Elinor's hand. Realizing that his grandfather was more likely to be angered over a scene than anything, Charles grudgingly gave way.

"My dance, Lady Kingsley?" Lucien de Clare asked her. Even as he spoke, his hand closed over hers, effectively settling the matter. "This week I can still bring you into fashion. Next week I am more like to put you beyond the pale."

Despite his words, his black eyes were cold, nearly repelling her. Out of the corner of her eye, she caught her husband shaking his head, and that decided her. Forcing a smile up at the darkly handsome earl, she nodded. "I should be pleased, my lord."

It was one thing to practice with a dancing master, or to count out the steps with a boy her own age, but Lucien de Clare was quite another matter. She felt wooden and utterly self-conscious, afraid to speak lest he think her a complete ninnyhammer. All she could think of was how warm, how alive his hands were. How very different, how much more exciting he was than Arthur. But she did not have to worry about appearing accomplished—flirting was apparently not on the wicked earl's mind at all.

She had scarce begun to relax, to give her body over to the rhythm of the music, when he asked harshly, "Where is your father?"

"Papa?" She nearly lost her step. "I told you—he's in attendance."

"When we are done, I shall expect you to find him for me."

"Oh, but I don't—"

"No games, my dear—I am in no mood for them." He turned her expertly, then as she came back to face him, he leaned close enough to whisper, "You would not wish Kingsley to know everything, would you? It might throw a spoke in your little wheel."

She gasped and did lose her place. "Of all the—"

"I could almost wish you had caught Bell Townsend," he added brutally. "It would have served him well."

"The fault was not mine, sir," she managed stiffly.

"I've not forgotten, you know."

"There is no need to be insulting."

"Find me your father and I'll acquit you," he offered.

"I would not know where—"

"Cut line, Lady Kingsley! I am not here to argue with either of you." He swung her around, then caught her hands to lead her the length of the extremely interested set.

"Somehow I cannot think you in need of the money, sir."

"The question is rather one of who owes whom," he retorted.

"But Papa hasn't—"

"A gentleman does not play where he cannot pay."

Even though his fingers were strong and his clasp warm, his manner was aloof, detached even. Aware of the curious glances from the other dancers, she felt her face grow hot, and she wished the music would end.

"I cannot think why you wished to dance with me," she blurted out finally.

He favored her with that faint, almost derisive smile, then shrugged. "Well, you are a beauty, you know—not to mention I saw no other way to avoid Kingsley's hanging over your shoulder."

Mercifully, it was finally over. She would have pulled away, but Longford tucked her hand in his arm. "Not until I see Ashton, I'm afraid."

"But I don't know where—"

"You'll find him."

The rooms around the ballroom were filled, making movement through them difficult. At one point, she could see Arthur Kingsley trying to gain her attention, and she deliberately pretended not to note him. Charles, looking quite harried, threaded his way toward her, but Longford pushed her through a door before they could be caught.

"Where do you think he would hide?" he asked tersely.

She hesitated but a moment, then guessed, "Perhaps the library."

"The library? Why there?"

"Well," she admitted ruefully, "he seldom reads, I'm afraid—says it gives him the headache. It would be the last place he'd think any to look for him."

"Where is it?"

"Across the hall."

The library itself was dark, almost eerie, with the musty smell of several hundred books mingling with the odor of stale tobacco smoke. As the slice of light from the hall chandelier cast long shadows on the wall, Elinor peered in.

"Papa—?" she inquired cautiously. "Are you in here?"

"Shhhh." A solitary figure sat hunched forward in the darkness. "Go away."

"Is aught amiss, Papa?"

"I'll be out directly, puss—just resting my eyes."

The earl stepped past her. "Fortuitous, don't you think, Ashton? Now we can conduct our affairs out of Kingsley's eye—unless, of course, you would prefer I applied to him."

"Longford!"

The earl offered a mocking bow. "Your servant, Thomas," he said softly.

"What are you doing here?" her father demanded peevishly.

"Light a candle," Longford ordered.

"You wasn't supposed to come!"

His body framed by the light, the earl appeared briefly absorbed in removing a bit of lint from his dark blue coat. When he looked up, his eyebrow rose. "As I recall it, it was you who sent me the card. Or was that merely to fob me off?"

When her father did not move, the younger man walked to the small fire in the hearth and bent to ignite a bit of kindling. Carrying it with him, he returned to light the brace of candles on the reading table. Shaking the flame out, he dropped the kindling into a dripwell.

"Well?"

Her father was going to weasel and she knew it. "Papa—"

"You keep out of this, puss!" He looked up at Longford defensively. "Roll you for it," he offered.

"No. I believe it's two thousand, Ashton. If you cannot pay that, you cannot afford to lose four."

Her father's face went a pasty gray despite the warmth of the candlelight. "Have to wait—I ain't got it. The settlements—"

"I don't give a damn about your settlements," the earl declared impatiently. "I have not the whole night, sir."

"Got to wait—Kingsley's clutch-fisted—got me on an allowance, in fact." He could see Longford's jaw tighten ominously. "Dash it, but you are richer n' Croesus, my lord! It's a paltry sum to you! Can't say you are done up, 'cause I'll not believe it!"

"That, my dear Thomas, is irrelevant." Once again, the softness in the younger man's voice was almost menacing.

Her father licked his lips nervously. "Give me a week."

"No."

"No?" he fairly howled. "It ain't like you got to have it now, is it?"

"Psssst! You in there, Elinor?" Charles Kingsley's low voice carried from the hall. "Dash it," he hissed, "but it ain't the thing for you to go off with Longford!"

"You'd best go, puss," her father told her. "Wouldn't do it if Kingsley was to be vexed with you, you know."

"Elinor?" Charles came in. "Dash it, but you cannot be that green!" Looking past her to the earl, he declared importantly, "Lady Kingsley is a kinswoman, sir, and as such, I cannot allow—"

Longford shrugged. "With her father for duenna, I cannot think Kingsley can complain." Turning his attention back to Ashton, he sighed. "I'm afraid it's tonight, Thomas. You see, I shall be leaving before the week ends."

"Send it to London—I promise. Get it to your man of affairs before next quarter day."

The earl looked pained. "I shall be gone from the country, Ashton. I shan't be in London."

"Told you he'd have to run!" Charles crowed to her, forgetting himself. "Told you he couldn't stand the scandal!"

"Shut your mouth, you young fool!" Thomas Ashton shouted at him. "It's Longford! Don't listen to him, my lord—he don't know what he says."

Stung, Charles retorted, "I know he's sued Diana Fenton for divorce—had it of her own brother! Going to flee, ain't you?" he directed to Lucien. "Got to!"

There was an arrested moment as the words hung in the air, then Longford met the boy's eyes. "Actually," he drawled, "I have been given a regiment."

"You're going to fight Boney?" Charles demanded incredulously.

The earl inclined his head slightly. "Someone has to, don't you think?"

"Then you ain't getting the divorce?"

"This ain't fit for Nell's ears, boy!" Ashton roared. "Take her out of here!"

"I despise *contretemps*, Charles," Lord Kingsley announced coldly from the door. "You will take Elinor back to attend our guests. And close the door behind you, if you please."

The boy flushed to the roots of his hair, and he hung his head. "Your pardon, sir."

Elinor looked to her father. "Papa—?"

"You heard both of us, Nell. Go on."

She nodded, then raised her eyes to the earl. "Godspeed you in the war, my lord."

As she followed the chastened Charles out, she heard her elderly husband remind her father, "My wife's name is Elinor, sir. Any common housemaid can be called Nell."

In the hall, she and the boy exchanged looks, and it was obvious that neither of them wished to return to the party rather than hear of Longford. She hung back a moment, and it was all the encouragement Charles needed. Together they leaned against the wall and listened.

"The war, sir?" they heard Lord Kingsley inquire.

"Fool cannot leave well enough alone!" her father snorted. "Got to throw decency to the wind and cause a scandal he cannot survive, and damme if he ain't going off to fight the Corsican!"

"I don't believe either my character or my folly is anyone's concern but my own," Longford said. "The matter is two thousand pounds."

"Told him I ain't got it," Ashton declared. "Have to wait until your man of affairs settles it, Arthur."

"Was the debt on the list?" Kingsley asked him.

"Yes—of course. You will recall—"

"Then I will settle for you that Longford may go." The elderly baron's voice betrayed his contempt for his son-in-law. "I will, however, deduct a like amount from our agreement, Thomas. I trust you are satisfied, my lord?" he asked the earl.

"I still do not see why this cannot wait," her father protested. "It ain't like he needs the money."

"Unfortunately, my dear baron," Longford murmured, "I have my own settlement to make—and I'd rather give your money than mine."

"Humph! From all I have heard, you ain't repining," her father muttered.

"Actually, had not poor Bell come along, I should have strangled her to gain my freedom." Apparently the earl turned to Kingsley, for his next words were, "My thanks." Then, "I wish you joy of the little chit, Arthur, but I would not share your shoes for the world."

"He's coming out!" Charles hissed into her ear. "Come on."

"Not yet."

But the door opened, and the earl stepped out. For a moment, his black eyes betrayed a trace of amusement. "Still lost, my dear?" he gibed at her. "I should have a care how I went on, you know, for I suspect Arthur does not mean to be a complacent husband."

"Uh—" She groped for a suitable rejoinder, but he was gone before anything came to mind, leaving her to feel like the veriest child caught out of school.

"What'd he mean by that?"

"Nothing. I suspect it's naught but his ill temper." She started back toward the ballroom.

"Elinor!" Kingsley said sharply.

She spun around at the sound of his voice, and the color rose in her cheeks. For a moment, she considered lying to him, but Charles hastened manfully to her defense. "Wasn't Elinor, sir—it was me. I—uh—I wanted to know where Longford was going. Wish it was me going to fight Boney, that's all."

"That will be all, Charles."

It was the boy's turn to redden. "Dash it, but she didn't do anything!"

"Charles—"

"Oh, all right—be glad enough to get back to Harrow!" Turning on his heel, the boy stalked off.

"I cannot say you have had a good effect on my grandson," Kingsley murmured. "Do come in, my dear." He turned back to the library. "As for you, Thomas," he added coldly, "I suggest when you are returned to Edgehill that you recall the amount of your allowance. I shall tolerate no more scenes like this."

"The voucher was on the list," her father protested.

"And it is paid—this time. Good night, Thomas."

Her father rose reluctantly and passed by her in the doorway. Her heart sinking at the thought of another interview with her elderly spouse, Elinor appealed to him.

"Papa—"

"Ain't nothing I can do about it, puss—it's your husband as has got the purse," he muttered resentfully. "Got to be a good girl and do what he tells you."

Her hands were suddenly damp and her heart seemed to be beating against her rib cage so hard she could hear it. Taking a deep breath, she wiped her palms against the expensive taffeta.

"Come here." Moving to lean against the mantel, Kingsley gestured toward a chair. "Sit down, my dear."

She hesitated, not wanting to hear the peal she knew he would read over her. "The guests—"

"Your concern is commendable, I am sure," he said dryly, "but I shall not require your attendance overlong."

"Yes, sir." She sank into the chair, sitting forward on the edge of the seat.

"No."

"No?"

" 'Yes, Arthur,' " he reminded her. "Say it."

"Yes, Arthur. About Lord Longford—he asked—or rather—"

"I have forgotten that matter already."

"You have?" For a moment, she could almost breathe her relief.

"Your wont of conduct in general is quite another matter." He moved away from the fire and came to stand behind her. His thin fingers smoothed a stray strand of hair against her neck, sending a shiver of renewed apprehension through her. "On the morrow, my dear, we shall begin your instruction. I'd have you understand what I require of you."

"I don't need a corset board, sir—Arthur."

"I was rather thinking of other things, Elinor. Before I can take you to London, I should like to know you are as accomplished as your father represented. You will demonstrate your abilities on the pianoforte—as well as your proficiencies in your studies."

"Papa said you did not want a bluestocking!" she blurted out.

"On the contrary, my love." His hand slid to the topaz necklace, tracing the gold filigree chain at her nape. "I want more than a bluestocking, Lady Kingsley. In fact—" His voice dropped, then he paused for effect. "In fact, I shall require a paragon. When I am done, you will be a credit to me in all things. You will comport yourself with grace at the pianoforte, on the dance floor, and in the best salons in London." Again, there was a lengthy pause. "You will be worthy of all I bestow on you, little Elinor."

"Arthur—my lord—," she began desperately. "I cannot be other than what I am."

"There you are quite wrong." He walked around to

face her, then lifted his cane, and she fought the urge to duck. "It's the last time I forgive your childishness, my love. For what I have paid for you, I have a right to expect beauty, charm, and a fair amount of wit, don't you think?" Lowering the silver-tipped staff, he held out his other hand. "Come—it's time we supped with our guests, dearest Elinor. I have it on Mrs. Peake's authority that the lobster patties are sublime."

She swallowed. "Could I—that is, perhaps my sister Charlotte could stay—for just a few weeks?" she dared to ask.

"I am afraid you will not have the time to entertain the child," he answered. "And I cannot say I will miss any of your family, my dear, for they are not the least credit to me. Now—I am understood, am I not, on that head?"

"Yes, sir," she mumbled glumly.

"Arthur," he reminded her again.

He waited until she rose from the chair, then gave her his arm. As her fingers closed over it, she could feel the bones beneath his coat sleeve. The chill once again seemed to tighten about her heart, making her breastbone ache, and she felt anew the acute loneliness. And she knew if she were to survive, she'd have to become what he wanted.

"Yes, Arthur," she repeated for him.

London: May, 1812

"IT'S A PITY the fashion for perukes has passed," Arthur Kingsley murmured regretfully as Daggett attempted to arrange the gray wisps into a sort of feathery Brutus. "What do you think, my dear?" he asked, turning to Elinor.

He was vain, and she knew it. She cocked her head to look at his hair, then answered noncommitally, "It will do."

"Yes, well—it's not precisely the effect I had wanted." He reached a bony finger to poke at the fine fringe, then sighed, "Aye—it will have to do. Come over here that I may have a better look at you."

She moved closer, the emerald satin of her evening gown clinging seductively to her thin petticoat. "I know I wear green too much, but I have always liked it."

"It becomes you," he decided, nodding. He favored her with his thin smile. "You have acquired my taste, my dear."

It was his greatest compliment, and one that he tended to repeat more often these days. She inclined her head. "Thank you."

"In fact, you are becoming quite the Toast. I had it of Sefton that Brummell calls you the Titian Beauty."

"Well, I should not call my hair 'titian' precisely."

"The point is, my dear Elinor," he declared patiently, "that you have gained his favorable notice, and given what he has been known to say about others, I must count it a triumph. Lady Sefton also declares him an admirer of your eyes."

"People refine too much on his whims, I fear. I for one count him a shallow person in a shallow society. Anyone who would give up his commission because his regiment was posted to Manchester—or wherever it was—"

"I do hope you do not mean to bring up the war again," he interrupted her impatiently. "It's too unpleasant for social discourse, you know."

"Thankfully not everyone feels as you do, Arthur," she murmured. "George Ponsonby chose to go—and Longford also."

"Humph! All the Ponsonbys tend to the military, I am told." Turning to peer into the mirror Daggett still held for him, he fluffed the gray wisps one last time. "As for Longford, my dear, I hope you do not mean to hold him up as an example for anyone. There was not much else he could do to escape the scandal," he reminded her mildly. "Indeed, but even then the tale does not die."

Rising, he gestured for his evening coat. He shrugged into the expertly tailored coat, and settled his stooped shoulders as Daggett smoothed the cloth over them. "Come," he added with uncharacteristic conciliation, "you are far too lovely to worry over that which you cannot help, Elinor. It is more to the point to plot your continuing success." His hand reached to touch her cheek lightly. "I shall not be satisfied until everyone admires you as much as I do."

"Fiddle, my lord."

"Ah, my dear, but do you not see?—it's part of your charm that you are unaffected." For a long moment, he surveyed her critically, then he turned to his valet. "What say you, Daggett—is she not exquisite?"

"Exquisite, my lord," the man agreed with him.

"I see you chose the emerald and diamond collar again," Kingsley observed. "I should rather have thought the other diamonds spread above the satin . . ."

"Well, Sally Jersey seems to admire these every time she sees them," she countered, knowing what would persuade him.

"Ah, yes—the Jersey. I am glad to see that she has been won over, for with Lady Sefton with us also, I cannot but think you will receive vouchers for Almack's."

"Brummell says it's nothing but stale cake and lemonade."

"It would not matter if it were bread and water," he

responded dryly. "You are not made until you have been there."

"I think I should prefer Hyde Park, Arthur," she murmured, betraying a trace of asperity. "At least there one can look at the flowers among the Pinks."

"Nonetheless, I shall be satisfied with nothing less than Almack's, my dear."

There was a definiteness in his tone that did not invite further discussion, so she forebore disputing the matter. His thin smile curved his mouth again and he nodded. "Just so, dearest Elinor. You will conquer that last bastion also."

"Your stick, my lord," Daggett reminded him, handing him the gilt-handled ebony cane.

Kingsley leaned heavily on it, testing his leg as he took a step. Satisfied, he offered Elinor his arm. "Ready, my dear?"

"Of course."

"You are unfashionably prompt," he chided her.

"You would be vexed otherwise."

"What time is it, Daggett?" he asked his valet.

"Seven, my lord."

"Seven," he repeated. "And it's a musicale at Lady Broxton's, is it not?" He sighed. "I suppose we shall merely take the long way, for I'd not arrive before it's a squeeze."

"The Candotti sings, Arthur," Elinor protested. "If we are too late, we shall not have seats."

"See and be seen," he reminded her again. "There is nothing like a late entrance to gain one notice."

"At Almack's, I am told they will not even admit the Regent late."

"Well, when we are for Almack's, I shall remember that."

* * *

After four years of marriage to Arthur Kingsley, Elinor knew the oft-repeated scene by heart. Ever conscious of the entrance they made, Arthur led her inside to greet the host or hostess, in this case Lady Broxton, then moved through the crowd slowly, stopping to acknowledge anyone of social standing, until finally they reached a chair along the wall. As always, he urged her, "Enjoy yourself, my dear, and do not forget to be all that is proper before Lady Sefton—and Lady Jersey, of course." For a brief moment, he searched the room eagerly, then sighed. "I do not see Princess Esterhazy tonight, but I am told the Drummond-Burrell woman is to be here, much good she will do us."

He sat down to watch her, his faint smile betraying of the satisfaction she gave him. It was, she reflected wryly, as though she were a top on a string, and once he pulled, she was expected to spin gaily among the glittering *ton*, displaying his wealth for him. And all the while she was to be the epitome of style and wit.

Arthur's gaze followed her, taking in those who spoke to her almost jealously, wishing the acceptance he'd pursued so long had not come so late. But it had finally come—the beautiful, exquisite creature of his creation had given him that which his fortune alone could not buy. She had made most of the *ton* if not actually forget, then grudgingly forgive his humbler origins. Birth was everything, and even an impecunious baron was less suspect than he was. But Elinor was changing that for him. She had been worth the wait.

She was particularly in looks, clad in the low-cut, high-waisted gown that accentuated her slim body enticingly. On her neck blazed the spectacular collar of emeralds and diamonds, and above it all, her copper hair shone beneath the soft light of the chandeliers. The hair represented his only refusal to bow to the dictates of fashion—she could wear it up, pinned back, or twisted, usually at the nape of her neck, but he would not allow it to be cut above her exquisite shoulders. This time, she'd chosen to have it knotted on the crown, its severity relieved by a few artfully curled strands that softened her fine, almost perfectly chiseled features. Yes, she was his beauty.

Then he noticed the man who approached her as she stood conversing with Lady Jersey and Lord Palmerston, and he frowned, hoping she had the good sense to cut Longford. Knowing he could not get there in time to avert a social error, he held his breath.

Already stung by the icy stares and the whispered asides behind his back, Lucien had been contemplating cutting his losses and leaving when he saw her. For a moment, he did not recognize her, then it dawned on him that woman with Sally Jersey was Ashton's daughter. Old Kingsley's wife. The change was striking—the pretty child bride had become an utterly stunning woman. And judging by the jewelry and that gown, she was costing the old man a fortune. On impulse, he made his way toward her.

"Venus," he said low behind her.

In front of her, the fine-boned woman's mouth drew into a taut line of disapproval, and then her expression went distant. And Palmerston, after nodding curtly, looked away.

"What—no greeting, Sally?"

Lady Jersey did not answer. Elinor turned to look up into the Earl of Longford's face, and despite the time that had passed, she knew she would have recognized him anywhere. He was still the handsomest man of her memory, still the one who haunted her dreams. Momentarily, she wondered if he even remembered that awful night at the inn. But aloud she said, "I thought you were in the Peninsula, sir."

His eyes raked over her, and a faint, barely discernible smile played at the corners of his sensuous mouth. "I did not know you had followed my career. I must count myself honored, Lady Kingsley," he murmured.

Thinking he mocked her yet again, she closed the ivory-handled fan she carried, then answered coolly, "I shouldn't say *your* career precisely, sir—I have but read the papers, and if you happened to be in them . . ." She let her voice trail off as she shrugged her fine shoulders.

The smile deepened, but did not warm the black eyes. "You must give my compliments to Arthur, my dear. You have aged exceedingly well."

"Impertinence, sir. I am but nineteen—soon to be twenty," she answered easily.

"Ah, but you have been wed an age—nearly five years, is it not? And under Kingsley's tutelage, you seem to have blossomed." Before she could think of a suitable response, he'd turned to the man beside him. "You recall Leighton, do you not?"

"Of course." She favored the viscount with her most

dazzling smile. "Lord Leighton and I are forever crossing paths, are we not?"

"Everywhere," he agreed. "Lady Kingsley has become the reigning Toast—after you, of course, Sally," he added gallantly to Lady Jersey.

"Stuff," Elinor retorted. "I am but a poor reflection."

"Beauty, art blind," the viscount murmured before addressing the countess. "Shocking squeeze, isn't it, Sally? Hallo, Palmerston."

Lady Jersey unbent slightly. "Yes, George, it is. It would seem that Maria Broxton is more intent on quantity rather than Quality."

Lord Longford inclined his head slightly to Elinor. "Your pardon, my dear—I believe I see Bell over there. See you at the clubs, Henry," he told Cupid Palmerston.

As he crossed the room, Sally Jersey shook her head. "What can Maria have been thinking? And Townsend here also!"

Leighton followed her gaze. "If you are expecting a set-to, you are wide of the mark. He and Bell are reconciled."

"Reconciled?" For an instant, Lady Jersey was diverted. "My dear George, I have not heard it." She tapped his sleeve with her own fan and leaned closer. "It's a hum, isn't it? Henry, did you know this?"

He shrugged. "Bellamy Townsend paid damages, and Lucien forgave him, I believe."

"And who's to forgive Longford?" she demanded archly. "I am sure *I* shall not! When I think of poor Diana—"

"It was poor Diana as played him false," Leighton reminded her.

"All the same Maria—"

"I brought him," he interrupted her curtly. "And I'd not hear of it. Your servant, Sally. Lady Kingsley. Henry."

"Humph!" As he left, Lady Jersey turned to Elinor. "It's all of a piece, I suppose. Men will make excuses for men. I for one count him a dangerous man."

Elinor's eyes followed the earl curiously, her gaze flitting to where he spoke with his wife's former lover, then she shook her head. "I cannot credit it—cold perhaps, but I should not call him dangerous, I think."

"Oh, my dear, but you are mistaken," Sally warned her, "Longford is exceedingly dangerous to a woman, for he cannot be brought to care about anything."

"Humph!" Palmerston snorted. "You may count it a fault, dear Sally, but it's what saves his hide. His very detachment no doubt serves him well on the battlefield. Indeed, but he has distinguished himself to the point that Prinny himself means to decorate him for valor."

"Now *that* is the blood," Lady Jersey retorted. "His father—"

"Now there you are wrong," he contradicted her. "Mad Jack de Clare was hell for anything—utterly rash, if you want the truth of it—and the consequences be damned. A more reckless, unprincipled fellow I am sure I never met."

"And the ladies all loved him," Sally insisted. "It was not the same—I am sure he would never have divorced his wife."

"He didn't have to."

Sally Jersey snapped her fan shut. "If you are meaning to give me that farradiddle that Elizabeth died of a broken heart, I don't mean to listen. We were speaking of this Longford, after all."

But Palmerston merely smiled. "One would think you yourself had cherished a *tendre* for Mad Jack," he chided.

Lady Jersey turned to Elinor and shrugged her bared shoulders expressively. "Did I not tell you that men will forgive men anything? It does not matter to Henry that Longford consorts with all manner of opera singers—and that Harriette Wilson also—and yet he could not forgive Diana an understandable indiscretion."

To Elinor, it was much a case of the pot and the kettle, given that Lady Jersey was known to have had more than a few discreet affairs of her own, but she managed to hold her tongue. "It's an old tale now, and Longford's been away for years, after all," she murmured instead. "Perhaps he thought it was all forgotten."

"Forgotten?" The other woman's voice rose incredulously. "My dear, it cannot be forgotten! Not with this latest scandal!"

"The divorce was long ago," Elinor reminded her. "And he is not the first man ever to have been divorced."

"It was the way he did it," Sally Jersey pronounced awfully, turning on her as Lord Palmerston escaped. "To have dragged the Fentons through all that when the matter could have been scotched. The girl was a ninnyhammer—I admit it—but I daresay he had to have known that when he wed her."

"Perhaps he was young."

"And it was not as though he did not neglect her," she went on, ignoring Elinor's feeble defense of Longford. "But I am not merely speaking of the divorce, my dear—though that alone is quite enough in my book. It's what he does now that I find utterly repugnant," she declared flatly. "And I for one mean to give him the cut for it."

"I have heard nothing," Elinor confessed.

"I'm afraid Arthur keeps you far too sheltered, my dear, when he ought to warn you instead." The other woman leaned closer to confide, "There is to be another hearing."

"If he is divorced from her, I cannot see—" Elinor stopped. "Surely he is not being named correspondent in another instance, is he? I mean, he has been out of the country."

"Of course not," Sally retorted. "Most men are not so foolish as Longford. No, this is quite another matter." Her mouth flattened into a thin line of disapproval once more. "There is a child, I'm afraid."

"A child?"

"Probably more than one, if the truth were told, but no, you mistake my meaning. Diana has returned, asking for a settlement upon her daughter, and Longford means to fight it—he told Cowper so, in fact. Said it was why he was back." She waited for Elinor to express shock, and when the younger woman said nothing, she went on, "Do you not see? It will be the *on-dit* all over again, and how the Fentons are to stand it, I am sure I don't know."

"But is the child his?" Elinor wondered aloud.

"It does not matter," Lady Jersey declared dismissively. "As it is a girl, he ought not to quibble over it. If Oxford can accept that miscellany Jane has presented him, then Longford should pay for the child and not create such a fuss. It would be ever so much better to avert the scandal, but then he is certainly no stranger to that.''

''But if it is not his, it scarce seems fair,'' Elinor pointed out reasonably. ''Why should he acknowledge an heiress simply to avert unpleasant gossip?''

The countess smirked almost derisively, then retreated behind her fan. ''My dear, you are an innocent,'' she murmured. ''I daresay you must be faithful to your lord also.''

Perceiving the comment to be censurious, Elinor felt the color rise in her face. ''Yes,'' she said simply. Out of the corner of her eye, she could see Arthur beckoning her, and she excused herself. ''Your pardon, Lady Jersey, but my husband needs me.''

''A pity. There are so many eligible gentlemen to amuse oneself with.'' The older woman sighed expressively. ''But you are right, of course, for Kingsley has but the one heir. He might be rather vexed should another come in by the side door.''

''I can assure you that will not happen,'' Elinor muttered dryly. ''I think Arthur is ready to leave,'' she added, retreating. ''Perhaps he is not feeling well.''

''My dear, one should never live in one's husband's pocket,'' Sally Jersey warned her. ''It only breeds contempt and boredom, not to mention it's unfashionable.''

The crowd shifted to make room for the grand entrance of the Italian diva, and Elinor found the way suddenly blocked. Threading a narrow path among the press of bodies, she trod on someone's foot. ''Your pardon, sir—I—'' Her gaze traveled up to the coldly handsome face. ''Oh.''

''Lady Kingsley,'' he murmured, favoring her with that faint, seemingly derisive smile.

''Lord Longford.''

''You risk much acknowledging the pariah, you know.''

''Fiddle, sir.''

His manner changed abruptly, and he looked to the elegantly clad gentleman with him. ''Bell, have you been presented to Kingsley's Venus?''

''No. Been out of the country some,'' he reminded

Lucien rather pointedly, "but I've heard of her—conquered London, if the Beau can be believed."

Turning back to Elinor, Lucien made the introduction. "Lady Kingsley—Bellamy, Viscount Townsend."

"Charmed, Lady Kingsley, I assure you."

"Thank you."

"Were you presented at Court this year, Lady Kingsley?"

"Last year—and I still shudder when I think of the hoops and feathers," she murmured, smiling at him. "I looked a shocking fright, I am afraid."

"Daresay you weren't alone in that. Don't know why the females have got to dress like they was French royalty before the Revolution. Gentlemen either. I never did favor knee breeches and buckles." His eyes met Elinor's and there was no mistaking the open admiration in them. "How is Lord Kingsley, by the by?"

"He is here. In fact, I was on my way to him just now."

"Oh. Yes—well, perhaps I might call—to further the acquaintance, of course," Townsend ventured hopefully.

"We should be honored, I am sure. Your pardon, gentlemen, but I must find Arthur before the lights are doused."

Both men watched her disappear into the crowd, then Bell sighed. "Seems a shame, don't it? Beauty's wasted on an old man like that, don't you think?"

Longford's eyebrow rose. "My experience with elderly husbands is that they are inclined to keep everything they have bought, Bell."

"Bound to be bored with the old gent, I'd think," the viscount mused. "I wonder . . ."

"The girl's green. I doubt she would know how to play the game."

"You don't know that," Townsend retorted.

"Leave her alone, Bell—she's not up to your weight." Even as he said it, Lucien wondered why he bothered. If Kingsley's young wife got herself into a scandal, it was none of his affair. As soon as the new unpleasantness with Diana was over, he was going back to the Peninsula where things really mattered.

"It ain't like you to throw a spoke in a man's wheel," Townsend complained.

''You've thrown too many spokes in the wrong places, Bell,'' Lucien reminded him. ''You cannot afford another misstep, you know.''

But Townsend wasn't entirely convinced. He stared for a moment, then shrugged. ''Some things might be worth the risk,'' he decided, plunging into the crowd after her. ''Lady Kingsley, perhaps you'd care for a turn about the park?'' he asked, catching up to her. ''Got a new equippage and a splendid pair.''

He was a handsome fellow, there was no denying that. ''Well, I—''

''Perhaps tomorrow?''

''Not tomorrow, I am afraid. It's my day to go to Hookham's.''

''Good night, Townsend,'' Arthur told him coldly.

''Set down, Bell?'' Longford murmured at the viscount's elbow.

''Not precisely.'' Townsend's gaze followed her and Kingsley all the way to the door. ''A pretty plum ripe for the picking, I'd still say.''

''You've picked too many plums, Bell,'' was the dry reply. ''I doubt the baron will be as complacent as I was.''

* * *

Ensconced in the carriage and leaning back against the green velvet squabs, Elinor waited for the inevitable peal, and it was not long in coming.

''You little fool! You would ruin all I have striven for!'' he hissed at her. ''What were you thinking of?''

''I am not a child,'' she retorted, turning to stare out the window.

''When you saw the Jersey woman give him the cut direct, you should have also!''

''Who?'' she inquired, feigning innocence.

''Longford! Don't know what Leighton was thinking of either, for the earl is not received. But it isn't the same—a man can survive the association!'' He leaned across the seat and reached to lift the emerald collar with a cold fingertip.

She held herself very still, not wanting him to touch her. ''I have enough credit to survive, I think.''

"I'd not have it said my wife lacks breeding, Elinor. I do not pay for you to throw yourself at Longford. Townsend either."

"I should scarce call a few words throwing myself, Arthur," she responded coldly.

"I have made you, Elinor, and I'd not have you forget it. Without my money, Ashton would be rotting in Newgate, and your family would be on the rolls." When she said nothing more, his anger began to ebb, and he leaned back. "Well, I have said enough on that head, I think. No doubt you were too green to know what to do," he conceded finally.

She'd heard him say it before, not often, but still it rankled. She considered lashing out that she'd rather be free than rich, but it would serve no purpose. Instead, she watched the glowing yellow balls of the gaslights that lined the street.

For all that she'd vexed him, he did not want to further a quarrel, not when he needed her. "You must be exceedingly tired," he said after a time.

She wasn't, but she knew what to expect, so she merely nodded. Once home, he would order warm milk and honey for her and a glass of port for himself, and given that it was Saturday, he would join her in her bed. She considered saying that she did in fact have the headache, that she felt fever coming on, but that also would make no difference. He would tell her he was "healthy as a horse—always have been, in fact," and he would sleep with her for the sake of appearance, because his vanity required it.

She pulled the evening cloak about her, folding it over her arms, and told herself she was merely blue-deviled. She ought to give the man across from her credit—he'd made her into the envy of half the ladies in London. He'd showered her with jewels and pampered her with every convenience. He'd seen that nothing was too good for her. He'd guided her into the chancy waters of a gay, almost brittle society. It was altogether true—everything she was, he'd made from a green, scared fifteen-year-old girl, and yet despite all he'd given her, she was restive and bored with much of her life. She wanted more—she wanted someone to hold her, someone to love her for more than her face and form.

''Chilled, my dear?'' he inquired solicitously. ''Perhaps a toddy would be more useful than milk tonight.''

''I don't want a toddy.''

''If I have criticized you, it's for your own good, Elinor. I'd have you know how to go on.''

She wanted to cry out that she didn't want to know how to go on, that she wanted to know how to *live*. As it was, she was growing old within a body that was not yet twenty.

Once home, as soon as he took her cloak, the butler informed Kingsley, ''Master Charles is at home, sir.''

''The devil he is,'' Arthur muttered, clearly displeased by the news. ''Gone up to bed, has he?''

''No, my lord—he awaits you in the bookroom.''

The old man's face creased into a deep frown. ''You'd best go on, my dear,'' he told Elinor. ''I shall be up directly. Tell Mary when she fetches your toddy that I'd take half a glass of port and no more. Got a twinge of the gout tonight, I'm afraid.'' Leaning over, he kissed her cheek. ''Best have her put another blanket on the bed.''

As she climbed the stairs, she heard him enter the bookroom, and she stopped on the landing to listen. At first, there was the indistinguishable murmur of voices, then the sounds of a quarrel rose acrimoniously as Arthur shouted at his grandson and was answered angrily. Charles had been sent down from Oxford, and it did not appear that he was sorry for it. He could not study, he declared, not when England's finest were fighting for her life and honor. All he wanted, he cried, was for his grandfather to buy his colors. There was a stunned silence, then Arthur thundered, ''I have reared an ingrate—an ingrate—do you hear me? You are my heir, Charles—I have built an empire for you!''

''You don't understand me! I cannot—''

''There is nothing to discuss, Charles! I forbid this nonsense! I did not send you to Harrow and Oxford for this!''

''I won't go back!''

''You won't go to Spain either! Let the poor fight the Corsican upstart! No grandson of mine goes!''

The door opened, and she hastened up the stairs. Behind her, the young man trod angrily, catching her at the top. Below, Arthur shouted for him to come back.

"Guess you heard," Charles muttered at her shoulder. "Damn him! Sorry—shouldn't have said that before you. But he doesn't care what I want—he doesn't care what anybody wants! It's all his plans—*his* plans! What about mine? I don't want to sit around waiting for him to die! I want to live my own life, Elinor! I'm ready to fight Boney—I'm ready to fight for England!"

She turned around to face him, and as she looked up into his angry, troubled eyes, she felt an instant sympathy. She knew exactly what he meant.

"I know."

"You cannot know! You are a female!" he retorted.

"I thought you were going to bed, Elinor," Arthur observed from the bottom of the stairs. "As for you, Charles," he said coldly, "I will speak with you again in the morning."

The young man's face flushed, but he managed to hold his tongue. Impulsively, Elinor reached to touch his arm, whispering, "You are not alone, Charles." Then, knowing that her husband came up, she moved quickly to her bedchamber.

"The young master's home," Mary observed as Elinor sat down before her dressing table.

"Yes." Elinor tried to hide her exhilaration at the news. For a time at least, she would have someone to talk with, someone to laugh with, someone young enough to understand.

"Jeremy, the lower footman, says he got sent down fer a prank."

"I don't know."

"Well, it don't matter—he ain't the first," the maid went on as she began taking the pins from Elinor's head.

"No."

"I heard ye in the hall, so's I ordered the milk fer ye." She paused a moment to drop the pins into an enameled box. "I knew as how ye didn't like any toddy."

"Thank you."

"Stands to reason—if ye'd wanted toddy, he'd ordered milk, don't you see?" When Elinor did not answer, Mary continued, "I got laudanum if you was wanting to lace his port, ye know."

"What?"

"Well, it's his night to come to you, ain't it? And if you wasn't wanting to—well, thought maybe ye'd want the laudanum."

It occurred to Elinor then that the maid really did not know that Arthur did not touch her as a wife. "No—but I thank you, Mary," she said sincerely.

"I'm sorry, my dear—I did not mean for Charles to disturb you," he murmured, coming into the room. "An unfortunate matter, but I don't mean to bend."

He was waiting to watch her undress, and she knew it. A shiver crept down her spine, sending a shudder through her. But as always, he turned a chair to face her. "Do go on," he directed Mary. "By the by, I sent back the milk, and James is fetching the toddy. It will warm her."

"DON'T KNOW WHY it had to be Hookham's," Charles muttered behind her. "Damme if I ain't had enough of books for a while. If you are not wanting to take a turn about the park, I can think of a dozen other places besides a damned library. Sure you would not rather go to the Mint—or the Menagerie at the Tower?"

"No."

She was already halfway up the steps. Sighing, he hastened after her. There was no accounting for female tastes, he decided, for it seemed as though every one of them among his acquaintance was addicted to the Gothic Romance. And he did not understand the appeal at all, particularly after a fellow in his hall at Harrow had smuggled one in and read it aloud after hours. He could still remember the snickers that had brought old Humphrey's rod down on them.

"Good afternoon, Lady Kingsley," the gentleman behind the desk greeted her, rising. "I have obtained the book you requested." He held up the leather-bound volume. "Miss Austen's *Sense and Sensibility*. Highly recommended by the ladies—we've scarcely kept it in since it came out last November."

"Thank you. When I am done browsing about, I shall come back for it."

"No!" Charles protested. "Dash it, but I ain't—" He was too late, for she'd already started into the reading room. It was going to be a long afternoon, and he knew it.

"Females!" he uttered, rolling his eyes at the clerk.

"Do you have a subscription, sir?"

"No—and I don't want one neither. Thought I was going for a drive, if you want the truth of it. Said she wanted to stop in here, but how was I to know she meant to stay, I ask you?'' he demanded, aggrieved. Then, perceiving that the clerk's expression was rather censurious, he muttered, ''Don't suppose you even got any military books, do you?''

''Oh, yes—yes, indeed, sir. In fact, there is an excellent volume on Marlborough. And Rogers's diaries, I believe. And Caesar's campaigns. And an excellent study of—''

Afraid he was going to be treated to a cataloging, Charles cut him short. ''You don't say.''

''Perhaps if you do not wish to subscribe, Lady Kingsley might—''

''Lud, I don't think so. Tell you what—I'll just sit and wait for her in there.''

She was opening a book to the last pages and reading it. Discarding it, she picked up another one and did the same. Finally, he could stand it no longer. ''Dash it, if you was to know the end, why would you want to read it?''

''I don't read anything where everybody dies,'' she replied. ''I despise tragedies.''

''Every one of 'em is a tragedy, if you was to ask me.'' Just then, a solitary gentleman caught his eye, and he brightened. ''Egad—Longford!''

''Shhhhh,'' someone hissed behind them.

''Dash it, but it's Longford!'' he shot back, unrepentant. ''Fellow's been in Spain with Old Douro!''

''*Will* you be quiet, Charles?'' Elinor whispered.

''Think I'll see him,'' he mumbled. ''Ain't nothing else to do here.'' Ambling diffidently to where the earl sat absorbed in a book, he cleared his throat. ''Sir?''

The black head snapped back almost warily, and the black eyes narrowed when they saw Charles. ''I don't believe—'' he began coldly.

''Kingsley—Charles Kingsley, my lord. We met in Cornwall some years back—in the winter—party at Stoneleigh,'' he offered, trying to prompt the earl's memory and yet hoping Longford would not remember his boorish behavior then. As the dispatches and news accounts had come in, Charles's earlier censure had turned to outright admiration. To him, Longford was more the hero than Mad Jack had been.

"Ah, yes. Kingsley," Lucien murmured. "The old man's son."

"Grandson." Charles dropped to a chair across from Longford. "Were you at Talavera, sir?" he blurted out.

"Yes."

"And at Cuidad Rodrigo?"

"I was."

"And at Badajoz last month?"

"Yes." Uncomfortable, Lucien snapped his book shut and started to rise.

"Don't go, sir—please. I'd know what it was like—with Wellington, I mean. I'd know what it was like to beat the Frogs."

There was no mistaking the eagerness in the younger man's eyes, and despite the adulation he saw there, Lucien felt compelled to dispel it. "It was hell," he said succinctly.

For a moment, Charles was taken aback by the flatness in Longford's voice, then he brightened. "We did give 'em hell, didn't we?"

"It was hell all around—for all of us." Lucien sat back down and stared for a long moment. "Hell," he repeated softly. When he looked up, Charles Kingsley still watched him, his face a mirror of boyish innocence. "You wouldn't like it," he said abruptly. "There is a stench to it—smoke, blood, animal offal—not very glorious, I'm afraid. And it's noisy—first there is the awful cannon fire, the rockets, the shouts—and when it's over only the cries of poor dying devils break the deafening silence."

"How can you say so when it's for the honor of England you fight?" the younger man cried.

"Honor?" It was little more than a snort. "Not for honor—nor glory neither."

"But—"

"Make no mistake about it—it's to stop Bonaparte before England stands alone."

"Well, I know that, but—"

"I'm ready now, Charles." Elinor hesitated, then spoke to the earl. "Hello, my lord—it's a pleasure to see you again."

She was as stunning in her bronze lustring walking dress as in her evening gown, and wisps of her bright hair framed her oval face beneath the pleated brim of her matching bonnet. The thought crossed his mind that not many could wear the color. Hers was, even to his jaded taste, an unusually appealing beauty.

But though her words were polite, her copper eyes darted nervously to the door, as if she half-expected Kingsley himself to appear. Lucien rose politely, inclining his head.

"Lady Kingsley."

Knowing that the earl was probably not received, Charles flushed guiltily, yet he was loath to leave. "Been talking to Longford a bit while I waited. His lordship's been everywhere."

"Everywhere?" One of her brows arched in disbelief, then she smiled impishly, making Lucien wonder at the easy discourse between them. "I shouldn't think quite everywhere, Charles. I mean, there is India—and America—and China—"

"In the war—Talavera—Cuidad Rodrigo—"

"Suffice it to say I have been in the Peninsula," Lucien cut in curtly.

"You staying home now?" the younger man wanted to know.

"No." Briefly, the earl appeared absorbed in the stamped title on his book, then he looked up, meeting Elinor's eyes. "A bit of business, then I am back, I'm afraid."

"Wish I were going with you," Charles declared.

"Be grateful that you are not," Longford retorted. "War steals a man's soul. And the last thing we have need of is more idealistic fools, for they seldom survive." He reached for his beaver hat and adjusted it over his black hair to suit him. "Your servant, Lady Kingsley. Kingsley."

Noting the flush in Charles's face, Elinor said stiffly, "I'm afraid you are not very civil, sir, when you are in the presence of an admirer."

The black brow rose quizzically. "You—or the boy?"

Perceiving that he meant to glean more than was there, she felt almost foolish. "Charles, of course."

"Oh, I did not take it amiss," Charles hastened to assure him. "Know what you meant—too many green 'uns sign up, don't they?"

"Precisely." Bowing slightly, Lucien looked intensely

into Elinor's eyes again. "My compliments on your social success, my dear. And no, I have not forgotten our first meeting. You have a face that lingers in a man's memory." Pushing his chair back under the table, he turned to leave.

Later, she could not think for the life of her why she did it, but she called after him, "I wish you Godspeed, my lord. England depends on men like yourself." And once again, she felt the fool for saying it.

He turned back, and for a moment, the derisive smile curved his mouth. "Don't let Sally Jersey hear you," he advised softly. Then he walked to the counter, where he handed the clerk his book, and left.

Bemused, she stared after him until Charles tugged at her elbow. "What the devil did he mean by that? Damme if I was not at Stoneleigh also. But there's no denying he's a handsome fellow, I suppose—you just got to remember he's a rake, that's all. Dangerous to the females. Mad Jack's son, after all." Propelling her toward the desk, he muttered, "You ain't up to his weight, I hope you know."

"I am not entirely green, Charles. And I don't think Lord Longford was attempting a flirtation." Perceiving that the young man had been more than a little affronted by his hero's manner toward her, her eyes twinkled as she assured him, "From my *vast* experience in the matter, I have found amorous men much more inclined to flatter, so I think you can acquit Lord Longford."

"Which amorous men?" he demanded suspiciously.

"All of them."

As Elinor laid her selections before the gentleman behind the desk, Charles tried to read the title of the one Longford had handed in. *Marlborough*. "Er—I should like to borrow that one," he decided. "On her subscription." Seeing that Elinor stifled a smile, he retorted, "Dash it, but you ain't the only one as can read, you know. I ain't been to school for nothing."

Once outside, he looked up at the sky, and shook his head disgustedly. "Here I got the old gent's smartest cattle, and it ain't raining, and we ain't going anywhere."

She felt sorry for him, for like her, he'd been constrained far too much in his nineteen years. "Well, I don't suppose a turn in the park would do any harm," she conceded. "I did tell Arthur that I would be at home this afternoon, but I suppose he will not refine too much if I am late. 'See and be seen,' he is forever telling me."

"That's the ticket. See and be seen—and Hyde Park's the place for it."

"But we shall be a bit early for the crowd."

"That don't matter. Thing is, we got a bang-up equippage to ride in, and it don't hurt m'credit to be seen with a Toast—be the envy of every fellow as sees me, in fact," he added gallantly. He stopped and looked back at her. "You know, for all I didn't like his saying it, Longford's right—you got a face a man don't forget—deuced pretty, you know."

"Spanish coin—but I shall accept it."

"Beauty," he declared solemnly. His blue eyes warmed as they met hers. "Thought you was the prettiest chit I'd ever see when you first came to Stoneleigh, you know, but I was wrong—look better every year."

"Now I *know* you are giving me Spanish coin, Charles," she told him severely.

"No, I ain't." Then, realizing that he'd probably said too much, he took her arm. "Come on—the rest of the day is waiting for us. And if there ain't anybody in the park, we'll repair to Gunther's for ices. And tomorrow, we'll go to the Mint—and maybe the Tower."

"Tomorrow I am being fitted at Madame Cecile's," she demurred.

"For what?" he fairly howled. "You keep the woman in business!"

She sighed. "I know, but Arthur would have it that I am in need of a new muslin or two—and some day dresses—and perhaps a new gown for the Devonshires' ball next month—not to mention a new riding habit."

"You cannot tell me you do not have more clothes than you can count," he snorted.

"Ah, but I have already been seen in most of them, you see."

He stopped to stare at her. "He don't let you wear 'em more'n once?"

"Not in public, I'm afraid."

"Egad."

"I find it a sad trial, if you would have the truth of it," she admitted. "It is such a waste that I have taken to sending my cast-offs to my sister Charlotte, though they are a bit old for her. And Mama has written me saying that I must economize more—as though I have the choice.''

The liveried tiger brought the two-seater up to the curb and jumped down to take his place on the rear step. Charles handed Elinor up, then climbed onto the seat beside her. ''Here—hold m'book, will you?'' Taking the reins, he twisted them around his wrist, then flicked the small whip. ''Always did like to drive,'' he told her, settling back against the leather seat.

The park was thin of company, allowing Charles to give the pair their heads. The air against Elinor's face was exhilarating, providing a feeling of freedom that the staid outings with Arthur lacked. As they turned a corner precariously, nearly oversetting a flower stand, the wind caught the brim of her bonnet, whipping it back from her face, and before she could catch it, the ribbons came loose. It sailed directly into the path of a single rider. On the instant, the rider shouted for them to halt as he reined in but inches from the hat. He dismounted to retrieve it, then walked toward them.

''Lady Kingsley,'' he murmured, holding it up to her.

''How kind of you, my lord. My thanks.''

Bellamy Townsend bowed, but not before she saw the speculative glance he cast at Charles. ''On your way to Hookham's?'' he chided her meaningfully.

''Actually, already been,'' Charles answered for her. ''Saw a friend of yours there, in fact.''

''Oh?''

''Longford.''

If he'd intended to embarrass the viscount, he was wide of the mark. Townsend merely smiled. ''There is no ill-will there.''

''Glad to hear of it,'' Charles muttered. ''Servant, sir.''

But before he could flick the reins, Elinor caught his arm, then leaned forward to address Townsend. ''Forgive the lapse, but you are acquainted with my husband's grandson, are you not?''

''I have not had the pleasure, I am afraid.''

''Charles Kingsley. And I am certain you have heard

of his lordship. It's Viscount Townsend, Charles,'' she murmured.

''We ain't been in the same circles,'' the younger man said stiffly. ''But I know all about him.''

Bellamy Townsend favored him with a patronizing grin. ''No—it has been some time since I was a schoolboy, I admit. Oxford—or Cambridge?''

Perceiving that he'd been set down, Charles bristled. ''Neither—I am come to town. Been thinking of signing up to fight the Frogs, in fact,'' he added importantly.

One of Townsend's blond eyebrows rose. ''Shouldn't think you'd like it—it's a dirty business best left to those below us.''

''Longford don't think so,'' Charles retorted.

The eyebrow rose higher. ''Sometimes Longford is a fool.'' Abruptly turning his attention back to Elinor, the viscount's manner changed, and he flashed her an engaging smile. ''Had I known you did not mean to tarry at the library, I should have offered to take you there myself, Lady Kingsley. Is it too much to hope that you will be at home tomorrow?''

''No, she ain't,'' Charles cut in quickly. ''Going to the Mint—and the Tower. After Madame Cecile's.''

Ignoring the younger man, Townsend addressed Elinor again. ''Then perhaps the day after?''

''That would be fine, sir. Indeed, but I am quite certain that Arthur would welcome the company.''

The viscount tipped his hat rakishly, letting the sun show his blond Brutus to advantage. ''Until then, Lady Kingsley—and do give my regards to Arthur.''

''What were you thinking of, Elinor?'' Charles demanded as Viscount Townsend remounted his horse. ''Man's a damned dolly mopper!''

''I beg your pardon?''

''Sorry—he's in the petticoat line—been beneath too many petticoats to count 'em, if you want the truth of it.''

''Charles!''

''Sorry,'' he said again, but his manner was anything but repentant. Looking again to where Bellamy Townsend rode down one of the paths, he frowned. ''Ain't any way to wrap it up in clean linen for you, I'm afraid. And I don't care if you have been about the town, you are as green as I am—greener, in fact, 'cause m'grandfather don't give you much leash."

Affronted, she declared stiffly, "I merely said he could call. Anything less would have been uncivil. Besides"—she gazed after the retreating rider—"besides, he does not look so very dangerous to me."

"Humph!" he snorted. "Shows what you know, don't it? Man's got no principles—none. Look at the Longford thing—every one of 'em had to leave the country! And that don't even begin to count the others!"

"What others?" she asked.

"Not the sort of thing I can tell you—ain't fit for a gel's ears."

"He is more received than your Lord Longford," she reminded him, "so there cannot be much to the tales."

" 'Cause there's too many as wouldn't want him to talk out of Church, don't you see?"

"Sally Jersey—"

"Especially Lady Jersey. Lady Oxford also, to name but two of 'em. No, he put himself beyond the pale for me over the Longford affair, I can tell you. Man don't dally with his best friend's wife—and certainly not before there's an heir." He shook his head in disgust. "How'd you think Longford was to feel if Diana Fenton had a-given him a son by the side door? Man wants his own blood to inherit, and his wife owes him that, you know. You can blame Longford for the scandal, but I can see why he did it—the gel was an utter ninnyhammer to do a corkbrained thing like carrying on with Bellamy Townsend!"

"Five years ago you did not like Longford."

"I was a boy. Got to admire him now."

"Because he serves with Wellington," she observed dryly.

"Respect him. He took the risk and paid the price."

"Yes, I saw the price last night. Sally Jersey looked through him as though he did not exist."

"Lady Jersey's got her gall—how many lovers do you think she's had?" he demanded indignantly. "Been away at Oxford, and even I've heard the tales! She's even dallied with Prinny!"

"It seems to be the way of things, doesn't it?" she sighed. "Sometimes I think I must be sadly out of fashion, you know. The only requirement appears to be discretion—and the heir, of course. Although Lady Sefton took it upon herself to remind me that it is always a good notion to have a spare—just in case, mind you—before one embarks on an *affaire de coeur*."

"Egad. She didn't."

"You have no idea how many ladies of the *ton* have seen fit to advise me how I should go on—using the excuse of my youth and inexperience, you understand."

Charles cast another glance at Bellamy Townsend, who had rounded the path and was again headed their way. With one hand, he flicked the whip, urging the horses to speed, and with the other, he reached to cover Elinor's fingers, squeezing them.

"Deuced good thing I came home, ain't it? If I cannot go to the Peninsula before I am of age, I might as well protect you from the likes of Bell Townsend."

"Thank you, but I don't think—"

"And you ought to call me Charley—everybody but you and the old man do, anyways." Squeezing her hand again before he released it, he smiled. "You make the place bearable, you know."

There was unexpected warmth in his blue eyes, and for a moment, Elinor was drawn to it. Unlike the jaded blades of the *ton*, he was open, honest, and without guile.

"Take you everywhere," he promised. "Show you everything you want to see, 'cause I know Grandpapa ain't done it. Even take you to the parties, if you was to want, but I got to warn you—I ain't learned to dance one whit better than the day you were presented at Stoneleigh."

"Well, if you are to go about in society, you will have to learn the new German dance," she teased him.

"Don't want to learn anything German," he maintained stoutly. "Bunch of clunches, if you was to ask me. Only got to look at the royal family to know that."

"It's quite the scandal in London, you know. Charles, you will not credit it, but the gentleman actually holds the lady's waist."

"You don't say!"

"Unmarried females must be approved by the patronesses at Almack's before they can do it publicly—as though that makes it right. Only fancy—" She giggled.

"Only fancy—just last week, the rector at St. Paul's railed against it, saying it was but a license to lechery."

"You got to show me when we get home. And just because you are approved, it don't mean you got to do it in public, after all. You save that for the family."

She cocked her head and looked sidewise at him. "If you were not relation, I'd think you jealous."

"Just don't want you letting Bell Townsend hold you, that's all," he shot back, reddening. "Kingsley honor, don't you know?"

"Well, I'll teach you the waltz, anyway," she decided. "Then if I am ever given vouchers to Almack's, I can watch you lead out the unmarried females."

"Don't want to lead 'em out. Rather dance with you. Make me the envy of every man there," he insisted sincerely. "Prettiest female in London, after all."

"Well, you are not precisely a shab yourself."

"You don't think so?"

This time, she turned in her seat to face him, and for a long moment, she studied his straight, clean features and the soft brown of his hair. Then she met his blue eyes squarely.

"Not at all. You'll set the heart of every female on the Marriage Mart to fluttering, Charley. And since you are his only heir, it will not be long before the matchmaking papas are courting Arthur for your hand." Her fingers clasped his briefly, and she smiled. "You'll have your pick of all the pretty girls."

His flush deepened. "Don't want any of 'em," he declared firmly. "There ain't another like you."

ELINOR STARED PAST her mirror, out her bedchamber window, scarce seeing the profusion of flowers in the garden below, her thoughts on Bellamy Townsend—and on Charles Kingsley. For the past ten days, the dashing viscount had fairly haunted the house, and his presence was an unsettling reminder of what her marriage denied her. There was a vague ache, a certain loneliness that no matter how Charles tried, he could not completely dispel the sense of the emptiness that was her life. But God knew Charles did try, and she could not help loving him like a brother for it.

Poor Charles, she reflected wearily. He'd set himself up at every juncture as her protector against Lord Townsend to the point of utter rudeness. It was as though he saw himself as some sort of rival, and his determined concern was beginning to come to the notice of Arthur. Already there were signs of a widening gap between her husband and his grandson, particularly since he'd caught her and Charles coming back from watching the fireworks at Vauxhall. He'd told his heir angrily that it was not a place for Baroness Kingsley, and they had quarreled.

Still, she admitted to a certain bond with the younger man, for she knew what it was to wait for someone to die—she knew the resentment—and the guilt. Not that she wished any harm to come to Arthur, of course. Nothing of the sort. If she were free, she did not care if he lived forever. Even that candid thought yielded guilt, for she suspected that he could not help what he was, that the years of making his fortune had given him a singleness of purpose that precluded any degree of intimacy with anyone. For all his wealth, Arthur Kingsley was a man apart, a man alone.

"Blue-deviled, my lady?" Mary asked, breaking into her thoughts.

Elinor sighed. "I suppose I am."

"It's a lovely day."

"Is it?"

Elinor wanted to cry out that it did not matter that the sun shone, or that the flowers bloomed, for it would be but a day like any other. She would drink her chocolate, dress, then wait aimlessly for Charles and Arthur to join her for a light nuncheon, where Arthur would dampen any attempt at lively conversation. After four and one-half years of marriage, it still mystified her that he expected her to be witty, gay, and scintillating among the *ton*, but he preferred her to be quiet, almost subdued at home.

And after she and Charles stared at their plates, mumbling naught but the merest pleasantries for exactly one-half hour, she would escape to look forward to the stilted, always correct calls. Most of the time, she counted it a mercy when the cards were merely left in the silver salver in the hall, and she was spared exchanging the merest commonplaces with empty-headed titled ladies, whose only interests seemed to be exhibiting their husbands' money on their backs and titillating each other with the latest *on-dits*. And today she simply had no interest in more fatuous gossip. If someone were to say that Prinny's latest favorite was the dean of Canterbury's wife, she'd not care.

No, she'd much rather racket about seeing London with Charles, doing those things that vexed Arthur, like the excursion to the Royal Mint, which had turned into an entire afternoon—or like entertaining Viscount Townsend, whose manner was pleasing and whose conversation was amusing.

She had to admit to a certain liking for Bellamy Townsend, for he was as handsome, witty, and engaging as her husband was not. Unfortunately, he was also becoming assiduously obvious in his attentions, and it would not be long before Arthur drew the line there also. That would leave only Charles. And if Charles did not cease guarding her like the proverbial bone . . . well, it did not bear thinking. But already Arthur had remarked mildly but definitely that he was afraid they were inadvertently inviting gossip.

"Ye got the headache again," Mary murmured, drawing the brush through the tangled copper hair. "I can see it."

"No."

"The master said ye was to know he means to be out."

"Oh?"

"Gone to meet with his solicitor, he said, and then to his club." The brush hit a snarl, and the maid had to stop to carefully separate it with her fingers. "But he's to be home before Almack's, he told Daggett to tell ye."

Almack's. The last bastion for Arthur Kingsley to storm before he counted himself a success. Despite the honor of Sally Jersey's voucher, Elinor found herself strangely loath to go. Perhaps it had been the three days' discussion of what she would wear, to whom she must speak, of how she must comport herself, but she was heartily sick of the place before she ever stepped inside it. Like much else in her life, she expected it to be a crushing bore, another aimless night of being seen. But to Arthur the invitation was her greatest triumph.

Mary held up a lock of Elinor's hair, surveying it critically in the mirror before them. "Don't know why he wants the diamond pins with the peach gown," she grumbled. "Me—I think ribbons would show better. I mean, ye got the diamonds on yer neck, don't ye? Too many of 'em and they's looking at the stones instead of ye."

Elinor sighed. "My dear Mary, by now you surely must know that were it possible, I should have to wear the entire vault to please him. I am but the display case for his money, after all."

There was no mistaking the bitterness in her young mistress's voice, and for a moment, the maid was taken aback. "Ye don't give a fig fer any of it, do ye?" she murmured sympathetically.

"Oh, I do not deny that some of it amuses me," Elinor admitted, "but much of my life is always the same." She twisted her head to look up at the maid and forced a smile. "How ungrateful I must seem to you, when I have so much."

"Well, I wouldn't mind being ye, if it wasn't fer his

lordship,'' Mary conceded. ''What ye need is a wee one in yer nursery. But I don't spose—well, guess he's too old ter get one. Guess he ain't got as much—''

''What an improper thing to say.'' Shaking her head, Elinor returned to disabusing the maid of the glamour of her existence. ''You might not think so, but you would soon tire of the life. The smiles are false, the friendships shallow, and everyone waits for a misstep that he may amuse himself over it. And there are only so many dresses one can wear. It's a shocking waste—all of it.'' Looking again to the mirror, Elinor made a face at her reflection. ''One day I shall be as empty as they are, you know.'' And as she said it, she knew it for the truth.

''Ye cannot say Lord Townsend does not admire you,'' Mary murmured slyly.

''I suspect Lord Townsend admires the chase more than the chased.''

''Or the chaste.''

Both women turned at the sound of Charles Kingsley's voice. Moving into the room, he apologized, ''Didn't mean to intrude before you are dressed, Elinor, but I thought perhaps later we might watch the balloon ascension in Hyde Park.'' His blue eyes took in the copper hair that cascaded over the shoulders of her embroidered silk wrapper, and his mouth went suddenly dry. Despite the race of his pulse, the catch in his breath, he managed to grin crookedly. ''Look good *en deshabille*. Truly.'' Even as he said it, his face flushed, betraying him. ''So—want to go?'' he asked eagerly.

''You know there will be callers,'' she reminded him.

''If you are speaking of Bell Townsend, he can dashed well leave his card,'' he declared brutally. ''Fellow runs too damned tame in this house to suit me, anyway.''

''Arthur—''

''Won't know of it—I swear.''

''Like he did not know of our visit to Vauxhall?''

''Thought he was going to stay at his club. How the deuce was I to know he'd be home early? And you cannot say it was not great fun. Besides, it's day—and I'll have you back for Almack's,'' he coaxed. ''And I won't let anybody ogle you, I promise. Be good to go somewheres besides the modistes.''

It was tempting, but she did not want to be the cause

of another peal read over him by his grandfather. Reluctantly, she shook her head. "I don't think I should—not today."

For a long moment, he stared at her, and his flush deepened. "I see," he declared stiffly. "You would rather exchange inanities with Bellamy Townsend than go anywhere with me."

"Of course not, but—"

"You need say no more on that head, Elinor." Gathering his affronted pride about himself like a cloak, he turned on his heel and stalked out. "I ain't a complete fool yet," he flung over his shoulder.

"Charles—oh dear—" She half-rose, calling after him, "Charley—it's no such thing!" When he did not answer, she sank back onto the padded seat. "Do you think I ought to go?" she asked Mary uncertainly.

"If ye do, his lordship ain't going ter take it kindly," the maid pointed out reasonably. "Seems ter me as he's already vexed with the boy."

"Yes." Elinor exhaled heavily. "And I am afraid it's my fault."

"No, it ain't. Ye cannot help it that the boy's head over heels fer ye."

"It's no such thing, and I'd not have you repeat it." But even as she said it, Elinor did not quite convince herself.

"Humph! Only the blind as don't see it."

"We are relation, after all," Elinor retorted. "And neither of us has anyone else for company much of the time."

The maid shrugged. "Most young bucks haunt the clubs."

"Arthur would like that even less, for he is opposed to gaming. He keeps nearly as tight a rein on Charley as on me, if you would have the truth of it."

"Mebbe so," the maid acknowledged noncommittally.

Before Mary could pursue Charles's growing attachment further, Elinor turned the subject. "I'd best get dressed."

"And which was ye wanting ter wear t'day? The master favored the blue-figured muslin, Daggett says."

Daggett says. *Daggett says.* She was heartily sick of the valet. In fact, she was heartily sick of everything. On this, the day of her supposedly great triumph, she longed not for the approbation of the patronesses at Almack's, but rather for a life like anyone else's. She wanted to be a schoolgirl again, to laugh and tease with other girls, to be free to wear what she liked over and over again.

"You really think ribbons?" she asked, looking into the mirror again.

"Tell ye what Lady Landsdowne's dresser said ter me—'it's the simple as is elegant'—and she has an eye fer it. But his lordship—"

"Where would you go for ribbons?" Elinor wondered slyly. "I mean—if *you* were to buy them, where would you shop?"

"Me? I don't—well, I ain't got the money, but—"

"*If* you had the money," Elinor interrupted impatiently.

Not following her mistress's reasoning, the maid decided, "Well, if it was after quarter day and I had me wages, I'd get m'brother Tom ter take me to th' market."

"What market?"

"St. James—got stalls of everything, they do, but it ain't a place fer a lady—" Mary blushed. "Got everything fer sale in Market Lane, ye know—everything," she added significantly.

"But you shop there?"

"Ain't no place like it," the maid said solemnly. "Got everything from smuggled lace and purled ribbons to th' gimcracks fer the females—and Tom says a man can get anything from dressed to tumbled there. Aye, and if ye was to look fer 'em, ye can see the opium holes along the alleys." Then, deciding she'd said too much, Mary's mouth flattened with disapproval. "But it ain't no place fer a lady," she declared, repeating herself.

But the lure of the forbidden already beckoned, bringing an uncharacteristic sparkle to the amber eyes. Compared to the stuffy, effusively condescending atmosphere of the premier modistes, there was a certain fascination for a place where one could get *everything*. It was ever so much more exciting than the confining life at Kingsley House.

"Ribbons, you say?" Elinor inquired impishly.

"Lor' luv ye, but he'd clap us both of if ye was to go there!" Mary cried, alarmed.

"We'll take Charles," Elinor decided, "and thus there will be none to spy on us."

"The tiger—"

"I shall have Charles insist that we do not need him." Elinor rose again, this time going to the door. "Charles! Charles!" When he did not appear in the hall below, she turned her attention to Hensley, the front butler. "Have you seen Master Charles?"

"I believe he has gone out, madam."

"Did he say where?"

"Wilson said he slammed the door before he answered."

"Oh."

"Would you have a footman sent up when he returns?" he asked politely.

It could be hours, nightfall even, and she knew it. "No."

When she retreated into her chamber, Mary merely murmured her relief. "Guess we ain't going anywheres. Besides, ye got Lord Townsend a-coming."

The image of the handsome viscount came to mind and with it the knowledge that he meant to pursue her openly. And already his flattery was taking its toll. In a moment of cowardice, Elinor shook her head.

"We'll take Jeremy, the youngest footman, for he'll not tell. And we shall have the carriage set us down near Carlton House. There can be no exception to that, I should think. It will be considered that we mean to admire the flowers and perhaps walk to Marylebone Park."

"I don't think—"

"And I shall of course give you five pounds to spend on yourself—it will be an escapade between us," Elinor went on eagerly.

Five pounds was a considerable sum to a lady's maid. As Mary contemplated the unexpected windfall, she wavered, then capitulated. "Well," she conceded slowly, "I ain't ever had no trouble there. But ye got to promise me a character if the master was to find out and discharge me."

"Fiddle. As if I should let him." Elinor's eyes met her skeptical maid's for a moment. "I have but to refuse to go to Almack's with him, you know," she declared mischievously. "Besides, we won't let him discover where we have been, so naught's to worry over, is there?"

NOTHING IN HER SHELTERED life had prepared her for the dirty hurly-burly of the streets around the St. James Market, and Elinor thought it inconceivable that such a place could be situated so close to the Prince of Wales's home. Market Lane itself was narrow, strewn with filth, and crowded with an assortment of street urchins, pickpockets, beggars, and bargain hunters who elbowed their way from stall to stall to examine all manner of wares. Ahead of her, a fellow haggled over two shillings for a silk waistcoat, calling it robbery.

A dirty hand caught at her skirt, pulling it, and when she looked down, a toothless beggar grinned up at her. With his free hand, he gestured to his ragged, empty pantleg. "A penny fer a soldier—a penny fer a soldier," he chanted, singsong. His eyes were glassy, his grin almost vacant. Mary started to brush him away, but Elinor fumbled in her reticule for some coins.

"Don't—"

But before she could stop her, her mistress was bending to hand him a shiny guinea.

Jeremy looked back uneasily, then bent close to Elinor to whisper, "Don't be a-showing the gold, my lady."

"Thankee. Thankee." The fellow's grin broadened, showing white gums. Holding the guinea up for all to see, he struggled to stand, then leaning on his gnarled staff, he hopped toward an alley.

"Humph! Going to smoke opium, or me name ain't Mary," the maid muttered.

Stung, Elinor snapped, "The man lost his leg for England! Would you let him starve?"

Noting the curious stares of the people around them, the young footman caught Elinor's arm and pulled her past the haggler, who'd got the price of his prize down to one shilling, seventy pence. Suddenly conscious of what he'd done, Jeremy dropped his hand and mumbled, "Your pardon, my lady, but I'd not see you robbed—or worse." He looked down at the bulging reticule. "Best tuck that under your arm," he advised nervously.

"Here"—Mary removed her plain brown shawl and draped it over Elinor's arm to cover it—"too many flash coves as would cut our throats fer that."

"Did you see the price of that waistcoat?" Elinor asked, betraying her awe. "Arthur must pay fifty times that."

"Daresay it could be flashed," the footman said.

"Flashed?"

"Filched," Mary explained. "A flash is a thief."

It was a different world, this enclave of enterprise that thrived within a stone's throw of the fashionable houses in Piccadilly. And for all that it was seedy and seamy, it was nonetheless exciting to explore. Stopping from time to time to feel of silk scarves "from Norwich," cloth openly described as having eluded "Boney's blockade," colored kid slippers of every description, soft gloves, artificial flowers, dyed ostrich plumes, exquisite laces, and purl-edged ribbons at a fraction of the price at Grafton's. It was a veritable paradise to one used to the sedate establishments Elinor patronized.

"Ye paid what he asked!" Mary fairly howled after the purchase of a fine Norwich shawl. "Before we are to the end, they'll all know ye fer the gentry mort ye are! They'll up the price when they see ye."

"A gentry mort?"

"A lady," Mary muttered in explanation. "Leave the ribbons and laces ter me." To demonstrate, she stepped up to a stall displaying what was marked as "Belgian lace." Winking at the proprietor, she gestured to Elinor, "Me n' the duchess'd like some of the wide."

"And me and the Queen'd be pleased to sell," he shot back. "Six shillings to the yard."

Elinor nearly gasped at the cheapness, but Mary retorted, "We ain't here to be robbed. Three."

The fellow lifted the delicate lace, letting them see the pattern. "It's worth six," he insisted.

"Come on, my lady," Mary murmured. "Old man Grosset's got the same thing fer less."

"Five shillings—it's my best," the merchant whined.

"It's lovely," Elinor said, reaching to touch it.

"Wait until ye see Grosset's."

"Five shillings," he repeated.

"Come on," Mary insisted. "We can do better."

"How much better?" he asked, wavering.

"Four."

"You only offered me three!"

"Well, if he was to start at four, I expect he'll come to three, don't ye know?" the maid countered practically.

"Four."

"And thread to match."

'A penny a spool."

"Come on, my lady." Looking across to the nearly apoplectic proprietor, Mary shook her head. "And ye could have said ye had her Grace fer a customer."

He exhaled heavily. "And the thread."

"Done."

It wasn't until Jeremy had the paper-wrapped lace tucked beneath his arm that Elinor dared to speak. "Why did you say I was a duchess?"

"Because he knows it'll look good on his sign," Mary answered blithely.

"But it's a lie!"

The maid shrugged. "It's the way it's done."

"Does Mr. Grosset have it cheaper?"

A slow smile spread over the maid's face, then she giggled. "Mr. Grosset is the barber in my village, but he don't know that."

"That's dishonest."

"No, it ain't—he expects it." Unchastened, Mary winked at her. "No telling what duchess he'll claim fer patroness, ye know."

A painted woman gestured invitingly to the young footman, and he reddened. Another one, bolder than the first, stepped into his path. Pouting prettily, she leaned into him, but the effect was spoiled by the smell of sweat. Mary pushed the woman aside, chiding her, "Here now, ye hussy—keep yer hands off me husband!"

The footman's flush deepened, and he choked as though he were strangling, but Mary grasped his arm firmly, propelling him past. "Ye don't want one of 'em," she advised him low, "fer they are like ter give ye the clap."

"What's the clap?" Elinor wanted to know.

Jeremy indulged in a full fit of coughing, but the maid merely shook her head. "Ye ain't got ter worry about it, 'cause the master don't consort with any of them."

About that time, the footman happened to notice that two men seemed to be following them. Marking them for cutpurses, he grasped his mistress's arm, urging her, "Run!"

"What?" She started to pull away, then realized he was indeed serious.

Mary looked back over her shoulder. "Oh—Lor!"

"I don't see—"

But Jeremy thrust Elinor ahead of him, muttering a curse she could not understand. When she looked up, she could see that the street ended in an alley.

"There's no way to go!"

But he pulled her into the alley, then paused to look for the way out. Even in daylight, it was a dark, dingy place, littered with beggars and men hunched over, their faces blank from rum or opium. Now there was no mistaking that they were being followed, for as they ran, so did those behind him. Panicked, the young footman yelled at Elinor, "Try to reach Jermyn Street beyond, and I will attempt to delay them!"

"Where?" Frightened, Elinor half-turned back, but the young man was determinedly blocking the narrow alley, his fists raised.

"Come on," Mary muttered, catching her mistress's arm. "Ye got ter turn at th' end."

The two women half-walked, half-ran deeper into the filth-filled footway. A sot grabbed for Elinor's slim skirt, streaking it with dirt, and she stumbled, tumbling into a drug-befuddled fellow. Scarce losing a stride, Mary pulled her up and continued dragging her along.

"This way," she panted, indicating a blind corner. "It's Jermyn Street—it's the way out!" For the briefest instant, Elinor looked back, but there was no sign of Jeremy or of the men who'd followed them. "Ain't no time ter waste!" Mary gasped. "We're marked!"

At the corner, a milling group of ruffians waited, their ragged clothes betraying a different desperation. Some still wore dirty, tattered bandages. For a moment, Elinor hung back, but Mary yanked the reticule from her wrist, then pushed her straightway at them.

"Ye got ter run inter the street!" Opening the fringed silk bag, the maid flashed the gold coins, tossing one out into the lane. It rolled into a garbage-filled puddle, where a dozen hands groped and clawed for it. "Go on!" Mary shouted. "I'll see ye out there!"

The mob surged forward, their interest in Elinor gone as her maid turned the purse inside out, scattering the money. Reaching the open street, Elinor looked back, seeing nothing but the crush of bodies scrambling like pigs for the slop. And she knew she could not leave Mary in that.

"Well, now—" A hand gripped her shoulder, spinning her around, and the smell of cheap rum nearly overwhelmed her as a man leered into her face. "Fancy—a gentry mort! Tad, we's got us a gentry mort!"

She jabbed him with her elbow, catching him in the stomach, then broke and ran directly into the street. Behind her, another fellow grabbed for her, only to roll away as a smart equippage careened around the corner. The driver and tiger shouted and cursed as the horses reared, and she fell, scrambling frantically on her hands and knees in the muddy street to escape the flailing hooves. The wheels rolled over her newly purchased shawl, grinding it into the mire, and the ironclad wheel spokes rattled past her head, catching one of the ribbons of her hat. It jerked free, tumbling her hair into dirty water.

Almost as quickly as she realized she lived, she knew she had to flee. She stumbled blindly for the opposite side, tearing her narrow skirt. Grasping it, she pulled it up, and gulped for enough air to sustain another run.

This time, when she was caught from behind, she turned to flail at her attacker, hitting and clawing blindly at him. "You little fool!" he shouted furiously, shaking her. "You could have been killed! Egad—Lady Kingsley!"

Despite the mud, despite her tangled, dirty hair, despite her ruined gown, she was still a beauty. Just staring into those amber eyes, he felt as though he could drown in them. Telling himself she was but a spoiled, pampered female like any other, he managed to sustain his anger. "What the devil are you doing here?" he demanded harshly.

She looked up into the Earl of Longford's face, then caught both his arms, choking, "We were robbed! My maid—I've got to go back for my maid!"

"The hell you do." For a moment, he steadied her, then looked to his tiger. "We've got to get her out of here," he muttered. When he perceived that she was still shaking uncontrollably, his fury faded. "You are all right—I'll see you home." Before she knew what he meant to do, he swung her up and dumped her into his open carriage. "Get down," he ordered curtly. "You can't be discovered, or there'll be the devil to pay."

"No!" She pushed open the door on the other side, and darted back toward the alley. "I've got to find Mary!"

"What the deuce—?" He had half a mind to leave her then, but as one of her earlier attackers ran after her, he knew he could not. "Hold the horses!" he shouted at his tiger, then he took off in pursuit.

As the fellow caught her, he was yanked back rudely from behind and sent sprawling against a wall. He started to rise, his hands balled into fists. "Try it," Lucien growled, "and I'll draw your cork." This time, when his hand grasped Elinor's, he held on. "There's naught you can do—come on."

"No! You don't understand—it was my folly—and they've got Mary—and Jeremy!" Tears streamed down her dirty face, streaking it, as she struggled to free her hand. "If anything's happened to them, I shall never forgive myself!"

He looked into the alley, seeing the melee as ruffians fought with beggars over a few gold coins. "You can't go back, you little goose," he muttered, pulling her back toward his open carriage. "You've got to get out of here."

"I cannot leave without them!" she cried, her voice rising hysterically. He slapped her then, and she stared in shock. "You hit me!"

"Get in."

"No!"

He uttered a long, unsatisfactory oath, then pushed her

toward his bemused tiger. ''Hold her—if you have to sit on her, hold her,'' he ordered tersely. His black eyes met Elinor's momentarily. ''And if you run back in there, I'll leave you to that mob—do you understand me?''

She nodded mutely as the boy held both her arms from behind.

''What does this Mary look like?''

''She—she's got on a brown dress—and a cap—and a bonnet—brown-checked, I think,'' she mumbled. ''Oh—please—''

Her concern moved him far more than her tears, for it reminded him of the battlefield, where men risked their lives to retrieve the wounded. He grasped his driving whip. ''All right.''

''And Jeremy—'' But he'd already started back across the street. ''Blue livery—he's got blue livery!'' she called after him.

He strode into the alley, shouting for the mob to make way, and for a moment, it looked as though they meant to turn on him. But as he raised the coach whip, one of the ragged men yelled, ''It's Longford! It's the major! He was at Talavera!''

''He's a swell!'' someone countered, crouching as though he meant to jump.

But several of the others restrained him, then looked down, their eyes on the garbage and refuse in the alley. ''Got no pension,'' a man muttered. ''Got to eat.''

It was the same everywhere, and Lucien knew it. He hesitated, uncomfortable with this reminder of how England rewarded those no longer able to fight. ''Come round to my house in Berkeley Square—and I will see you are fed,'' he offered, ashamed. ''But for now, I'd take the woman.''

''What woman?''

''Brown dress and bonnet—she was with the lady.''

''He means the one with the money,'' someone decided. ''She ain't here—tossed the purse and ran.''

''Where?''

''Back.''

''No,'' someone else contradicted. ''Into the den—over there.''

The man who'd recognized him first held out a bright

guinea in his dirty hand, but Lucien shook his head. "Keep it—she can afford it."

A crone lurked in the doorway, her face seemingly frozen in a vacant grin. Behind her, a small, wizened man, his face cracked and seamed, spoke up. "A tuppence fer a pipe—make a man fergit 'is troubles."

He pushed past both of them into the narrow room. It was dark and reeked of the smell of human refuse, vomit, and sweat. In the shadowy hell, men hunched against the wall or bent over the opium pipes, and as his eyes adjusted to the dimness, there was no mistaking the dreamy escape in their faces.

"Mary?" he asked, scanning the room.

In a corner, a woman rose, wiping her muddied face with a corner of her shawl. "I ain't—" she began, afraid the proprietor had sold her. Then she realized he'd used her name. "Aye, sir."

"Come on—your mistress is safe."

The woman began to cry. "He'll turn me off—I know it!" she wailed. "I oughter not let her come!"

"Nonsense," he said brusquely, reaching for her. "Come on."

He had to blink when they emerged again into the light, but the woman clutched his sleeve excitedly, shouting, "It's Jeremy—it's Jeremy—oh, praise the Almighty!"

The young man looked as though he'd been in a mill, but there was no mistaking the concern on his face. "The mistress?" he asked anxiously.

"Safe," Lucien told him. "But we've got to get her out of here."

"Oh—aye." The footman nodded sheepishly. "Knew we ought not to come, sir."

"Perceptive of you," Lucien muttered dryly.

Once outside in the street, he frowned. "I'd take you up, but I'd not draw the attention." He looked to where his tiger maintained a determined grip on Elinor Kingsley. "The trick will be to get her home undiscovered." He hesitated briefly, then dug into his coat pocket, drawing out a couple of small coins. "Can you hire a hackney, do you think?"

"Aye, sir," the footman answered, "but the mistress—"

"I'll take her—discreetly, of course. I'd have you get there first, if you can, that you may smuggle her inside."

"Aye, sir."

Leaving them, he crossed the street. "I'm sending them home in a hired conveyance," he told her abruptly. "Get into the carriage."

"But—"

"If you are fortunate, they may be able to get you into your house before any more harm is done. We'll take the long way to give them time."

"I'd go with them."

"Don't be a fool, Lady Kingsley." Catching her about her waist, he lifted her up into the open four-seater, then climbed in after her. She started to sit only to be pushed into the floor. "Lie down," he ordered. And before she could protest, he threw a lap rug over her.

"I cannot see!"

"You don't need to." To insure that she lay there, he raised one leg to rest on the seat across from him. The other foot he placed on her back. When she tried to rise beneath his calf, he growled, "Don't be a ninnyhammer—if you are seen with me, you are done."

But she could scarce breathe beneath the weight of his leg. She tried to wriggle her head from beneath the rug, only to have him yank it back over her. "Lady Kingsley, I am seldom inclined to aid foolish females, and if you insist on drawing attention to yourself, I will wash my hands of you—do you understand me?" Taking her muffled reply for assent, he reached for the reins, clicking them.

The pair of horses surged forward, throwing her flat against the floorboards. Twisting beneath the leg that pinned her down, she grasped his boot and held on, heedless of the impropriety. The carriage sped for several blocks, then slowed to a leisurely pace, and she could hear the earl exchanging occasional greetings with other drivers as though nothing were amiss. Apparently, in the absence of females, gentlemen did not feel it nearly so incumbent to give the notorious Longford the cut.

After the initial shock of lying beneath the shaft of his boot passed, she became acutely aware of the masculine weight above her. It was nothing like the occasional brushing of Arthur's thin, bony leg against hers. There was something alive, virile, something utterly forbidden about Longford's leg resting on her back.

It brought back the girlish memory of his kiss, the memory of his body against hers, and for a moment, she allowed herself to imagine what it must be like to be loved by someone like him. And the thought, once freed, frightened her with its very existence. It was as though the thought alone could damn her. She had to remind herself that he cared about nothing.

"Riding all right?" he asked, his voice abrupt, as if he really did not care.

"Yes."

But an idea, however preposterous, once born did not die easily. Despite everything she knew of him, she was fascinated by the feel of him, by the masculine smell of leather. Yet any association with the earl, even an innocent one, would be utter folly—and anything more than that would be ruinous. Longford, Sally Jersey had declared, was too dangerous to touch, for he simply refused to acknowledge the rules.

"Lucien!" someone hailed him.

"Hallo, George."

Lord Leighton peered curiously at Longford's extended leg. "Hurt yourself?"

"It pains me sometimes. I must be getting old."

"At nine and twenty?" Leighton snorted. "I beg you will not say it, for we are of an age." He shook his head. "Must be the war. That the leg that took the ball?"

"Yes—but nothing serious."

"You really going back?"

"Monday."

"Don't know why—it's not as if you had to, is it?"

Lucien shrugged. "The Corsican still straddles Europe—and I see no reason to remain here. Suffice it to say I am going back where I am welcomed."

"You and the Ponsonbys," George sighed, then grinned. "Guess it's in the blood—Mad Jack's son, after all. He was hell-bent for anything good or bad, I am told. He stopped, collecting himself, then added sheepishly, "Sorry—didn't mean—"

But the earl's breath seemed arrested, then he exhaled sharply, releasing the sudden tension in his body.

"There's nothing you could say about him that I don't know, George."

"Shouldn't have said it anyway. You coming to dine tonight?" Leighton asked, turning the subject.

"If you can stand the association."

"I've got good credit—too many matchmaking mamas hanging after me. If I was a gazetted murderer, they'd forgive me for m'fortune, I daresay." He hesitated, then blurted out, "Bad business about Diana. You'd have thought after all these years, she'd have let it lie, wouldn't you?"

"Yes."

"You seen the brat? Sefton said it don't look like Bell, but that don't mean—"

"No—I haven't seen her. And I don't mean to."

Perceiving that Longford did not want to talk about that either, Leighton tipped his hat. "Until tonight, then."

As the carriage moved on and silence descended once more, Elinor finally dared to ask, "Where are we?"

"Going through the park. I'd advise you to be still, for we are not alone." To prove his point, he hailed another conveyance, calling out, "Hallo, Bell! You are like a bad penny come 'round again. Just talking about you."

"Talking to yourself, old fellow?" Bellamy Townsend chided.

Longford smiled wryly. "It comes from a lack of society, I suppose, but no—it was Leighton." His eyes narrowed. "You look a trifle pulled."

"The pursuit goes slowly. First female as didn't swoon over me within the week."

Elinor's leg cramped, and she tried to shift her weight to ease it. Longford's foot pressed down, warning her. Then he spoke to the viscount more loudly. "You cannot win every ladybird, you know. Perhaps you ought to cut your losses and go for another, more amenable female."

"Really want this one."

"You want them all," Lucien reminded him.

"But this one's different—if she wasn't wed, I'd think her a virgin. Downright skittish. But," he added smugly, "the plum will be plucked before fall, and you can put your money on it."

There was a brief pause as the earl smoothed the lap

rug over his leg, then he met Townsend's eyes coldly. "I should not advise putting it on the books, Bell. Old men tend to be jealous."

"He won't call me out."

"No." Lucien's hand rested on Elinor's back for a moment. "But this time I don't think you can afford the damages. He is not like to be as complacent as I was."

"Complacent?" Townsend howled. "You made a dashed scandal of it!"

"Take my word for it—Kingsley would see you ruined—and he's got the money for it." Before the viscount could respond, Lucien flicked the coach whip lightly. "Cannot leave the cattle standing," he murmured apologetically. "Good day, Bell."

"Wait—you going to White's tonight?" Townsend shouted after him.

"Leighton's! You?"

"Almack's! Then to White's!"

The four-seater rolled down the lane, leaving Bellamy Townsend to stare after it.

"We are about out of the park," Lucien told Elinor.

"May I get up now?"

"No. Did you hear enough?"

"My knees are cramping. And he did not say it was I, did he?" she countered.

"Your backside ought to burn. If Kingsley had any sense, he'd apply the cane to it." He was silent for a time, then he spoke again. "What the devil were you doing there?"

She didn't like his tone. "I could ask the same of you," she muttered.

"I was at Carlton House." Later, he was to wonder why he did it, for he was not particularly proud of it, but he reached into his coat pocket and drew out a pin. Tossing it beneath the blanket, he explained, "It's because I have survived."

This time, when she lifted a corner of the lap rug, he did not stop her. She stared at the pin. "The Regent decorated you?" she asked, betraying her awe.

"I told you—I am alive. And you have not answered me."

"I went to buy ribbons."

"One would think you could afford Grafton's," he said sarcastically, "or does Arthur keep a tight purse?"

"Sometimes I tire of the life I lead," she said simply.

"The bored widgeon. I pray you will spare me the tale, for rich, useless women pain me."

"I do not expect you to understand, my lord," she responded stiffly. "And if I am rich, it's because Papa took your advice and sold me."

"You seem to have done rather well."

"I have naught to do but shop and be seen."

"An enviable lot to most—did you not see those poor devils back there?" he asked almost angrily. "They have fought for an ungrateful nation, it would seem. And when Prinny has his way and the stalls are torn down, they will probably perish."

"Parliament—"

"Parliament be damned!"

"It's not my fault they are poor. Indeed, I—"

"You are the problem—aye, and all the rest of us."

"At least I have never been embroiled in an unsavory scandal," she retorted. His leg tensed, and she wished she could call back the uncivil words. "Your pardon—"

"There is no need to apologize for the truth, Lady Kingsley."

"But I did not mean—that is, I understand that the circumstances—"

"You don't know the circumstances."

Apparently, for all his seeming indifference, his divorce pained him still, and she pitied him for it. "She must have been very lovely," she said lamely.

"Very."

"I'm sorry."

He snorted derisively. "For what? I assure you I value my freedom above my pride."

"Perhaps she was merely led into it," she murmured, thinking perhaps that would make it less painful for him.

"I rather think it a mutual leading." He lapsed into a strained silence again. He could scarce blame Townsend, for Elinor Kingsley was an Original—a beauty lacking the insipidity he despised. And if he'd had the time, he might have cast a few lures that direction himself. But he didn't—and he had no business thinking it. No, it was better to pursue those who knew how to play the game—

or those who made pursuit unnecessary, the sophisticates among the *demimonde* who understood a business arrangement.

He looked down, seeing the bright, mud-streaked hair, and for all that he told himself he disliked rich, bored females, he could not resist moving his hand to touch the silk of it. And despite what he'd thought scarce a moment before, he considered the possibility he might interest her in a brief liaison. His hand moved lower, brushing the bare skin where her hair fell away from her neck.

She shivered involuntarily, then held her breath, knowing she ought to duck away. Instead, she closed her eyes as his fingertips traced lightly, making her long to be held by a man. If his barest touch could do that to her, she dared not think what his kiss would make her feel now.

He forced himself to remember that she'd been the only one to speak to him, and for that alone he owed her more than this. Reluctantly, he leaned back, warning her, "A word to the wise, my dear—your friend Bellamy is possessed of an utterly inconstant heart. He will lead you to grief, if you allow it."

"It would seem like the pot warning of the kettle," she retorted, trying to hide her embarrassment. "You have not precisely been absent from the tattle-tongues yourself."

"No, but I never promise that which I am unprepared to give. I've never offered any woman constancy to get beneath her petticoat."

"How very crude you are, sir."

"At least I make no pretense of being anything other than what I am. But no doubt the Jersey has warned you to stay away from me." He noted the street. "You can sit now, but you might wish to cover that hair. You can use the rug."

He shifted his legs, and she pulled herself into the seat across from him. "I shall look the veriest quiz," she muttered. Nonetheless, she pulled the woolen blanket over her head.

"I should rather say a ragamuffin."

"What a lack of address."

"Being an outcast, I have little need of any."

"No, I suppose not."

"That's your house, isn't it?"

"That one—yes." She pointed to the large Georgian mansion, its red brick contrasting with the white pillared portico. "Oh, dear." She swallowed, then said hollowly, "Arthur is home."

"Would you have me set you down here?"

"Yes—no—" Her hands twisted the soiled material of her skirt. "It does not matter—he will read me a peal, anyway."

"What do you mean to tell him?"

Her amber eyes widened, then she answered, her voice low. "The truth—and I pray he will not discharge Mary and Jeremy for it. I shall of course make it plain that the scrape was mine, that they attempted to dissuade me."

He stared, oddly drawn to the smudged face and the dirty hair that clung to her neck, and he felt the familiar stirring within. Reminding himself again that he had neither the time nor the inclination to pursue another man's wife, he murmured regretfully, "I should not tell him you were with me, you know."

"I'd not be caught in a lie, my lord."

The carriage had stopped, and the tiger had jumped down to open the door. For an instant, she hesitated, then she held out her hand to Lucien, blurting out, "You must not think me ungrateful, my lord, for had you not come along, I know not what would have happened to me. Indeed, but—"

"It was nothing," he declared brusquely. He tipped his hat, then reset it over his black locks. "Good day, Lady Kingsley."

She stepped down, then turned back to look up into the black eyes. "Goodbye, sir—and Godspeed."

He watched her smooth her muddy, torn gown over her slim figure as though she could somehow lessen the damage, then she squared her shoulders and walked toward the Kingsley house. Telling himself that for all her looks, she was probably as empty-headed as the rest of her sex, he snapped the reins, and as the pair started forward, he looked down to discover the ruined shawl at his feet. For a moment, he considered going back, then decided against it. Even if he were inclined to help her now, he could not. He did not see her stop at the corner, nor did he see her turn back to watch him go.

Her eyes followed him until he was out of sight. He

was a strange man—cold and bitter—and yet if even a fraction of the stories told of him were true, his bitterness did not stop him from enjoying the companionship of Cyprians and opera dancers, she reminded herself. But despite his own warning, she knew he was not entirely bad, for he'd come to her aid, and he'd gone back for Mary. And, dangerous or not, there was that about him that still intrigued her.

She stared absently, wondering if he even remembered kissing her in the inn. He could not know that for nearly five years, her memory of it had lived, promising her that when Arthur was gone, there had to be someone a bit like Longford for her.

"TOWNSEND DO THIS TO YOU?" Charles demanded angrily. "Afore the Almighty, I'll call him out over it!"

"*Will* you be quiet?" Elinor whispered loudly. "You'll alert the whole house!" Acutely aware of her dirty, disheveled appearance, she edged toward the stairs. "I shall explain later."

"Did he force you?" he asked, moving in front of her.

"I said I would speak of this later," she muttered, exasperated, as she tried to pass him. "It was no such thing, I assure you."

"No you don't, my girl—I shall not be fobbed off so easily," he insisted, catching her arm.

"Charley—please!" she hissed desperately. "Later!"

"Unhand her, Charles," Kingsley said.

They spun around guiltily, and his grandson dropped his hand before stepping back. She took a deep breath and waited silently, knowing that she had been too late.

"I have discharged Mary."

The old man's voice was controlled, but there was no mistaking the edge in it. His faded eyes rested on her disdainfully, and she wanted to flee from the coldness in them. "When you have made yourself presentable, Elinor, I should like a word with you."

"But Mary is blameless! The fault was mine!"

"It's to be hoped that Agnes can repair your hair and face before tonight," he went on, ignoring her outburst.

"I won't have her! Mary—" But he'd already turned away, and leaning heavily on his stick, he had started back toward his bookroom. She bit her lip to stifle the pain she felt. "Please, Arthur," she whispered. "Mary does not deserve this—I pray you—"

He did not mean to listen to her, and she knew it. In his anger, he'd not even bothered to ask if she were hurt.

She wanted to run after him, to plead, to explain, but she knew it would be to no avail. Her shoulders sagged and she fought the urge to cry. Without Mary, she would be at the mercy of his spies. She looked mutely to Charles, unable to speak for the ache in her throat, then she walked past him.

"Where were you?" he asked behind her. When she did not answer, he followed her. "I ain't about to be put off, Elinor—where the devil were you?" he repeated more loudly.

"It doesn't matter," she responded wearily.

"Doesn't matter! The deuce it don't! You cannot go to the balloon ascension with me, but you can come home like this!"

"I would you lowered your voice, Charles. Please."

"The driver said he set you down in Marylebone, then Mary came home without you—in a hired conveyance in fact, when she don't have any money! It was an assignation!" he declared loudly, daring her to dispute it.

He was going to make things worse with Arthur. Pushing her mud-caked hair back from her face, she retorted, "It's none of your affair. Now, if you will pardon me, I mean to bathe."

"No!" His hand closed over her arm, pulling her back. "I got to know, Elinor—I got to know!"

He was looking at her like the veriest mooncalf, and for a moment, she could only stare at him. "Even if I owed you an explanation, which I do not, I would not dignify such an accusation," she responded icily. But as he reddened, she felt sorry for hurting his feelings. "Do you really think that Lord Townsend would do this to any female?" she asked more kindly.

"Fellow's a dashed loose screw! Been with half the females in London! And you don't know what you are about!" His fingers tightened, pressing painfully into her arm. "You are green, Elinor!"

"Oh, for—" Disgusted, she shook free. "Look at me, Charles Kingsley! If I took a tumble, it was in the street—and I very much doubt that even a—a seasoned rake like Bellamy Townsend would be so crude as to maul me in the mud! Given his reputation, I should expect a gentler, more persuasive approach," she added tartly. "Wouldn't you? Or are you too blinded to reason to think on it?"

His color deepened, then he dropped his gaze to stare at her ruined slippers. In his jealousy, he was making a muddle out of everything. "No, I guess not," he mumbled finally, "but I was out of reason worried, you know. And when the maid came back—and she wouldn't answer—well, dash it, what *was* we to think?"

"I would have hoped you cherished a higher opinion of me." As soon as the words were out of her mouth, she wished she'd chosen better ones, for she'd given him an opening she didn't want him to pursue.

"Do cherish you," he insisted. "Alway have—always will."

His voice had dropped, and there was no mistaking the warmth in it. "Then do not be so quick to accuse." Afraid he meant to say more, she started down the hall toward her bedchamber.

"How'd you get home?"

"I was rescued," she answered simply.

He watched her go, a sickness in the pit of his stomach, an ache somewhere beneath his breastbone, feeling the hopelessness of the impossible passion he'd nursed ever since his return. It was foolish to feel what he felt for her, but he could not help it, not even knowing that once the old man was gone, he still could not have her, not in England.

"Wait—"

She stopped, but did not turn back. "What?" she asked cautiously.

"Are you hurt?"

"Only my pride—but I thank you for asking, anyway."

"I hope Agnes can cover the bruises, for he still means to take you to Almack's," he said lamely. When she said nothing, he exhaled heavily. "Don't favor cake and lemonade myself, but I'll go also. Been practicing the waltz," he added diffidently, "so I won't embarrass you."

"After today, I doubt anything could embarrass me."

"You want me to speak to him of Mary?"

"No." Her shoulders slumped slightly. "No," she repeated tiredly. "I shall have to make him see the fault was mine. Later, when I feel more the thing, I mean to try again to make him understand."

"He didn't catch Jeremy, you know."

"I'm thankful for that, at least."

Afraid she was still angered with him, he didn't want to let her go. "Look—I'm sorry, Elinor—truly I am. I didn't mean to—"

"It's all right, Charley."

At least she still called him Charley. "Best have Mar—best have Agnes take a look at that place on your arm. Looks nasty." He felt like an idiot when the words came out. "I mean—"

She looked down at the ugly bruise above her elbow. "No—no, you are quite right. I shall have to wear a winter gown, I fear."

He let her go then, wishing that somehow he could do something for her, but he was in no better case than she was—the old man controlled the purse strings. Reflecting resentfully on the miserable hand Fate had dealt him, he turned to go back downstairs. Had he been like Byron, he'd have thrown a scarf about his neck, rumpled his hair wildly, and affected the air of a tragic figure. But Elinor would probably think he was making a cake of himself.

Instead of going to her bedchamber, Elinor climbed the back stairs to the servants' quarters above. Mary was packing her few things into a worn wooden and leather portmanteau. When she looked up, her eyes were swollen and red. "Oh, mistress—it's sorry I am ter leave ye!" she burst out, her face contorting as she tried to hold back tears. "But I didn't tell 'im where we was! I was a-tryin' ter sneak in fer ye, so's ye could come in the back way—and Jeremy was a-paying the hack!" Unable to control the flood now, she turned away and sobbed.

Her own throat tight with emotion, Elinor moved behind her maid, touching her shoulder. "The fault was mine, Mary, and—"

The girl turned into Elinor, clinging to her. "It don't matter now—and—and I ain't got a character! He said he ain't giving me one!"

For a moment, Elinor held her, patting her, making clucking sounds like her own mother was used to do. Finally, she stepped back, holding the maid at arm's length. "I won't let you go," she promised. "I swear it."

"But ye ain't—" The girl sniffed, then wiped her

streaming eyes on her sleeve. "He don't listen to nobody!" she wailed, dissolving into tears again. "He don't!"

"He cannot drag me to Almack's."

Hope flared briefly in Mary's eyes, then she shook her head. "He'll beat ye."

"On the day of his greatest triumph? No, I don't think so." Elinor looked to the ancient portmanteau. "You'd best put your things back, then come down to make me presentable."

The girl stared. "Ye ain't going to beard him, are ye?"

"Yes."

"Oh—mistress!"

"Now, if you will but cease watering the flowers, and tidy yourself up, we shall both be all right."

Before the maid could throw herself into her arms again, Elinor retreated to the door. But once outside, she stood for a moment, trying to control her own shaking. In the four and one-half years of her marriage, she'd not dared a direct confrontation with Arthur—not once. Taking a deep breath for calm, she forced herself to march back downstairs before she lost her resolve. Outside the bookroom, she stopped to wipe damp palms on her dirty skirt, then went in to face him.

He was sitting before the empty fireplace, his hands over his waistcoat, his fingertips touching each other, and his eyes were closed. She walked around to face him. She felt as though her insides had turned to jelly.

"My lord—"

He looked up, took in her muddy, tangled hair, and frowned his displeasure. "You look like a street whore after a parade," he muttered sourly.

It wasn't going to be easy, and she knew it. "I went to the market," she began, trying to keep her voice calm. "When she could not dissuade me, Mary went also. She went to protect me, Arthur."

"I have no wish to hear this," he said coldly.

"As your wife, I have the right to speak, else I am no more than that clock on the mantel to you."

"I said—"

"I wanted some ribbons for my hair, Arthur—and I wanted some excitement. I wanted to see the market. I tire of this life I lead, and—"

"I give you everything!" he snapped. "Everything! You had no need!"

"I want more! I want to see things—I want to do things!" She swallowed hard, and lowered her voice. "Can you not see? Arthur, I tire of dressing up and posturing before these shallow people you would have me know. I'd not be forever in your leading strings. Indeed, until Charley came home, I'd seen and done nothing beyond this world you would keep me in."

"I have made you what you are, Elinor."

"You have made me into a pretty *thing*—an expensive possession—nothing more, Arthur—nothing more." She held out her hands then dropped them. If she did not cease confronting him on this, she would lose. "But we were speaking of Mary, I believe. My lord, she was blameless—she tried to stop me."

"She could have come to me. She did not have to abet your folly," he reminded her coldly.

"You were not home. It was but my innocent mistake, else naught would have happened. I opened my reticule where all could see, and we were set upon." When he said nothing, her voice rose. "You have not even asked how I fared—you've not offered one word of concern, have you? We were robbed, Arthur! Had not Mary thrown the money at them, I know not what would have happened! Do you not see?—it was Mary as saved me! I had to crawl into the street to escape them!"

"I do not tolerate scrapes, Elinor. The girl goes."

"Then I shall return to Stoneleigh." She had the satisfaction of seeing him look up at that. "Without Mary," she went on evenly, "I have no interest in Almack's—in Prinny—or Brummell—or any of your ambitions." To control her shaking hands, she clasped them tightly before her. "There—I have said it. I do not go to Almack's tonight—or ever."

"You cannot go to Stoneleigh unless I allow it," he retorted.

"Then I shall go to Edgehill to visit Mama and the girls." Despite her thudding heart, she managed to meet his eyes steadily. "I will not have Agnes, Arthur. I don't like the woman, for she spies on me without cause." She pushed back her dirty hair. "And while we are about it, I should like to increase Mary's income to forty pounds."

He could scarce believe the young woman before him. Gone was the pleasant, almost docile girl he had groomed so carefully. He considered that she gambled, but he was loath to discover how far she would go. It had taken him too long to get her a voucher to Almack's. But neither could he yield completely, for weakness invited defiance. And he would not be ruled by a willful young wife. He stalled.

"How did you get home?" he growled, scowling.

"Lord Longford."

"Longford!" he choked. "Elinor, I forbid—you know you cannot be seen in his company!"

"He was coming from Carlton House—the Regent decorated him there, I believe. I collect he is some sort of hero."

"That's outside of enough, Elinor! Longford!"

"There was no one else," she pointed out reasonably. "And he was careful of my reputation, I assure you, for I rode home against the floorboard with a carriage rug over me, so you have naught to worry on that head."

"Still I cannot like the association. You were forbidden—"

"I could scarce remain in the street, Arthur," she reminded him calmly. "It would have been a greater scandal had I perished there."

He favored her with a look that bordered on dislike, then turned to stare into the empty fireplace. "Humph! Tell the woman she can stay if she can make you presentable tonight," he muttered grudgingly. "At thirty pounds."

"Thirty pounds! Arthur, she cannot live on that!"

"I am fining her for her folly."

She knew if she argued, she would set his back up, and Mary would go packing. He had to win—in everything, he had to win something—or else someone had to pay. But this time it did not matter. She would make up the difference out of her own allowance.

"Thank you, my lord," she said quietly.

"In the future, you will not take the carriage without my permission. And if you go out, you are to take both Mary and Agnes."

"Arthur—"

"Perhaps in a month or so, I may relent, but just now

I can only say you have disappointed me, my dear. Now I can only hope none will note it when you are not in your best looks tonight.''

''I shall have Mary make use of the haresfoot.''

''See that she does. I have paid too much for this opportunity to waste it.''

As she trod the steps up to her bedchamber, Elinor's fatigue was mitigated by a sense of triumph. Though the battle had been small and not entirely decisive, for the first time since she'd met him, she'd won something of him.

The woman Agnes looked up when she entered the room, and her mouth flattened into a thin, disapproving line, then she smirked. ''His lordship said I was to tend ye, my lady.''

''And what else did his lordship say?'' Elinor inquired silkily.

''That things was to be a bit different now.''

''Oh?''

Agnes nodded. ''Ye ain't to be gadding about without me.''

''I think you are mistaken,'' Elinor said coldly. ''Mary accompanies me.''

The smirk faded. ''But his lordship said—''

''I have spoken to his lordship and it's settled that Mary shall stay.'' Elinor waited for the import of her words to sink in, then added, ''I require loyalty, you see, and I've no wish to be spied upon without reason.''

The older woman stared, her disappointment evident in her face. ''But he said—''

''That will be all, Agnes.''

Affronted, the woman left, and Elinor sank into a chair and held the arms tightly to steady herself. Utterly, completely drained, she closed her eyes. For a time, she savored her little victory, then her thoughts turned to the Earl of Longford, remembering the feel of his leg against her body. And she felt a certain yearning, a wish that instead of Arthur she'd been wed to a younger man, to someone who wanted a wife rather than a possession. She wanted to be held. She wanted to be loved.

In the bookroom below, Arthur Kingsley stared moodily into a glass of brandy. Since Charles had come home, the house had been at sixes and sevens, and now Elinor had begun defying him also. Perhaps it had been a mistake to make the boy stay. Perhaps they were too much of an age—perhaps the high spirits of the one was rubbing off onto the other. Well, he would not have it. He'd meant what he'd said to her—he'd paid too much to gain acceptance, and neither she nor the boy were going to interfere with his keeping it.

BRUMMELL'S OVERHEARD ASSESSMENT had been right—the atmosphere at Almack's was rather disappointing. But if Arthur noted the plainness of the assembly rooms or the bare dance floor, he gave no indication as he smiled and bowed his acknowledgment to each of the patronesses. And even the haughty Mrs. Drummond-Burrell, though she merely extended two fingers, did not snub him. He almost forgot his pique with Elinor for not being in her best looks. He was seeing and being seen in that ultimate bastion of snobbery to which he had so long aspired.

Using paste and powder and a skillful application of rouge from the pot, Mary had managed to cover most of the damage done at St. James Market. And, having decided against a winter gown, Elinor draped a silver-shot silk shawl about her shoulders, pulling one side down to conceal the bruise on her arm. That, coupled with the simple peach silk gown Arthur had chosen, set off her flaming hair to advantage.

While the musicians played softly from a stand, a number of young girls, most shepherded carefully by their mamas or older sisters, circulated about the room, displaying their requisitely demure muslin gowns, smiling shyly at the bucks, trying to fix an eligible *parti's* interest. It was perhaps the first time in her life that Elinor was grateful she'd not been paraded in this most exalted of all Marriage Marts.

On this Wednesday Assembly night, the cream of the *haut ton* appeared to be there. Even Brummell, for all his disparagement of the place, stood conversing in a corner with Lady Sefton and Countess Lieven, the Russian ambassador's wife, who had created the recent stir of introducing the waltz into London. And despite the railings of clergymen and moralists, the dance had become the rage, with hopeful girls eagerly awaiting approval of the patronesses to engage in the shocking exercise publicly.

The slim, impeccably plainly attired Brummell looked up when he saw Elinor. Excusing himself from the two ladies, he made his way to her.

"Ah—Longford's Venus," he murmured over her hand.

As the Beau always seemed to tread a thin line between manners and malice, Elinor was uncertain as to how to answer him. But knowing that Arthur would never forgive her if she did not attempt Brummell's approval, she smiled.

"I should not say Longford's," she responded, "for I scarce know him."

"My dear lady, you were quite the only female to acknowledge him at Maria's."

As Arthur tensed by her side, Elinor's smile deepened, warming her amber eyes, and she dared to touch the Beau's arm with her fan. "I try not to refine too much on old scandals, sir."

She could almost feel her husband's relief when Brummell smiled back. "You are possessed of a kind heart, Lady Kingsley."

"I hope so."

"Venus," he murmured, considering her. "Longford was right—it suits you better than Titian Beauty. I shall have to remember it." He leaned closer as though he spoke to her alone. "Have you heard the latest, my dear? It's said that Bell Townsend is pursuing a certain lady. I wonder . . ." He let his voice trail off speculatively.

"From all I have heard, Lord Townsend's pursuit of any lady ought not to cause comment," she countered. "It's only to the point when he gets her, don't you think, sir?"

Brummell shrugged. "Unless it's entered in the books."

"Then I should think the lady would cut him, costing those foolish enough to wager a great deal of money," she answered smoothly.

It was obvious that he'd learned what he wanted to know. "Oh, I am more like to wager over which duck will cross the road first than on a lady's honor," he assured her. Turning to Arthur, he nodded. "My congratulations, sir—your wife is indeed an Original."

After the Beau moved on, turning his gossipy interest to Lord Alvanley, Arthur beamed. "You are made, my dear," he whispered proudly.

"Fiddle. If words can make so quickly, I am sure they can destroy also." But when she looked up, Mrs. Drummond-Burrell favored her with a frosty smile, a singular distinction that did not go unnoticed. "Nonetheless, I am glad you are pleased, my lord."

"Pleased? I should count it nothing less than a triumph."

"Yes, the Beau is not noted for admiring kind hearts, is he?" she murmured, exasperated by her husband's open pandering to a man she could not quite like. "One day his rudeness will go too far, and no one will care a whit what he thinks—or what he bathes in—or even from whence comes the shine on his boots."

"Lady Kingsley," a masculine voice drawled behind her, "do you waltz?"

Charles, who'd gone to procure glasses of the weak lemonade for them, moved quickly to intercept Lord Townsend. "Hallo, Bellamy." As the viscount's eyebrows rose at the perceived familiarity, Charles thrust a glass into Elinor's hand. "Waltzing with me," he declared importantly. "Family."

"The second dance, then?" Townsend addressed Elinor.

"Well, I—"

"Belongs to m'grandfather. Her husband," he added almost truculently.

Elinor choked on her first sip of lemonade, for it was commonly known that Lord Kingsley did not dance. But the viscount continued to regard her expectantly.

"If it amuses you, my dear—," Arthur began.

"It don't," Charles insisted brusquely. He looked to Townsend. "Sorry for it, but you got a bad rep with the females, don't you know, and we don't want her name bandied about."

"Charley!" Elinor gasped.

"Truth of it," the younger man declared. "No sense in trying to wrap it up in clean linen, is there? Plain as a pikestaff what he's up to."

Afraid of a scene, Arthur Kingsley sought to intervene. "Er—don't you think it's up to Elinor to decide, Charles?" Turning to her, he added mildly, "I shall not refine too much upon it, I assure you."

"Then you are a fool, Grandpapa!" Charles protested. "Pays her too much attention already—wouldn't surprise me if it was on the betting books."

"Charles!" Her face reddening, Elinor apologized to the viscount. "Your pardon, sir—I am sure he did not mean—"

"Every word," Charles muttered.

"That will be all," the old man told him sternly. "You are drawing unnecessary attention."

"No, I ain't—he is."

A quick glance about the room revealed a number of interested stares. Afraid for the consequences should his grandson irritate Arthur further, she held out her hand to Townsend. "I am sorry, my lord. Perhaps another time—when I have learned the steps better." Smiling up at him, she tried to mollify him. "But I shall be at home tomorrow. Perhaps Hyde Park?"

"Done, dear lady—shall we say four?"

"Yes."

"Until tomorrow, my dear," he murmured, kissing her hand gallantly. He bowed toward Kingsley. "My lord." Then nodding stiffly toward Charles, he said, "Good night, *Mister* Kingsley," an obvious reference to the boy's lack of title.

Charles flushed, then as the viscount walked away, he muttered something about "drawing his lordship's cork for him," under his breath.

There was a strained silence between the three of them, until the old man finally spoke to his grandson. "Perhaps you ought to get Elinor a bit of cake."

"It's stale. And there ain't anything else but bread and butter to be had. Ain't even a supper," he added, disgusted. "Don't see what—"

"No doubt you would have enjoyed White's more." There was no mistaking the ascerbity in the old man's voice. "I had supposed you came to inspect the Season's beauties, but I can see I was quite in error."

"Bunch of empty-headed ninnyhammers!" the boy snorted.

Arthur opened his mouth to say something, then closed

it as Lady Jersey approached them, her still-handsome face wreathed in a smile. "There you are, my dear Elinor! Shocking squeeze, isn't it? Fortunately not all our little assemblies are so well-attended." She held out her hands, possessing both of Elinor's, then turned to the old man. "Is she not lovely tonight?"

"Quite."

"Ravishing," Charles declared sincerely.

For a moment, the woman was nonplussed, then she recovered, lifting an eyebrow questioningly. "I'm afraid you have the advantage of me—?"

"My grandson," Arthur supplied quickly. "Home for the Season." He looked down to his ebony cane briefly, then added, "Company for Elinor, you know, as I cannot dance. Bad knee."

"Oh, yes—of course. It is an old complaint, is it not?" Before he could answer, she faced Elinor. "I do hope you have learned the waltz, my dear, for if you have, I can think of at least a dozen gentlemen willing to oblige. And as you have been out an age—"

"Been practicing with me," Charles answered. "Take her out onto the floor myself—family, you know."

"Sally!"

Lady Jersey was diverted by a mama eager to push her daughter, and as she turned away, the old man hissed, "Don't make a cake of yourself, boy!"

"Well, I ain't going to stand here and watch 'em ogle her, if that's what you mean," Charles muttered.

La Jersey fluttered away, her silk scarves trailing after her, as the musicians began to strike up the first strains of the highlight of the evening—the scandalous, seductive waltz that everyone had been waiting for. As "Cupid" Palmerston appeared to be headed their way, Charles grasped Elinor's hand firmly.

"You heard her—you been approved. Come on before the floor is too crowded."

But somehow practicing at home and executing in public were two very different things. As he counted out his steps to get started, he felt stiff, awkward, and graceless. To make him more at ease, Elinor leaned into him, whispering, "Remember the first time we danced at Stoneleigh?"

"When you told me spirit compensated for style?"

"Yes. And it still does—you have but to pretend you like it."

Her gloved hand was warm in his, her body alive beneath his touch. As the sweet scent of roses wafted from the soaked cotton tucked in her bosom, he lost his awkwardness and thought of the woman in his arms instead. For the moment, he would forget she was his grandfather's wife, that she was beyond his touch. With a passion born of youthful idealism, he pulled her closer, savoring the exquisite intimacy.

"I think I have always loved you," he murmured, his lips scandalously close to her ear.

She missed her step and nearly tripped. "Oh, Charley—I pray you will not—"

Jarred back to reality, he recovered, saying gallantly, "Deuced pretty, you know—ain't a fellow out here as don't envy me right now."

But he was too late, for his grandfather had been watching, his face wooden, and he was not watching alone. As Charles twirled Elinor about the floor, Arthur overheard Lady Jersey remark, "For all that Bell thinks otherwise, I should say that Baron Kingsley is more like to be cuckolded at home."

When the music ended, there was a sudden awkwardness as Charles dropped her hand. He stood there, his blue eyes intent on her. "I know I should not have said it," he spoke finally, "but I'm not sorry."

"Lady Kingsley—?"

"Lord Palmerston," she murmured, relieved.

"May I?"

She did not look at Charles. "Yes—of course."

"Get you some lemonade," the younger man promised.

"Thank you."

Heartsick, afraid now that the words had been spoken that somehow Arthur would know and blame her, she tried to divert his attention by dancing not only with Palmerston, but with Lords Sefton, Alvanley, Roxwell, Barrasford, and half a dozen others. To the chagrin of a dozen mamas and at least as many acknowledged beauties, she could truthfully have been described on this night as the Reigning Toast. Even Brummell deigned to dance with her, not once but twice. She had finally given

Arthur Kingsley his greatest social triumph, and she hoped he'd been too exhilarated to note anything else.

"Exhausted, my dear?" he asked solicitously during the carriage ride home.

"Yes."

"Ain't no wonder—it's nigh to three o'clock, and you didn't miss a dance," Charles muttered. "Only one as you did not dance with was Bellamy Townsend, and he went home early."

"You were much admired—everyone remarked it," the old man told her proudly, ignoring his grandson. "You are a credit to me." His hand closed over hers, squeezing it.

Despite the darkness, she blinked. It was perhaps the first time in her marriage that he'd ever paid her her due. Always before, it was he who had made her.

"It was your money," she said simply.

"No—it was breeding. They only note those born to it."

"Well, if you was to ask me, I'd say it was her looks," Charles offered.

"I do not recall asking you," Arthur said coldly.

It was as though Elinor's hands had turned to ice. He knew. She groped for some means to save Charley from the old man's wrath and could find none. An abrupt, nearly deafening silence descended within the elegant coach, leaving only the sound of the wheels against the cobbled streets. And the steady beat of her dreading heart seemed to reverberate in her ears.

Once home, Charles mumbled "good night" and started up the stairs, only to be stopped by his grandfather's clipped, curt voice.

"A word with you—it will not take long," Arthur told him. Looking to Elinor, he added, "You go on to bed, my dear—there is no need to wait up for me."

Exhausted, Elinor dispensed with everything but undressing, then slipped between cool sheets to lie listening in the dark. Oddly, there was no sound of an argument—only footsteps on the stairs, a slammed door down the hall, and finally nothing. For once, she was torn between dreading Arthur's Wednesday night visit and a need to know what he had done.

Finally, when she had decided that he did not mean to come to her, she heard the door creak inward, then close. She rolled over to see him, his nightcap drawn down over his wispy hair, his nightshirt hanging past his knees. He was carrying a candle, its glow heightened by a brass reflector. When he saw she was still awake, he set the candle on a table near the bed.

"I told you you did not need to wait up for me."

"I was too tired to sleep."

"I'm afraid I was too blind to see it. I should have known after Vauxhall. He would live in your pocket, if you let him."

"He is but a boy—it's calf-love, Arthur. Think on when you were twenty," she said softly.

"I was making my way." He sat on the edge of the bed, then leaned to blow out the candle. "I did not go to Harrow—nor Oxford—nor Cambridge—nor anywhere else. My father could not afford to send me. What I have learned, I have taught myself."

"You did well."

"And I had none to thank for it. My grandson, on the other hand, would play me false with my wife, forgetting what I have done for him."

"It's but the first pangs—the beginning of his salad days, if you will," she pleaded. "Arthur, it will pass, and we shall but be amused by his youthful foolishness."

"I am not amused, Elinor."

"No doubt next month he will have thrown his hat over the windmill for someone else," she persisted. "He is too young to know his own heart—there will be dozens of imagined passions before—"

"No." The bed creaked as he lay down beside her. "Next month I expect he will be on his way to Spain." Turning away from her, he pulled the covers up over his thin shoulders. "He's had his way, you know—I am buying his colors." His voice was flat, toneless. "He would be a dragoon like Longford."

Alarmed, she sat up. "Arthur, he is too young! Do not punish him for a passing fancy—he will outgrow it!"

"He can outgrow it elsewhere. I'd not be laughed at while he makes a cake of himself."

She reached to touch his shoulder. "What if he perishes? You cannot—"

He pulled away. "Your concern is suspect, Elinor," he said coldly. "Mayhap the dragoons will do for him what I cannot—mayhap they will make him grateful for what I have given him."

"Arthur—" She took a deep breath, then let it out slowly. "You cannot be jealous of Charles. He is your grandson—your heir—your own flesh and blood."

"Mayhap I am. And if so, there is no use for more than one jealous fool here."

It was no use. He would not change his mind, and any argument she offered now would only make it worse for Charles. A new loneliness washed over her—and an acute fear. While she did not think she cherished a *tendre* for him, she knew she genuinely loved Charles Kingsley like a brother, and Arthur was sending him off to war because of her.

She lay still, listening to the ticking of the ormolu clock on the mantel, hearing the Earl of Longford's words echo in her mind. *The last thing we have need of is more idealistic fools, for they seldom survive.* Arthur was buying a commission in the dragoons—the cavalry that led the charge into battle. Every week, the papers listed those who had perished, citing their bravery, lauding their sacrifice.

Longford would know of that, for he had served with them—was going back, in fact. She thought of his medal—it was because he had survived, because he'd lived, he'd said. But Longford was cold, Longford was hard, and Charles was not. Charles was kind, lighthearted, and too young. He would believe that he would make a difference in whether Napoleon ruled or not.

She recalled his almost worshipful adulation of the earl—and Longford's attempts to dampen it. Longford. In the darkness, her mind seemed to race ahead of rational thought. Longford was an officer—he could perhaps see that Charles did not get sent to the front. If she sought him out, if she spoke with him, he could perhaps see that the boy was safe in someone's train at the rear.

She lay there, almost afraid to breathe lest Arthur somehow would know of her preposterous plan. But he was snoring softly at her side. Sometimes she wondered if he ever doubted anything he did.

LUCIEN WAS ENDURING a final fitting of his new uniforms when the unwelcome news came up that Diana waited below. Peering into the cheval mirror, he adjusted the braid-trimmed epaulets.

"Tell her I am not receiving," he ordered brusquely. Turning to the tailor, he wondered, "Not that it matters on the field, but does it seem that they are even?"

"Precisely, my lord—I measured them myself. It's the gorget that sits askance."

Lucien adjusted the symbol of his rank over his collar, then nodded. Extending his hands, he checked the length of his sleeves. "Much better, I think. Fellow in Spain had them half over my hand." Satisfied, he shrugged out of the jacket and waistcoat, then nodded to his batman. "Pay the man." Perceiving that the lower footman still waited, he frowned. "I thought I told you to tell her I would not come down, Tompkins."

"Before I came up, she insisted she would not leave—she asked that I tell you she is prepared to remain until hell freezes." He coughed apologetically. "I did not think you would wish her forcibly removed, my lord."

"The devil I wouldn't," Lucien muttered.

He was in no mood to face her, not after the last hearing, but there was no help for it, he supposed. No doubt she'd come to beg now that the court had ruled the child was not his. Leighton had suggested then that perhaps the way to be rid of her was simply to pay, but he'd be hanged if he'd do it. Let her bleed the brat's father.

He'd been exonerated, absolved, and he wanted no discourse, nothing that could maintain any tie between them. But it always seemed that just when he'd thought he'd severed everything once and for all, she managed to tie a knot, tangling the threads of his life again.

"She said she'd set up a screech if I was to lay a hand on her."

And she would. This time when she'd come back to London, she'd played the wronged woman with the art of a Siddons. And while she was generally cut, there had been a couple of Whig wives who seemed inclined to support her, decrying the laws that let a man discard even a promiscuous wife. And the presence of the child had gained her a great deal of sympathy, even from those who pretended shock at the scandal.

"Do you want me to try, my lord?" the fellow asked. "I suppose me'n' Burdette could push her out the servants' door."

"No." He sighed his displeasure. "I'll tend to the matter this time."

He did not bother to don his coat, choosing to show his contempt for her by his shirtsleeves. After all that had passed privately and publicly between them, it was unthinkable that she would be there, waiting for him in his own house. Taking the carpeted stairs almost silently, he crossed the hall into the front saloon. She was standing with her back to him, but as he closed the door, she spun around.

She had obviously dressed with great care, wearing her best gown, the same one she'd worn to court, trying to hide her now straitened circumstances. But there was a hardness to her eyes, a brittleness to her beauty that betrayed the harshness of her exile. She forced a smile when she saw him.

"Madam," he acknowledged curtly.

She licked her lips nervously, then spoke. "You look well, Luce."

"I've not aged much since last week. I believe you sat at the table across from me, did you not?"

"No—no, of course not." Clasping her hands before her, she moved closer. "You always were a handsome devil, you know. Had you been at home, there'd have been no need . . ." Her husky voice trailed off.

"What do you want?" he interrupted harshly. "I leave Monday and there's little time."

In the face of his coldness, her composure slipped briefly, then she recovered. "I was your wife, Luce. Can we not be civil?"

"Was—and no. If you are come for money, you waste your time—it was settled in court long ago, and nothing has changed that I am aware of."

"We did not mean to hurt you," she said softly.

"It was done before that. I don't care about Bell—I don't care if you've been with a hundred fools since."

"You loved me once," she reminded him. As she spoke, she loosened the ties of her bonnet, letting it slip to the floor. "You know you did."

"No. The choice wasn't mine," he reminded her bitterly.

Her fingers worked the small buttons at her breast, revealing the creamy skin beneath. "We don't need to part enemies, Lucien. I—"

His hands caught her arms, holding them above the elbows, forcing her back. "When I want a whore, I'll find one."

"Lucien, I shall starve! And—and Papa will not keep Lucy for me!"

"Lucy!" he snorted. "Clever choice of a name, but it did not work, did it? You'd have been better advised to name the brat Belle, don't you think?"

"She isn't Bell's."

"She isn't mine."

"Luce—"

"We both know she could not be, don't we?"

Tears welled in her eyes and spilled for effect onto her cheeks. "Lucien, I have nothing! Have pity—Mad Jack—"

"Mad Jack be damned! Leave him out of this!"

"He would not have wanted—"

"I don't care anymore what he wanted—do you hear?—I don't care! Don't you see?—I have never forgiven *him*!" He caught himself and lowered his voice. "In any event, it's over—all of it."

"He was dying, Lucien, else he'd not have done it." Her lower lip quivered. "He loved me."

"Humph! Jack loved no one." He swung away and went to stare out the window. "I owe you nothing, Diana."

"I tried to be a good wife to you, but you would not let me." She spoke hollowly, flatly now. "We could have put that behind us—we could have—well, I am not the first wife to take a lover. Sally Jersey—Lady Oxford—everyone—"

"There was no heir."

"I tried, Luce! But I could not get one by myself!"

"I was not prepared to take my father's leavings," he retorted coldly.

"I know you do not credit it, but I loved him." She came up behind him to touch his shoulder, but he shook her off. "I would not have done it else."

"You lied to him, and he lied to me. There was no babe!"

"Lucien, I am telling you that I have nothing—that I can scarce feed my daughter!"

"Sue her father—or was it the groom—or the lower footman?" he asked sarcastically. "It must have been someone you could not bleed."

"He's dead."

"A likely tale."

"At Talavera." As he turned around, she nodded. "If you tell it, I shall deny it, of course, but it was Rothesay."

"My wife the whore," he muttered. "How many others laughed to my back?"

"I don't have to answer that—I only know I could not stand your coldness. But I pray you will not tell me to go to Lady Rothesay, for she did not know of it."

One corner of his mouth went down. "How very considerate of you to protect her, my dear."

"Is everything a jest to you?" Her voice rose as the tears began to course freely. "Have you no heart? Can you not forgive a youthful mistake?"

"Mistakes," he reminded her brutally. "And quite a lot of them, if the servants can be believed."

"If you aid me, I shall go away."

"Where?"

"I don't know—the Indies—Canada—somewhere. I know I cannot stay here, for Lucy will never be accepted. Indeed, but Papa will not even speak to me now."

"Find a generous lover," he advised. "You still have your looks."

"As if any of them want a small child! She is of a difficult age, when she will not be still."

"Then you ought to have foisted the brat onto Townsend."

"She is dark—like you."

The pain he felt when he looked at her had little to do with what she had done, he told himself. She was merely the instrument of his destruction, the chalice of gall he had been forced to drink. But when she was not around, when there was no gossip of her, he could forget what his father had done to him. Despite all his public words to the contrary, if he truly believed she would go away, he could almost count it worth the money. That—and if he did not have to acknowledge her child. When he had an heir—or heiress—he wanted it to carry his blood.

"How much?" he asked finally. "To go away forever—how much?"

"I—I need an allowance, Luce. I cannot manage large sums of money."

"Obviously."

"A thousand pounds per year would—" She stopped, aware that he glowered. "Well, I cannot live on much less—Jack would not have wanted me to! He—"

"I told you—leave him out of it!"

She swallowed. "But—"

He didn't want to grant her an allowance. He didn't want anything that had to be renewed, that had to remind him. But after a time, he nodded. "Your passage—and five hundred pounds paid annually through my solicitor—and a public acknowledgment that the child is not mine, that you concede what the courts have ruled." Even as he said it, he was angered with himself for giving her anything.

"Lucien!"

"Take it or not." Not wanting to prolong the audience, not wanting to hear her plead for more, he turned to leave. "If you choose to accept, you will be paid on the last day of each year. And if you come back, if you so much as attempt to contact me again, all payments will cease. Good day, Diana."

"You weren't always so cold to me!"

He did not stop. "My mistake, wasn't it?"

"You have no heart!" she flung after him. "It's not a wonder that you are called Lucifer! I hate you—do you hear—I hate you!"

"Four hundred pounds, then. And if you continue shouting like a fishwife, I shall have to reconsider that."

"Lucien!"

His hand was on the doorknob. "Do you want me to say three?"

She had not a doubt that he would do it. Choking back the tears, she bent to collect her bonnet lest he change his mind altogether.

Furious with her, furious with himself, furious with the world in general, he started the climb up the stairs. He was nearly to the top when he heard her slam the saloon door. Damn her! Damn Jack! Damn the both of them! Voices floated upward—her loud sobs, the murmur of his butler and someone else, then the front door closed after her. Oddly, he could still hear Burdette's apparent denial, and for a moment, he stopped to listen.

"His lordship is not at home, I'm afraid," the butler declared stiffly, sniffing his disapproval.

"But I must see him! Perhaps I could leave a card—no—no, of course that will not do, for he cannot return the call." She hesitated, then blurted out, "Perhaps if you would tell him it's Lady Kingsley—he will remember me, I think."

"Madam—"

Afraid she would lose her resolve, she forgot her manners. "And I know he is in, for I collect he received the lady who was leaving."

"You are mistaken, Lady Kingsley," Lucien said coldly from above. "Diana is not a lady."

"Diana—?" For a moment, she was nonplussed, then she recalled the name. "Oh—your wife."

"No. The encumbrance exists no more."

His eyes raked over her, taking in her expensive walking dress, her Norwich shawl, the exquisite bonnet that framed her face, the almost fiery hair that peeped beneath it. He considered telling her to go on, that she ought not to be there, but she was incredibly lovely—and he did not doubt for a minute that she sought a bit of diversion from her elderly husband, that their earlier encounter at the market had encouraged her. She would not be the first bored female to throw herself at him, after all. Indeed, but it seemed that they all had a certain fascination for the forbidden, for the dangerous—and for all her beauty, Lady Kingsley was apparently no better than the rest.

"You are better advised to seek out Bell, for he plays the game more correctly than I."

"Bell—?" For a moment, her eyes widened innocently—a clever ploy—then she appeared to make the connection. "Oh—I collect you mean Lord Townsend." She found him singularly unencouraging, and she began to think she'd made a mistake. Clasping her reticule tightly, she tried to speak calmly. "I have come to seek a favor of you, my lord."

He'd given her her chance to flee, and she'd been too much the fool to take it. And there was no denying she was beautiful, making him the greater fool if he turned her away. Even as he looked at her, she set his pulse to racing. And in five days he would be leaving, perhaps to perish in a brutal war halfway across Europe. No, if she were rash enough to offer, he was rash enough to take. It had been a long time since he'd lain in the arms of anyone half so lovely as Elinor Kingsley.

Coming down the wide, curved staircase, flanked by portraits of a rather imposing collection of ancestors, he seemed even bigger than she had remembered him. It was perhaps that he wore no coat, that his shirt lay open at the throat, showing dark hair beneath the curved gold bar that hung across his neck. Or was it the effect of buff breeches so carefully tailored that they did not crease over muscular legs? Or possibly the tall, highly polished boots that covered his calves to his knees?

When he stopped before her, his black eyes were so intent that the pupils were barely discernible from the irises. And yet she could not help noting that his black hair was rumpled, giving him a boyish look totally at variance with the faint, familiarly derisive smile that played at the corners of his mouth. There was something about the contradiction that made her afraid.

"I should not have come," she ventured nervously.

"No, you should not," he agreed. "But you seem to be here, don't you?" he added softly.

Suddenly shy, she did not know how to broach the matter of Charles to him. She took a deep breath, then ran her tongue over parched lips. "I—uh—I'm afraid I did not thank you properly for yesterday," she began lamely. Looking up, she saw his butler's interested expression. "Er—do you think—that is—is there some place where we may be more private? There is a matter of some delicacy I should like to discuss."

It surprised him that she was not one of those who beat about the proverbial bush. Nodding, he walked past her to hold open the saloon door. As she ducked beneath his arm, he looked to Burdette. "The best madeira for myself and the lady—and then I've no wish to be disturbed."

Instead of taking a seat, Elinor moved to the empty fireplace, staring into the bare iron brazier for a moment, then turning back to face him. "It must seem odd that I am here, I know—"

"Not at all," he assured her. "Though I must admit that I seldom entertain ladies in my home." He smiled wryly. "Usually I meet them somewhere. It's considerably more discreet."

"Oh." Her gaze darted about the room before returning to him. "I hope you will not think me improper, but—"

"I own the thought *had* crossed my mind," he admitted, "but no doubt given the circumstances, you have your reasons, my dear." She was as skittish as an unbroken colt, making him wish that Burdette would return with the wine. "Er—perhaps you would care to sit?"

"Oh—no."

"You look as though you are about to bolt, you know."

"Do I? Yes, I suppose I must, but this is quite new to me. You must understand that I am not in the habit of visiting gentlemen unattended." She smiled nervously. "But had I brought Mary, and Arthur discovered it, she should be discharged on the instant. Indeed, but she very nearly was over yesterday's scrape. And there was no one else who would not tell him, you see. I'm afraid I am surrounded by spies."

And with good reason, no doubt. But aloud he assured her, "You may count on Burdette's discretion, Lady Kingsley."

"How fortunate for you."

The butler entered with the tray, and an awkward silence ensued as he uncorked the bottle of madeira and poured two glasses. Lucien favored Elinor with a faint smile, then addressed Burdette.

"Take her ladyship's bonnet and shawl, will you? No doubt she would be more comfortable without them," he said smoothly.

"Uh—no."

"Nonsense, my dear. There is no need for formality, is there?"

To her surprise, the earl himself reached to tug at the ribbons under her chin, untying them, then pushing the hat from her head. The chipstraw caught one of the pins, pulling it, and part of her copper hair fell about her shoulders as he tossed the offending bonnet to the butler. She hastily reached to secure the loosened locks with another pin.

"Sorry," he murmured.

He was looking at her in such a way that she wished she had not come, but as she was there, she was determined to pursue her purpose.

"You are going back to the war, aren't you?" Even as she said it, she felt utterly foolish, for he'd told her he was but the day before.

"Yes." He handed her a glass of the wine, then lifted his own. "To the days between now and Monday."

She heard the door close, and she realized she was now utterly alone with him. To hide her unease, she sipped the madeira tentatively. "Uh—about why I am here—"

"I know why you are here." He set his own glass aside and moved closer. "And I do not mean to disappoint you."

Before she knew what he intended, he'd reached around to the back of her head, loosening her pins, letting her hair cascade over her shoulders and down her back. "Did none tell you how very fashionably you wear this, Lady Kingsley?" he asked softly as he combed it with his fingers. "It's like silk," he murmured, bending his head to hers.

Alarmed, she leaned back, but his hands twined in her hair, holding her. "Uh—I don't think—" Her words died against his lips, and her glass slipped from her hand, spilling the wine onto his boots. Her eyes widened in surprise, then closed, as she was overwhelmed by the hard, masculine feel of his body against hers. Later, she was to count herself an utter fool, but for the moment, she savored the passion of his kiss, the feel of his arms holding her, and she knew this was the way it was meant to be between a man and a woman.

Lucien de Clare's mouth teased hers, pressing, probing, tasting, sending tremors coursing through her until she was breathless, and all the while, she could only hold on, first to his arms, then to his waist. When he finally released her mouth, he moved along her jaw to her earlobe, nibbling it. His breath rushed loudly in her ear, and shivers traveled down her spine, nearly chasing rational thought from her mind.

"Lovely Elinor," he whispered hotly. "So little time . . . so few days . . ."

She arched her head away from his, only to have him find the sensitive hollow of her throat. She was drowning, falling into the maelstrom of a new, intense, answering passion. It was a heady, utterly overwhelming sensation that seemed to possess both mind and body—until she became vaguely aware that his hand had found the hooks at the back of her walking dress. Reluctant reason reasserted itself, and she stiffened.

"No!" She pushed him, backing away from him, nearly tripping over an andiron behind her. "No," she panted. "It's wrong! Arthur—"

"Arthur be damned! You came for this—admit it," he croaked, his voice thick with his desire. He moved closer, catching her, pressing her against the cold marble of the fireplace facing, and this time, his kiss was ruthless, demanding, daring her to deny him.

Panicked, she struggled against him, pounding at his chest, crying, "Let me go—I pray you—let me go!"

Telling himself that she was like so many others—that she wanted to be courted and conquered, absolved of any responsibility for what happened, he did not listen. He moved his hands over her, smoothing her dress and petticoat over her hips, pressing her body against his, feeling the firmness of her breasts against his chest, knowing that before he was done, they would sate each other's desire.

She twisted and turned, but he was far too strong for her, and she knew he meant to ravish her. This time, when his hand sought the hooks, she had nowhere to go, no escape. "Damn," he mumbled, fumbling with the metal fasteners.

For a moment, she sagged against him as though she meant to yield, then she murmured, "Let me do it."

Panting, thoroughly aroused, he released her, thinking she meant to undress for him. Instead, she bolted for the door, screaming for aid. He caught her from behind and clamped a hand over her mouth. She bit down hard, catching the fleshy part behind his thumb.

"What the devil—? You little vixen—you bit me!"

"Mmmmmmph—mmmm—nnnnnhhhh!"

As he took his hand from her mouth to shake it, she struggled in his arms, kicking backwards, catching his shin through his boot. She was slender, small in comparison to him, and yet she fought as though her life depended on escape. His ardor dampened by the realization that she resisted, that she was not being merely coquettishly coy, he pushed her away.

"I don't know your game, but I don't mean to play it," he growled, sucking the blood that trickled from the bite.

"Game!" she shouted, outraged. "Game? You would have ravished me!" Putting distance between them, she accused him, "You, sir, are no gentleman!" Her coppery hair fell forward in disarray, and she pushed it back angrily. "Never in all my life have I been subjected to such—such utter *importunity*!"

"You came here! You led me on like a penny whore!"

"Not for this! And I did no such thing!" Her bosom heaved with indignation, and she had to swallow to control her fury. "It's no wonder you are cut, sir! I came to ask a favor—not to sell my person to an—an—" Words failed her for a moment, then she finished furiously, "—an unprincipled rake!"

His jaw worked, but he managed to tell her stiffly, "Your pardon, madam. I thought—"

"It's obvious what you thought," she retorted acidly. Her chin came up as she sought to restore a semblance of her dignity. "And it's equally obvious that I should not have come to you for help. If you would be so good as to require my bonnet and shawl of your butler, I will go."

Her anger heightened her color, giving her beauty animation, as she stood there like an affronted goddess. He regarded her regretfully for a moment, then sighed. "We could have had such a good time of it, you know."

"How dare you—*how dare you*? I have never betrayed my marriage vows, sir!"

"You must surely be among the few," he observed sarcastically. But it was obvious that her indignation was very real, and he knew he ought to make amends. "All right. You have established my miserable reputation, Lady Kingsley." He bent to pick up her glass, then set it aside. Pouring more of the wine into his, he held it out to her. "It will make you feel more the thing."

"I don't—"

"Drink it," he ordered curtly. "Despite what you think, I am not given to rapine—cut or not, I don't have to. Go on," he urged her, "it's quite the best the smugglers can manage."

She still regarded him suspiciously. "No. I think I ought to leave."

Her manner intrigued him. "This favor—what was it?"

"I cannot think you would care."

"Sit down."

"No."

"Look, I seldom apologize for anything, Lady Kingsley, but you find me reasonably contrite—disappointed, but contrite. Clearly I misread the situation."

"Clearly," she retorted acidly, reaching to repin her hair.

"But I am not a complete fool, I think—if it was of great enough import to bring you here, it surely must be worth the telling now." He gestured to the chair again. "If you like, I shall sit across the room—at a safe distance," he promised.

She hesitated, staring into his black eyes long enough to satisfy herself that he meant it, then she took the chair, sitting forward primly, ready to run if he moved again. It was not until he dropped to a settee some distance away that she exhaled her relief. He regarded her soberly. "Well?"

"Charles tells me you are in the dragoons," she blurted out finally.

"Charles?" For a moment, he was perplexed. "Oh—the boy."

"Yes."

"And—?"

"Well, you must have some influence! I saw your medal, sir, and—"

"You want me to get him a commission?" he inquired incredulously. "My dear Lady Kingsley, it's no soiree over there, but a war!"

"Of *course* I don't want him to have a commission, but Arthur is sending him—a cornetcy, I think—and I am afraid for him! And Charles has chosen the dragoons because of you!"

"Me? Acquit me—I scarce know of him even," he retorted.

"But he admires you!" she insisted, exasperated. "And he is ill-suited to the task—he is but a boy!"

"How old?"

"Not quite twenty—and he has had no training."

"Cannon fodder!" he snorted.

"Precisely. And—and I could not bear it if he were to perish. I'd not have him dead because of me," she added more calmly.

"Because of you?" Once again, his eyebrow rose.

"That, my lord, is none of your affair—indeed, I should not have said it."

"But you did."

"It's too preposterous to tell the tale, and I'd not dignify it in the repeating."

He leaned back lazily, studying her stiff demeanor, then nodded. "The old man wants no rival, eh?"

She started to deny it, then sighed. "Yes," she said simply.

He felt an unreasoning stab of jealousy. "So that's how the land lies, is it?" he asked cynically. "You and the boy but wait for the old man to die, eh?"

"No, of course not! Charley and I are of an age—and it's but his salad days! There's naught—"

"Spare me the Cheltenham tragedy!" he snapped, sitting up. "I know not what you think I can do if the boy is determined, so I am afraid you have wasted your time and mine."

"You are an officer!"

"There is more than one regiment, Lady Kingsley—and it's scarce likely he will be assigned to me." He rose and moved to stand over her. Seeing her recoil visibly, he felt anger. "I cannot aid you."

"You mean you would not," she contradicted him.

"Probably not."

"But you could use your position to see he is kept from the fray," she insisted, watching him warily. For a moment, she feared he meant to touch her again, but instead he pulled the bell rope beside her. "You know you could."

"Burdette! Burdette!" he shouted.

"Aye, my lord—?" the butler responded promptly.

"Lady Kingsley's bonnet and shawl, if you please."

The butler cast a sidewise glance at her and seemed surprised. "Of course."

"Even if I could, I would not, I am afraid," Longford declared coldly. "I don't mean to be nursemaid or mentor to any young fool. I have enough to do staying whole myself."

"But—"

"No."

As the butler presented her things, she rose stiffly. "I had thought better of you, my lord. I had thought you might care that a boy goes to fight unprepared."

"Your mistake."

"Sally Jersey is right—you cannot be brought to care for anything, can you?" She stared into his hard countenance, then added bitterly, "But no doubt had I been more amenable, you might have tried."

He bowed slightly. "I might—but I doubt it. I am not easily bought, Lady Kingsley." Again, one of his black eyebrows lifted slightly. "Never say you are thinking of relenting, my dear?" he drawled.

She tied her bonnet carefully beneath her chin, then draped the shawl about her arms before she replied. "No—I am not bought at all, sir—and even if I were, in your case, I should count the cost too great."

He had to admire the setdown, to acknowledge the girl was pluck to the bone to even be there. He waited until she was in the foyer, then he followed her. "How do you mean to get home?"

"The same way I got here," she answered truthfully. "I shall walk. It's no great distance, after all."

"Burdette, have Tompkins hail a hackney for her."

Her chin came up and her eyes met his, betraying her contempt for him. "Lord Longford, I should rather walk, I think. I'd not have it said I trespassed on your grudging *kindness.*" There was no mistaking the derisive inflection she gave the word. Her back held straight, she turned on her heel and marched out the door, too angry to note anything beyond the fact that she'd made a fool out of herself before Longford.

A carriage rounded the corner, and for a moment, the lone occupant could only stare at her, then at the house from whence she had come. After brief consideration, he decided to lean back and pass her unnoticed. But there was no mistaking Bellamy Townsend's chagrin to learn that Longford had stolen the march on him. It was not until he was well past her that he could see a certain advantage in what he'd witnessed—the lovely Lady Kingsley was not nearly so unattainable as was generally thought—and Longford was leaving town.

And with that realization, Bell's mouth curved into a slow smile—with what he now knew, he did not doubt that it would be but a matter of weeks before she was his also. He need no longer play the game as though she did not know what he was about. And if she continued to keep him at arm's length, he could always lay down this new card and repique her. Not that he wanted to, of course, for he preferred to conquer with charm.

Inside the brick-faced mansion, Lucien returned to the saloon, poured himself another glass of the madeira, and half-sprawled on the settee to drink it. Damn Elinor Kingsley! he thought resentfully. Why couldn't she be like the rest of her sex? Why did she have to act as though she thought he had a conscience? Or cared if he did?

He held his glass up, staring at the amber-colored wine, thinking that the color reminded him of her eyes. "To the *virtuous* Lady Kingsley," he muttered defensively. "A pox on her!" But even as he drank, he did not want to forget that momentary, soft, yielding feeling of her in his arms—until it brought back memories long buried, memories of another woman who'd held him quite differently, reminding him that they were all weak creatures, capable of betrayal in different ways.

His eyes strayed to the portrait of the lovely woman that still hung almost defiantly over the mantel, and his black eyes locked with the painted blue ones. Lifting his glass once more, this time toward the image of a woman he barely remembered, he murmured, "Mother, I would that you beheld what you and Jack have made of me." And the old, bleak bitterness washed over him, confirming yet again that despite his wealth, there was very little else in this world for him.

THERE WAS NO SIGN of Charles when she returned home, and she assumed he'd gone out. And Arthur, having been told by a nervous Mary that Elinor had merely stepped outside to potter in her garden, had accepted the explanation and merely left word that he intended to spend much of the day at Watier's. It was a retreat from unpleasantness, but Elinor didn't care—it was enough that he was gone from the house

As she moved about the large, seemingly cavernous mansion, it was as though Charley were already gone, as though she might never see him again, and she didn't know if she could bear it. In the short time he'd been at home, it had been as though a door had been left ajar in her prison, providing her a glimpse of life beyond the sterile, empty confines of existing with Arthur. Instead of the continuing round of visits to the modistes, there had been the Mint, the menagerie at the Tower, a visit to the undercroft at Westminster Abbey, a barge ride down the Thames on a fresh spring day—and the fateful but utterly exhilarating excursion to watch the fireworks at Vauxhall. With Charles she could share the exuberance, the liveliness of youth.

But the door was closing once again, forcing her back into the glittering emptiness Arthur craved so desperately. For a moment, she tried to imagine what it would be like when she were finally free, when she would be a wealthy widow in control of her own destiny, then guilt washed over her, making her feel like the lowest of God's creatures.

"Where were you?"

She spun around, and her heart lurched at the sound of Charles's voice. "As it's not raining, I went for a walk. I did not know you were at home."

"I guess he must've told you I was leaving, didn't he?"

"Yes—and I'm sorry—truly sorry." She swallowed, trying to drown the lump in her throat. "I know not how I shall go on without you."

"I ain't going forever, you know." He grinned, then sobered. "Funny, isn't it? I wanted to go, and he would not let me. Then I spent a couple of weeks with you, and it was like always—you're a great gun, you know—and now he won't let me stay."

"Perhaps if you told him—if you promised—"

"No." He crossed the room to her and took her hands, holding them. "He's right—I cannot stay—not now." His fingers were warm, surprisingly strong. "I guess you are the only one as did not see it," he said softly. "The hat's over the windmill, and there ain't any way to get it back, Nell."

It was the first time anyone had called her Nell since Arthur had forbidden it. "Charley—"

"No. Got to say it, don't you see? I'm head over heels for you—have been for a couple of years—maybe longer even." As she opened her mouth to speak, he shook his head. "And don't be saying it's but my salad days, 'cause it ain't." His clasp tightened as he drew her closer. "I love you, Nell—if it wasn't for him, I'd be shouting it from the rooftops."

She fought the urge to cry. "Oh, Charley—I—"

"No. You don't have to say anything—not yet."

"It's impossible, Charley." She bit her lip to still its trembling. "Even—even if—oh, I could not! Do you not see? I cannot betray my marriage vows!"

"But it ain't impossible. Been thinking—been thinking about it a lot, and it stands to reason he ain't going to live forever."

"But—"

"Oh, I know it ain't legal in England, but I'd take you away from here—maybe marry you in America, if you'd have me." Releasing one of her hands, he reached into his pocket and drew out a folded paper. Opening it, he showed her a simple pearl ring. "Want you to have something to look at while I am gone, so's you don't forget me."

"Oh, *Charley*! As if I would! But—" Her lower lip quivered, and her eyes spilled tears onto her cheek.

"Stoopid," she choked, "you know I love you, but not like this!"

"Here now," he said gruffly, "can't go turning on the water pot, Nell. And the time for 'buts' ain't now. All I'm asking for is that you don't forget me. Then when the war's over—when the old man's gone—I mean to ask you to marry me. Until then, I ain't wanting to know whether you want me or not." His voice was earnest, his eyes intent. "I know I can win you, Nell."

He possessed her right hand and slid the ring on her middle finger, then stared at it. "Ought to be diamonds, but it wouldn't look right—not yet."

"It's—it's beautiful."

His hands slid up her arms to her shoulders, then he hugged her close, enfolding her against him, murmuring, "Been wanting to do this a long time, you know."

She returned his embrace, clinging to him. "I'm afraid for you, Charley. What if—?"

"Shhhhh." One of his hands tilted her head back, and he bent his face to hers. His warm breath brushed her cheek, then his lips pressed gently, tenderly against hers. Then he stood back. "Ain't half of what I'd like to do with you, but I ain't about to dishonor you—or the old man. We got time, Nell—we're young."

She heard the footmen moving something heavy down the stairs. "Charley, you are not leaving *now*? Not yet—surely—"

He nodded. "Got to. The old man's paid for lodgings at the Pulteney until the papers are done. He don't want me under the same roof now."

"But I'll see you again before you leave?"

"Don't know. Rumor's got it that something big's about to happen in the Peninsula—chance is good that once I am signed, they ain't going to want to wait to ship me over."

"But surely—I mean, you are not trained—and—"

"Ride as good as the best of 'em," he assured her. "Good shot, too."

"Charley, it's war!"

"Going to write to you—every day, in fact. Oh, I know they don't dispatch 'em like that, but I'll keep a journal—mail the pages when I can." Once again, he lifted her chin. "You going to write to me, Nell?"

Her throat ached almost too much for speech. "You know I will," she whispered.

"Good. Word of you will mean everything to me."

"Charley, go back to school—don't—" She choked, unable to go on.

"Can't. Too late for that. Tell you what though—come back a captain for you."

There was a discreet tap on the facing of the open door. "Begging your pardon, sir, but the carriage is waiting."

"Oh—tell 'em I'll be right along." This time, he leaned to place a quick kiss on her cheek. "Wait for me—it's all I ask," he whispered. "You don't have to love me—yet."

This time she knew he was gone. She stood at the window and watched as the big, black-lacquered carriage pulled away, then disappeared down the sunlit street. As she turned away from the cross-panes, she was nearly overwhelmed by the sudden dreariness, the emptiness of the ornately decorated room. And a new, chilling isolation seemed to descend like a mantle over her.

Heavy-hearted, her mind in turmoil, she climbed slowly up the stairs to her bedchamber, where she sat staring unseeing for a time. It had happened too quickly, this brief glimpse of freedom and fun, and now it was gone. Had she done wrong? Had she somehow caused this? Did she love him—or would she even know if she did? Of course she loved him—who would not? But was it because he was the brother she'd never had—or was it because he cared about her?

She crossed her arms, holding herself, telling herself there was more to life than the inane, petty existence Arthur Kingsley gave her—that there was the comfort, the solace, and the excitement of a man's arms about her that every woman needed, and she did not have. She wanted someone to ease the aching loneliness that had settled into the hollow between her breasts.

But as she leaned back in her chair and closed her eyes, Charley's tender kiss faded in the remembered heat of Longford's passion. Where the one had been sweet, gentle, almost pure, the other had been ruthless and demanding. And as much as she believed she loved Charles Kingsley, as much as she now despised Lucien de Clare, she had to admit the earl's passionate embrace had been far more exciting.

Forcing both men from her mind, she rose determinedly and moved to her writing desk. She had to pour out her heart to someone or go mad. Sitting down, she drew out a crisp sheet of vellum and uncorked the inkpot. Dipping her pen into it, she began, "Drst Mama—" then faltered. What could she say? That her husband's grandson had declared his love for her and was going off to war for it? That she could not bear to go on being naught but a decorative accessory to her husband's life?

"My lady—?"

She looked up, startled. "Yes?"

"Jeremy said I was to tell you that Lord Townsend awaits ye below."

Townsend. She'd forgotten him. She glanced at the clock, sighing. She'd forgotten her promise to go riding in the park with him at four. For a moment, she considered going down to beg off, then thought better of it. If she had to explain, she would cry.

"My lady?" Mary came close, peering into her mistress's face. "It's overset ye are, ain't ye?"

Elinor started to deny it, then buried her head in her hands. "Just go away," she choked out miserably. "I—I shall be better later."

"I'll tell him ye've got the headache and are abed," the maid decided.

Ordinarily, Elinor would have despised the lie, but this time, she said nothing. Mary touched her shoulder, patting it briefly, then murmured, "Ain't none of us likes it, ye know—it ain't right." Then she stepped back. "When Lord Townsend is gone, I'll bring ye a bit of toddy."

Elinor straightened and wiped her wet cheeks with the back of her hand. "I'm not cold."

"It will ease yer mind if I was to put a dab of butter in it, ye know."

"I cannot be disguised when Arthur comes home, Mary—he cannot stand a female sot."

"Humph! If it was left ter me, I'd give him a dose of laudanum and leave 'im ter sleep it off. Then we don't have ter listen ter what he can't stand."

"Mary—"

"I'm a-going," the maid insisted. "Do Jeremy good ter tell his lordship ye ain't coming down."

When Mary returned a few minutes later, Elinor was still sitting, her eyes fixed on the sheet of vellum. "He said I was ter give ye these, my lady—he brung ye flowers. Roses from the flower monger down the street, I think."

"They are lovely," Elinor replied without enthusiasm.

"And Jeremy's ter bring the toddy—make ye feel more the thing. Though it ain't going ter seem right without the young master, is it?"

"No."

"Thought it was good fer ye to have somebody yer age about, but I guess—"

"It was my fault, Mary."

"Yer fault?" The maid's voice rose incredulously. "And how might that be, I ask ye? Ye ain't a boy caught in his first calf-love."

"I welcomed him—I was glad he came home."

"And well ye ought to be! Place's like a tomb when there ain't any but the old master about," Mary sniffed. "If he still had his eyes, he'd know—"

"Mary—"

"Guess it ain't proper to talk about it," the maid conceded reluctantly. "Guess ye just got to drink the toddy and try to fergit it, huh?"

"I don't know—Mary, I don't *know*!" For a moment, Elinor's face seemed to crumple, then she regained her composure. "You'd best see what keeps Jeremy."

As soon as the maid left again, she redipped her pen and scratched across the page, "I am the most miserable of females, and I see no end to it."

She stopped to stare at the words, then put her pen in the inkwell. She could not send that, not when her mother was powerless to do anything to help her. Wadding the vellum into a ball, she threw it to the floor and took out another sheet and began to write again.

Drst Mama,

I trust you, Papa, and the girls are well. As for Kingsley and I, we are fast becoming all the crack, and the pace is quite exhausting. Charles has been home for several weeks, but is leaving to join a regiment of dragoons, and I shall miss him in the extreme. Indeed, now that I have become used to a young person in the house, I know not how I shall go on without one.

I know that Charlotte is not yet out, but I have been thinking perhaps that she might enjoy a visit to London. There is so much to see here, Mama, that you cannot imagine it all, and although Charlotte cannot go about to routs and balls before she is presented, I am sure I can keep her tolerably amused. And it will do no harm to see that Madame Cecile takes her measurements for her court presentation next year, after all, for there is quite a waiting list.

You must not worry over the expense, for I am sure Arthur would frank the entire trip were I to ask him. And you must think of it not as a favor to Charlotte, but rather as one to myself. I assure you I shall delight in taking her about.

Do tell Papa and the girls that I think of them often, and that I wish it were possible to see them also. And you have my leave to tell that awful Mrs. Pangburn that I have waltzed at Almack's, for I quite know it will set up her back and afford you a bit of amusement.

Until we are met again, I remain yr obedient dtr,
Nell Kingsley.

She read it carefully to discern if there were anything that might offend Arthur, then decided there was nothing beyond her use of the word *Nell.* If anything, it was rather vacuous, utterly concealing her pain and loneliness. Sitting back, she felt a small bit of relief—with Charlotte there, she would have an excuse to avoid Lord Townsend. And after what had happened with Longford—not to mention the guilt and loss she felt over Charles—she did not welcome any sort of flirtation, however fashionable Sally Jersey might think it.

IT WAS EARLY and White's was relatively quiet, with the usual gaming over baize-covered tables, the gentlemen who merely conversed, and those who were already more than half-disguised with drink. In a solitary corner, Bellamy Townsend sat hunched over a bottle of port, his handsome countenance marred by his ugly temper. From time to time, his friends Sefton, Alvanley, and Skeffington approached him, trying to draw him into a game of faro, and each was equally rebuffed.

Brummell glanced across to him from his exalted place at the bow-window and suggested loudly that "Poor Bell has either lost his last farthing or been thwarted by a female," at which the drunken viscount lurched to his feet, demanded the betting book, and rashly entered a wager that "Bellamy, Viscount Townsend, shall mount Lady Kingsley before the year is out, taking her away from the Earl of Longford." When done, he read his entry loudly, as though he dared any to dispute it. For a moment, there was relative silence, then a ripple of murmurs, followed by considerable speculation as to the virtue of the lady in question.

"I have it on authority that Longford's Venus is rather unattainable," the Beau said coolly.

"You?" someone snorted. "She rebuffed *you*?"

"Of course not—but I should take the Jersey's word for it, for she knows everything. She says La Kingsley is an innocent."

"I can take her away from Longford!" Townsend snapped.

"Who says she is Longford's?" Skeffington asked. "First I ever heard of it."

"Much you know," Bell responded sourly. "Saw her at his house myself."

"I hear Longford's going back to the war," someone else spoke up.

"How much you want to wager, Bell?" Freddy Pinkham demanded, drawing out his money. "Think you must be mistaken."

"A hundred pounds," Bellamy muttered truculently.

"Well now—that don't make it worth the space in the book," Freddy complained.

Leighton, who'd half-observed the wager between casts of the dice, started to rise. "Bell's gone too far, Luce—if you don't mean to queer his lay, I do."

Lucien raked in his winnings, and shook his head. "Best leave it—Bell's got a damnable temper when he's foxed. And if I stand up, the rumor will be counted."

"Damme if I'll stand for it—it isn't right. Not a reason in the world to think—besides, Townsend's outright accusing you, Luce!"

"Don't be a fool—let it die." Lucien's hand snaked out, holding down Leighton's arm. "He'll lose, George."

"Dash it, but I *like* Lady Kingsley! Feel sorry for her. I mean, who'd blame her if she did put horns on the old gent? But it ain't something I'd bet on."

"No," Lucien muttered dryly.

"A man ought to stand up for a woman's honor, Luce." Then, "Why'd he call her your Venus? You been up to something I don't know? That dancer—Emma Land—pale for you already?"

"No." Lucien shrugged. "Malice—wit—who knows? I told you—I mean to ignore it."

"But if it's not so, it isn't right!"

"Forget it."

"She's not up to his weight at all," Leighton protested. "Gel's an innocent."

The earl favored him with a pained look. "Are you playing or not?"

"How deep am I?"

"About ten thousand."

"Got to come about—blasted run of luck lately." The viscount shook his head in disgust. "Went down about the time you came back, you know."

"My dear George, I never advise playing against me," Lucien murmured mildly. "If you had hoped to win, you ought to have sat down with Bell."

"Fellow's three sheets into it," Leighton snorted.

"Precisely."

"And what am I supposed to make of that?"

"You ought to stick to your cards. Would you care to try faro?"

"Lud, no! You fleeced me the last time! You know what, Luce?—you've got the devil's own luck."

"I hope so—considering where I am going."

"It makes no sense to go, Luce. Just because your father—"

"It has nothing to do with him."

"Diana, then."

"Nor Diana."

"Look, if you'd stay and face 'em down—if you'd do like Rotherfield did and brazen it out—"

"George, I don't give a damn if I am never received again," Lucien cut in coldly. "It was worth the price." He picked up the dice, weighed them in his hand, then cast them onto the table, rolling a seven. "Well worth it."

"Maybe you asked too much of her. I mean, you are a cold fellow, and—"

But Longford's attention had strayed to the door. "Damn!" he muttered under his breath.

"What—?" Leighton blinked, then followed his glance. Perplexed, he frowned. "I don't—oh, young Fenton. Hope he doesn't mean to make a scene."

"No. The one with him—Kingsley."

"Kingsley? But he's—"

"The old man's grandson."

"Ten to one, he'll not be amused by the wager."

"Not at all," Lucien agreed grimly.

For a moment, he could see Elinor Kingsley sitting forward in her chair in his saloon, acknowledging that her elderly husband was jealous of the boy, that he was sending him off to war because of it. And as the two young men walked unsteadily, betraying an early start on an evening of drinking, Lucien forsaw disaster. He tossed the dice again, paying no attention to the ivory cubes, telling himself that even if the boy quarreled with Bell, it was none of his affair. Almost idly, he handed the dice to Leighton.

"Well, George?"

"Done up for tonight, I'm afraid."

"Your vouchers are always good with me."

"Heart's not in it. I get tired of losing." Leighton started to rise. "If you want to fleece somebody, take Bell. Think I'll see what Alvanley means to do."

"I can tell you—they are all going to Watier's to sup, provided Prinny is not in attendance there. The coolness between the Beau and our Regent continues, I'm afraid."

"Watier's?"

"Rumor has it that it's to be lobster patties and apricot tarts—and you know what that does to Alvanley," Lucien answered. "They but wait for a coachman to come back to advise them on Prinny's presence."

"Dash it, but you cannot know that! You been sitting here with me, and I did not hear it," Leighton protested.

"Acute hearing is sometimes useful, George."

"One would think the cannon would have dulled it by now," his friend muttered. He looked up. "Oh-oh. Fenton's wanting to enter something in the book—no doubt it's a mill or some such thing."

Despite his self-professed disinterest, Lucien half-turned to watch as the attendant brought out the book. Fenton started to write, then said something to the other boy, whose face reddened visibly. Before he could be stopped, Charles Kingsley started across the room toward Bellamy Townsend. And it was obvious that in his present state, he wasn't entirely rational. There was a public and ugly quarrel in the making.

But you could use your position to see he is kept from the fray. It was as though Elinor Kingsley's words echoed in his mind. *I could not bear it if he were to perish. I'd not have it said he died because of me.*

Lucien groaned inwardly. He'd refused her once, and rather shabbily, and what there was of his conscience still pricked him for it. Reluctantly, he heaved himself up to head the fool off. "Kingsley!" he called out.

But he was too late. With Tom Fenton urging him on, Charles Kingsley already confronted the inebriated viscount, who was sprawled back in his chair. Weaving above him truculently, the boy demanded, "Take Lady Kingsley's name from the betting book, damn you! Take it back!"

Bell blinked. "Wha—? Don't—can't." He tried to sit

up, then fell back. "Oh—it's you." He grinned foolishly. "Ain't her husband—not your affair."

"She is my kinswoman, and I'll not stand to have her name sullied, sir!" Charles shouted. "It's an insult not to be borne!" Retrieving his glove from his coat pocket, he was about to strike Townsend in the face, when Longford caught his arm.

Leaning close, the earl murmured, "A duel will keep the tale alive."

"What the devil—? Longford!"

Diana's brother spun around in disbelief, then his jaw jutted out belligerently. "Ain't your affair, Luce!"

Bellamy looked up, blinked again to focus reddened eyes, then sneered. "Never shay you mean to de—defend the ladish honor, Lu—Luce? I saw her, you know—and—"

He never got to finish. Lucien's hand caught him under the chin, lifting him from the chair. Bell's neck seemed to lengthen above his starched cravat, and his eyes bugged out. He moved his lips, but could not speak.

"No, but I am prepared to defend mine," Lucien said almost softly. "Before you accuse, you'd best ask."

"But—"

Lucien's grip tightened as the viscount's face purpled. Alarmed, Leighton threw his arms around his friend, trying to hold him. "For God's sake, Luce—the man's disguised!"

"Gentlemen, not here!" the proprietor implored them. "If you must quarrel in your cups, go outside."

But Lucien's black eyes were on Townsend's. "Is there a quarrel, Bell?" he asked silkily.

"N-no," the other man gasped. As the earl relaxed his grip, Townsend slipped back into his chair and began rubbing his neck, looking up balefully. "Did—didn't have to cho-choke me, Luce."

"You saw nothing, Bell—nothing."

The other man's eyes dropped. "Must've been mistaken," he muttered. "Got no quarrel with you." When he perceived that that was not enough, he added, "Could've been the Wilson woman—got red hair, too, you know."

"Precisely." As though nothing had happened, Lucien adjusted the cuff of his shirt beneath his coat sleeve. "I'm glad—I should not want to put a hole in you before

I leave the country.'' Turning his back on Townsend, Fenton, and Charles Kingsley, he walked over to where the attendant still held the book.

Awed, Charles followed him. ''I say, but—''

''I'd have the pen.''

The proprietor himself produced one—and an inkpot. ''Was you wanting to lay a wager, my lord?''

But rather than answer, Lucien took the pen and scratched out Townsend's entry, inserting instead the motto of the Garter, *''Honi soit qui mal y pense.''* As those around him exchanged perplexed glances, he snapped the book shut. ''I suggest you give him back the money you are holding for him,'' he told the man coldly. When nobody moved, he added, ''I believe it was one hundred pounds.''

''What the devil—? You cannot expunge his wager,'' Sefton protested.

''I just did.''

''I say, Luce—but—'' Once again, Bellamy Townsend tried to rise, supporting himself with his table. ''It was about La Kingsley—not—'' He stopped, aware that Charles Kingsley glared at him.

''Suffice it to say, Bell, that if I ever read my name—or Lady Kingsley's name—in any of the betting books again, I shall choose to make a wager of my own—shall we say ten thousand pounds that I can score a solid hit at twenty paces?''

''Who the devil'd take that?'' Alvanley demanded. ''Crack shot.''

Fenton turned to Charles and whispered, ''What'd he write?''

''Honi soit qui mal y pense,'' Charley hissed back.

''What?''

''Shame to him who evil thinks—or something like that, if I remember it right.''

''Well, he ought to know about shame,'' Fenton muttered.

''Still doesn't settle the matter,'' Charley began, only to realize that Longford had his arm again.

''You're foxed,'' the earl declared coldly. ''You'd best go home.''

''But I ain't—''

''We'll speak of it in my carriage.''

It was Charles's turn to blink. "Your carriage? You'd take me up?"

"I'm leaving anyway."

Despite the earl's awful reputation, Charley considered it a signal honor. "Going to the Peninsula with you, you know," he confided as Longford propelled him toward the door. "Dragoons."

"You won't like it."

"Be a hero like you," the boy mumbled. "Come home a hero to Nell."

There was a low murmur as Lucien passed, a muttered "Lucifer" under someone's breath, and Bell Townsend proclaiming loudly to any who would listen that he wasn't afraid of Longford. To which the usually taciturn Earl of Rotherfield, a rather sinister fellow himself, replied that even he was not such a fool as to quarrel with Lucien de Clare.

Charley stumbled as he tried to step up into the conveyance, and Lucien had to boost him up. "Love her, you know."

"You're in your cups." Lucien looked up at his driver. "Kingsley House."

"No—cannot go there," Charley protested. "The Pulteney."

"You ought to go home."

"Old man won't let me—don't want me in the house because of Nell."

"Nell?"

"Elinor." Charley leaned back against the squabs and closed his eyes against the dizziness he felt. "Lady Kingsley. Mean to marry her, you know."

Longford surveyed him soberly for a moment, then shook his head. "When it comes to women, there are two kinds of foolish fellows, Kingsley—the very young and the very old."

"It ain't like that. Nell's different—great gun—only he don't see it. Won't let her—" The boy swallowed hard, trying not to disgrace himself before Longford, but he couldn't. Grasping the door handle, he wrenched it open to hang outside, where he was heartily, thoroughly sick. When he was done, he pulled himself back in, and fell back against the seat. There was no mistaking his misery.

"What was I saying?" he mumbled.

"It doesn't signify."

But Charley wasn't to be denied. "No—it was the old man—you don't know—keeps her a prisoner."

Longford's eyebrow rose. "Coming it too strong—half the females in London would welcome such a prison."

"He don't even want her to think. Got to be what he wants—always got to be what he wants. But he ain't living forever, you know—make it up to her. Mean to marry her," he repeated.

"What you are suggesting is incest," the earl reminded him.

"Take her out of England—America maybe—start over." Charley's blue eyes opened briefly to meet Longford's dark ones. "Don't care if I'm a baron or not. Just want to support her. Love her," he insisted almost defiantly.

Salad days, Lucien thought privately. But he'd not yet seen a youth ready to part with his idealized dreams of a female. That came later, sometime after the conquest, when the poor fellow discovered that one woman was in truth much like any other. The only things that separated Sally Jersey or Lady Oxford from courtesans like Harriette Wilson and her sisters were money, aristocratic birth, and complacent husbands.

Nonetheless, he found himself inquiring hesitantly, "Er—Does Lady Kingsley return your regard?"

"If you are asking if there's anything havey-cavey between her and me, there ain't." Once again, the blue eyes met Lucien's, and this time they were almost sober. "But I know she loves me—cried when she found out I was going to war. Going to wait for me."

There was something earnest, something quite appealing about the boy, possibly the innocence Lucien had never had. When he remained silent, Charley thought to add, "She ain't the sort as would cuckold the old man, you understand. Got character. And for all that he'd make her like the rest of 'em, she don't want to be like that."

Lucien thought of her as he'd last seen her—her bright hair straggling where she'd missed some of it with her pins, her bonnet tied slightly askance, her straight back as she'd sailed out his door—and he felt a twinge of conscience once more.

Sally Jersey is right—you cannot be brought to care

about anything, can you? Once again, her words seemed to echo in his ears, stinging him with their truth. *I have never betrayed my marriage vows . . . I am not bought at all* . . . She'd offered him nothing—nothing at all—when she'd asked his aid, not for herself but for the boy. It would not have required much effort on his part, but he'd rebuffed her. Now, facing young Kingsley across the seat, he felt almost sorry for it.

The carriage rolled to a halt, and a coachman promptly hopped down to open the door. "The Pulteney, my lord."

Charles reached unsteadily for the pull-strap, then sprawled back. "Sorry—had too much—gone to m'head."

Cursing inwardly, Lucien helped him lean toward the door, advising the coachey to catch him. Then, jumping down after the boy, he thrust a shoulder beneath his arm, supporting him.

"Deuced good of you—," Charley mumbled. As Lucien dragged him through the elegant lobby, the boy drew attention to them by rousing, calling out, "It's Longford—going to be a dragoon like him! Come back a hero like Longford—come back a—" The earl's free hand covered his mouth, stifling his ramblings.

"Get someone to help him, will you?" he growled at the nearest liveried attendant. When the fellow moved forward, Lucien shoved Charles Kingsley into his arms, then palmed a coin into his hand. "Put him to bed."

He turned to leave, ignoring the stares of the curious as the boy called after him, "Be like you one day, you know—dragoon just like Longford!"

"Going back to one of the clubs, yer lordship?" Lucien's coachman asked politely.

"No."

"But ye ain't supped, have ye?"

"No. I'm not hungry."

Lucien swung back up into his carriage and leaned back against the squabs. He wasn't going to sup—he was going home to bury himself in his cups. As the carriage bowled down the street, he reflected resentfully that he'd managed to survive nearly thirty years without help from anyone. When one only counted on oneself, one was seldom disappointed—it was when a fool embroiled himself in the lives of others that he suffered. If he'd learned naught else from his father, that had been a lesson well-learned.

And yet when he got home, after he poured himself a rather large glass of brandy, he sat staring for a time into the empty brazier. Outside, it had begun to rain, and the sound of wind and water against the windowpanes reminded him of the night he'd first met her. She'd been a little chit then, her face nearly as white as her nightgown. Briefly, he wondered if his life would have been any different if Ashton's ploy had worked, if she'd come to him instead of Kingsley. But she wouldn't have, for there was Diana—and even then he was beyond caring, beyond acting out of honor.

It wasn't until after his third glass that he rose to move to his desk. And, whether from drink or some other weakness, he sat down to write a single line to her.

"I'll do what I can for the boy."

He left it unsigned, telling himself she would know from whence it came, and he'd not cause her any more difficulty with the old man. When done, he glanced up to the blank space above the cold fireplace, the place where Jack's portrait had once hung. Despite fresh paint, the sooty outline of the frame could still be discerned.

"You think me a fool, Papa—don't you?" he said, his voice harsh. "Damn you, Jack—damn you! It isn't the war that takes my soul—it's you!"

He knew not how long or how much he'd drunk, but after he finally managed to stumble up to his bed, he lay there in his rumpled clothes, remembering first Elinor Kingsley's plea, then the boy's almost fawning admiration, and somehow it amused him to know that he was not entirely immune to flattery, that somewhere deep within him, perhaps he could be moved to care. With that drink-induced, maudlin notion, he turned over to cradle his head against his pillow. His last rational thought was that he was going to pay for the brandy on the morrow.

SHE CAME DOWN to luncheon to discover her opened letter on her plate. From the end of the table, Arthur watched her sourly. She looked up, surprised. It was obvious that he was vexed with her.

"I have no intention of franking that, I'm afraid."

"But why? Surely you cannot object to my sister."

"I have no patience with children still in the schoolroom," he told her coldly. "And I'd as lief not remind any of the connection."

For a moment, she could only stare, then she felt anger. "Arthur, my family has held property under patent longer than yours. Papa's title—"

"Oh—I have no objection to the breeding, my dear—it's the parent himself I fault."

"It's the same!"

"Not at all. Thomas Ashton is a wastrel—a waster of his substance—and I tire of his hanging on my sleeve. It's enough that I said I would give him the allowance he chooses to waste in the hells."

"Arthur, you said I could bring Charlotte out! You promised!"

"Lower your voice, Elinor."

"But you said—"

"The girl's still in the schoolroom," he repeated. "And I said I should not object to assisting her in making a good marriage—perhaps next year. Your mother can take her to Bath for the short season." He looked up at her, and there was no mistaking the displeasure in his eyes. "Sit down that I may eat."

She felt ready to cry. "Arthur, now that Charley is gone, I shall have no one."

"Apparently you have no need of anyone else to get yourself into a scrape, my dear." He began carving a slab of cold tongue, slicing it thinly. "It's enough that I had to send Charles away."

"Charley and I did nothing! A trip to Vauxhall to see the fireworks—to sit under the stars—to buy food from the stalls—it was all, Arthur—all! It was utterly harmless! We did not even go near the Dark Walk! And as for Almack's—"

"I was not speaking of Charles alone, my dear."

"The market was—"

"Nor the market."

She sank into her chair, temporarily dispirited, for she knew whatever maggot he'd gotten in his brain, he would keep it. And she was at a loss as to the source of his manner. "I know not what you have been told, my lord, but I can only think it was a lie. I can think of nothing—"

"How long have you been seeing Longford?" he asked abruptly.

"Longford! But I haven't—I—" She stopped, wondering who could have told, who could have spied on her. Her chin came up almost defiantly. "I collect you are referring to yesterday, and if you wished to know of that, you had but to ask."

"The reason is immaterial—it's outside of enough that you were seen."

"I walked there to ask that he look after Charley."

"A likely tale!" he snorted. "Longford would not put himself out for anyone. He could not even be brought to his father's bedside in the end."

"Well, he could not be said to be very pleasant," she conceded. "But I did not know that when I went." Trying to control her shaking hands, she reached for the bread rack. "He turned me away."

His eyes narrowed, he regarded her shrewdly. "A likely tale," he said sarcastically. "No—I did not bring you to town to disgrace me, Elinor."

"And I have not. Arthur—I have not!" She wet her dry lips with her tongue, trying again. "Please—I'd have Charlotte. She'll not vex you, I promise!" But even as she spoke, she knew he did not mean to let her have any company beyond his. She felt a sense of defeat. "Indeed, but she'll give you no cause—Arthur, she is a quiet, biddable girl!"

"You will lower your voice when you speak to me."

"Then you will not accuse me of baseness, my lord."

"I may accuse you of anything I wish, my dear—you would forget what I have given you. I have made you the envy of every female in London."

"I should rather be poor, I think," she muttered bitterly.

"You would not like the life." He pressed his fingers together and continued to stare at her. "But you are like Charles, are you not? I have made it too easy for you."

"Easy?" Her voice rose incredulously. "*Easy*? Do you think I like this life you have given me?"

"I'll not have your name bandied about like a common whore's."

Somehow she knew he was getting to the heart of the matter, and she was perplexed. "What? Arthur, I have not the least notion—"

He favored her with an impatient frown. "There was a great deal of excitement at White's last night, I am told. In the guise of friendship, Lord Sefton stopped by rather late to report of it." He waited for her to react to that and was disappointed. "I understand Townsend placed a bet that he would have you when Longford was through."

"*What*? Townsend?" She nearly choked. "When Longford was through—? Arthur, I can assure you it's no such thing! The earl rebuffed me—that is"—she amended hastily—"he refused to help Charles. All I wanted was for him to keep Charley safe, Arthur!"

"Sefton is neither deaf nor given to invention, Elinor."

"This is preposterous! And I care not who wagered on it—it's not true!"

"You have made me a laughingstock!" he snapped. "And I'll not stand for it!"

Her color rose in her cheeks, and her own anger made her reckless. "No more so than when you wed me, I should think," she bit off precisely. "And what of Sally Jersey? Or Lady Oxford? Or the Melbourne woman? It would seem infidelity is the fashion, so I cannot think any would refine overmuch on it."

"Then it's the truth."

"Of course it is not! I am sure Lord Longford, having taken me in dislike, would most certainly deny it. And as for Lord Townsend—well, I cannot account for his malice. Indeed, but I thought him a friend."

"He has run tame here for weeks," he reminded her.

"Because he is fashionable! Because he amused me a little—but certainly for nothing more. You did not discourage Lord Townsend, Arthur!"

"I warned you about Longford, Elinor! Make me appear the fool and I shall take you back to Stoneleigh," he threatened.

"I would that you did!"

"When I discovered you, you were but a pretty, striking chit," he told her, lowering his voice. "I made you a beauty—an Incomparable. And that's the thanks I get for it. I am surrounded by vipers—vipers I have nurtured at this very table!"

"You wanted men to admire me—you said so yourself!" She rose and moved to stand over him. "Look at me, Arthur! Do you not know that I would rather be plain? That I would have the pox if it would mark me and free me from this?"

"Lady Jersey, sir!" the footman announced.

"Tell her to leave her card," Elinor muttered. "No doubt she has come to ferret out the gossip."

But Arthur shook his head. "It's early, but I'd not send her away. Sit down and try to recall that you are a lady," he advised her. When she did not move, he hissed, "For God's sake, sit!"

"Kingsley! Elinor dearest!" The countess swept into the room, her scarf trailing over her walking dress. "I came as soon as I heard!"

"Heard what?" Elinor asked without enthusiasm.

"About that dreadful wager, my dear." Sally turned to the old man. "Never say you have not been apprised?"

"Sefton told me," he answered.

"Well, I do not believe there is an excessive amount of damage, for it's off the books, in any event." Her gaze flitted to Elinor, and for a moment, she could not contain her interest. "Longford, my dear? I *told* you he was dangerous. But I must admit it was rather generous of him to see it removed."

For once, Arthur came to Elinor's defense. "Lady Jersey, I do not refine on it at all, I assure you. The earl is scarce the sort to appeal to a sensible female."

Sally fixed him with a glance that indicated he must be daft. "Nonsense," she declared flatly. "But that is quite beside the point. We must see that the matter is met headlong, that there is nothing to it. I have sent quite a peal to Bellamy, I'm afraid. I cannot think what he was about! And but two days after I sponsored dear Elinor at Almack's."

"It's very kind of you, Lady Jersey, but—"

The countess turned on her. "Kindness has naught to do with it, my dear! It was *I* as recommended you to the patronesses, after all. Lud, but what a smirk I shall expect from Mrs. Drummond-Burrell—"

"I collect you think she can recover," Arthur cut in, interrupting her rattling.

"Of course! She is not the first wayward wife, after all," she declared in understatement. "The unforgiveable is not the deed, but a lack of discretion, and certainly that must be laid upon Bell's head rather than hers. And since Longford forced it from the books, we must all brazen the matter through."

"Lady Jersey, there is naught between Lord Longford and myself," Elinor protested. "Indeed, I cannot say I even like the man."

"Of course not, my dear," Sally responded, indicating clearly that she did not believe her. "Though I cannot say he is noted for that sort of association—not since Diana. No, Longford has consoled himself rather more with the likes of those Wilson women."

"Viscount Townsend, my lord!"

"Here?" Elinor choked. "How dare he?"

"What the deuce—?" Arthur frowned.

"I asked—no, I *commanded* him to come," the countess said. "He began it—he can very well scotch it."

The usually impeccably tailored, always perfectly groomed viscount entered the room almost sheepishly. And on this day, his blond hair looked as though it had been combed with his hands, while his coat appeared to have been slept in.

"Caught me still at White's—haven't been home to change," he murmured apologetically, looking to Lady Jersey. "Trying to come about, you know." Casting a sidewise glance at Elinor, he reddened. "Hallo, Lady Kingsley. Your pardon for my appearance. Kingsley."

"You, sir, are an utter blackguard," Elinor told him with feeling.

Chagrined, he could see his anticipated conquest slipping beyond his grasp, and he sought to retrieve the situation.

"Dear lady, I assure you—"

"Loose lips and full cups are the bane of civilized society," Sally declared spitefully. "I'm afraid they know, Bellamy, so there is no need to shilly-shally over the matter."

He flushed uncomfortably. "Foxed—only excuse for it—dashed disguised. Didn't mean—"

"Sir, were I younger, I should call you out for it," Arthur growled. "Half a mind to, anyway."

"And you should look the veriest cake at your age," Lady Jersey said. "No—it will not do at all. We must draw together, putting out that it was but a hum to embarrass Longford." Completely taking charge, she directed the viscount, "This afternoon, Bellamy, you will take both Lord and Lady Kingsley up—about five, shall we say? And do make it the open carriage."

Townsend's blond eyebrows lifted. "Even if it rains?"

"It's not a time for levity," Sally snapped. "And the three of you really ought to attend the opera together—no, no—it would be better if there were four—perhaps young Kingsley—"

"No," Arthur retorted curtly. "Charles is unavailable."

"Oh." For a moment, the woman was diverted, then she returned to the matter at hand. "But you must see and be seen, the more places the better, I should say. Perhaps Bell ought to bring a pretty female also," she mused, "and when it's noted there is no rancor—"

Her advice was slow to sink in for Bell, and when it did, he gave a start. "Five today? I've not been to bed! I shall look deuced hagged."

"Five," Sally repeated. "Everyone is there then."

But Arthur remained unconvinced. "Who's to say I shall not be pitied like Will Hamilton?" he protested. "He let Nelson flaunt Emma before the world, and afore God, I'll not stand for that!"

"No—no, of course not. I shall set it about—a little discreet gossip here and there—that it was a jest played upon Longford that got out of hand. After all, no matter what is said there must surely be some small bit of bad blood betwixt Bellamy and Lucien de Clare."

Elinor looked from one to the other of them as though they were mad. "Well, I have not the least intention of going so far as the corner with Lord Townsend—not after this!"

"Told you—in my cups." He smiled crookedly. "Would not have hurt you for the world, you know."

"You—you *wagered* on my reputation!" Turning to Arthur, she declared, "I should very much rather return to Stoneleigh, my lord. Your pardon, Lady Jersey." Without so much as a glance at the viscount, she walked from the room.

"I will trust you to reason with her," she heard Sally say. "But I must go—Emily Cowper and I are to meet at Gunther's, you know." There was a brief pause, then she added, "You must not dispute it when I set about a long-standing acquaintance between you and Townsend, you understand."

Beginning to see the possibility of salvaging the Season, the old man nodded. "And you may rest assured if Longford so much as shows his face, she will give him the cut direct." His eyes met Townsend's momentarily. "As for you, sir, I should rather take you up, for I have no wish to ride in your carriage. And I cannot help but feel it would be less obvious."

Bell sighed. "I shall try to be ready at five then."

It was not until after Lady Jersey and the viscount left that Arthur made his way upstairs to his wife's sitting room. "They are gone," he announced curtly.

"To perdition, I hope."

"You are behaving like a spoiled child."

"You have not given me the opportunity to be anything but a child, my lord," she responded coldly. "And I don't care if I go home in disgrace."

"Stand up."

"What?"

"Stand up."

Baffled, she did as he asked. "I don't see—"

"The dress—take it off."

Her hands went cold and her mouth went dry. "Arthur—"

"Now."

Reluctantly, she began working the buttons on her bodice, then turned her attention to the grosgrain band that criss-crossed beneath her breasts, loosening it. "What—what do you mean to do?" she asked nervously.

"Step out of it."

She did as he bade her, then in her zona and petticoat, she turned away to hide her embarrassment. He raised his cane and brought it down hard against her back. She flinched but managed to hold back tears. Again and again, it came down, striking her hips and buttocks.

"You'll not make a fool of me again! Behave as a child, and I shall treat you as one—do you hear me? You'll not shame me before Lady Jersey again—or any of the others!"

He struck her perhaps ten times, venting his anger, then threw the cane across the floor, reminding her of that other time, the humiliation of her wedding night. And she hated him for it.

"I'll have no whore in this house!"

"And you have none," she managed through clenched teeth.

He seemed to recall himself then, and as he walked to pick up his cane, he spoke more calmly. "Despite your rash behavior, we shall come about, Elinor. I have come too far and spent too much to retreat in disarray to Stoneleigh." Moving closer, he reached to brush her cheek lightly with the back of his hand. "You are to be admired, my dear—but not touched. You are Kingsley's Venus—not Longford's."

Near Salamanca, Spain: July, 1812

IT HAD BEEN HOT, almost unbearably so, for days, and Wellington had taken successive defensive postures, drawing his smaller force back from the city, despite having been welcomed enthusiastically but days before. It was the first time any could remember the sober, iron-disciplined general being nearly unhorsed by a horde of admiring ladies.

But now they waited cautiously in the Spanish hills for the French under General Marmont to move. For the time being, it appeared to be a Spanish standoff, with the French trying to stay until harvest, thus supplying their army for another year, and the English considering withdrawing again into Portugal to protect their own supply lines.

For a fortnight, they had faced each other across the shallow Douro River, feinting and parrying under cover of darkness, until Wellington gave the order to draw back again. And for another six days, the two armies had played cat and mouse beneath the blazing Spanish sun, so close that an occasional sniper could bring down an enemy on either side. Above, expectant vultures circled, waiting, providing grim targets and macabre jests for the army.

For Lucien, used to his general's less than glory-seeking tactics, the wait was rather ordinary. For Charles Kingsley, eager to join the fray, eager to beat the Frogs, that same wait was interminable. And now as rumor filtered down through the ranks that Wellington meant to withdraw again, giving up much of what they had won, he and many of his fellow dragoons were disappointed. Though not under Longford's command, whenever he encountered the earl, which was not as often as he would have wished, the boy complained bitterly. On this day, the twenty-first of July, he could scarce contain his ire.

"If we run back to Portugal, it'll be another year before we can take 'em. Don't see why we don't attack and end it."

"Supply," Longford told him tersely, tired of having to justify Wellington's orders to his own grumbling men. "An army eats—and drinks. It's why I would have you go with Walton—supply is the utmost—"

"Don't want to," Charles grumbled. "Dash it—if *anything's* to happen, I want to be here! And so I told Major Barry! I didn't come over here to guard wagons—I came to fight!"

"Then you are a fool," Longford told him. "If it gets too hungry, an army does not fight at all."

Knowing that the earl was vexed with him, Charley tried to control his own anger at the man's meddling. "All the same—" But there was no denying that they were already hungry, cut to three-quarter rations and a pint of rum every other day now.

"Well, she cannot say I did not try," Lucien murmured, shrugging. Turning on his heels, he walked away.

Charles shaded his eyes against the white-hot sun and watched him go, wondering what he'd meant by that. Somehow, and he knew not why, he'd expected Longford to understand, to know what it meant to win his spurs as a man. But the earl seemed almost detached from the war, as though he was there because there was nowhere else to be, as though the glory he'd achieved meant nothing to him.

The war, or what he'd seen of it so far, was not what Charles had expected. His woolen serge uniform itched in the heat, his shirt was soaked with sweat, and he stank until he could smell himself. Moreover, given the conservation of rations, it seemed to him that he was in a constant state of hunger. To make matters worse, the blanket that passed for his bed was infested with fleas, the tent that sheltered him torn and tattered. And, being the most junior of junior officers, many of whom had served together since Talavera and before, he was constantly lonely.

"Cold 'un—don't snap under fire. Ain't a man as I'd

rather serve under, including Wellington himself,'' a man observed as Longford left.

''Aye,'' another agreed, ''ain't afraid like some of the swells, ye know. Guess he got it from Mad Jack.''

''Don't know how, but he survives.'' A fellow spit on the hardened earth. ''One of fifteen as came back outer five hundred.''

''Aye.''

Charles unbuttoned his sweat-soaked coat and loosened his sticky cravat, pulling it away from his neck to cool his chest. They could call fighting hell, he reflected grimly, but he was ready for anything to take his mind off the heat—and the loneliness. It seemed that there was not a waking hour when he did not long to pour out his heart to Nell, either in thought or on paper.

Evening came and clouds began rolling in, blackening the sky in contrast to the layered orange sunset. Charles propped his secondhand tent, unrolled his blanket, and leaned back against his saddle to write, first in his journal, and then to Elinor.

In the beginning, he'd written her daily, but as one day became so very like another, and there was only so much one could say about heat and flies and fleas, he'd taken to keeping the journal, filling it with anecdotes of experiences like his first attempt to milk a goat, or the scrawny chickens that had mysteriously appeared despite an order not to plunder, tales of the foibles, the fears, and the hopes of his fellows, and long passages of his longing for her. It would be a record of sorts, something to share with her when he got home again. Who knew? Maybe he could publish his account of the summer of '12.

This night he wrote of his near-quarrel with the earl, for Longford had spoken earlier with Major Barry about sending him to accompany the empty supply carts back to the safety of Portugal. There was no glory in guarding flour wagons, he wrote resentfully, not when the fires of the French were so close that the smoke mingled with theirs. If only the French would move, if only they could be engaged, he would taste the glory of battle, he would feel it had been worth what he'd endured.

Despite his taciturn manner, Longford felt something was about—Charles sensed it. And despite his resentment of the man's interference just now, he still admired him above the other officers. If only Longford would understand that he wasn't a boy in need of protection, not anymore. All he needed was the chance to show the others that he could ride and fight with the best of them. He wasn't going with any supply train, thanks to his own plea to Barry. He was going to stay and be a man like the rest of them.

As lightning flashed closer and the thunder rumbled ominously, he finished describing his day, then tore a blank page from the back of his journal book and began a separate letter to Elinor, taking care that should it fall into his grandfather's hands, the old man would not throw it away. But he could not refrain from addressing her informally, his own way of establishing a degree of intimacy, he supposed.

Drst Nell,

After weeks of waiting, it now appears that you will get your wish, and I shall be safely returned to Portugal to await the winter there. It's a waste, but for all that I would have it otherwise, I am far too low for Wellington to listen to me.

Your letter of the 24th last reached me yesterday, heartening me greatly, though I cannot like it that you are still subjected to the importunities of a man like Bellamy Townsend. When I am come home, I mean to speak to Grandpapa about it, for it seems singularly ill-advised to allow a rake to be forever in your company. It's like inviting a viper to strike.

Today I saw Longford, and for all that others see him as cold and distant, I must admit he has tolerated me rather well when we are met. In fact, when one gets to know him, he can be droll in a macabre way. One of his leftenants is oft-quoted, insisting that God spares him for not even the Devil would have him, but there's not a man as would not follow him against the Frogs. I would that I had had the fortune of serving under him rather than Barry.

Since last I wrote you, there was a bit of a turn-up in Salamanca itself, when a senorita made sheep's eyes at poor Longford, and her family was determined that he should marry her. He entertained her father armed to the teeth, his rifle over his shoulder, his cartridge case slung at his waist, his saber at hand, saying that he had no objection to the match—provided she did not mind carrying his gear into battle. The girl's interest waned on the instant, providing us with a great deal of amusement when she called him a savage. Hargrove—my leftenant—said Longford looked as fierce as a Cossack, but never having seen one, I cannot attest to that.

I do hope you are well, and I would have you know that I miss you greatly—both of you. You cannot know how much your letters mean to me. But as it grows darker, and the wind smells of rain, I'd best seal this that it may go out in tomorrow's dispatches. I do feel sorry for the regulars, those miserables whose lack of rank gives them naught but a bit of rum and a bowl of beans at day's end. I at least am allowed to share the officer's mess, albeit at the far end of the table, for I am a junior and like to remain one else there is a battle.

But they are a jocular lot, these common soldiers of England. How they can go on, I know not, for while they speak often of wives and sweethearts, being uncommissioned, they never receive letters from them. I feel almost guilty when each new dispatch bag brings me word of you and my grandfather.

Until the next time, I am yr. affectionate kinsman,
Chas. Kingsley.

Even as he rolled the letter up and dipped it in wax to seal it from the weather, the lightning intensified, lighting up the sky and illuminating the hot, airless plains below. The dragoon horses, tethered within a rope pen, reared and neighed, frightened by the ensuing thunder, and their handlers sought to calm them, dodging between flailing hooves, calling each by name.

It was going to be a miserable night. He ought to have told Nell how much he hated Spain, how much he hated the heat and the rain, he thought morosely, but he did not want to burden her again. No doubt she was already sick of hearing about the place.

"Here."

He looked up, surprised to see the earl standing over him, a canteen in his hands. Despite the dusty earth, Longford dropped down on his haunches, and unscrewed the cap. "Port," he said succinctly. "The rum's bad. Oily."

"No worse than the food, which tastes like day-old oatmeal." Nonetheless, Charles proffered his cup. "My thanks, my lord."

"It's going to come a hell of a rain," the earl offered.

It occurred to Charles that in his own way, perhaps Longford himself was lonely. He moved over, giving him room beneath the tilted canvas. "It's all of a piece, isn't it? Only choice is between the heat and the flies—or the mud and the worms. You'd think they'd drown, wouldn't you?—the worms, I mean, but they come forth in hordes every time it rains. Ground's full of 'em."

"You ought to have taken the supply train," Lucien tried again. "There's as much honor in seeing we are fed as in taking a ball on the field."

Charles stared at the flickering sky, then shook his head. "I'm a dragoon—not a sentry."

Longford took a deep swig from his canteen. "You make me a liar, you know—I promised Lady Kingsley I'd see you stayed in the rear. She would have you safe."

"It wasn't her place to ask—nor yours to give, was it?"

"No. But I thought you might wish to know of her concern for you." His black eyes met Charles's blue ones soberly. "Some things might be worth staying alive for."

Charles was silent for several seconds, then he nodded, sighing, "Devil of a coil, ain't it?—a man waiting for his own grandfather to die. Makes you think less of me, don't it?"

"No. There are times I wish my father had perished sooner," Lucien admitted." He looked away, his expression distant. "Blood can make unreasonable demands on us."

"If he treated her right, I could stand the wait." When Longford did not respond, the boy sighed again. "Sometimes I think I hate him, you know—and that ain't right."

"I don't know—I cannot say I felt much for my father after my mother died," Lucien admitted.

"Mad Jack?" Charles asked incredulously. "But he

was—I mean, everybody knew—'' He stopped. ''Guess it ain't right to ask why.''

''Honor. Without a man's honor, he's damned—and Jack left none.'' Longford looked down to the plains. ''I wonder what Marmont means to do?'' he asked softly.

''He ain't going to do nothing,'' Charles responded, disgusted. ''We are going to sit here looking at each other until one side goes home.''

Lucien shook his head. ''The French put too much stock in glory. I should be surprised if they let us retreat unscathed. Marmont will want to posture before Napoleon, and how is he to do that if we go?''

''Damme if I don't wish for the fight,'' Charles muttered. ''Better'n sitting here getting ate by fleas. Been praying for it ever since I got here.''

Longford took another pull on his canteen, then wiped his mouth with his scarlet coat sleeve. ''It was the only thing of worth Mad Jack ever told me—'be careful what you ask for, boy, else you might get it'—though it was said in a different context, as I recall.''

''M'father died when I was in short coats.'' Charles hesitated, then blurted out, ''What was he like? Mad Jack, I mean.''

Lucien's jaw worked visibly, and for a moment, Charles did not think he meant to answer. ''Sorry—ain't my business, is it?''

''No.'' Lucien squared his shoulders, then stared into a jagged ridge of lightning. ''He was as big a bastard as I am.''

''But you ain't—''

His words were drowned in a sudden, howling wind that brought a volley of rain. The earl muttered a curse, then rose.

''Going to be a mire on the morrow,'' he said. He hesitated as though he would say more, then clasped Charles's shoulder. ''I hope you don't get your wish, you know—I'd not fight in this.''

He was gone as abruptly as he'd come, leaving Charles to stare after him. He'd said the wrong thing, and he knew it. It seemed that as much as he wanted to know Longford, as much as he admired him, he never knew what to say to him. But he was not alone—no one claimed any great degree of friendship with the man—not even his batman.

The wind caught the tattered canvas, ripping it from its rickety poles, blowing toward the smoldering, smoking coals of the fire set to ward off the pests. Charles lunged for it, then struggled against the sheet of rain to fold it beneath his arm. The sky poured now, soaking the stinking wool serge, the linen underneath, and the blanket he'd folded for his bed. There was no sense even trying to reset his tent.

Like everyone else caught out in the storm, he tried to unroll the canvas, then lay down, pulling it over him like a blanket, cradling his head on his arm, smelling the wet wool and the earth beneath it. But amid the howl of the wind, the force of the rain, and the hardness of the ground, he did not think he could sleep.

His thoughts turned again to Nell. Come hell or high water, both of which seemed possible now, he was going to make her proud of him. And when he went home, he'd surprise her, for the boy that had left would be a man.

Around him, the lightning flashed, the thunder crashed, and the frightened horses bolted, some of them charging riderless toward the enemy on the plains below. Those assigned to them ran frantically, trying to catch them, shouting, adding to nature's mayhem.

His neck hurt, and the rain ran down his face in rivulets, dripping into the blanket beneath him. Finally, unable to stand the steady flow of the water, he pulled his saddle closer and used it for a pillow, then drew the soaked canvas higher, creating a pocket of protection from the storm. Sometime in the night, his aching body adjusted to the discomfort and the din, and he managed to sleep fitfully, his dreams carrying him away from that awful place.

Then, before dawn broke, a scout rode through to report that the French were on the move, that they were trying to skirt the right flank, and that was that. Waterlogged and sullen from a lack of sleep, Charles groped groggily for his weapons. At first light, his leftenant shouted, the French would either fall back or they would begin to fire.

"Kinda like the fireworks at Vauxhall, wasn't it?" another dragoon observed, dragging his saddle toward his horse. "But I cannot say I liked the seat."

It still rained, but not so violently, and now there was no lightning to illuminate the movement of the French. Despite a certain stiffening of the hairs on his neck, Charles felt a sense of exhilaration. For the first time since he'd come to this godforsaken place, he was going to get to strike a blow against the enemy. And, afore the Almighty, he was going to show everybody he could do it.

There was a sense of urgency all around him, for every man there knew they were the only regular army England possessed, that to fail would be disastrous. Riders circulated, distributing Wellington's orders, shouting that the attack was coming from the west, on the right flank, that the Fourth and Fifth Dragoons and the light cavalry were to throw themselves to the center, next to Cotton and in front of the Portuguese. Already, the air was filled with the sound of French cannon pounding the hillside, softening it for the attack. Gunsmoke mingled with the rain, giving it a musty, sulfuric odor.

Under the overall command of Cotton, the dragoons mounted, taking an offensive position between the French and the Third division, as the Portuguese and the British infantry fanned out to cover their flanks. It was a battle plan that had been discussed, but not executed, and as Charles rode to his position, he could see the lighter cavalry forming to his left. They would go in on second charge. At that moment, he knew they were not going to defend, that they were going to attack. For the first time since he'd arrived in Spain, his heart was in his throat.

They moved slowly, in a solid wall of red over the hill, dragoons, hussars, infantry, fusilliers, grenadiers, across a shallow depression, and down from the crest to face the superiority of the French guns. Shells raked the scarlet line as the British descended, the awful din of the volleys compounded by the eerie wail of bagpipes from a Highland regiment. The noise obliterated shouted commands, the acrid smoke burned eyes and lungs.

It was clear that Marmont had not expected the British to come down from the hills, that he had expected them to hold their positions, and his armies, though superior in number and artillery, were not yet fully in place. In an effort to surround the Anglo-Portuguese forces, he'd left a mile-wide gap yet to be closed south of the Light division. As the sun came up, Wellington could look through his telescope and be pleased with what he saw.

He ordered an even greater slowing of the advance, a thinning of the line near the center, and by early afternoon, he was rewarded when the French, perceiving what they believed a weakness there, charged, furthering the lag between their divisions. It was then that Wellington called for the advance of his reserves, and the charge of the Fourth and Fifth Dragoons.

The dragoons, which had moved with almost precision slowness, their horses picking their way downward despite the enemy fire, saw the order given to the Portuguese cavalry, and the mounted force surged forward, rifles raised, shouting, cutting across a large body of surprised French infantry, overrunning them. It was brutal—bloodier than anything Charles could have imagined.

He fired, stabbed, bludgeoned, and reloaded, all the while under a steady barrage of cannon fire, grenades, and small arms fire. A grenade loaded with nails exploded but a few feet from him, and he saw a fellow dragoon fall, horse and rider mortally wounded. Another took a direct hit, nearly severing his torso at the waist. There was a stench to that too—and now agonized screams added to the terrible cacophony that deafened his ears. Despite the almost constant exhilaration, the fear, there was the fleeting thought that Longford had been right—they were in the bowels of hell.

Another comrade fell, his horse shot from under him, and the man scrambled to escape the charge of his own men. Charles saw him take a ball in the shoulder, stumble, and go down to his knees. It was Beatty, the company wit, a fellow with a wife and children at home. On the instant, Charles leaned down, trying to grasp the man's arm, shouting to him to throw himself up. His hand closed over the other's, and as he straightened, he felt the sudden, hot, searing pain in his neck. He reeled in his saddle, lost his grip, and slumped forward. His head against his horse's neck, he could see his blood pour downward, and he wondered why he was cold, why he did not hurt. Ahead, the light nearly blinded him, a bright beacon beckoning, pulling him. His father and mother stood there, waiting for him. He didn't want to go, but he was already in the tunnel, and they would not let him go back. "Nell," he gasped.

Down the line, Lucien de Clare struck with his bayonet, jabbing his way through a wall of infantrymen, smelling the awful stench of blood, sulfur, and smoke. He saw a Frenchman raise his rifle, but he was too late. The report was deafening, and he knew he'd been hit. He snapped back from the impact, and as the hot pain spread through his body, a wave of nausea hit him. A second bullet half spun him around, then he fell forward, clinging to his saddle. He could not breathe—he was drowning. He tried to cough, to clear his chest, and red-flecked pink foam spewed from his mouth. The French bastards had hit a lung, and he was going to die. And the awful irony was not lost on him—for all that he'd done, Jack had died at home in bed.

"Major! Gawd! The major—Longford's been hit!"

Someone grabbed his reins, pulling his horse from the fray. He swallowed, then reached to hold left his shoulder. Numbness was spreading down his arm, and blood filled his hand, trickling between his fingers.

"Can't help—me," he managed to gasp. "Don't leave—your position—I—" He coughed again, tearing his chest out, and more of the bloody foam came up. He hunched forward, trying to conserve his strength, clinging to his life, as a captain and another dragoon turned his horse between theirs. "Cannot—" He leaned, trying to use his knees to guide the animal, and fell, sliding headfirst into the mud. One of his men dismounted, shouldering him, and began carrying him back to the rear. "Save yourself," he choked. "I'm done."

"And how's it to look if I was to let Mad Jack's son die?" the fellow shot back.

Someone else caught Lucien and helped. Between them, they staggered, zigzagging across the field, dodging fire and the shrapnel from exploding grenades, until Lucien's consciousness disintegrated into black oblivion. He never knew when they caught him up, a man to each extremity, and ran for the hospital tent, calling out that Mad Jack's son was dying.

He lay on a pallet, its blanket stiffened with his own blood, his mind somewhere between blackness and a dim awareness that a surgeon worked on him, muttering that it was bad—that a lung had collapsed.

"Put that piece of wood in his mouth that he does not swallow his tongue," someone barked.

His chest and shoulder were on fire, and still the foam welled in his throat, choking him. He tried to protest, to tell them to save someone else, then he felt the probe and everything went utterly, completely black.

"Mercifully he's fainted," the surgeon mumbled.

"Can you save him?" the woman hovering over Lucien asked.

"No—bullet got the lung. Unless it reinflates itself, there's naught I can do but get the ball out and pray."

"Then—"

"Mad Jack's boy!" he snapped at her. "Got to try."

Lucien regained consciousness slowly. All around him, he could hear cries for help, mumbled prayers, whispered words of comfort—and somewhere in the dark distance, the sounds of the battle faded to sporadic fire. But there was the stench—the stench of blood and death there with him. He tried to open his eyes, but they were swollen from the smoke. He was parched.

"Water," he gasped weakly. "Thirsty. Cannot breathe—"

There was the muffled rustle of skirt against petticoat, then someone leaned over him. "Major—can you hear me?"

"Yes," he croaked. He forced his eyes open, trying to focus through the slits, and recognized Leftenant Wilson's wife. Her eyes were red, her face streaked, either from smoke or crying.

"My arm?"

"Shoulder's hit," the surgeon declared from behind her. "May be stiff when it heals. Bled like a pig, though—lucky to have lived." He did not tell him about the lung—he'd seen too many give up when they knew.

Mrs. Wilson dipped a rag into water, then dribbled it into the corner of his mouth, waiting for him to swallow. She repeated the process again and again until he pushed her arm away. He coughed, and she wiped his mouth quickly, before he could see the blood.

"John—?"

Her face contorted hideously, then she managed to control herself. "Johnny's dead," she whispered.

"I'm sorry."

"There are so many—such need—there is not time to grieve." Once again, she dipped the rag and held it to his lips. Her own chin quivered. "Johnny would not forgive me if you perished now—he was proud to have—to have served under you, my lord."

"You ought—"

"No. Alone, I should have to think about it."

The doctor moved to him, kneeling to feel for the pulse in his neck, then he straightened, apparently satisfied. "Strong for a big fellow," he muttered. "Usually, it's the big ones as perishes. And God knows there've been a lot of 'em today."

The boy. Lucien remembered Kingsley. He coughed, trying to clear his throat. "Damn!" he uttered, lying back, closing his eyes for strength.

The woman moved away, then returned with a tin cup. "It's laudanum," she murmured.

"Best drink it," the doctor said without turning back. "Had a devil of a time going for the ball."

He hated the taste of the stuff—always had. But as the pain brought tears to his eyes, he managed to gulp it down. His other hand closed over the woman's, holding it, drawing and giving strength.

"I'm sorry," he repeated.

"It was quick—at least it was quick. There were others—not so fortunate." Her voice was so low he had to strain to hear her. "How strange it seems to speak of dying quickly as though it were a blessing. Johnny was proud of what he did—best regiment—best cavalry, he always said."

He lay there, blocking out the sounds of the suffering, holding her hand, trying not to think of any of it. It seemed it took the laudanum a long time to take effect, but finally the warmth, the detached dizziness began to take hold of his body and mind. Only then could he bring himself to ask, "Word of—young Kingsley? Word of—the boy? With Cotton too—"

Her fingers tightened in his, and she took a deep breath. "There was nothing to be done, I'm afraid." Her voice quavered, then she managed to go on, "He took a ball in the neck."

"Bled to death," the doctor confirmed. "Painless way to go. After the first instant, he didn't feel it."

Whether it was from the drug or from the pain, Lucien thought he hallucinated, for he could see Elinor Kingsley as clearly as if she were there. And he didn't want to tell her that he'd failed.

"The battle?" he gasped.

"Won it," the surgeon answered. "Fifth Dragoon Guards—and the Fourth and Fifth Dragoons won the day—cut up the French line—your charge, in fact. Killed 'em three to one." His hands pressed against the thick bandage tied to Lucien's chest. "Bleeding's slowed—good sign," he muttered. "Won it," he repeated. "Marmont's dead—four generals also—got so many prisoners can't tend to 'em." Seeing that the massive dose of the opiate was taking hold, he rose to move to another.

"Good," Lucien managed to mumble behind him.

He slept, his hand in Leftenant Wilson's widow's, not knowing when she left to tend others. His laudanum-induced dreams were fitful nightmares, bizarre flashes that faded from one to another. He was on his mother's lap. He could hear the quarrels, the threats. The room was dark, she lay upon the bed, as white and bloodless as the linen beneath her, and Mad Jack pulled him away, saying she'd fallen suddenly sick and died. But there were overheard whispers—it was too much opium, someone said. There was Diana, screaming that Mad Jack was too young to die, that it could not be, not now, not when—and there was Jack asking him to marry her, to cover her shame, to give his father's babe a name. They were all there, tormenting him. He wasn't alive—he was in hell.

"Major—"

Cool hands lifted his head, holding a canteen of sour wine to his lips, urging him to drink. Somewhere in the distance, he could hear someone say they would have to bury the dead there, and a sort of panic assailed him. He fought in the woman's arms, trying to shout, but no words came.

Stronger hands forced him down and held him. "Here now—you are all right," the doctor said gruffly.

''Kingsley,'' Lucien gasped. ''Don't—don't bury him.''

''Man's delirious.''

''No—got to send him back—''

''He's dead.''

''Got to take the body—she'll want it—'' He choked, then coughed. ''Cannot breathe—''

The doctor and Mrs. Wilson exchanged glances, then she leaned over him, speaking directly into his ear. ''It's the heat, my lord—there is the danger of cholera—they will wish to burn it.''

''No—pay to—pay to seal the box.'' His hand clutched hers. ''Don't let them—bury him here.''

She glanced up questioningly, and the doctor shrugged. ''Rich boy, wasn't he? Aye—old Kingsley can pay the passage.''

His grip relaxed, and once again, Lucien felt himself slipping toward the abyss. To stop his fall into the pit, he forced himself to think of Elinor Kingsley. And he knew she would want him to bring the boy's body home to her, and if he survived, he meant to do it. Later, he would try to discover what had become of young Kingsley's journal. He'd like to take that also. But first he had to live.

SHE SAT THERE, twisting her hands in her lap, looking down to see the ring he'd given her, not wanting to believe the scarlet-clad officer who stood before her. Beside her, Arthur slumped in his chair, seeming to have shrunk, to have aged even beyond his sixty-five years within a few minutes. He said nothing, nothing at all.

"Believe me, I convey my own as well as Lord Wellington's condolences," the stiffly correct Captain Moore told them. When Baron Kingsley did not respond, he murmured, "Under the circumstances, I shall of course leave you alone in your grief."

Elinor's throat ached, the lump too great to swallow even. As Jeremy showed the captain out, she clutched the arms of her chair, holding on as though she could somehow stem the rising hysteria. Charles was dead—dear, sweet, fun-loving Charley was dead—gone forever. That could not be right—there must've been some mistake—only yesterday, she'd received a letter from him. A letter she'd shared with Arthur—and with Mary—and all the while he'd already been dead for days.

She wanted to scream—to cry out to God that it could not be! Not Charley—anyone else but Charley! Dear God—not Charley!

Without speaking to her, Arthur rose from his chair, and leaning heavily on his cane, he walked slowly from the room. Already word had spread in whispers through the house, and now silence descended, as though everything within had stopped.

Outside, in the street, there was a near carriage wreck, shouted accusations, and angry threats. Moving as though she were in a trance, she rose to close the window against the hot city air. The August sun shone brightly, the street was alive with people who did not know, who continued living their existences without a thought for Charles. She fastened the shutters angrily. Why could it not have been one of them? Why Charley? Why? Why? *Why*?

The Earl of Longford would be accompanying his body back, the captain had said. Longford had been wounded also—so grievously that he'd been expected to die. But now it appeared that he was recovering. There was no justice—Charley had perished while a man who cared about nothing had lived. And she could not help feeling a deep bitterness for that.

"My lady—?" Mary inquired timidly from the door. "It's sorry I am fer ye." She entered the room, moving closer. "Are ye all right? Perhaps a bit of laudanum—"

"No." It even hurt to whisper.

"I ordered some tea fer ye."

"Thank you."

There was such a sense of unreality that Elinor thought she had gone mad. She was going to drink tea, she was going to go through the motions of living, knowing that Charley was dead. Three months ago, she was laughing at the antics of the animals in the Tower menagerie with him. Three months ago, she'd sat beside him to watch the splendid fireworks at Vauxhall, had shared ices at Gunter's, had—she couldn't go on thinking about those things—she couldn't. And yet when she closed her eyes, she could see him standing before her, she could hear him again.

I ain't going forever, you know . . . come back a captain for you . . . Now he was not coming back at all. She stood there, seeing his earnest face, that ruffled brown hair, the intense blue eyes, the fun-loving boy Arthur had sent to war because of her.

She looked down to her hand again, to the pearl ring that Arthur had disparaged as looking plain and cheap, saying he did not know why she chose to wear it when she had so many that were finer. *Want you to have something to look at while I am gone, so's you don't forget me.* As if she ever could.

I love you, Nell—if it wasn't for him, I'd be shouting it from the rooftops . . . I love you, Nell . . . I love you, Nell . . .

She felt an intense loss, an intense guilt that tore at her insides as surely as if she had been stabbed—an emptiness as real as if something had been wrenched from her body. She'd not even been able to tell him that she loved him as he'd wanted, and she regretted that now. Not because she loved him like that, but because he'd died for her. And she felt a bitter, overwhelming resentment of Arthur. How dare he waste other's lives?

"I brung the tea," Mary offered. "Ye'd best sit down to drink it."

"Thank you," Elinor murmured absently. "Later, perhaps."

"Cook put a bit extra in it—ter make ye feel better," the maid coaxed. Setting the tea tray down, she took Elinor's arm and gently pushed her toward Arthur's leather chair. "Just a dab—not much, mind ye," she insisted, pouring the dark amber liquid into the cup. Not to be denied, she held the steaming cup to her mistress's lips. "A wee bit—ter revive ye."

But Elinor had no wish to be revived. Still, at Mary's urging, she managed to take a sip. "Ugh—it's not tea!" She choked, pushing it away.

"Aye, it's—just doctored a bit. Now ye'd not have me take it back a-saying ye didn't try it, would ye?" She held the cup to Elinor again. "Got honey and butter and rum—and a touch of spices in it."

"And laudanum—I can taste the laudanum."

"Ye ought ter sleep, so's God can heal yer heart," the woman murmured. "Just a bit more."

"I don't want to be senseless!" Elinor cried. But she did—she wanted to wake up and discover it was but a nightmare. She wanted to discover another letter from Charley in the post. She exhaled heavily, then took the cup and drained it. Maybe she would not wake up at all.

But Mary poured another. "If ye was ter go to sleep down here, I'd cover ye. Come on—one last drink."

Elinor obeyed as though she were a child, then pushed it away. "It's all—I'd take no more." She leaned back, but this time did not close her eyes.

Outside, in the foyer, she could hear voices—a polite dispute of some sort. The butler, backed by the footman, was insisting that "Lady Kingsley is not receiving, sir—there's been a terrible tragedy. Neither she nor his lordship will be going about with you, I'm afraid."

"I heard—saw the captain leaving." Bellamy Townsend was in the door. Behind him, Jeremy protested, hissing that she was unwell, then apologized to her, "I tried, my lady, but—"

"It's all right," she responded woodenly.

Bell had started to go when he'd encountered the captain and heard the news. Instead, he'd changed his mind and chosen to stay, to steal a march on others who would come to offer condolences, but when he saw Elinor, he was stunned. There was no mistaking the utter anguish in her face. And for all that he was an unprincipled rake, he felt a surge of genuine sympathy for her. He crossed the room quickly, then dropped to his knees at her side, taking both her hands.

"Dear lady, I came as soon as I heard. There are no words—" He cut himself off, sensing that it was no time for flowery speeches. "If there is anything I can do—anything I can get for you, you have but to ask."

"There is nothing."

"Arthur—?"

"I know not—he went upstairs."

"I am here for you, Elinor," he said quietly, knowing that he meant it.

It was the first time Bell had ever felt utterly helpless before a woman. Knowing that he would look the fool should any see him, he nonetheless sat there on the carpet, saying nothing, just holding her hands. A shudder, not of revulsion, but rather like a chill, passed through her. He looked up to where her maid hovered.

"She needs a throw—a blanket."

The woman shook her head. "It's the medicine—she'll sleep soon enough."

He nodded, and his fingers tightened over Elinor's.

For the moment, she forgot that she did not really like him, that she merely tolerated him for Arthur and Sally Jersey, that she had only played the acceptable game, the superficial and utterly meaningless social discourse with him. As he held her hands, she took what measure of comfort she could in his presence.

"I am afraid I am poor company," she murmured.

Already the room seemed to be moving around her, and while she felt cold inside, her extremities seemed to warm. Her palms felt hot, her mouth dry. She blinked, trying to reattach herself to reality, then leaned back, closing her eyes against the spinning world.

"I think she's swooning," she heard Bellamy say from a distance.

"It was a lot of laudanum," Mary told him.

With an effort, Elinor forced open her eyes and tried to focus them, struggling to sit up. "Got to lie down," she mumbled thickly. "Got to get to bed." She fell back, defeated by the drug. "Charley's coming home," she whispered through dry lips. "I know it." Then everything went black.

Rising awkwardly, Bell glanced toward the maid. "She ought to be abed. Kingsley—?"

"Locked himself in his bedchamber. But Jeremy—"

The slender young man stepped forward. "Me'n the others'll carry her up."

"No. Just help me get her out of the chair."

"It ain't seemly," the woman protested.

Elinor Kingsley was nearly dead weight, scarce moving, protesting unintelligibly when he lifted her. She lay back over his arm, her neck arched, her head dangling, her red hair spilling toward the floor, and he feared he'd break her neck. Shifting her manfully, he managed to throw her up against his shoulder, bracing her head.

"Where?" he asked tersely.

"Upstairs."

Although he was surprised by her lightness, it was no mean feat to carry her up, and, his vision blocked by her body, he nearly stumbled several times. Behind him, two footmen followed, ready to catch him, and ahead, the maid led the way, throwing open the door, scurrying to turn back the covers on the four-poster bed. He laid her down, then pulled the sheet over her, covering her morning dress.

"How much laudanum did you give her?" he asked curiously. "She's out."

"Fifteen drops in rum tea."

"Egad." Despite the bright hair that spread over the pillow, she was pale against the white sheet. "It must've been a dreadful shock—they were of an age, weren't they?"

Mary nodded. "He turned twenty last week, and she will in September."

"A pity. One could tell he was quite attached to her."

The maid's head came up and she met his eyes soberly. "They grew up together."

"Yes, yes—of course." But he could not ask a servant what he most longed to ask. He could not ask if Elinor had returned young Kingsley's regard—if there had been more than familial devotion between them. "It will take time to ease the pain she and Arthur must feel," he said lamely.

"We all liked the young master," Mary responded. "He was a good, honorable gentleman."

"I did not mean otherwise," he said quietly. He wanted to stay, to be the one there to comfort Elinor Kingsley when she wakened, but he knew he could not. Still, he lingered. "Would you see that Arthur is told I came by?"

"Yes."

He had already intruded beyond anything that was proper, and there was nothing to do but leave. Reaching into his coat pocket, he drew out a gold guinea and held it out to her. "I should welcome news of how she fares—and Arthur also," he added quickly.

Ignoring the money, she shook her head. "I cannot—it would cause comment." Seeing that his face fell, she relented slightly. "But perhaps Jeremy could tell yer footman . . ."

"All right."

As he trod the stairs downward, it was perhaps the first time he'd regretted his miserable reputation. He was getting older, he decided—perhaps his salad days were growing to a close. Mayhap it was time he turned his efforts from pursuing every new beauty to loving one.

Stoneleigh: August 20, 1812

THE ANCIENT CHAPEL was airless, hot, and oppressive, and more than one of the neighbors come to mourn Charles Kingsley shifted uncomfortably in their seats, fearing they'd faint before the vicar finished waxing eloquent about "the bloom of youth cut short." A few craned their necks to watch as Elinor sat, red-eyed but quiet, between her parents, then whispered among themselves at the curious absence of Lord Kingsley himself. Indeed, but no one, not even those neighbors who'd called to offer condolences, had seen the baron since his return to his country home. There was a rumor afoot that upon hearing of his grandson's death, the old fellow had gone quite mad. And there were some who had intimated that the attachment between the old lord's wife and his grandson was more than a familial one. But today it was impossible to tell much for Lady Kingsley's tear-streaked face was obscured somewhat by her black veil.

The prayerbook lay precariously in Elinor's lap as her hands clenched and unclenched, creasing the black crape skirt of her mourning dress. She stared straight ahead, her eyes on the wooden box. In there was Charley—or what was left of him. It still did not seem real, not even knowing that his body lay there. Perhaps if she'd been able to see him, to actually bid him farewell, but it was too late, and rationally she knew that after a month of summer heat, she'd not want to. Despite the pitch seal, there was a faintly unpleasant odor coming from the casket, an odor that compounded the discomfort of the closeness.

Arthur should have been there, she thought resentfully. He ought to have to see for himself the pain he had wrought. But he wasn't. He was in his bedchamber, the drapes pulled against the light, sitting alone, staring, leaving her to grieve by herself. Oh, her mama and papa had come, but they did not understand—to them, Charley had merely been Arthur Kingsley's grandson.

Indeed, her father had looked about the huge mansion, shaking his head, saying it was a pity she'd not increased, for now the old man had built himself an empire for naught. "Be like the Romans," he muttered, "gone to ruin for lack of any to rule it."

"As I recall it," she'd retorted, "it was not for *lack* of a ruler, but rather from too many aspirants that Rome was weakened."

"What I mean," he agreed, nodding. "When the old gent's gone, there's going to be a vultures' feeding for the two-thirds as don't go to you. Old man must have distant relations somewheres, you know."

As if she cared. She didn't want his money—she didn't want anything of his—except Charley. And Charley was dead.

A wave of loneliness, of self-pity washed over her, sending a tear trickling down her cheek. Poor Charley. Poor her. Now she would never know if she was but the first passion of his youth, the onset of his salad days, or if she had truly been the love of his life. He'd not even lived long enough for her to know if she could have come to love him as he'd wanted.

Her mother passed an embroidered lawn handkerchief to her, then reached to hold one of her hands. And Elinor wanted to turn against her, to bury her head in her mother's shoulder, and to weep loudly for him. But she couldn't—she was no longer a child, but rather a woman who neared her twentieth birthday. She was past being held by her mother.

Mercifully, the service ended, and the pallbearers, their noses covered with perfumed handkerchiefs, carried poor Charley out into the tiny churchyard. There had been speculation that Arthur Kingsley, in his desire to maintain the image of being born to the manor, would have the boy interred beneath the floor as were the previous owners and their families. But as Arthur had not responded when asked, Elinor had chosen a place outside, a place beneath a spreading oak, one she thought Charles might have liked. As if he even knew it.

They filed out silently, and when she looked up, she

could see the earl's scarlet-clad back. In a way, it surprised her that he had come, for she'd been stunned when he accompanied Charley's body home. He still looked terribly ill, pasty beneath his sun-bronzed skin, and his black eyes seemed to be set more deeply, the planes of his face harsher, more angular. He'd been wounded—almost mortally, if the papers could be believed, but she supposed they exaggerated in their need to make heroes. If he'd taken a ball in the lung as reported, he surely would have died, for who had ever heard of a lung healing? She felt a new surge of resentment—how could he have survived the impossible when one bullet took Charles?

Behind the earl was Viscount Townsend. Indeed, but his kindness had surprised her, for he'd nearly haunted her since the day they'd heard about Charles. He'd even gone so far as to wangle an invitation to stay with Lord Leighton nearby, that he might support her through this, he said. It was as though Charley's death had somehow made him aware of his own mortality, and he was bent on rediscovering his own soul. Now, instead of flirting outrageously, instead of importuning at every available instant, he was actually showing himself capable of compassion.

Even Leighton, whom she had barely known before, had been kindness itself, riding over daily to inquire as to whether there was anything he could do for either her or Arthur. But Arthur would not see him. Arthur was shutting her and everyone else out, punishing her still for his own folly.

The air was warm, the sun bright, the sky blue and cloudless—as though the Power that was did not care that Charles Kingsley had perished, as though He decreed that life went on regardless of the pain.

"Best go on," her father murmured, taking her arm. "No need to watch, puss."

"Oh, Papa—I cannot! I—" As the earth was shoveled over the wooden box, she lost her composure completely. "No! Not yet!" she cried hysterically, pulling away. "Not yet!"

Lucien, who'd watched such scenes a hundred times and more, moved between her and the grave, blocking her way. Catching her with his good arm, he held her apart from him, pushing her back. She struggled, and for a moment, he reeled, then righted himself.

"There's naught more you can do for him, Lady Kingsley," he said. Despite the gruffness, there was a measure of sympathy in his voice. "Go with your parents."

"But—" Her lower lip quivered and tears spilled freely from her eyes.

"Go on—I will see it done." His black eyes met hers for a moment. "You don't want to remember this." When she did not move, he added gently, "He'd have you think of him as he was, you know." Looking past her to her father, he nodded. "Take her home, will you?"

With her father pulling, she half-stumbled away, and Lucien could hear Ashton muttering, "Don't know who the devil he thinks he is, telling me what's right to do, puss."

Bellamy Townsend started after her, but Lucien stopped him. "Leave her to grieve alone a bit, Bell."

"It's none of your affair!" the other man retorted. Then, he turned back apologetically. "Sorry—you been through hell also, haven't you?"

"Something like it." They faced each other across the open grave. For a moment, Lucien looked down as a laborer tossed a shovelful of earth over Charles Kingsley's casket, obscuring a corner of it. "Something like it," he repeated softly.

"She took it hard, you know," Bell murmured. "Boy meant a lot to her. Children together, I guess."

"She meant a lot to him also."

Bellamy's gray eyes rested on the bulky bandage that stretched the shoulder of Longford's regimental jacket. "Heard you'd nearly bought the beyond yourself."

"So they tell me."

"Heard it was the lung—that you were spouting blood."

"Bell"—Lucien growled uncomfortably, then relented enough to tell him shortly—"it seems to have healed itself once it filled with air again."

"Cool about it—say that for you. Ought to earn you another medal from Prinny, from what I hear—wouldn't even surprise me if you were to be received now."

"I don't mean to put it to the touch," Lucien muttered dryly.

"Thinking about rusticating, are you?"

There was no mistaking the disappointment in the other man's voice, for it was obvious Bell wanted no rival, no matter how unlikely. Lucien smiled faintly and nodded. "Let us just say I mean to rest awhile."

"You going to be at home this afternoon?" Leighton asked, interrupting them.

"I can scarce go anywhere," Lucien retorted, then sighed. "I suppose you were thinking of visiting me?"

"Only if you are up to it."

Lucien looked down to where the box was nearly covered now. "My dear Leighton, I am going to get myself utterly, totally foxed—so disguised that I do not mean to know my own name," he declared flatly, "but you and Bell are welcome to join me in the enterprise."

"Man ought not to drink alone," Leighton murmured solemnly. "Bell?"

Townsend watched Thomas Ashton help his daughter into a small, open carriage for the ride back to the house. Behind them, Elinor's mother and sisters mounted a larger conveyance. If he visited her today, he would be intruding, and he knew it. Besides, whether he wanted to admit it or not, he also knew Longford was right—Elinor Kingsley needed time, and in putting himself constantly forward, he was probably making her heartily sick of him.

"Might as well—got nothing else to do at the moment."

Lucien followed his gaze, thinking that he ought to take Charles Kingsley's journal to her. On the morrow, when he felt better perhaps . . .

* * *

It had been a long time since Bell had been in any of Lucien's houses, not since the affair with Diana. He looked around the elegantly appointed saloon approvingly. "Surprised me to hear you'd bought an estate in Cornwall," he murmured.

Lucien shrugged. "It was Langston's—poor fellow was quite run off his legs—and I could not complain of the price. But let us move to the bookroom—it's better suited to the sport of drinking." He held the door open, and as Bellamy passed, he said, "I rather favor the wildness of the coast, you know. When it storms, the waves beat upon the rocks with a fury you cannot imagine. It rather soothes one's soul."

"Thankfully, I cannot say it has stormed since my arrival."

"Bell prefers only the maelstroms of his own making," Leighton observed, dropping into a leather-covered chair.

Townsend took a chair opposite, and twisted his head to look back to where Lucien's shaking hand poured port. "Actually, I have been thinking of settling down."

Lucien's eyebrows raised. "You? I shouldn't think the life would suit you, Bell."

Townsend nodded. "I'm thinking of marrying Elinor Kingsley," he admitted. "Getting too old for the pursuit—pretty soon I'll be an old roué. Nothing worse than that, you know—always hate to see the old gents in their corsets trying to play the lover."

Lucien's hand stopped midair. "I was under the impression that Kingsley was merely indisposed—not dead."

"He ain't going to last forever—can't. Besides, nobody's seen him since word came about the boy."

"My dear Bell," Leighton advised him, "those kind do last forever—think of our poor king. How long has he been mad this time?—nearly two years, I think—and that does not count—"

"It's not your affair, George! Besides, the old gent's sixty-five if he's got a day on him."

"It's my affair if you mean to set up a flirtation from my house," George retorted. "I'll not countenance it."

"The honorable Leighton." Bellamy sneered. "Tell me—are all the Maxwells so devilish straitlaced? Must be that dour Scots upbringing, I suppose. I always heard that the Presbyterians were a bloodless lot."

"He hasn't been to Scotland in years, Bell," Lucien murmured, carrying three big cups and two bottles of the fortified wine to them. "He doesn't like the cold."

Leighton took his and stared at the cup for a moment.

"Not too elegant, Luce. Must be two glasses' worth in here."

But Bell took his and grinned. "Man's into some serious drinking, George—when he says he means to get foxed, he means it, don't you, Luce?"

"Precisely."

"Shoulder paining you?" George asked Longford.

"Yes. Interminably." Lucien pulled a chair up between them, then reached for his own cup, wincing. Leaning back, he lifted it, murmuring, "May Russia swallow Boney before the year is out. Pray for a hard winter, gentlemen."

Bell snorted. "Don't you have anything but the war to think on, Luce? It's over for you, you know." Nonetheless, he drank to it.

"I should like to see you go there," Leighton observed.

"Me? Un-uhhh. I should not be able to take my tailor, I'm afraid. Besides, I don't want a ball in me. Look at Luce—fellow's deuced peaked—and dashed fortunate to be breathing."

"Your patriotism overwhelms me, Bellamy," Lucien observed sardonically.

Thinking that the other two might get into it over the war, Leighton tried to turn the subject back to Elinor Kingsley. "So you came in pursuit of the baroness," he murmured, sipping of his port. "And I thought it was my friendship you courted. I agree with Luce, you know—you are better advised to wait for the old gent to pass on."

"Going to steal the march," Bell insisted. "Bound to be a passel of fortune hunters after her when he's gone. Besides, the woman's an innocent, George—an utter innocent! She won't know the bad ones from the good ones."

"And you mean to be there to help her sort them out?" Lucien queried incredulously. "My dear Bell, who's going to warn her about you?"

"She cannot be a complete innocent," George decided.

"Oh, I own that I thought Longford—that there was something there—but I have since concluded I was mistaken. Devilish straitlaced female, if you would have the truth of it.'' Townsend looked at Leighton over the rim of his cup. ''If I'm not mistaken, I don't think she even knows how it's done.''

''Don't be absurd, Bell—the gel's been wed an age,'' George retorted.

''Look, I've been flirting with her for months—and she can't even get those interesting *entendres* a man throws out to show his intentions.''

Lucien shrugged. ''Maybe she's stupid—or wise. If she pretends not to understand, she doesn't have to answer—did you never think of that?''

''She's not stupid,'' Bell insisted truculently. ''Got brains to match the beauty—spouts Latin and Greek as good as old Master Downey in grammar school. But—'' He fixed his eyes on the earl, who now appeared more absorbed in his port than anything. ''But I *would* like to know what she was doing at your house that time, you know—and you ain't fobbing me off that it was Harriette Wilson I saw.''

For a moment, Lucien stared into the dark wine, remembering how she'd stood there when he'd removed her bonnet, not knowing what he was about. ''She came to ask me to look after the boy,'' he answered simply. ''I did a miserable job of it, didn't I?''

''Then you know she's an innocent!'' Bell crowed.

''Yes, I know.'' He sat up and reached for one of the bottles of port. Pouring himself another cup, he regarded it briefly, then met Bellamy Townsend's eyes. ''There is still Arthur Kingsley, Bell—and I fail to see how you mean to get around that.''

''Wait for him to die.''

Devil of a coil, ain't it?—a man waiting for his own grandfather to die. Charles Kingsley's voice echoed once again in Lucien's ears. He lifted his filled cup, spilling a little of the wine onto his buff breeches. ''To Arthur Kingsley's long life,'' he murmured before tossing the contents off.

''Well, I won't be drinking to that! You hear him, George?'' Bell demanded plaintively. ''Wantin' to drink to the old gent's long life!''

''She deserves better than a rake.''

''Since when did you appoint yourself the protector of

decent females? I ain't the only rake in this room, you know! Besides, I told you—reformed rake."

"And I can tell you from bitter experience that rakes do not reform, Bell—they merely age," Lucien told him tiredly. "Whether you have a wife or not, when you are fifty, you will be chasing females less than half your age. Until your corset creaks," he added significantly.

"Don't know how you'd know," Bell muttered. "Since Diana, you aren't chasing any of 'em as don't want to be caught. Nothing but demireps and fashionable impures—like you aren't wanting a lady. Threw away Diana—tossed her my way, in fact."

"Diana wasn't a lady!" Lucien snapped "At least with the demireps, one knows what one is getting, which isn't much—but the arrangement is an honest one—one does not have to pretend what one does not feel. Not that you would know about that, Bell."

"Whatever happened to Diana, by the by?" Leighton asked.

"I neither know—nor do I care."

Bellamy shook his head. "Named the brat after you, you know. Made me nervous for a while—thought she meant to lay it at my door."

"Bell—I have no wish to discuss Diana."

"All right—all right." He ran his fingers through his blond hair, ruffling it, then dared to meet Lucien's eyes again. "But I don't know why you got to blame me, why you think I cannot change. Dash it, but Elinor's all a man could want! It isn't like you think!"

"Elinor?" One of Leighton's eyebrows rose. "Elinor?"

"Oh, I don't call her that to her face—not like we are familiar or anything. Not often, anyway—got to be careful, particularly after the thing about the bet."

Lucien drained his cup and poured yet another. Staring hard at Townsend, he declared angrily, "You are like my father, Bell—you take what you want, then damn the rest to hell. Elinor Kingsley deserves better than that—you'd do to her what Jack did to my mother. A few years with you and she'd wither, waiting for you to give up your barques of frailty."

"If she hasn't withered with Arthur Kingsley, she's not going—"

"It was a long time ago, Luce," Leighton said softly. "You've got to forget about Jack."

But Lucien had come to his feet, towering over Bellamy, weaving. "What you and Jack don't understand is that it's never over, Bell! Never! You wreck lives, Bell!" He started to cough, but his healing lung hurt too much. Pressing his balled fist against his side, he managed to hold it back.

Stung, Bellamy pressed his body back against the tufted leather, and retorted defensively, "You said you did not care about Diana! You said—"

"I had no wish to be a laughingstock! I had no wish to be pitied, Bell!"

"Well, if I'd have known—dash it, but you made yourself the laughingstock! You wanted rid of her! I gave you the chance—that was all!"

"If I had not, it would have been the same!"

"You're disguised," Bellamy muttered. Ducking Lucien, he managed to rise. "As for Mad Jack, you are more like him than you would have us think! I don't see you riding to rescue any fair ladies yourself, Luce!" His face now red, he sneered, "You are as bad a fellow as he was, you know. Your neglect made Diana ripe for the plucking."

"Leave Elinor Kingsley alone!"

"Aha! You got designs on her yourself, don't you? Well, there you are out! I've not played Galahad so's I could step aside! You hear me, Luce? She's mine!"

Leighton threw himself between them. "All in our cups, that's all. Come on, Bell—got to go before you regret it."

"If you think I mean to let him insult me—to tell me—"

"Fool if you was to try to do anything about it." Leighton caught Townsend by both arms, forcing him back. "For God's sake, Bell—let's leave it. Luce's wounded—daresay it's affected more'n his shoulder, that's all."

"I meant what I said."

"Coming it too strong, Luce!" Bell shouted. "You got no right—you haven't even been here!" Shaking free of Leighton, he faced Lucien angrily. "And I'm not afraid of you—I don't care if they do call you Lucifer!

Throw a spoke in my wheel where she is concerned, and before Almighty God, I'll call you out!''

''That's enough, Bell!'' Leighton insisted loudly.

''Stay out of it, George! He's got no right—''

He jabbed Lucien's left shoulder, and for a moment, the earl went white beneath his tan. Holding his shoulder, he closed his eyes against the pain and soreness there. A wave of dizziness, of nausea hit him, then passed. He ought to be beyond this by now, but he wasn't. He was far sicker than he wanted to admit.

This time, Leighton moved behind Townsend, grabbing his arms, pulling him away from Longford. ''I'm not burying either of you—d'you hear me? You've got to stop this—both of you!''

Lucien caught his breath, then released his shoulder. ''Leave her alone,'' he repeated evenly.

''My intentions are honorable!''

''Hell will freeze before I believe it!''

With one arm still around Bellamy Townsend's waist, Leighton leaned to reach the hat on the table. Slamming it crookedly over Bell's disordered blond locks, he dragged him toward the door. ''Got to sleep it off—that's the ticket—get you some air—''

''She's mine, Luce—d'you hear me? When Kingsley's gone, she's mine!''

''Shut up, Bell!'' Leighton snapped. ''I said I did not want to bury you—leastwise not while you are a guest in my house.''

''He can't—you saw him—I ain't afraid of him, I tell you,'' Bellamy protested.

Lucien stood there, rooted to the floor, listening as the front door slammed. He wasn't foxed—he wished he were, but he wasn't. His shoulder throbbed like the very devil, and he was as weak as the proverbial kitten. If Bell had actually landed a blow, he'd have fallen. Damn! He ought to be better mended than this. But he felt ill, weak in spirit and body still. Maybe the damned doctors had been right—maybe he hadn't been healed enough for the journey, but he'd wanted to bring the boy home. It was a sort of atonement, he supposed, an atonement for what he had not been able to prevent.

Holding his arm, which now felt almost too heavy for the shoulder, he returned to pour himself another cup of the port. As he sank back into the chair, he waited for the weakness, the dizziness, the sweat that came with it to pass, then he wondered why he'd provoked the quarrel with Townsend. It certainly wasn't the obvious—no matter what either of them thought, it wasn't over Diana. They couldn't know that if he'd found her lying in a London gutter, he'd step over her, that he hated her almost as much as he hated Mad Jack.

He supposed it might be a certain admiration for Elinor Kingsley. Even as he sat there, as sick as he was, he could still remember when she'd come to him in London. How she'd been surprised, shocked even, by his mistakenly amorous overture, how she'd only come to ask his aid for the boy. And having known Charles Kingsley, and having seen her at his grave, he was prepared to believe she'd loved poor Charley.

He lifted his glass, mocking himself. Whether Bell mounted her or not ought to matter not one whit to him. But it did. She'd asked him to protect Kingsley, and he had failed so miserably that the boy had fallen in his first battle. Now it seemed as though Charley haunted his thoughts in turn, asking him to do no less for her, begging him to protect her from someone like Bell Townsend. It was a jest of sorts—rather like the wolf being asked to tend the sheep. But he had to try.

He hadn't wanted to—and he'd not wanted to quarrel with Bell. Sitting there, he felt a surge of resentment. Neither she nor Charley had ever had any right to expect anything of him, to make him feel guilty for anything. And yet since the boy had fallen, he'd known no peace.

His gaze moved around his bookroom, taking in the extraordinary library Langston had possessed and prized, then his eyes rested on the bound journal that lay upon his desk. Like a thief, he'd read it, sharing the dead boy's innermost thoughts, his hopes and dreams, letting himself forget his own cynicism for the moment, to live vicariously a youth he'd never had.

At twenty, he was already living down his father's rep. At twenty, he'd already lost all innocence. Sometimes he wondered if he'd ever been green. Only when Jack had persuaded him to wed Diana, to give her nonexistent brat the family name. It was Dame Fortune's ironic jest—he'd survived while decent fools like Charles Kingsley had not.

He sat there, drinking the port, striving for oblivion, for release from the physical and mental pain, telling himself that he would take her the boy's journal on the morrow, for it was not the sort of thing that could simply be sent. Somehow he thought the old man might keep it from her. Besides, he owed it to her to tell her how Charley had died honorably, doing what he thought he wanted, but in his heart, he knew that would provide little comfort.

If only he felt better, if only the insistent pain, the heat of the wound would go away. He wondered if he'd picked up something in Spain, some debilitating weakness that meant to linger. Whatever it was, he could scarce breathe for it, and it was affecting his temper. He'd begun to think he was possessed of but two moods—one belligerent, the other morose.

He rose unsteadily, then sank back down, defeated by a body weaker than his mind. Surely tomorrow would be better. It had to be. Otherwise, he was going to die.

"My lady?" Surprised to hear Daggett's voice behind her, she turned around. "Yes?"

"It's his lordship." He looked down, appearing almost diffident before her. "I can do nothing with him—nothing," he declared dramatically.

She sighed. What did he want of her? What did he think she could do about Arthur's strange behavior? Did he not know that she did not care what became of her elderly husband? Anything she might have been able to feel had died with Charles. She shook her head, saying aloud, "He does not listen to me."

"But he will not have the light, nor will he eat or bathe," the valet complained. "He does but sit or lie and stare."

She didn't want to talk about Arthur. She did not even wish to be reminded of his existence. Not now. Not yet. "It was a shock to him—as to all of us," she murmured, starting away.

"Lady Kingsley, he cannot go on like this!" Realizing that he'd raised his voice to the only authority now in the house, he apologized. "Your pardon, my lady, but I am out of reason worried about him. It has been four weeks since his nails were pared, and—"

"Mr. Daggett—"

"He fasts himself to bones!"

"What can I do about it?" she cried. "It's he who sent Charles to die, and I'd not—"

"It's a grievous price he has paid for it. Please, I pray you will attempt reason with him. Just once. Perhaps when you have seen him, you will wish to summon a physician—or the vicar. All I know, my lady, is that something must be done, else he will die."

She did not want to see him. She could not look at

him without remembering how he'd sent Charley away, how he'd caned her for the innocent attachment between them. Indeed, but it had been almost a relief when he'd disappeared into his room, when he'd insisted on taking a separate carriage to Stoneleigh.

"Here now—what's this?" her father demanded, coming out into the hall.

"I have asked Lady Kingsley to see to his lordship's welfare," Daggett sniffed.

"Well, of course she will! Won't you, Nell? Knows her duty, Mr. Daggett!"

"Papa—"

He leaned closer, and she could smell the wine on his breath even though it was early in the day. "Don't be a fool, puss," he advised her low. "Estate ain't entailed, you know."

"I don't care," she muttered.

"Got sisters to think of—see he takes care of 'em before he pops off. Go on—be all that is proper—God'll reward you for it," he murmured, pushing her toward Arthur's bedchamber door.

"God, Papa?" she asked incredulously. "As He has done the rest of my life?"

"Hush—it's blasphemy to doubt it. Besides, you owe it to him."

"Owe—? Papa, you are mistaken, I assure you," she told him coldly. "I have paid for every trinket, every gown, and—"

"It don't bear saying now, Nell. Man's got one foot in the grave and dragging the other that direction, if half the servants can be believed."

"Is that all you can think of—his money?" she demanded angrily.

"Feel for him, Nell—go on, puss," he urged her. "It ain't like he was a stranger to you."

"You forget he does not like for you to call me that," she retorted. Nonetheless, she reluctantly reached for Arthur's door, telling herself that even after nearly five years, he was a stranger, an almost sinister being she could not, had not ever loved.

The room was dark and musty, the air stale save for the smell of the chamber pot. Daggett hovered behind her, whispering, "He would not have it emptied—would not have the chambermaid within. Wants no noise."

She wrinkled her nose against the odor. "Naught's wrong with you, is there, Mr. Daggett?" she demanded acidly. "I'd have it emptied—and cleaned *now.*" Moving farther into the darkened room, she looked for her husband. "Arthur—?"

There was no answer, but she found him sitting slumped in a chair, and for a moment, she thought him dead. "Arthur," she said more loudly, shaking him.

His eyes opened, the darkness making them seem almost malevolent, and he regarded her balefully. "That stench—it's death," he muttered, looking away.

"It's no such thing." Moving purposefully to the window, she pulled back the heavy hangings, letting in the light.

"Don't." He lifted his hand weakly, then dropped it. His head fell forward until it seemed to rest upon his chest.

She turned back, prepared to accuse him, to rail at him, if he so much as said an unpleasant word to her. But she was unprepared for the sight of him. He seemed so old, so frail, so unkempt—like the poor creatures described by Hannah More after a visit to an asylum. Her anger faded to pity, and it occurred to her that she was no longer afraid of the human husk he'd become. Gone was the arrogance, the ambition that had consumed him for as long as she'd known him.

She reached to touch his shoulder again. "Arthur," she declared forcefully, "it's time this stopped—it serves nothing now. You will be bathed, put into clean clothes, and brought downstairs. This is not grief—it's insanity!"

"Witch!" he spat at her. "Ought to have seen it—you bewitched him!"

She wanted to strike him, but somehow she managed to hold both temper and tongue. "Mr. Daggett, you will see a bath is drawn."

"Don't want one!" the old man declared. "Get out of here before I take m'cane to you!"

"You are in no condition to take a cane to anyone, my lord," she told him. Nonetheless, she moved the walking stick safely out of his reach. "Get up—I think you have soiled yourself."

"Don't care," he muttered mulishly. "Go on—leave me be, I said!"

"No. Daggett, get a footman, for I am not at all certain he can stand unaided." When the valet did not respond, she looked up. "Now. And tell Mrs. Peake that he must have clean linen on his bed. I shall have Mary and the other maids air this room out before he retires tonight."

"Humph! Mrs. Peake won't—"

"It does not matter what Mrs. Peake likes. You asked, and I am here," she reminded him coldly. "We are going to give him a bath, dress him, and see that he is carried downstairs," she repeated.

"Cannot turn me up sweet," the old man's voice rasped. "Cost me Charles."

A month of bitterness welled, then overflowed. "It was not I who sent him to die!" she snapped. "And think you you grieve alone? Well, you do not—you do not! At least Charley loved me—at least he cared! If any lost Charles, it was I! But you do not care for anyone, do you? You will not even let me share the pain I feel! You cannot even grieve with me!"

"Love!" he snorted. "It was his salad days—nothing more."

"Then why did you send him away? Why? Arthur, it was you that sent him to Spain!" Telling herself that it served nothing to provoke him now, that it was too late to bring Charley back, she swallowed hard, trying to stifle the anger she felt.

"Whore!"

Her hands shook as she reached to unbutton his soiled vest, but she managed to say more evenly, "I shall choose to ignore that, counting it but the deranged state of your mind, Arthur." As the footman came into the room, she ordered him, "Stand him up, if you will. Those clothes have to come off him."

"My lady, it's unseemly—" Daggett began.

"I have seen most of him before." Seeing that Arthur pulled away, she began to relish the thought of controlling him this once. "If you have let him get to this state, then someone must take charge," she said tersely. While the footman struggled to both hold and undress her husband, she returned to the window, this time to throw up the sash. "This cannot wait for Mary. Indeed, but a little air might help us all,'' she muttered. ''I know not how you have stood it, Mr. Daggett.''

''His lordship forbade—''

''But *you* are of sound mind,'' she said coldly. ''He obviously is not.''

''He don't like—''

''At this point, I should think what he likes or dislikes to be quite immaterial.''

''Nell?''

She looked up to see her mother standing in the doorway. ''It's all right, Mama—I have everything quite in hand.''

Nonetheless, her mother came inside, wrinkling her nose. ''Oh, dear—I had no idea—oh, *my*!''

''Overwhelming,'' Elinor muttered.

As the valet and footman removed Arthur Kingsley's small clothes, his pale, sunken eyes sought Elinor. ''Whore!'' he flung at her again.

''Arthur, if you are going to behave as a child, I shall see you treated as one,'' Elinor retorted. ''And I am not above washing your mouth with soap the next time you use that word.''

''Nell!'' her mama gasped.

''Well, it's the truth,'' she shot back, unrepentant. ''When he says such, he sullies Charley as much as me.''

''Madam''—Daggett addressed Lady Ashton—''perhaps you would wish to remain outside. I cannot think it seemly—''

''Pish,'' that lady declared. ''I have been wed twenty-one years and borne children, sir—he does not have anything I have not seen.'' She looked to her daughter. ''I am here to support you, dearest. Between us, we shall set this place to rights—and Lord Kingsley also.'' Her eyes flitted to the stained small clothes, and she shuddered. ''I had no idea,'' she repeated, ''none at all.''

''Madam—'' Daggett tried again.

''You ought to be turned off to let him get into such a case,'' Lady Ashton muttered. ''If you would be useful, I'd have you fetch the soap.''

''I wash my hands of this!'' he declared, sniffing.

''If you do, it's all you have washed,'' Elinor's mother told him with feeling. Moving closer to the nearly naked baron, she announced to him, "I did not rear my daughter to endure filth of mind or body, my lord."

He blinked almost childishly. "Don't want—"

"That, sir, is immaterial. When you are recovered, no doubt you will wish to apologize for your behavior. Nell—"

"Yes, Mama?"

"You'd best discover a clean nightshirt for your husband—for I am not at all certain Mr. Daggett can be trusted to do it."

Affronted, the valet looked from Elinor to her mother, then back again. "Which is it to be, my lady? Are we to dress him or ready him for bed?"

Elinor had meant to force him into company, but she supposed the bath itself would be all the unpleasantness she'd wish to endure. "The nightshirt—he can come downstairs tomorrow."

One of the footmen finished removing the baron's stockings, and for a moment, he stood there, his whole body shivering, the loose flesh of his flanks quivering. Mercifully, the footman threw a blanket about him, and helped him to sit while the bathwater was poured into the copper tub. Lady Ashton drew a breath, then made a face. "If you are possessed of Hungary water—or cologne even, I pray you will put a bit of it into his bath," she ventured hopefully.

As Daggett busied himself in Arthur's cabinets and the footmen tested the water, Elinor whispered, "Thank you, Mama."

"Nonsense," Lady Ashton told her, "you were doing quite well without me."

When they were ready, the men eased Arthur Kingsley into the tub of water, where he sat hunched forward, still shivering. Wetting a cloth, Elinor began working up a lather from the soap. Leaning over him, she started with his back, sudsing it. Looking down to where his hands clutched the rolled edge of the tub, she could see his long, filthy nails.

"Sally Jersey ought to see you now, my lord," she murmured.

"Sally Jersey is a whore," he muttered.

"You did not think so when you sought her favor."

He closed his eyes against his tears. "That was when I had a reason to live."

* * *

It was the summer's heat, he told himself. Lucien reined in at the crossroad, considering whether he ought to go back. He felt like the very devil, more so than yesterday even, for his shoulder ached unbearably, his arm felt hot and heavy, and something within his head pounded like a hammer. For a moment, he swayed in his saddle, then he straightened, holding himself tall, militarily correct. He'd come too far to turn back. He'd come to bring Elinor Kingsley the boy's journal, and no stupid complaint would keep him from that. From Jack, he'd learned a contempt for weakness, and for his own more than anyone else's. He jerked the reins almost savagely, wincing as the hot, tearing pain traveled from his neck to his elbow, and he turned the horse down Stoneleigh's lane. He'd not give in to the nausea he felt—he had but to master it. But he did not mean to tarry overlong at Stoneleigh. He had to get home before he fainted.

The horse plodded, settling into a pace between a walk and a trot, jarring every bone in Lucien's body, adding to his misery. He passed a weary hand over his eyes, trying to bring the world back into focus, trying to rid himself of the spots that seemed to dance before his eyes. It was not much farther, he promised himself.

Afore the Almighty, it was hot, so much so that he could scarce stand it. His shirt seemed to cling under the scarlet regimentals, making him wish he'd worn something else. Sweat poured from every pore, soaking his hair, his face, his whole body now. Spanish fever—he was coming down with the Spanish fever. He mustn't pass out from it.

Holding the reins with his good arm and hand, he brushed at his hat with the other. It toppled, falling to the ground, rolling like an errant bandbox. Mumbling a curse, he let it go. He'd begun to feel as though if he dismounted, he'd be too weak to pull himself back into his saddle. When he got to the house, he'd have to entrust the journal to whoever came out, hoping it reached her hands. Otherwise, he'd not get home again.

He shouldn't have come—he knew that now. He'd be deuced lucky if Shakar could find Langston Park unaided. He leaned forward, resting his good arm on the Arabian's saddle. When he looked up, the huge country house was there.

A hostler came running, then stopped when he got to him. "Yer lor'ship—ye all right? Jock! Jock! Come aid his lor'ship! It's Longford!"

"No." Lucien tried to unbutton his coat to retrieve the bound journal, but the nausea overwhelmed him. He was going to be terribly, utterly sick, and there was naught he could do to stop it.

"Gor! Fetch Mr. Peake!" the hostler shouted. " 'E's swoonin'!"

"Humph! It ain't Mr. Peake he needs—Mrs. Peake neither," his companion snorted. "It's the doctor!"

"No—give—" With an effort, Lucien managed to pull out the leather-covered volume. It was already stained with his sweat. "Here—" He leaned to hand it, and his world went black, plummeting him into oblivion.

The two men caught him, dragging him free of his stirrup, and eased him to the ground. "Lawk-a-mussy! Big'un—ain't he? Lud, Davy, but what's ter do now?"

"Best get all of 'em," the other fellow advised. "Earl, after all—can't leave him lie."

Someone else came up to stare. "Must've et sommat bad," he decided.

Elinor, her dress soaked, had just finished buttoning her husband's clean nightshirt, when Mrs. Peake appeared to announce somberly, "My lady, there has been an accident."

"An accident?"

"Lord Longford has fallen from his horse." The woman could not help adding, "Disguised, no doubt."

"Longford is fallen from his horse?" Elinor repeated incredulously. "Where?"

"Below—outside."

"Here?" she asked foolishly. "Whatever—? Has anyone gone for Dr. Beatty?"

The woman nodded. "I sent a footman, but Peake would have it that you must be apprised."

"Yes, of course." Elinor stood there, momentarily

baffled. Longford was below and he'd fallen from his horse. It was absurd. "How—how bad is it?"

"Peake said he was out of his head. He don't know where he is—keeps a-talking about the cannon—tells 'em to stay low," Mrs. Peake muttered.

"Mr. Daggett, you will put my husband to bed."

"I'll come with you," her mother offered.

Once it sank in that the earl had suffered an accident there, Elinor raced down the stairs, holding her gown indecorously high. There, on the front portico, Longford lay where he'd been dragged. She stopped when she saw him. His skin was slightly gray and utterly pale in contrast to the red of his coat and the black of his hair. Kneeling quickly, she could see the beads of perspiration, but when she touched him, he was quite hot, two circumstances that did not match. She looked up at one of the hostlers.

"How did he fall?"

"Didn't fall 'xackly," the fellow mumbled. "Me 'n' Jock caught 'im afore he hit the ground. He was a-looking real queasy-like, ye know."

"Get me a cloth."

"Yes'm."

"What do you think, Mama?"

"I think he's a very sick man—a very sick man," she repeated.

"Were you expecting him, madam?" Peake inquired, clearly irritated that anyone, particularly the notorious Longford, should choose to faint there.

"No—of course not. We are scarce acquainted." As someone, possibly one of the downstairs maids, passed her a dampened cloth, Elinor leaned over Longford to wipe his face. "Can you hear me, my lord?" she asked loudly.

"Out like a snuffed candle," one of the hostlers insisted. "Dunno what's ter do."

"Well, we cannot very well leave him to lie upon the stones, can we? We shall, of course, carry him up to bed and await Dr. Beatty."

Mrs. Peake looked down on the earl, then uttered disapprovingly, "Lord Kingsley would not—"

"Lord Kingsley is himself indisposed!" Elinor snapped.

"Nonetheless, I cannot think—"

"The man is sick—or hurt, Mrs. Peake! I know not which, but we shall certainly offer him aid," she added more stiffly. "He obviously is in no condition to ride home."

"There is the carriage."

"That will be all, Mrs. Peake. You will see to it that a room is prepared on the instant, and then we must have him carried up."

Affronted, the woman marched inside, muttering something to the effect that his lordship would be displeased when he heard of this. At the door, her husband could be heard warning her to hold her tongue.

Lucien awoke surrounded by the curious and the concerned. Blinking, he tried to collect where he was and struggled to rise, but Elinor Kingsley pushed him back against the hard stone floor of the portico.

"What—?"

"Apparently you have fallen from your horse, my lord," she told him. "And you are burning up."

"No—cold," he contradicted weakly. "Was hot—cold now."

"I think you are fevered."

"Got to get—got to warn Wellington—Clausel's moving toward the Fifth. Going to attack," he gasped.

"Not here. You are at Stoneleigh, my lord," she assured him.

His black eyes darted about him, then he shook his head. "Spain—Spanish summer—remember the heat."

"Outer his head," Jock muttered.

Lucien caught at Elinor's hand. "Got to get to Cotton—tell him—"

Cotton had been in charge of the dragoons at Salamanca. She knew that from Charley's letters. For a moment, she looked to her mother, then she squeezed his hand reassuringly. "I shall see he is told," she declared. "Promise."

"Cotton's got to move up—he—cannot let 'em break the line—got to attack—"

"We shall tell him that also."

"I—I—"

"You have been wounded, sir, so you had best lie still until you are carried up."

He seemed to accept that. He relaxed slightly and closed his eyes. "Tell Cotton to give 'em hell."

"We are winning."

"Good. And the boy—the Kingsley boy?" he whispered. "Any word—?"

She could not bring herself to answer.

"Lost 'is mind," Davy whispered. "Heard o' that, ye know."

"If he is out of his head, it's the fever—he's hot," Elinor muttered, not bothering to look up. "See if Mrs. Peake has a bed turned back yet."

He swallowed, then his jaw worked. "Got to get back—"

"No, you are done this day. If you would live to fight again, you must let the doctor tend you."

"Kill as many as they save," he gasped. His eyes fluttered open. "My arm—cannot feel—is it—?"

"You still have it," she murmured. Once again, she glanced toward her mother. "Mama—"

"You are doing all you can, Nell."

Longford turned his head against her knee, touching her wet gown, then mumbled, "Got blood on you, Mrs. Wilson."

"It's water."

"Blood," he insisted. "Mine."

One of the lower footmen came out to announce, "Mrs. Peake says she is as ready as she's going to be." He looked down at Longford dubiously. "Take more'n me and Simpson to bring him up."

"I suspect it will take four of you. Jock, Davy—get his feet, if you will."

The four men carried him up the stairs with Elinor and her mother trailing them. At the top, Mrs. Peake indicated the chamber at the far end of the hall. Daggett came out, surveyed the earl, then shook his head.

"Got nothing to fit him."

"Can you undress him?"

He looked at Longford again. "With aid—aye."

"Here now—what's this, puss? Heard that Longford—" Elinor's father stopped. "Egad—so it is."

"Can you help Mr. Daggett get him into bed, Papa?"

"It ain't my—"

"If you don't, Mama and I shall have to try."

Already they'd managed to lay the earl upon the bed and were struggling to remove his high boots. "Dash it, but what's Arthur to think?" he complained.

"Arthur does not think much of anything these days," she snapped, betraying more than a trace of asperity. She looked down at her wet dress. "Please, Papa—I have already struggled with Arthur. And before you say the others must do it, I'd remind you there are none here but Daggett and yourself who are aware of what ought to be done." She moved closer, then added for his ears alone, "At least your hands have not been cleaning the stables."

Knowing it would be highly improper to watch, she and her mother went back down to await Dr. Beatty. Dropping dispiritedly into a chair, Elinor eyed Arthur's brandy decanter for a long moment, then sighed. "I do not suppose it would be at all the thing to be discovered disguised, do you, Mama?"

"No."

A wave of self-pity washed over her, and once again she fought the urge to cry. "I would that Papa would let you stay with me."

"Nell, I cannot." Her mother leaned forward to clasp both her hands. "I dare not."

"Then why not Charlotte?" Elinor bit her lower lip, but could not maintain her composure. "Mama, I don't want to be alone with him! At least for a time there was Charley, and now there is no one!"

"Lord Kingsley sent money that Charlotte could be sent away to school, Nell. Perhaps one of the younger girls . . ."

"As if they would understand," the girl retorted bitterly.

"Nell . . . Nell . . ." There was no mistaking the sympathy in her mother's eyes. "Do you think I would not wish to stay with you? That there is even a day that passes that I do not feel for you?" she asked softly, sighing.

"Mama, if you loved me, you would stay!"

"If I stayed, there would be nothing, Nell," the older woman declared sadly. "As it is, I must guard every farthing, else the girls shall have nothing."

"Arthur gives him an allowance!"

"Once a gamester, always a gamester, I'm afraid. And now he has taken to drinking to excess. He cannot accept that the allowance is all Lord Kingsley means for him to have."

Elinor stared through tears. "Papa has debts *again*?"

"Yes." Her mother looked away. "More than twelve thousand pounds that I know of, and God only knows how much more than that."

"Oh, Mama! Arthur will not pay any of it—I know he will not!"

"For nearly five years he has lived on expectation of Arthur's dying."

"And what would he have done had Charley lived? Did he never consider that? I could not—I would not have asked Charley for the money, you know."

"Nell—" The slender, bony hands smoothed the younger ones, then patted them. "Promise me this—promise me that no matter what he asks of you, you will not give him money. Rather than settling his debts, he will attempt to come about—and he cannot."

"Mama, I could not let you suffer for his folly. If—if Arthur does not recover, there are my jewels—and all manner of things he has given me. Surely—"

This time, it was her mother's turn to be bitter. "If you loan him anything, he will not repay it. If you give him anything, he will squander it. No, I should very much rather die of shame than see him bleed you for that which you have earned so dearly."

"Mama—"

Her mother forced a smile. "Besides—you did say that I and the girls might live with you, did you not?"

"You know it, but—"

"Hush. One of these days, we might need to."

"It would seem the day is now, Mama. Indeed, but I should like—"

"Lady Kingsley, Dr. Beatty is without," Peake announced.

"Go on—see him up," her mother urged her. "And do not worry—leave Thomas to me. Indeed, but I should have said nothing of this to you—not at a time when your plate is already full."

Elinor rose, then turned back. "Mama, you are welcome wherever I am."

"I know, dearest—but now is not the time. I cannot leave else he would sell Charlotte. Later, when this is past, when the purse strings are yours, we shall hold the better hand, Nell."

WHILE ELINOR SAT, her face averted, the physician examined Longford, grunting and murmuring to himself occasionally. From time to time, she stole a curious glance at the earl, who tossed fitfully beneath Dr. Beatty's probing. Finally, the doctor stood up.

"Fellow's burning up," he declared.

"But he was sweating when he arrived."

He nodded. "A grave sign—body's in distress."

"Grave?" she asked, alarmed. "You do not think that he—?"

"Seen it before, and lost 'em. Final shock, you know."

"But what—?"

"Spanish fever, I'd say, but there's more than that wrong with him." His eyes met hers and his expression was troubled. "You ever see a bullet wound?"

"No—of course not."

"Suppose not," he agreed.

"I collect you think it is his wound, then?"

"Don't see anything else." Walking back to where Longford fretted beneath several blankets, he turned them back to expose the earl's shoulder and chest, revealing two still angry scars. "Ain't pretty, is it?" He pointed to the lower one. "A wonder he lived this long—had to have got the lung. Usually takes 'em right then and there, but I guess he was fortunate—for a time." He turned his attention to the shoulder. "I'd say it was this one," he murmured. "See where it appears to have healed?"

There was an irregular scar just below the joint itself. And while the skin around it was pale, ashen, the wound itself was reddened, strangely shiny, and as smooth as if the skin had been stretched to cover the bullet hole.

"Feel that—go on," the doctor urged.

There seemed to be something daring, almost obscene about touching the man's body, and she hesitated. Then she reached gingerly, tentatively to examine where Beatty had pointed. Longford's shoulder bore little resemblance to Arthur's. He was bigger, more solid, harder. She drew back and looked up questioningly.

"Blood poisoning. See the streak that runs to his arm?"

"Yes."

"I'd say that in their attempt to save his life, they tended the lung first and missed something in there." As he spoke, he reached for his bag. "I'll need assistance, Lady Kingsley. Perhaps a footman—or a maid even."

Blood poisoning was usually fatal. Guilt washed over her for wishing him dead in Charley's place. "I—I shall not mind doing it." When he looked up in surprise, she added more definitely, "I am not of the least squeamish nature, I assure you."

"We'll need water to wash the mess if I am right." He stopped, listening to the earl's tortured breathing, and he shook his head. "That does not sound good either. I hear rales."

Rales? The death rattle? Elinor's hands shook as she went to the washstand. The bowl and ewer were empty. "Mary!" she called out. "Dr. Beatty'd have water!" When she turned back, the physician had assembled an evil-looking collection of instruments on the coverlet.

"You might want to ask for towels to protect your bed-covers also," he added.

"And towels!" she shouted.

"I brung 'em," the maid answered. "And I'm right here as where ye needs me." She looked at the earl, then back to Elinor. "He don't look—"

"Hush." Elinor's eyes dropped to the instruments on the bed. "Do you think we ought to notify someone, sir? I mean, before you—"

"There's no time, Lady Kingsley. As it is, it's a race with the reaper."

"Oh. Yes—of course."

Longford suddenly tried to sit, scattering scalpels and probes, shouting, "Forward! Got to charge! Come on!" Then he fell back, mumbling, "Cannot see for the smoke—damned smoke—"

"Get a footman—no, best make it two footmen," Beatty barked. "Cannot have him thrashing about."

"Laudanum?" Elinor asked.

He shook his head. "Body's under too much distress already. Time enough to dose him when it's done."

Mary did not have to go far for the footmen—full half the household hovered just outside the door. A strapping fellow Elinor scarce knew and the lower footman in charge of the silver stepped inside.

Beatty did not look up. "Hold him down—one to each side—and for God's sake, stay out of my way. Lady Kingsley, if you insist, you may hold the basin—though if I am right, I don't know what good that will do."

"What am I to do with it?"

"Try to catch the stuff when I drain it. And the maid—is the maid still here?"

"Aye, yer honor," Mary answered.

"Tell someone to find a piece of salted meat—pork preferably—then come back. I'd have you ready with water and a cloth."

"Damn you, Jack! First it was Mama—and now it's me!"

Elinor leaned down and tried to soothe the earl. "You are all right, sir—everything's going to be all right."

"Cannot reason with him," Beatty muttered. "Just try to keep him as still as possible." He selected a small, sharp knife, and held it poised above Longford's shoulder. "Got him, boys? No matter what, you've got to hold him down." Satisfied, he moved the knife, then stopped. "Damn—got to have better light. You"—he pointed to Mary—"hold a candle close. You can wash him later."

"Aye."

He waited only until she returned with a lit candle, then with one hand, he guided her arm, showing her where he'd have her hold it. He sucked in his breath, then plunged the knife directly into the healing scar on Longford's shoulder. The earl's body stiffened, then went limp as the two footmen pushed him into the feather mattress. Elinor gasped, recoiling as the abscess beneath spewed the fetid corruption, spraying everything around it. As some hit her face, she gagged. "How—how do I catch it?" she choked.

"You are nearly too late," he grumbled.

The wound smelled both sweet and foul, reminding

her of meat that had spoiled. Swallowing the gorge that rose in her throat, she forced herself to tip the basin slightly and hold it steady. Beatty pressed the outer edges of the scar, expressing more of the greenish ooze. It welled, then drained again and again.

"Don't know how he got home in the first place," the doctor muttered more to himself than to her. "Ought to be dead." Finally, when the wound began to yield only thin, watery blood, he exhaled his satisfaction. "A wet cloth."

"Aye, yer honor." Mary passed it to him.

He washed the area carefully, pressing and frowning, then he dropped the cloth onto the coverlet and reached for the thin-pointed probe. "Got to be something in here somewhere," he murmured. He dug deeply into the hole. "Bring the candle closer," he ordered. "Got to be a piece of the ball or something." He stopped, thinking he felt something, and exchanged the probe for pincers. "Ahhhh—yes, yes." There was no hiding his excitement as he drew out what appeared to be a small bit of bloody cloth. He leaned back, holding it up.

"What is it?" Elinor asked curiously.

"Wadding."

"And that made 'im sick?" one of the footmen wanted to know, clearly disbelieving it. "It ain't hardly nothing."

"It's foreign and contaminated by lead and black powder," Beatty snapped. "A lot of fellows have died from less."

"Gor!"

"I'm not going to try to sew it—not yet. Need to see if we got it all. Right now, I'd have a hot compress to draw it, then we'll put a piece of salt pork over it—salt tends to pull the pus, you know."

"No," she admitted.

"Well, it does." He began putting his instruments away. "Though by the sound of his chest, we've got as much to worry about there. I'd say he's been afraid to cough, and now he's given himself pneumonia."

Pneumonia. A foul abscess. Blood poisoning. Spanish fever. Any one of them sounded bad, but together, they made Longford's case seem hopeless. Elinor swallowed. "Will he—? That is, now that you have drained the wound—?"

"Lady Kingsley, I am a physician—not a prophet. In the first capacity, I should say I think it unlikely—but sometimes we see God's hands work in mysterious ways. Sometimes those we have quite given up survive." Then, recalling the recent loss of Charles Kingsley, he tried to soften his prognosis. "There is a lot to be said for a strong man—and there is much to be said for assiduous care. Between the two of them, we can be surprised. I am sure you have a number of competent staff to attend him."

"Yes, of course."

But the overriding thought that echoed within her mind was that Longford was going to die, that he was going to die at Stoneleigh with her watching. A new wave of guilt washed over her, for had she not begrudged him his life? Had she not wished him dead instead of Charles? But now if he died, after what had happened to Charles, she was afraid she'd go mad. It already seemed that she clung to sanity by little more than a fine thread. And with Arthur's bitter withdrawal and her mother's leaving, there would be none to fight the battle with her.

* * *

The room was dark, the silence punctuated only by the earl's labored breathing and episodes of hallucinogenic raving, none of which made much sense. From time to time, he chilled so hard that he shook his bed, then he would toss, mumbling of the heat. Twice already, she'd summoned footmen from their beds to change his sweat-soaked gown and sheets.

He cursed, he rambled obscurely, he mumbled. He was in hell, he was leading a charge on the battlefield, he was bringing Charles home. Then he was silent again, and for a moment, she feared the worst, that he was perhaps dying. But when she leaned over him to wipe his face, his eyes opened, and his hands caught at hers.

"Mama?" he croaked.

"No."

"Can't leave—can't go." His fingers curved over hers. "Don't leave me, Mama." As he spoke, tears welled in his eyes. "Don't—don't want to be left with him." Despite the weakness, there was a degree of urgency in his voice.

According to Bell, Longford's mother had died long ago. Indeed, but he'd hinted darkly that there had been rumors of a scandal quickly hushed. But it seemed as though everything about Longford had been touched by some sort of scandal. "You are all right, my lord," she murmured soothingly, pulling away her hand.

She'd only meant to come up, to ask Mary of his progress, for she was nearly too tired for thought herself. But the maid had been afraid, saying she didn't want to be left sitting with a corpse, and in the end, Elinor had stayed. Now she herself thought she felt the eerie presence of death. Beneath her fingers, he burned, his skin nearly too hot to touch. And in the hour or so that she'd been there, he'd not responded rationally to anything. It was as though he were already in that valley between, seeing and speaking with those who'd gone before him.

"Nell?" her mother whispered. "How is he?"

"Worse, I think."

Her mother came into the room. "You ought to be abed. Arthur—"

"Nobody deserves to go like this, Mama."

Lady Ashton reached to smooth the black locks at his forehead and drew back from the heat. "Have you sent for the doctor?"

"I told Mary to ask one of the hostlers to go." She looked up. "There must be something—"

Her mother considered being brutally frank, of telling Elinor that she'd never heard of anyone recovering from such a massive infection, but there was something in the younger woman's face that gave her pause. For three weeks, Elinor had grieved herself to the point of illness herself, and now there was Longford. Whether the earl could live or not, it seemed to her that he could for the time being provide her daughter with a reason to care about something beyond her own pain, that perhaps God in His mercy had given her the fight for Longford's life.

"He does not know where he is, Mama."

"It's the fever." Lady Ashton looked about her. "Where's the basin?"

"Here—on the floor."

"He must be cooled. When Charlotte had the fever,

Dr. Pearson prescribed a soaking in cold water. Of course we could not get Longford into the tub,'' she added practically. ''Fetch—what is that footman's name?''

''I don't know which you mean,'' Elinor answered wearily, ''and I'd not ask any of them to get up again.''

''Mary then.''

''Mary is afraid he means to die before her eyes.''

''Well, I daresay it's not a very pleasant notion, but it's something that we can all expect.'' Nonetheless, her mother bent to pick up the porcelain basin and ewer. ''At least she can fill this, I should think.''

''There is more water on the stand. I had her bring some before she retired.'' Elinor looked up, then sighed. ''I had thought perhaps he might thirst.''

''And no doubt he does. Would you get it for me, then?''

When Elinor came back with the pitcher of water, Lady Ashton already had Longford's borrowed nightshirt unbuttoned past his waist. ''Help me with this, will you?''

''Mama! What are you doing?'' the girl gasped.

''Undressing him,'' her mother replied calmly. ''While I should not under ordinary circumstances consider this, I cannot think him in any condition to mind.''

''No, of course not. But—''

''And unless he is some sort of oddity, he is possessed of nothing we have not seen before,'' Lady Ashton continued mildly. ''Here—we need not remove it completely. We shall wash him to the waist first, cover him, then lift the bottom and do the rest.'' When Elinor did not move, she asked shortly, ''Well—what are you waiting for?''

''Uh-nothing.''

''There is no time for false modesty, my dear.''

''No—of course not.'' Elinor dipped the cloth into the cool water and began with Longford's head, wetting his hair over his forehead, then moving over his features down to his chin. Wringing out the cloth again, she did his neck and started to wipe his good shoulder. ''I—I am afraid I might hurt him,'' she said, reddening.

''Nonsense—the man is insensate.''

''Damn you, Jack,'' Longford mumbled. ''Damn you.''

''But vulgar,'' Lady Ashton observed. ''Here—if you cannot—''

''No—no.'' Gingerly, Elinor continued over his chest,

stopping at the poultice that had been tied over the drained abscess. Then she moved lower, beneath his ribs to the hard, muscular band beneath. Had he not been in such bad case, she would have been fascinated. "There." She raised her eyes to her mother's face, only to discover that Lady Ashton was engaged in lifting the nightshirt to expose Longford's legs. "Uh—"

"While you wash the rest, I shall rebutton his gown, Nell," her mother declared matter-of-factly. "And be generous with the water—the wetter you get him, the cooler it will make him."

His legs were long and well-muscled. Feeling very much as though she violated his privacy, Elinor washed them all the way up. An old wound, possibly the one that Leighton had mentioned that day in the park, had healed just below his groin. A few inches above and he might have bled to death from that. Her hands shook as they crept higher, passing over the curling hair, scarce touching his masculinity, and she averted her eyes, trying not to stare at it. It was difficult to believe that Arthur had ever looked like the man before her. By the time she had managed to drag the wet cloth over the flat, almost concave plain of his belly, she was perspiring from her own nerves.

"There," she said finally. "I have done it."

"Damn you, Jack!" the earl said more distinctly. "Damn you to hell for what you do to me!" he shouted.

"Surely he does not mean his father," Elinor whispered as her mother pulled his nightshirt down again.

"It's likely he does. From all I ever heard of him, Mad Jack was utterly unprincipled. There were tales—not all of which I credit, of course—that even decent females were not safe around him. Indeed, but—" She stopped. "It does not signify."

"What doesn't signify?"

"One should not repeat old rumors, dearest."

"You witch! You lying, cheating witch!" Longford called out. "You're no better than he is!" His whole body seemed to quiver, then he relaxed. "Get out of my house," he said clearly. Apparently, whoever he addressed spoke back to him in his mind, for he added, "Jack wasn't enough, was he?" Then, "I'll never touch you again—do you hear me?" His voice had risen to a near shout. "Never! No more lies—no more lies! D'you hear me? No more lies!"

"Lord Longford, you must try to lie still," Lady Ashton told him. "You are but fevered. Nell, get him a bit of the water—just a bit into the corner of his mouth."

"Here now—what the devil's going on?"

Both women looked up, startled by Thomas Ashton's voice. "We are trying to tend Longford," Elinor's mother answered quietly. "And do keep your voice down."

"Keep it down?" he roared. "No, afore God, I will not! Man cannot get a decent night's rest in the place! Tell *him* not to shout!" He reeled slightly, and his speech, for all that it was loud, was slurred. Clearly he'd been drinking.

"Thomas!"

"Papa, he is terribly ill. We have summoned Dr. Beatty again."

"Humph! No great loss if he was to die, if you ask me."

"That's enough, Thomas."

"Well, the man's indecent—left his wife—blood's bad, if you want the truth of it," he declared, unrepentant. "And I won't have either of you tending him, Nell—it's unseemly in the extreme!"

"Papa, he may be dying," Elinor whispered.

"Witch! Never wanted you—never—believed Jack, that's all! You can burn in hell for all I care!" Longford tried to turn, then fell back, mumbling, "Burn with Jack."

"Well, if he's dying," Thomas decided, "there ain't no doubt where he's going."

"Papa!"

"Boy died," the earl whispered. "Didn't mean for it—tried—"

"Hush, my lord." Elinor leaned over him, placing her mouth near his ear. "You are at Stoneleigh."

"Stoneleigh," he repeated, and for a moment, she thought he understood, but then he began to ramble again. "Couldn't stop it—couldn't—Wilson, Cox, Humphries—the boy—all dead. Too late. Couldn't take out the guns on the first charge—tried." He caught at Elinor's arm, clutching it, his eyes open but unseeing. "Don't let 'em take the arm—don't let 'em take my arm! Can't feel it—can't feel it at all."

"Your arm is fine, Lord Longford." Elinor poured a

small amount of water into a cup and tipped it into a pocket she made by pulling down his lip. "You are at Stoneleigh," she repeated. "You have an abscess, that's all."

He swallowed and choked. And when he began to cough, he nearly came up from the bed. It was as though the force of it racked his whole body.

"I never heard the like," Thomas Ashton muttered.

"It's pneumonia—his bad lung is inflamed also."

"Then he's a goner," he said brutally. "And I don't want either of you here to see it. You get that maid—or the Friday-faced housekeeper. You ain't got no business—"

"Go on," Longford whispered.

"See—even he don't want you here."

"He's confused, Papa."

"Go on," the earl said again. "I saw the blood—take care of the others—I know, Sarah—I know. It's my lung."

"Who's Sarah?"

"I told you he was confused, Papa."

"Sorry about John—good man. Sorry about the boy—she was right—he was a good boy." His hand came up as though he meant to wipe his mouth, then fell back to the bed also. "Damned funny—Jack died at home, Sarah—I'm going in Spain." He coughed again. "Tell her—tell Kingsley's wife—I tried to save the boy."

"Here now—what's he doing talking about you, puss? Don't like the sound of that."

"Go to bed, Thomas."

"Ain't going without you," he maintained stubbornly. He stumbled toward a chair. "Going to sit until you come with me—indecent for you to be here."

"Thomas—"

"Go on, Mama. I can manage—really. If there is any change, I shall waken you."

"No, you won't," her father declared belligerently. "Be good thing if he was to die. Can't have him talking about you, puss."

There was a loud pounding on the door below, the shuffling of feet, the murmur of voices, steps on the stairs. Dr. Beatty rapped on the doorjamb, then came on into the room.

"I collect there has been a change?"

"Man's ranting!" Thomas Ashton shouted at him. "Expect you to do something about it!"

The physician cast a quizzical look at Elinor. "My father," she murmured, embarrassed. "Papa—go to bed."

"Not without her!"

"I'm afraid he's been drinking," she offered apologetically.

"So I see. Yes, well, I should like all of you to leave—except Lady Kingsley, of course."

"What the devil d'you need her for?" her father demanded. "Ruining her rep!"

"She has a strong stomach—a rare thing these days."

"All right, Thomas," Lady Ashton said tiredly, "I am coming with you."

"Going home with me, too," he told her thickly. "Tired of the place. What with the old man a-staring and her forgetting what she owes her papa, it ain't anywhere I'd like to be."

As her mother dragged her father out, Elinor turned her attention to Beatty. "Perhaps I should not have sent for you, but I cannot get his fever down. He's so restless—his mind wanders—he sees things—"

He nodded, not unkindly. "It's to be expected, I'm afraid."

"And the cough—it's terrible."

"Aye." He leaned over Longford, frowning. "If it was but the wound—or the inflammation of that lung, I should give him a chance, but—"

"Is he—is he much worse?"

"You summoned me," he reminded her.

"Well, I thought perhaps there might be something to ease him—he cannot thrash about and shout all night." She felt utterly foolish, as though she ought not to have bothered him. "And he is so very hot. Surely there must be something that can be done."

"Even if he should get better, he will worsen first."

"Worsen? He cannot!"

"Lady Kingsley, he is corrupted with infection. Bring the candle over here."

She did as he asked, then leaned over his shoulder to watch as he unwrapped the shoulder. When he lifted the salt pork, yellow-greenish pus clung to the meat, and the wound beneath it was wet. And once again the rotted smell permeated the air.

"At least it still drains—there is no sign the abscess is reforming," he noted with some satisfaction. Noting her revulsion, he added, "I mean to change this in the morning." His manner changed abruptly. "How much is he coughing?"

"Quite a lot, I think."

"Bringing anything up with it?"

"You mean like blood?"

"I mean anything, Lady Kingsley."

"Not—not much of anything that I have seen."

He laid his head against Longford's chest, listening to the rales. "Too low—middle lung, I think. It must come up if he is to have any chance at all."

"How?"

But Beatty had lost interest in explaining. Instead, he rolled the earl over onto his side and began striking blows to his ribs in the back. For a moment, Elinor thought he too had lost his mind.

"You cannot—the man's sick!"

"If this does not loosen, he's dead," he retorted, continuing to beat on Longford's back. "Got to make it come up."

"But the pain—perhaps some laudanum?"

He shook his head. "It will impede his cough. You want him to cough—between the corruption in his shoulder and that in his chest, he's poisoned. Anything that can be got out of him in either area is to the good." He shifted the earl, hanging his head over the side of the bed, then began to thump his back anew, until his patient began to cough. It was a raw, deep bark at first, but as Beatty persisted, it grew productive. Longford gurgled, then gagged. Beatty looked up at her. "Think you could do this?"

"Yes—if someone can turn him over for me."

"Get one of the men for that. I don't want them pounding on him, for they don't know what they are doing. You don't either, but at least you are not as like to make the lung hemorrhage. You want to strike him here—and not too hard. The trick of it is to do it steadily until that stuff inside loosens."

"I see. But his fever—"

"Wipe him down with cool water. If it gets too high, get him into a tub." He pushed the earl back onto the bed, then turned to rummage in his bag. Taking out a small jar, he opened it. "You can try a bit of this powder—a teaspoon or so in water—but I have not much hope of its helping." He rose to stand over her. "I have left word with Mrs. Beatty that I shall be staying the night here. I require nothing fancy, Lady Kingsley."

"Yes, of course. I shall waken Mrs. Peake to show you to a bedchamber."

"No need—just direct me, and I shall find the way."

He wasn't going to sit up with Longford. She started to protest, then thought better of it. He was the physician, and when it came to treating the sick, she was little more than a green girl. At least he had come when she'd sent for him—at least he would be no farther than a few doors down the hall.

"There are several empty chambers, sir—there is one two doors to the left."

"No need to point it out—I can count that far, my lady," he assured her.

After he left, she sank back into the bedside chair and tried to stay awake lest Longford should need her. But he seemed to have calmed—whether from the bathing or from the thumping, he seemed to be resting more easily. She started to doze, only to be awakened by the awful, racking cough. At first her body would have her deny she'd heard him, then she forced herself to lean forward with a cloth to wipe his mouth.

"Helpless as a babe," he muttered.

Hope surged. He was not entirely unaware. But then he turned his head away, mumbling, "Tell Barry we need more powder. Damned sorry about the leg—meant to be there to the end."

Curious, she asked him, "What leg—do you mean your leg, my lord?"

There was no answer.

Sometime after that, she fell asleep and knew nothing until someone shook her awake. "Nell—Nell—it's Mama. Get you to bed, and I shall watch him."

"No," Elinor mumbled. "Cannot—got to thump him."

"What?"

"Thump," the girl managed drowsily. "His back."

"In the morning."

She opened her eyes and passed a weary hand over her face. "Is it morning?"

"No. The clock has but struck three."

"Can't go."

"You have to—Arthur will have need of you tomorrow."

"Arthur has no need of me, Mama. Don't you see? I gave him Almack's, and there's naught else he'd have of me."

"He grieves—as do you."

"Sarah, how fares the boy—how fares young Kingsley?" Longford croaked. "Told her—" His words disappeared in a fit of coughing.

"Mama, you go to bed, else Papa will be vexed with you. I am all right."

"Nell—"

"No—I am all right. Please."

"Nell," he whispered. "That's a pretty name."

Once again, she thought he was aware, but then his mind wandered. "Charley's Nell. Cannot write forever, you know—not that much to say to a female." He tried to turn and could not. "Thirsty—Sarah, I thirst."

She mixed the powder into a small amount of water and managed to give him a drink without strangling him. Then, throwing modesty into the wind, she did as she and her mother had done before, washing him down with cool water. And when she was finished, she leaned her chair back gainst the wall and closed her eyes. This time, sleep did not come as her conscious mind fought to survive. In the space of less than a day, Lucien de Clare, the despised Earl of Longford, had become exceedingly important, for a time crowding her grief from her mind. In her fatigued fancy, she was locked in an impossible battle for a man's life. And she was going to win.

Fleetingly, she wondered about Sarah—was she a woman he'd left in Spain? All the world knew of Diana—but Sarah? For a moment, she felt a painful stab of jealousy—not for the man, but for the woman Sarah. For the moment at least Longford lived, while Charles lay cold and still within the confines of a box. No, she could not think of that now. Later—later, when Longford survived, she would remember Charley.

OUTSIDE, THE EARLY MORNING rain pelted the house, while inside most of the household still slept. Exhausted, Elinor had sought her bed but a few hours before, leaving a reluctant Mary to watch over Longford. Now, too tired to sleep, she lay listening to the rain, wondering how a man could endure what the earl had and still live. For whatever could be said of him, he was not going tamely into his final good night.

As the days had worn on to a week and more, the duties of nursing him had had to be divided, until now even the stiff, cold Mrs. Peake unbent enough to take her turn watching him. But his progress, if any, had been minute, and if there was anything encouraging about his condition, it was that he still lived at all.

She'd thumped, bathed, spooned sustaining broths, and watered him, held his hand to soothe him, listened while he raved until she almost felt a common bond with him, a common struggle for each labored breath. But this night just past had been the worst—for his fever had soared, and he had cried out at unseen demons, denying them. Finally, she'd summoned two of the stouter footmen and between them, they'd managed to soak him in a tub of cool water. He'd calmed then, slipping into a quieter sleep, and she'd come to bed.

Every muscle ached, every limb was weak from wrestling him down. And to make matters worse, her father, announcing he did not mean to stay where the house was at sixes and sevens, had finally managed to drag her mother home with him, so that for the last two days the ordering of everything had been hers. Even now, when she thought of her parents, she felt guilty, for she'd been too tired to protest, too tired to weep even when they left. She could scarce remember her mother's tearful embrace, her whispered words of encouragement.

"My lady—?" Mary inquired tentatively from the doorway.

"I'm not asleep."

The maid came into the room. "I think we ought ter send fer Beatty."

Elinor sat up on the instant, her heart in her throat. "He—he's not worse?"

"He ain't doing nothing."

Throwing back the covers, Elinor hit the floor running, her mind racing silently, praying. *Please—not now—not after what he's been through—not after Charley. You took Charley—surely Longford must not go also.*

When she got there, the room was strangely silent, and she knew the worst had happened. She turned back to Mary. "Tell Dickon to run for the doctor."

"Already did," the maid admitted.

Elinor approached the bed gingerly, afraid of what she would find. The flickering light of a hastily lit candle cast an eerie orange and yellow glow to pale skin. Longford looked as though he'd been carved from white marble. Very cautiously, she reached to touch his forehead. It was cool, almost cold, and her stomach knotted.

"My lord—" She'd lost the battle, and now she was losing what little control she had over herself. She caught at his shoulders, shaking him, screaming at him, "You cannot die! Not now—not after all I have been through!" Her head went down, buried in his shoulder, and she began to weep hysterically. "Why? Why Charley? Why this?" she sobbed. "If there is a God, He does not listen to me!"

"Lady Kingsley!" Mrs. Peake gasped, shocked. "It's blasphemy!"

But the sobs racked the girl's body. "I tried—I tried!" It was then that she became aware of movement beneath her. He breathed.

"Cannot"—it was the merest croak—"breathe," he finished. "Heavy."

She sat up and wiped at her streaming eyes. "Longford—?" she whispered.

"Aye. Been to—hell." He coughed, and the loose rattle was like music to her ears. The congestion was breaking up. "Hell," he murmured again. With an effort, his eyes fluttered open, staring up into hers. "Mistaken—heaven." And he closed them again, leaving her to wonder if he was still out of his head.

"Gown's soaked," a still-dressing footman observed from behind her shoulder. "Ought to get him dry."

"Oh—yes, yes—of course." She rose self-consciously, aware now that she'd not even put on her wrapper over her nightgown, that her hair tangled in wild disarray, falling over her shoulders nearly to the dark circles of her nipples beneath the thin lawn gown. "Uh—if you will change him, I shall make myself presentable for Dr. Beatty," she mumbled, crossing her arms over her breasts. Her eyes flitted to Mary. "I think he's better," she offered in understatement. But even as she spoke, she exulted. Longford lived.

Half an hour later, the physician was confirming it—the fever had broken rather precipitously and showed no sign of coming up again immediately. And a new examination of the shoulder wound revealed that it had all but ceased draining. But most encouraging of all was that awful cough, for it was now producing, bringing up the congestion from his lungs.

"That'll be with him awhile, I expect," he decided, "but the inflammation's breaking up. Oh, that don't mean to say he's out of the woods yet, you understand, but I'd say he's got a damned good chance of living." He stopped. "Sorry—shouldn't have said that—forget sometimes—should have said 'deuced good chance,' I guess. Mrs. Beatty's always a-getting on me for it."

"Doctor Beatty, as long as you are telling me the worst is over, you can say anything you want," Elinor insisted gratefully. "Thank you. Thank you." Overwhelmed, she choked back tears.

"Lady Kingsley, if there is any credit to be given, it's to the Almighty—and you. And so I mean to tell his lordship." He looked at her and smiled. "Best brace yourself, though—fellow's a long way from well. Be weeks before he regains his strength, and in the meantime, he'll run a fever now and again. Still have to keep the lungs draining also, but God willing, he'll soon be able to help you."

"I beg your pardon?"

"Hang himself over the bed while the phlegm is being loosened. Got to keep that up, you know." He gave her a kindly pat on the shoulder. "Best get yourself off to bed and sleep while you can. He'll have bad times yet."

When she emerged into the hall, Mary was waiting, her lower lip quivering, and then the maid burst into tears. "We done it, my lady! We done it!"

"It's not over yet," Elinor cautioned her. "Dr. Beatty says it's weeks before he is well."

"But Dickon was a-listening at the door," the girl admitted. "Heard him say his lordship was a-going ter live!"

"We hope so." Elinor felt her own heart was nearly filled to overflowing, and she could maintain her calm no longer. "Oh, Mary! We *did* do it, I think!" She felt a hand on her arm, and when she turned around, there was Mrs. Peake, her sharp features quivering, her eyes red. Wordlessly, Elinor embraced her, holding the thin, stiff body. "Thank you," she whispered.

"Here now—it was nothing," that woman muttered gruffly. "Christian duty, that's all."

And there was Daggett waiting also. "My thanks, Mr. Daggett," she told the valet. "I know how very difficult this has been for you, what with my husband and—"

He nodded. "His lordship would speak with you, madam."

For a moment, she thought he meant Longford, then she realized it was Arthur. Arthur. In the week past, she'd scarce spared a thought for him. Well, whatever he said to her, whatever names he cast at her, he could not dampen the exhilaration she felt now, the exhilaration of knowing she'd actually done something worthwhile.

"Yes, of course," she murmured.

This time, her husband's bedchamber was dark not from being closed up, but rather from the gloomy rain outside. As early as it was, he was sitting, his thin body wrapped in a blanket, looking out the window into the garden below. She sucked in her breath, then exhaled it slowly before she approached him.

"Good morning, my lord."

"I hear Longford lives," he rasped.

"Yes—at least for now."

"Cannot see you." He lifted a bony hand, motioning her to come around him.

She moved to face him, standing at the side of the window. For a moment, she looked down, seeing the red roses that climbed the garden wall. When she looked back, her husband was watching her.

"Look like the very devil—I've seen harridans in the markets as were more kempt than you," he declared sourly.

"I've not had much time to attend my toilette, I'm afraid."

"Still got your tongue, I see."

"My sword and buckler, I suppose."

His hand reached for what appeared to be a tall, slender book in his lap. "I considered burning this, Elinor," he admitted, "but having read it, I have decided to let you have it."

"I beg your pardon?"

"The foolish ramblings of a foolish boy—no doubt worth more to you than to me." He held it out and looked away as she took it.

"What—?"

"Charles's journal," he said simply. "I collect Longford meant to bring it to you."

Her exhilaration, her exultation evaporated as she looked at it. Opening it almost cautiously, she saw the familiar scrawl and felt the painful tightening within her chest. She closed it quickly, not wanting Arthur to see her cry.

"Thank you, my lord," she whispered.

He stared out into the rain, and for a moment, she thought he'd not heard her. But finally he spoke. "It's sad reading, you know. I cannot recommend it."

Her chin quivered and the lump rose in her throat. "He loved you, Arthur."

"Aye—but you more than me."

The bleakness in his voice was unmistakable. "Arthur—"

"I scarce knew him, I'm afraid—or his father either," he mused slowly. "It was always my fortune as came first, and now it was for naught." He looked up at her, his blue eyes rheumy and reddened. "You behold a man with an empty empire, Elinor. A man builds for his heirs, and now I have none. It's all gone but the money.''

For all that he'd railed at her, for all that he'd accused her, calling her whore and worse, she pitied him now. ''Arthur, there is yet good to be done.'' She moved closer, laying a hand on his shoulder, and was surprised when he reached to clasp it.

''I did not build a fortune to establish hospitals or schools, Elinor—I built it for the Kingsley name—I built it for my blood. I'd thought to know there would be a Kingsley at Stoneleigh after me.''

She let Charles Kingsley's journal slip from her other hand and very gently she brushed the wispy gray hair back from his forehead. ''We cannot always have what we would, my lord,'' she said softly. ''God—''

''God!'' he spat. ''Pfaugh! What sort of god takes Charles and lets the likes of Longford live?'' he demanded angrily. ''Do not speak to me of God!''

Having felt much the same herself before, she had no answer. Instead, she continued smoothing his hair. He stiffened as though he meant to recoil from her, then both his hands came up to hold her waist. His thin shoulders shook, and it was as though their roles were reversed, as though she were the elder and he were the child. For a moment, he wept against her.

Abruptly, he collected himself and pushed her away. ''Go on,'' he ordered curtly.

The brief intimacy was over, leaving her once again separate and alone in her grief. She bent to pick up Charles's last recorded words and started to leave.

''Ought to have burned it,'' Arthur muttered behind her. ''But I could not.''

When she reached the door, she turned back, but he was once again staring out the window, mumbling something more about his empty empire, about how the only relations he had were distant, and every one of them smelled of the shop. What she did not hear was his avowed determination to see that they did not receive a farthing. To him, the notion of a clerk or worse as Baron Kingsley did not bear thinking.

WHILE LONGFORD SLEPT, Elinor sat by the window reading Charles's journal for the third time in as many days. The first time, she'd wept bitter tears, the second, she'd tried to picture him as he'd written it, and now she listened as his voice seemed to echo in her ears. Her heart ached terribly, but as she imagined he spoke to her, his words were a sort of catharsis, a healing purge, giving her not memories of a sealed box being lowered into the ground but rather of a boy full of life.

Mrs. Peake entered the room, her mouth pursed in disapproval. "Lord Townsend is most insistent, my lady, and he will not be denied."

Bellamy Townsend. Elinor colored guiltily, thinking of how many times she'd sent him away in these ten days past. She started to rise, then thought better of it. "Send him up—no doubt he will wish to see how Longford fares."

As she heard his footsteps on the carpeted stairs, she laid aside Charles's journal and waited. He crossed the room quickly, his concern evident, and took both her hands.

"Dear lady—" He stopped, shocked by the fatigue etched in her face. "Oh, my dear—had I only known—"

"I am quite all right, my lord," she murmured, repossessing her hands. "At least he rests comfortably enough that we can sleep at night."

"You should have allowed me—or hired assistance," he chided her. "It's beneath you to nurse a man of his stamp."

"He was dear to Charles," she replied simply. She gestured to the journal. "Charley idolized him, you see. That was what made him wish to be a dragoon."

From the moment he'd heard that the earl had collapsed at Stoneleigh, Bellamy had denied his jealousy, telling himself that Elinor Kingsley was a paragon merely doing the decent thing. Still, he felt an acute unease. It was one thing to rival a dead man, quite another to have to compete with a wounded hero who had the advantage of the field.

"Yes, well, the boy was an innocent—too decent to know what he was about yet. Terrible, terrible tragedy—my heart aches for you—and for Arthur, of course." Pulling a chair up beside her, he sat down. "How is Kingsley, by the by?"

"Better, I think. He seems less inclined to blame and more intent on disappointment."

He couldn't follow her. "Disappointment?"

"Yes. Now he is obsessed that he has none to leave his fortune to but me, I think."

"There must be other heirs surely."

"None that I have heard of." She sighed. "It's all so pointless, isn't it? After all these years of currying favor, of striving to be other than what he was born, he has achieved a title he is unable to pass on and a fortune he cannot take with him."

"Poor devil."

She looked up at that. "I suspect his awareness of those circumstances will make him determined to outlast all of us."

"I had thought him in serious decline."

"If I had learned naught else, my lord," she said tiredly, "it's never to underestimate my husband." Then, realizing how she must sound, she smiled wryly. "You must forgive me—I did not mean that I wish him to die."

"You could not be blamed if you did."

She was too weary to dissemble. "Oh, I cannot deny there was a time—when first Papa forced me to wed him—that I quite counted on his demise. But now—"

"Yes?" he prompted.

"Now that Charley is gone, it does not matter."

Once again, his hand sought hers, clasping it. "While that first youthful passion is seldom entirely forgotten, Lady Kingsley, I assure you it can be replaced with something far more lasting. Indeed, but I—"

He got no further. Longford roused, moaning loudly, crying out, "I thirst."

She pulled away and rose to tend him, leaving Bellamy Townsend in the awkward position of intruding in the sickroom. He rose, saying rather stiffly, "Under the circumstances, dear lady, I ought to take my leave. Perhaps on the morrow you would care to drive out? You have been cooped up far too long, you know, and the air would do you a great deal of good." When she did not answer immediately, he came up behind her as she poured a cup of water, putting his hands on her shoulders, massaging them lightly with an intimacy that ought to have gotten him a sharp set-down. "It will be fall before you know it. Come out while the flowers are still on the hillsides," he coaxed.

She had scarce breathed any air beyond the sickroom and certainly had had no conversation beyond Longford's illness and Charley's death. For a moment, she considered the invitation, then she nodded. "If it does not rain." As she looked up, she caught the warmth of his smile and added hastily, "And if you promise you will not behave improperly."

He dropped his hands and stepped back. "My dear Elinor, I shall be whatever you would have me. Indeed, but you must surely know of my regard—that I—"

Longford moaned again and tossed as though he were in great pain. "Your pardon, my lord," she murmured to Townsend.

"You know, I meant my earlier offer—I should be happy to attend him to spare you. For all that is in the past between us, I still count him a friend."

She started to tell him that there was nothing, then relented. "Perhaps you could help me clear his lungs."

"Anything, my dear—anything." He watched as she sat beside Longford and tried to lift him. "Allow me," he insisted, bracing Lucien while she held the cup to the other man's lips. "Weak as a newborn pup, isn't he?"

"Yes, but each day is better than the last one."

Longford swallowed, then began coughing, holding his sides against the pain. It was a deep, loose rattle. He looked up at Bell. "God's punishment for living," he managed.

She set the cup aside, ordering, "Lie him down and turn him over, will you? And if you do not mind it, I'd have his head over the side."

"Why?"

"We've got to bring that up else he will not get better."

Bellamy did as she asked, then watched curiously as she began pounding on Longford's back, cupping her hands so as not to hurt him, moving them rhythmically over his ribs. The coughing increased until the earl began to choke and spit.

"Catch that in the basin," she ordered brusquely.

"What?"

"The spittle. Dr. Beatty would see it."

The viscount was thoroughly revolted, but somehow he managed to slide a small basin beneath Longford's head. His eyes met hers. "Egad. I had no idea—is *this* what you do?"

"Yes. It's not precisely pleasant, but it helps."

"I'd think one of the maids—or a footman—"

"No. It must be done just so."

Finally, the earl ceased the awful coughing, and Bell laid him back. "Sorry, old fellow—didn't know."

"You'll need to turn him over and pull him up onto the pillows," Elinor advised him. "Otherwise he cannot breathe."

"And you do this by yourself?"

"Much of the time."

"You must be fagged nigh to death."

"Sometimes I think I am," she admitted. "But it keeps me from thinking of Charley."

"Yes, well, had I known it was like this, I should have been here to assist you, dear lady. As it is, I mean to come back in the mornings that you may rest."

"Oh, I don't—"

"Nonsense. I can contrive to keep him tolerably amused as he recovers, I assure you."

"But there is no need—that is, I—"

"Longford and I are old acquaintances, my dear." He reached to cover her hand with his. "And I do not mind it." He rose from the bed and started for the door. "Until the morrow, then. And if you have need of me, you have but to send to Leighton's." He looked to Lucien. "I shall look in on you in the morning. Is there aught that you would have me bring you?"

"No."

Longford dissolved into another fit of coughing, leaving Bell little to do but leave. "*Au revoir*, my dear," he murmured to Elinor.

She waited until he was gone, then turned her attention to Lucien. "This time, my lord, I think you are shamming it," she told him severely.

"Somehow the thought of Bell's declaring himself here and now seemed a bit premature, don't you think?" he inquired sardonically. His sunken black eyes nonetheless were alight with mischief. "Particularly since Arthur's mind appears to be on the mend," he added.

"You were listening earlier," she accused him.

"Well, as I could scarce go anywhere else, I could not avoid it."

"I thought you slept."

"Obviously." He closed his eyes, muttering, "Too weak for anything."

"Dr. Beatty says we may begin restorative jellies," she offered.

"What?"

"Restorative jellies."

He didn't open his eyes. "How very appetizing."

"Well, I expect it will be better than the gruel."

"Tell the old bonesetter that I require more food than he is inclined to give me."

"The 'old bonesetter' saved your life," she reminded him.

"My, how neither of you wishes credit for it," he murmured. "According to him, the blame belongs to you."

"Fiddle. I did but what he told me."

"Rather assiduously, I am told. A pity I was not awake to see you bathe me."

The bond that she'd felt she'd shared with him in his darkest hours had gone, leaving a self-consciousness in its place. He was fast becoming Longford again, Sally Jersey's "dangerous man," and she felt a pang of regret for it. For the last week and a half, she'd been needed, useful, something more than the crowning jewel in Arthur Kingsley's collection. Now Arthur was recovering his mind and Longford would soon be able to leave, and once again she faced being nothing beyond a possession.

He knew by her silence that he'd gone too far. "I know

what I owe you,'' he said quietly. ''And while I am not at all certain I am worth your effort, I thank you for it.''

''Sarah must think so.''

''Sarah? Who the devil's Sarah?''

''I don't know—it was you who called for her when you were out of your head with the fever.''

His forehead furrowed momentarily, then he nodded. ''Oh—*that* Sarah.''

''Your sweetheart?'' she found herself asking, then wished she could get back the words. ''Your pardon—I should not pry.''

''Sarah Wilson—Leftenant Wilson's wife. She tended the wounded at Salamanca.'' He tried to turn over and dissolved into a fit of coughing. She proffered a cloth quickly and he spat into it. Lying back, he waited to gain his breath. ''Wilson died there.''

''Oh.''

Both fell silent until he felt it incumbent to say something. ''Sorry for the boy.''

''I know.'' Her hands knotted the black skirt. ''I know,'' she repeated softly. ''I heard that often while you were sick.'' Again the silence was nearly deafening, broken only by the steady beat of the rain against the windowpanes. This time, it was she who felt the need to say something. ''He wrote often of you, you know.''

''A great deal of nonsense, I'm afraid.''

''You mean there was no Spanish lady intent on wedding you?'' she teased, trying to lighten the mood between them.

''He wrote of that, too—eh?''

''Yes.''

He grinned ruefully, then winced. ''Damned shoulder—too sore to move.'' Once again, he closed his eyes as though that would somehow help him gain strength. ''Near thing—family wanted to get her out of Spain.''

''But somehow the thought of trailing after you into battle deterred her.''

''No,'' he admitted baldly. ''It was the notion that I was a savage that convinced all of them. I wore every weapon I possessed, then announced that madness ran in the family.''

''You ought to be ashamed.''

''I told you—I make a damnable husband.'' He

coughed again. "God," he groaned, "it's enough to make me wish I had died."

"You nearly did."

"Too mean to die. It's the good that go."

"Except Mad Jack." Once again, she could bite her tongue for the words that slipped out. He lay there, his eyes still shut, his jaw working, the only sign that he'd heard her. "I did not mean to pain you, my lord," she said finally. She turned to leave. "Mary will be here directly to feed you."

"No."

"You cannot manage it yourself."

"No," he repeated. "You did not pain me—I hated him."

"Well, there are times I cannot say I care very much for my father either," she admitted. "But I am tiring you with speech."

He waited until she reached the door, and when he heard it creak inward, he spoke again. "Don't want the girl—spills too much on me."

"Mrs. Peake, then."

"Gives me indigestion."

She closed the door after her, taking some small measure of satisfaction in the notion that he still needed her for something.

He dozed for a time, waking only at the sound of the door again. Forcing his eyes open, he was surprised to see Arthur Kingsley himself, his bony hand pressing heavily on the ebony cane, his steps slow and measured as he crossed the room. The old man stopped at bedside and dropped into the straight-backed chair there. Leaning forward, resting both hands on the silver-handled walking stick, he peered into Lucien's face, studying it before he spoke.

"Longford."

"There is no accounting for survival, is there?" Lucien murmured.

"No."

Without preamble, the old man admitted, "I read the boy's journal, though I collect you brought it to my wife."

"I thought he would wish it."

Arthur Kingsley nodded. "I gave it to her, you know."

The faded eyes watched Lucien, then the baron mused, "He was the first I ever heard of as had anything good to say of you."

"My lamentable reputation."

"Regrettable." The old man cleared his throat. "I collect you mean to live."

"Apparently I am too mean not to."

"I always thought you a ruthless man—did what you wanted and damned those as objected. I like that. Shows—"

"A decided lack of character," Lucien said, interrupting. "I know what I am." Once again the awful cough racked his body, hurting him. He winced visibly."

"Come by it honestly. In the blood, after all. I remember when your mother died and it was said—"

"I know the rumors," Lucien snapped.

"Any truth to 'em?" the old man persisted. "Don't mind the other, you understand," he hastened to add as Lucien's color rose. "Just don't want any insanity in m'heir, that's all."

It occurred to Lucien then that Kingsley's mind had snapped, and that his recovery was physical rather than mental. Still, he forebore reminding him that Charles had perished.

"Well, I cannot say I have any great familiarity with your family," he conceded. "But there are not many who do not admire the size of your fortune."

"Elinor is a beauty—you got to admit that. When I took her to town, there wasn't a buck's head as did not turn."

"An Incomparable," Lucien agreed.

"Don't look like a milk and water miss—got color. Gave her style, too."

"Striking," Lucien murmured, wishing that Mary or anyone would come, for the old man was making him uncomfortable.

"Still in the bloom of youth—twenty next month. Isn't much for her to do here. Daresay she could be ripe for anything, don't you think?"

Somehow it angered Lucien that Kingsley could think that after all he owed Elinor he would be so base as to consider seduction. "You are better advised to discuss this with Bell Townsend," he declared stiffly.

"Don't want him. Fellow's a gamester, and I don't need that on both sides of the blanket. I did not work to see my money disappear at the likes of White's." He leaned closer, so close that his eyes were but inches from Lucien's. "I want an heir with wits enough to keep what I leave him."

The old man was crazed—his grief had made him mad. Nonetheless, Lucien answered, "Most empires fall, so you must not repine over what cannot be. Another generation and neither of us will be remembered."

"There will be a Baron Kingsley here."

"My dear Arthur—"

"Think I've lost m'mind, don't you? Haven't. Been thinking about it ever since I read the boy's journal, waiting to see if you meant to live." His eyes seemed to bore into Lucien's. "You can name your price, Longford—all you got to do is give me m'heir."

It was the first time in recent memory that Lucien could truthfully admit to being stunned. "Sir," he managed when he found his voice, "what you suggest is repugnant in the extreme."

"Elinor's got a soft heart," the old man went on as though he'd made no objection at all. "Ripe," he repeated. "Ready for a young buck like you. And you need not worry that I don't mean to acknowledge any babe you get of her, 'cause I've got nobody else I'd want to leave anything to." He leaned back, chuckling wryly. "Irony, don't you see?"

"No," Lucien snapped.

"Man my age getting a babe. But you must be discreet about it—I don't mean to be pitied. I'd have it thought it was mine." He stopped, smiling smugly. "Well?"

"Regardless of what you think me, I've no wish to take advantage of your wife in her grief. She cared for Charles, you know. And as you can see, I am in no case—"

"Not as you think, my dear Longford—not as you think." Kingsley cut him off. "Having observed them closely and having read his letters to her—and hers to him—I believe the passion was his."

"She mourns him!"

"Of course she does," Kingsley agreed. "But who is to say for what?" he added enigmatically.

"You sicken me, sir. If you would have an heir, I suggest you get your own."

The smile vanished. "If I could, I'd not ask you."

"No."

Arthur sighed. "I should not be hasty in denying what I offer. The child will have every advantage the Kingsley fortune can gain him." He rose slowly. "Think on it," he advised. "As you said, you are in no case to do much else yet, anyway. Otherwise, I shall have to encourage Townsend—or Leighton."

"George wouldn't do it," Lucien growled.

Kingsley shrugged. "A beautiful woman—a husband willing to be blind—are you quite certain?"

"What sort of man are you? You cannot just throw your wife at another man's head!" Again, he wished he'd not raised his voice, for now he nearly strangled from the cough. "No."

The old man smiled enigmatically. "The question, my dear Longford, is what sort of man are you? I had expected rather more from Mad Jack de Clare's son, I suppose." He started for the door, stopped, and turned back. "We both know what sort of man Townsend is, don't we?"

Long after the old man left, Lucien stared at the ceiling, telling himself he was so sick he'd imagined the whole thing. But he knew he hadn't. It was Arthur Kingsley who was sick—it was Arthur Kingsley who would push Elinor into Bell's all-too-willing arms. And he'd be damned before he let him do it.

HAD BELLAMY TOWNSEND been a praying man, he'd have asked first for Longford's immediate and total recovery, and second for an end to what seemed to be early and interminable rains. For despite his daily visits to Stoneleigh, she took him at his word that he meant to help with Lucien, and he seldom seemed to get Elinor Kingsley's undivided attention. It was beginning to wear on his temper. On this day, nearly three and one-half weeks since the earl had had the misfortune of nearly dying on Stoneleigh's doorstep, he not only was still there, but he did not appear anywhere close to leaving.

"Your move, Bell," Lucien murmured across the chess board. He sat back and waited. "You know," he chided, "I'd say neither your heart nor your mind is in the game."

"It's the rain," Bellamy muttered. He looked up resentfully. "Don't suppose as you've given any thought to removing yourself back to Langston Park?"

Lucien shrugged. "Beatty is against it."

"Country bonesetter!" Bell snorted.

One black eyebrow lifted. "If I did not know you better, I should suspect you see me as some sort of rival, old fellow."

"See you as a deuced dog in the manger!" Townsend leaned across the board and lowered his voice. "You've got no interest in that quarter, and you know it, but how the devil am I to pay court to Lady Kingsley when you are always about? Every time I suggest an entertainment to her, it seems I end up playing nursemaid to you," he observed with disgust. " 'I am sure Longford would enjoy that,' " he mimicked. He sat back and sighed. "Sorry—rain makes me out of reason cross, I guess. I know it's not your fault, but I don't seem to be any closer to fixing her interest now than before. And I didn't mind the pounding thing either, if it helped you." Having vented his frustration, he moved his queen.

"Quite certain you wish to do that?" Longford murmured, unperturbed.

"How the devil should I know? It's not my game. Now if you was to get out the dice—"

"You already owe me a thousand pounds this week," Lucien reminded him. "Check."

"I quit," Bell declared, disgusted. "Where the deuce do you think she is? Thought she meant to join us."

"I daresay she is attending to Kingsley." A faint smile twitched at the corner of the earl's mouth. "I believe she wished to give me the benefit of masculine companionship. She seems to think I must find being surrounded by females onerous."

"Kingsley!" Townsend fairly spat out the word. "How long can the old gent last, I ask you?" he demanded rhetorically. "A month ago he was out of his head."

"He seems to have recovered his wits," Lucien muttered dryly. "In fact, he comes to visit me."

"It's all of a piece, I suppose—like the Fates don't mean for me to have her."

"I suspect it's the pursuit that intrigues you, old fellow. If she fell into your arms, I daresay you'd be gone in a trice."

"Much you know of it. If we are speaking of constancy, I don't think you are noted for that either." Bell ran his hand through his blond Brutus, contributing to its fashionable disorder. "Thing is, I cannot stay with Leighton forever, you know."

"You could go back to London for the Little Season."

"And leave the field to you?"

"You have admitted I have no interest in that quarter," Longford reminded him.

"Daresay you could get one."

"I expect to be returning to the Park next week. Besides"—Lucien paused, waiting for Bell to react to that, then went on—"besides, I am not noted for seducing other men's wives, am I?"

Bellamy flushed. "Told you—got good intentions this time, Luce. If you was to get out of the way—"

The old man's words seemed to echo in Lucien's ears.

For all that he denied it, he'd thought often of Kingsley's suggestion. Indeed, but it was a good part of his reluctance to leave, but not for the reason the baron supposed. He knew if he went, the old man would encourage Bell. Before he returned to Langston Park, he supposed he would have to suggest to Leighton that Townsend had stayed overlong.

He rose and rubbed his still-tender shoulder. "I think I shall retire for a while, Bell."

That irked Bellamy also—while he cooled his heels waiting for Elinor Kingsley to favor him with her company, Longford ran tame in her house. And if Lucien went up, and she did not come down, he'd have to leave.

"Dash it, Luce! You go to bed, and I've got to go home in the rain!"

"Have you never thought that perhaps she finds your company onerous, old fellow? After the wager at White's . . ." He let his voice trail off meaningfully.

"Made it up with her and Kingsley," Bell retorted. "Sally Jersey saw to that." Realizing that the earl was indeed leaving him, he coaxed, "A hand or two of anything, Luce."

"My shoulder pains me." Lucien put his hand on the doorknob, then turned back. "The field is yours, Bell."

"In case you have not noted it, she's not down."

"I daresay you could wait."

Townsend wavered. "How long d'you think she'll be?"

"Well, I believe she is reading *The Iliad* to him."

"*All* of it?"

"As to that, I am afraid I cannot say," Lucien lied.

"Damn!"

The viscount sat staring at the chess board after Longford left. In all of his nine and twenty years, he'd never found a female yet that he could not bed. He had looks, wealth, style, and address, and he'd be hanged if he could tell that Elinor Kingsley had noted any of it. To give Longford his due, maybe he was right—maybe that was why he wanted her, maybe it was the difficulty of the chase. He was beginning to feel as though he were making a cake of himself over her, that maybe he ought to try a bit of indifference. Maybe Luce was right—maybe he ought to go back to London until she was done grieving over Charles Kingsley. If she had any interest in him at all, he'd leave word where she could find him.

A glance to the window told him what his ears had already heard—it was raining hard outside. He rose, sighing heavily, and called for his hat. If there was any consolation in the dreary day, it was that at least she could not be interested in a cold fellow like Longford.

Lucien heard the butler wish Bell a good day before the outer door closed. Stopping at Elinor Kingsley's door, he rapped lightly with his knuckles, then told her, "You can come out now, my dear—your swain is gone."

She opened the door sheepishly. "Is it that obvious?" she murmured. "And he is not my swain."

"Actually, I believe he aspires to be your *cicisbeo*."

"Don't be ridiculous."

That was one of the things he'd come to like about her—despite all that Kingsley had done to her, despite the extraordinary beauty she possessed, there was an utter naïveté about her—not a stupidity, but rather a desire to expect better of a man than she ought to.

She stepped out into the hall. "Actually, I do not mind Lord Townsend upon occasion."

"So I informed him."

"Well, I hardly think it *your* place to do so, my lord."

"Did you wish to?" he inquired, lifting one black brow.

"No, of course not. I could not."

"The difference between us, Lady Kingsley, is that I do not mind being unkind."

She looked up at him, regarding him almost soberly for a minute. "Perhaps it is that I know you now," she said softly, "but I should not count you unkind at all."

"Then you are a fool, my dear." As soon as the words were out of his mouth, he felt the greater fool for saying them. After all she'd done for him, she deserved better than that. "Your pardon—my unruly tongue."

"I daresay I have heard worse from you, my lord, so I shall not refine too much upon anything." She smiled faintly. "You forget—it was I as heard you rave and rant. You'd best have a care, you know, for I am possessed of your secrets."

"In truth, I don't think you a fool, Lady Kingsley."

"There is no need to dissemble with me, my lord."

Her smile broadened, dimpling her cheek at one corner. "Indeed, after London, I have had a surfeit of that." Impulsively, she held out her hand. "May there always be truth among friends, Lord Longford."

Even in her plain black mourning dress, with her hair combed about her shoulders as though she were a schoolgirl, she was incredibly lovely. He could almost curse Arthur Kingsley for insinuating that he could have more than friendship of her. Despite his best intentions to the contrary, it was beginning to affect his manner toward her.

When he did not take her hand, she dropped it awkwardly. She ought to have known better. Now that he was nearly recovered, she had no reason, no justification for touching him. Indeed, but he must think her quite forward. She felt a pang of regret, for she'd quite come to treasure the intimacy of sharing her thoughts once again with another human being, of being able to talk to him about Charley. In some ways, it was almost as though Charles had come home with him—and in some ways it was quite different. Where Charley had viewed the world expectantly, Longford seemed to expect nothing from it.

Damn Arthur Kingsley, Lucien reflected bitterly. He genuinely liked Elinor—in fact, she was the only woman of his memory he could say that about—and the old man had ruined it, making every word, every touch, every gesture seem to take on a different meaning in his own mind. If he'd done nothing else, the baron had given him thoughts that made him no better than Bell. Seeing her disappointment, he tried to retrieve the situation.

"Sorry. I guess Bell wears on my temper. Somehow having him nursemaid me leaves something to be desired."

"Oh, I suspect he means well enough," she conceded. "It's the rain that blue-devils us, I daresay." She started to retreat back into her chamber. "Perhaps we shall both feel more the thing before supper."

He did not want to let her go with the strain between them. "Well, if you are feeling low, I do not mind listening," he found himself offering.

She could no longer go to his sickroom with impunity, and she certainly could not invite him into her bedchamber. "I should not ask you to go back down."

"I don't mind—there's not much else to do."

Despite the nearly healed abscess, he was still weak from the lingering effects of the lung inflammation. As he started down the stairs, he experienced a momentary dizziness, and he stopped to hold the rail. She caught at his elbow, thrusting her slight body beneath his good shoulder to steady him.

"Perhaps you ought to be abed, after all."

"No." His good arm encircled her shoulder. "I am all right now."

"You are quite certain?"

"Yes." The faint smell of lavender wafted up from her hair, enticing him with the cleanness of it.

She felt his arm tighten, and she thought he feared to fall. "You can lean on me," she murmured, slipping an arm about his waist.

In all the days of his illness, after all the times she'd held him, lifted him, and tended him, it seemed to be the first time he'd noted how very slender she was. And then he recalled the feel of her body against his as she'd raised him to drink, and his mouth went dry. "I can manage," he told her curtly, drawing away. "I am too heavy for you."

The saloon where he and Bell had played chess was as gloomy as when he'd left it. She looked down, seeing pieces on the floor, then stooped to pick them up. "I collect he lost again?"

"What makes you think so?"

"Because you once told me you never play what you do not win. On the other hand, I suspect he is like Papa, and will play at anything."

"Not chess willingly."

"A pity."

"Do you play?"

"With Arthur. Though I cannot account myself very good at it," she admitted ruefully. Despite the grayness of the room, her amber eyes seemed to dance mischievously. "I much prefer whist, you see. When we were in London and Arthur was out, I played often with Jeremy, the lower footman."

"And won, no doubt."

"Well, I could have—but he had no money, so I pretended to lose often enough to let him win whatever he lost back.'' She looked out into the steady rain, then sighed. ''I daresay it will even rain on my birthday this year.''

''Arthur said it was this month.''

''Next week—the seventeenth, to be precise.'' She turned back. ''I shall be twenty. It's odd, but I feel ever so much older than that. Come December I shall have been wed five years.''

''It cannot have been much of a life for you.''

''You are the first to note it.'' She smiled and shook her head. ''The rest of the world seems to think I ought to be grateful for what he gives me.''

''There is a price to be paid for everything.''

''Oh, I have come to accept what I cannot change, my lord. I have learned what Arthur will and will not stand, what pleases him, what does not, what to wear, whom to acknowledge—''

''You acknowledged me,'' he reminded her.

''And he was not precisely pleased,'' she recalled. ''It's odd, but he seems inclined to tolerate you now. I suppose you must be coming back into fashion.''

''I would doubt that.'' He crossed the room to where the brandy decanter sat on a sideboard. ''Would you care for a glass?''

''Arthur does not approve of ladies partaking of much of anything beyond a light punch.'' Even as she said it, she felt a wellspring of rebellion within. ''He cannot abide a sotted female, he says,'' she continued impishly, ''so I think I might.''

''Good girl.'' He poured two glasses and held out one to her. Looking over the rim of his, he repeated her earlier words, ''May there always be truth among friends, Lady Kingsley.''

She sipped hers and nodded. ''It's strange, isn't it? You and Charley are the only friends I have had since—since I wed.''

He did not miss that she'd called Charles a friend. ''Surely not. What of Sally Jersey? Or Emily Cowper? My dear Lady Kingsley, even I have heard of your triumphs.''

''Fiddle. As if they care a fig for anything beyond their own consequence.''

''And their lovers,'' he reminded her.

"It's the way of polite society, is it not?" she countered acidly. "They promise devotion, then practice license."

She moved to take a chair in front of the empty fireplace. He carried the decanter with him and dropped into the chair opposite. "Poor Lady Kingsley—so very unfashionable in that respect, at least," he chided.

"Well, I cannot say I have truly had an offer—besides yourself, of course. And that does not count for I had not the least notion of what you were suggesting." Her amber eyes met his again over her glass. "And you did apologize for your mistake."

"There is always Bell," he said softly.

"Lord Townsend? No. Even if I were so inclined, I should not want a gentleman who could compare me with everyone." Then, realizing what she'd said, she colored. "That is—well, we were but speaking in theory, you understand. I'm afraid I'm not really suited to flirtation. I should probably hope for more than was there, you see." She finished her glass and stared for a moment into the empty fireplace. "No, if anything should happen to Arthur, I'm afraid I should be rather difficult to please. Silly of me, I suppose, but I still would wish for love."

He studied the dark liquid in the bottom of his glass. "I am not at all certain that there is any such thing."

The rain hit the windowpane like a spray of pebbles, sending a shudder through her. "Were it not so early in the month, I should wish for a fire to lighten the room. No doubt it's the gloom as makes for melancholia."

He shrugged. "As mistress of the house, I should suppose you can have what you like."

"Mrs. Peake would—" She stopped, then giggled like a conspiratorial schoolgirl. "No, you are quite right. We shall cook, no doubt, but at least we shall do so brightly." Reaching for the bellpull, she directed him, "Do pour me another glass, my lord—it's quite good."

Two more glasses of the brandy before a roaring fire, and she was feeling quite mellow. Kicking off her slippers, she drew her legs up beneath her into the chair. When she leaned forward, her hair fell over her forehead, and she had to push it out of the way.

"To friends," she declared, drinking what amounted to her fourth one down.

"And truth," he reminded her.

"And truth." She held out her glass again. "A pox on Arthur for his lack of compassion."

As weak as he was from his illness, he was beginning to feel the effects also. Nonetheless, he emptied the decanter, dividing the last of the brandy between them. "My dear Lady Kingsley, we are fast becoming foxed," he decided.

"Don't care. Hate being Lady Kingsley, you know," she confided. "Was always Nell, but he—he won't let anybody call me that."

"Nell." He stared at her for perhaps a minute, thinking what a lovely, appealing creature she was. Finally, he lifted his glass again. "To Nell." The word seemed to spill from his tongue easily. "It fits you."

"To Longford," she countered.

"Lucien."

"Sh—sounds French."

"It was. I think there was a Hugenot in the family somewhere."

Her manner changed abruptly. "Charley died fighting the French, you know."

"I know." Thinking to console her, he covered her hand with his. "He cared for you."

She pulled away and rose, going to stare out into the gray rain, saying nothing. He managed to pull himself up from his chair and moved to stand behind her. "He did care, you know," he said softly. "You have but to read his words to know it."

At that she burst into tears. "Charley loved me!" she choked out. "And I—I—"

"Nell—don't—"

"You—you don't undershtand! You don't understand!" She leaned forward, pressing her head against the cold panes. "I couldn't—couldn't tell him—"

As foxed as he was, he hurt for her. "Here now—" he whispered. "It's not—" His hands touched her shaking shoulders, stroking them lightly. "Nell, don't—"

She turned her face against his wound and sobbed as though a dam of tears had broken. Despite the physical pain in his own shoulder, he tried to comfort her. His hand smoothed her copper hair over her back, and his body tried to deny the feel of her breasts pressed against it.

"Shhhh—don't. Make yourself sick—" he mumbled thickly. "Nell, the boy loved you." He felt odd saying it, for he'd always believed love was nothing more than a myth. "It's all right, Nell—it's all right."

"No—" She shook her head against his shoulder, sending a sharp stab through it. "No—don't you see?—he loved *me*!"

"Make no sense." He tried to shift her to his other side, but she straightened up, raising brimming eyes. "Don't you see?" she whispered brokenly. "I couldn't tell him—I couldn't tell him! I couldn't let him know that I—"

"He knew—he *knew*. Sweeting, you have but to read—"

"What I did wasn't right—didn't want him to feel bad—" She stopped and tried to catch her breath. "I—I loved him—but—but not like he wanted!"

He caught both her arms, holding her back. "You cannot be blamed, Nell—it was not your fault."

She gulped. "I—I loved him like—like a brother! And—and he died for me! Lucien, he *died* for me!"

"It was a French bullet—you cannot be held accountable for that."

"No."

Flushing, Lucien half-turned to face Arthur Kingsley. "It isn't what you think," he growled.

But the old man was looking at Nell. Very carefully, as though he feared to fall, he walked slowly to face her, then stopped to lean, both hands on his cane. "No," he repeated. His gaze fell to the empty decanter. "Elinor," he said finally, "the blame is mine—and I have paid for it. If any sent him to his death, it was I." Looking to Longford, he exhaled heavily, as though admitting his own guilt had taken everything from him. "I'd ask you to help her upstairs, but you are in no case either."

Aware that she'd disgraced herself, that he must surely be displeased with her, she tried to compose herself. "I—I—"

"You are merely foxed," he said mildly. His bony hand touched her shoulder. "Do you want me to call Mrs. Peake?"

"No." Her nose was running and her face was wet. Heedless of either of them, she sniffed, then wiped her streaming eyes with the back of her hand. Trying to regain what dignity she could, she turned unsteadily, caught the arm of the chair for a moment, then walked in a decidedly irregular path toward the door. There she turned back. "I—I shall not be down to sup, I think."

Arthur Kingsley turned to Longford. "Somehow I had expected you to have a bit more style in the matter, my lord."

"I told you—it wasn't what you thought."

The old man ignored that. "And I told you I shall expect discretion. Disguising her with my brandy in my own house seems a bit indiscreet, don't you think?"

"Go to hell." Lucien towered over the baron, his hands clenched. "Go to hell," he repeated evenly. Then, with an effort, he walked carefully from the room.

Kingsley watched him go, then sank into one of the chairs before the fire. Nothing he could do would bring Charles back—nothing. For a long time, he sat there, staring into the red-orange flames. A litany of sins seemed to parade past him, the greatest of which had been his inability to know his son and grandson, and now in his old age, he was feeling the lack. It was as though he had known no one, and now there was none to care.

But if Elinor could be got with child, he'd have another chance. He'd know it had not been all for naught, that the wealth and power he'd gained would pass on, that there would be another Baron Kingsley at Stoneleigh. And this babe would be his in mind if not in blood. This child would be truly to the manor born, not some distant relation utterly unworthy of it.

His mind turned to the scene he'd just witnessed, and he felt a pang of regret for what he was doing, then consoled himself with the notion it would be worth it. One thing he knew—unless Elinor proved barren, the earl would provide the heir he wanted. For despite all Longford's protests to the contrary, Arthur did not doubt that he wanted her.

SHE'D NOT BEEN DOWN to eat, but then Lucien did not doubt she was sick from the brandy. He ought not have given her so much, he supposed, but there had been a shared, almost conspiratorial intimacy between them that he'd been loath to break. He lay there, staring through the darkness at a ceiling he could not see, wondering if she slept. He hoped so, for only sleep seemed to heal such pain as she'd betrayed earlier.

The rain had ceased, making the stillness almost oppressive. Willing his thoughts from her, Lucien forced himself to recall his father. There was scarce a breathing female on two continents Jack had not taken a run at, be she whore, serving girl, or lady, and he'd been damned proud of it. "Plucked roses from here to Philadelphia and back to Calcutta," he'd bragged. "That's what they're for, my boy." But there had been a cost—for all the admiration of his fellows, Jack had neither the love nor the respect of his wife and son.

Lucien closed his eyes, hearing again the whispers from his childhood. "She couldn't live with his roving eye, poor soul—it was laudanum, ye know." And Jack had not even had the decency to mourn her.

But were the women any better? For every "rose" he'd plucked, there'd been a willing female all too ready to yield it, all too ready to betray someone for the lies he told them. Like Diana. But Diana's betrayal had been before, and if he hated her for it, it was because she'd claimed she carried Jack's child. She'd wanted the title, the wealth, the name more than she'd wanted either of them, he supposed. And because she was supposed to be a "lady," he'd been forced to wed her when Jack could not.

Diana was as different from Elinor Kingsley as night

was to day. Tied to a cold, manipulative old man, living a sterile, empty life that held little joy for her, Elinor nonetheless clung to decency, using it as her shield.

But for all that he'd denied to Kingsley, Lucien knew he ought to be damned for his thoughts of her. Despite what he'd done when she'd come to his house in London, she'd fought for his life, she'd tended him as carefully as if he'd been a babe, asking nothing for it. It was for Charley, she said.

His mind relived those brief moments earlier, those moments when brandy had allowed her to give him a glimpse into the pain of her soul, and even now he hurt for her. He knew the pain of feeling responsible for what he could not feel.

Yet again he tried to force her from his consciousness and could not. He'd always been aware of her, but since the old man had offered her as though she were no more than chattel, Lucien's body tried to lead his mind. He could close his eyes and smell the lavender in her hair. He could lie there feeling her hands moving over his bare skin. He could feel her bright hair spilling onto his shoulder as she bent over him. And having held her, he could feel the softness of her woman's body, the press of her breasts against his chest.

If he did not leave Stoneleigh, he was going to be no better than Jack. The girl was fragile, nearly to the breaking point already, and he was the last thing she needed to complicate her misery. He owed her more than that.

If he'd not had so much brandy, he'd have taken enough laudanum to put himself beyond these thoughts that plagued him, but he dared not. Opium and distilled wine made poor partners, each seeming to intensify the effect of the other. Instead, he threw back his covers and rose to pour himself another brandy. If he had to, he'd drink himself insensate.

Somewhere down the hall, a door creaked and someone slipped softly over the carpet past his chamber. Then in the silence, there were light, almost muted footsteps on the stairs. He poured his brandy and carried it to the window. When he looked down, the lanterns on the portico were but haloed balls of yellow in the fog that had settled in after the rain. To his surprise, he heard the front door open, and he stared more intently, seeing a cloaked figure pass outside.

"What the devil—?"

For a moment, he was stunned, then he swore softly. She was in no case to be out there in the dark. He gulped his brandy, then dressed quickly, not bothering to discover waistcoat or jacket. If he did not hurry, she'd disappear into the fog, and he'd have no notion which way she went. It was wet and muddy out, the sort of weather that gave one consumption. He pulled on the knee boots he'd worn the day he'd come, and having no cloak, pulled a blanket from his bed and flung it over his shoulder.

He took the back steps two at a time, half-stumbling down them, coming out at the rear of the house. There was no sign of her—no sign of anything. Moving around to the front, he took down one of the lanterns and started across the wide expanse of lawn. In the distance, he could hear the wild roar of the sea as it rolled over the rocks, and he felt his stomach knot. It was no place to be in the foggy dark, not with the high, gray cliffs that plunged into narrow inlets frequented by smugglers. Fear seemed to clear his head, to pump strength into his body.

"Elinor! Elinor!" he shouted into the swirling mist. It was as though his words were swallowed.

Why would anyone, least of all a sensible female, be out on a night like this—or any night? And the answer, when it came to mind, did not bear thinking.

He cupped his hands, calling through them, "Elinor! Elinor! *Elinor*!"

He was dizzy from running, scrambling over the rocky land toward the sound of the sea. Visions of her broken body seemed to loom before him, forcing him on.

The moon was like a hazy beacon too weak to give much direction. Then he saw her. She was walking, her arms crossed against the damp chill, along the edge of the cliff. She stopped and looked downward into the churning sea. Not wanting to startle her, not wanting her to jump when she saw him, he dropped the lantern and came up to her from the side, then as she moved closer to the edge, he caught her, pushing her back, falling with her to the muddy ground.

"Lucien! What—?"

"You little fool! You damned little fool!" he shouted

at her, shaking both her shoulders until his fear ebbed. She stared at him, her eyes luminous, her expression one of total shock, then he enveloped her in his arms, holding her, rocking her against the wet earth. "It will pass—believe me, it will pass. Do you think this is what Charles would want?" Before she could answer, he pulled her closer, lying over her, twining his hands in her muddy hair. "Oh, Nell," he groaned, possessing her cold lips.

For a moment, she was bemused, then she clung to him, giving herself up to the exhilarating feel of his hard, masculine body against hers. Her hands moved over his shoulders, holding him, and she returned his kisses breathlessly, twisting beneath him, trying to get closer. And it was as though all the years of denial, all the years of yearning for someone to hold her were over.

He had never wanted anyone, never wanted anything as much as he wanted her now, and as her hands trailed fire across his damp shoulders, his body's need conquered thought. Pulling the blanket from his arm, he tried to spread it over the rough grass, all the while kissing her lips, her jaw, her ear.

His hot breath sent shivers of anticipation coursing through her, heating her blood despite the cold ground beneath her. As his mouth moved to the hollow of her throat, she arched her head, moaning, while every fiber of her being told her this was what she had been made for.

He forgot his resolve, he forgot the pain in his shoulder—everything was lost in his urgency to possess her. He rolled her onto the blanket, then slid his hand beneath her cloak to find the buttons at the neck of her nightgown, keeping his lips against her neck. When her hands came up between them, he brushed them away, croaking hoarsely, "Don't."

Somehow, he managed to get the neck of the gown open, to slip his hand inside. His palm brushed over a breast, tautening the nipple.

She gasped, for she'd felt nothing like this. Her eyes widened, then she squeezed them shut as though she would rather hide than stop him. His head moved lower, resting on her chest, as he turned his mouth to her nipple, teasing it with his tongue, sending ripples of pleasure through her. It was beyond anything she could have imagined. Her fingers caressed the thick black hair, opening and closing restlessly, as her head turned from side to side in the wet grass.

He tasted first one, then the other breast, as his hand moved lower, skimming lightly over her gown, tracing fire over her hip, her thigh, to the hem. Once again, his mouth possessed hers, eliciting a deep, hungry moan as she tried to move beneath him, to entice him with her body.

The gown came up, baring her pale legs, allowing his hand to move inside her thigh. When he found the wetness, he thought he would surely burst. He raised his head, trying to see her in the misty night, but her eyes were closed, her face damp either from fog or passion.

"Spread your legs around me, Nell," he whispered. "And kiss me."

"Just don't stop," she moaned, raising her lips to his. "Please."

With one hand holding her head and the other guiding himself, he took possession of her mouth and body at the same time. To his surprise, she stiffened as her body resisted momentarily, then he was inside, feeling the warmth of her close around him. Dimly, he realized she was a virgin, that he ought to wait, but he could not, as the feeling of her overwhelmed him.

She was being rocked, ridden, driven, pounded inside until she thought she could stand no more, and as the shock ebbed, she felt her own desire intensify. She cried out, begging him not to stop, and all the while she moved her hips, bucking beneath him, seeking a more complete union. She was hot, wet, and wanting with abandon.

He couldn't stop. He was going to explode. Grasping her hips with both hands, he held her as her body urged him home. He moaned loudly, then collapsed over her, exhausted, finally floating back to earth.

She felt the warm flood inside, and with it came the terrible realization of what she'd done. She didn't want to open her eyes, she didn't want him to see her.

After a time, he eased off her, but not before he saw her turn her head away. The passion was gone now, replaced by guilt. He knew he owed her more than this, that he had repaid her care with dishonor. And all the things he usually told his lovers were inadequate now, for even if he told her it was as good as he'd ever had, she'd probably think he lied.

She was utterly, completely mortified, thinking herself no better than the whore Arthur had called her. She wanted to cry, but somehow that would compound the humiliation she felt.

He rolled to sit, his back to her, giving her a chance to put her clothes back in order. "I'm sorry," he said simply.

Her throat tightened. He was sorry. "Why?" she managed to whisper, her face red in the dark. "Isn't that what men do to women?"

She had a right to be angry. He was angry with himself. "Nell—"

"No—I pray you will not make it worse, my lord." She managed to stand, pulling her gown down, and turned to button the neck. She could feel the warm trickle going down her leg. Pulling her cloak closer, she looked down at the foamy waves as they crashed over the rocks.

"I did not come for this," he said finally.

She crossed her arms over her breasts. "Why did you follow me?"

"I was afraid—I thought perhaps after what you said this afternoon that you meant to jump."

"No. Sometimes when I cannot sleep, I come to listen to the water."

"It's dangerous."

Her chin came up. "So Arthur says."

He picked up the muddy blanket and offered her his hand. "You still have my regard, Nell."

She didn't take it. Instead, she started walking back toward Stoneleigh. When he caught up to her, she seemed saddened. "I'm sorry I disappointed you," he offered her.

"No." For the first time since he'd had her, she met his eyes. "I disappointed myself."

They managed to get back into the great house undiscovered, but that was little consolation now. Whether Arthur Kingsley was apprised of the matter or not, it was going to be impossible to keep the servants from noting the laundry. At the bottom of the back stairs, he stopped.

"If you want, I will return to Langston Park tomorrow."

Her hand was already on the newel post. She turned back to him. "I think it would be best, don't you?"

Long after he heard her door close, he lay awake, cursing himself. Bell Townsend had been right—there was more of Mad Jack in him than he'd ever wanted to admit. And even if she forgave him, he knew that nothing with Nell Kingsley would ever be the same again.

She sat for a long time, her muddied cloak still pulled about her, staring from her bedchamber window into the thickening fog. She told herself that she hoped he left early, for she did not think she could face him in the morning. A sense of desolation settled over her, for now she'd lost not one friend, but two.

When she finally rose to clean herself up, she had only a bowl and pitcher of water to marshal against the mud. But she managed to rinse her hair, wash her face and hands, and wiped the unexplained blood and sticky seed from the inside of her legs. All the while, her mind accused her—he'd been *there*.

She'd given him that which he'd had no right to take. With the memory of what had passed between them came the nearly unbearable humiliation. She had not even the excuse that he'd seduced her, that he'd made her do that which she'd not wanted. Her own words echoed in her ears, reminding her that she'd begged him not to stop.

Finally, she went to bed to lay there, too awake to forget her shame in sleep. Instead, she closed her eyes, remembering the feel of Longford's arms around her, the intensity of his passion—the feel of his body inside hers. And the most shameful thing of all was that she knew she wished to feel it all again.

Although she'd not slept at all, she did not go down to breakfast, nor did she bid Longford farewell. She heard the carriage brought 'round, and she heard him tell Mary and Daggett goodbye in the hall. She even knew when he walked past her door, stopping as though he meant to knock, then finally going on. His booted steps took the stairs slowly, his voice carried from the foyer as he thanked Arthur and asked him to convey his "best wishes to Lady Kingsley." Then he was gone.

She rolled over onto her stomach and bit her knuckles to stifle the urge to cry. He was gone, leaving her once again with naught but Arthur.

"My lady—?" Mary entered the room and carefully closed the door after her. "His lordship said I was ter give ye this—and not ter tell yer husband."

"Go away," Elinor whispered.

"Aye." But before she left, the maid laid a folded piece of vellum on the pillow, then patted Elinor's shoulder sympathetically. "It's sorry I am ter see him go also," she murmured.

Elinor rolled over to sit and stared at the letter he'd left her. Finally, unable to stand it, she opened the sheet to read the bold scrawl.

My dear Nell,

There will never be any words capable of conveying my gratitude to you, for I know I owe you my life. And despite what you must now think, I'd have you know that you will forever have my highest, my most devoted regard. If there should ever come a time when you have need of a friend, I do pray that you will not hesitate to ask anything of me. I remain your obedient servant.

He had signed it simply "Luce."

That was it—nothing else. She read it again, thinking it sounded rather stilted, as though he'd felt he had to write it.

The door opened again, and this time it was Mrs. Peake come to inform her that before he'd left, "the earl had quite ruined one of the blankets."

"Yes."

The woman's gaze dropped to where Elinor had wadded her muddy, blood-spotted nightgown and thrown it onto the floor. Her eyes narrowed, making Elinor wish she could somehow disappear.

"That will be all, Mrs. Peake—Mary will attend to that," she said, not daring to look at her.

The housekeeper's mouth drew into a tight line, but she nodded, "As you wish, my lady."

No doubt before nightfall there would not be a soul in the house as did not know or at least suspect that she had been tumbling in the mud with Longford. It must surely be written on her face for all to see—"Lady Kingsley, for all the fine manners she has pretended to, is naught but a slut." She didn't want to face anyone, not now, not ever again. She pulled her covers up, covering her head, and turned to the wall.

There came an insistent tapping at the door, and for a moment, she considered ignoring it totally. But it did not cease, until finally she snapped, "Who is it?"

It was the last person on earth that she wanted to see. Arthur pushed open the door with his stick, then moved slowly to take a chair by her bed. Leaning forward, he lifted the sheet, waiting for her to turn to face him.

"Mary would have it that you are plagued with the headache, my dear," he murmured.

"Yes," she lied.

"Perhaps it was something you ate—or yesterday's brandy," he observed sympathetically. "In any event, I have ordered that you are not to be disturbed. A cool cloth—perhaps a cold collation for nuncheon later—and no doubt you will feel more the thing on the morrow."

"Thank you."

"You have worn yourself haggard nursing Longford, I'm afraid." He peered closer, taking in her reddened eyes. "He has left, you know."

"Yes."

"I made your apologies for you."

"Thank you." She clenched her hands tightly, wishing he would go away.

"And now that he has gone," he continued mildly, "I shall expect to return to the conjugal bed." She lay very still, wondering if he suspected also, but his next words dispelled it. "We both needed time to grieve, my dear. And Longford was so very, very ill, after all."

"It has been but two months," she managed, swallowing the revulsion she felt. "Charley—"

"Charles is gone, Elinor—and I cannot bring him back." He reached a bony hand to stroke her copper hair, smoothing it against her pillow. "I no longer blame you. After I read his journal, I could see it was boyish infatuation, nothing more."

She wanted to scream, to rail at him that she had no wish to speak of Charles, not now, not after what had happened with Longford, but she dared not. She could not let him know that she felt she'd betrayed what Charley had felt for her. She covered her eyes with the back of one hand.

"Please, my lord—my head aches until I can scarce think," she said.

"I quite understand your distress, my dear," he murmured, rising. "Until tonight, Elinor."

She held her breath as he walked past her soiled nightgown, but despite catching his cane in it, he did not appear to note it. It was not until he was safely out of her bedchamber that she dared to let it go.

Arthur was coming to sleep with her. It was a sort of justice, she supposed, God's punishment for what she'd done.

* * *

True to his avowed intention, Arthur sought her bed, not on the formerly customary Wednesday and Saturday night, but for a full week, until she found herself taking laudanum for sleep. And still there were times when she lay there, listening to his thin, reedy, whistling breath, thinking she was going mad. Times when he wrapped a bony arm about her, as though he sought the warmth of her body. Invariably, as she recoiled silently in her mind, she could not help thinking of Longford.

And the very memories that shamed her sent remembered heat coursing through her body until she ached while her sinful mind yearned for more. Sometimes, despite the wild, tumbling dreams of a drugged sleep, she'd waken, her body wet and hot with desire. It was as though, awake or asleep, she could think of naught else. The feel of him, the hardness of his body, the solid strength of his arms around her could not be forgotten, not when Arthur's thin fingers smoothed her gown over her hip, not when Arthur's wheezy breath sounded in her ears.

But if Arthur made her nights nearly unbearable, Bellamy Townsend did little more for her days. Almost as soon as he'd heard that Longford had removed himself back to Langston Park, the viscount had presented himself once more at Stoneleigh to pay her the lavish compliments of a lover. It was, she reflected wearily, as though he counted Arthur already dead and her a widow.

And it was not as it had been before—now she had a fair notion of what he was about. "Dear Lady, a kiss to treasure," he'd coax. But, when despite her protests, he'd stolen one, she felt nothing beyond an urge to struggle. As handsome, as well-muscled as he was, his presence could not replace Longford's.

For Bell, it was a novel experience, and one he could not like, for his inability to endear, let alone his inability to seduce, was wearing on him. He'd lost his touch, he told Leighton tiredly. To which his host had suggested a repairing lease somewhere else, pointing out the adage that absence was said to make a heart grow fonder.

He gave it one last try.

"Dearest Elinor," he began, possessing himself of her hands, "you behold a man besotted. Only say the word and I shall be the happiest man in England—I swear it."

"There are only two words I can think of," she answered, pulling away, "and neither seems quite proper."

"The only improper word is 'no,' " he insisted. "I should even count a 'perhaps' enough to sustain me."

"Lord Townsend," she retorted, betraying her asperity, "if you are asking me to wed, you are a trifle premature, for my husband is quite alive. And if it is something else, I shall count myself quite insulted."

"Elinor, I cannot wait! You are in my thoughts night and day," he protested. "Not since my salad days have I—"

"A-hem," Arthur coughed. When the younger man swung around guiltily, he fixed him with cold eyes. "Townsend, you are *de trop*," he said mildly. "Surely by now you must realize that Lady Kingsley neither encourages nor desires your company."

"Elinor—"

"Lord Townsend—Bellamy—" Drawing in a deep breath, she managed to look up at him. "I should always cherish your friendship, sir—but nothing more."

"It's Longford, isn't it?" he asked bitterly.

"Don't be a fool, sir," Arthur snapped. "She still mourns my grandson!" He lifted his cane, poking Bell with it. "I suggest you hang after someone else's wife. And a word to the wise—discretion, boy—discretion."

Bell looked to Elinor. "Until London."

"We are in mourning," Arthur answered for her.

It was not until the younger man had left, taking his wounded vanity with him, that the old man turned to her. "Two words, my dear?"

She sighed. "Yes."

"Perhaps and later?"

It was the first time she'd smiled since Longford left. She shook her head. "Go and away."

He caught her hand, lifting it to his lips, a totally uncharacteristic gesture for him. "My dear, your devotion honors me. I must surely be the most fortunate of men."

She eyed him suspiciously. "Bellamy Townsend is an unprincipled rake—I should be a fool to refine too much on anything he said, don't you think?"

"Most definitely." He looked outside, then sighed. "It rains again, and you are blue-deviled, aren't you?"

She started to deny it, then nodded. "Yes."

"Shall we say a game of piquet? A pound a point, perhaps?"

It also was not at all like him to put himself out to entertain her, particularly not since he hated cards, preferring the challenge of chess instead. "All right," she decided. Anything was better than sitting around, moping like a mooncalf over Lucien de Clare.

It was not until he'd dealt the pasteboards that he looked across the small table at her. "You miss him, don't you?"

There was no question who he meant. Not knowing where he meant to lead her, she considered pretending ignorance. "Yes," she answered finally.

"It was the common struggle." He discarded.

"What?"

"For his life, my dear—for his life. And now that he is nearly recovered, you miss that which has occupied so much of your time and thoughts."

"I don't—"

"You must not think I mind it," he went on. "Indeed, but I should not take it amiss if you were to pay him a call when the weather clears."

"Oh, I don't think—well, it's the country, and—"

"Precisely. There are not too many tattlers here." He met her eyes. "Your play, my dear."

It was always difficult to follow him, for one was never quite sure when he meant to close the trap. She tried to keep her voice light. "I am sure there is enough talk as it is, my lord, for he was here nigh to a month. You heard Lord Townsend, after all."

"An unfortunate guess—nothing more," he reassured her. "Do you good to get out of the house."

"Do you mean to go?"

"No. Leg pains me—stupid complaint." He threw down another card. "Take Mary."

"Actually, I had thought perhaps to go into Tintagel to order some black lace and ribbons."

"On your birthday? Surely not. Give Mrs. Peake a list and she may obtain what you need when she goes into the village for me."

She tossed down a card. "One birthday is very much like another, Arthur."

"Well, perhaps this one will be different. I understand that Mrs. Peake has ordered all your favorite dishes—even an apricot tart with raspberry sauce."

"You despise apricots, my lord," she reminded him.

"Ah, but it's not my birth anniversary, is it?"

She kept waiting for him to say something unpleasant, but he did not. Instead, when he tired of the game, he merely added up the points and paid off, taking a handful of guineas from his purse and pushing them across the table.

"I'm afraid I am not so good a player as Longford," he murmured.

It seemed as though every time he spoke with her, he mentioned the earl, until she thought she could not bear it. And every time, she had to appear disinterested, to sound noncommittal. Could he not see what he did? Could he not see she was afraid to even think of Longford? That Lucien's very name made her think of what they'd done?

"Yes," he said, putting away his purse, "I think it would be quite civil of you to call—and take Mary, of course."

THE SEVENTEENTH was a reasonably warm, pleasant September day. It was also the day she turned twenty. And yet for all that the household prepared to celebrate the occasion, she felt isolated, alone. She sat at her writing desk, trying to compose a letter to Charlotte, but it had been so long since she'd seen her sister, it was like writing to a stranger.

"Mrs. Peake is wishful of knowing if ye got yer list," Mary reminded her, interrupting her already elusive turn of thought.

"Tell her I have left it in the silver basket in the hall."

"It ain't like him to do it, you know," Mary added, shaking her head.

"Who?"

"Yer husband."

Elinor felt a brief irritation. "What is it that he's doing?"

"Gone with Mrs. Peake—said he favored a visit to the barber."

"For what? Daggett keeps him in trim. And I cannot think he wished to be bled."

"Like I said, it don't make sense." Mary moved to the wardrobe door and lifted out a gown. "Said you was to wear this when we go ter visit his lordship."

Elinor's fingers clenched, snapping the shaft of the quill. "I have not the least intention of calling on Lord Longford," she declared.

"It don't seem right—man ran tame here fer more'n a fortnight—and now it's as though he's fallen plumb off the earth."

"I doubt he feels much like being out and about," Elinor muttered.

"No—s'pose not. Then ye ain't wearing this?"

"No."

"Lovely day, ain't it?"

Elinor felt as though her nerves would shatter into pieces, leaving nothing of her sanity. She rose and went to the window. Below, the flowers still bloomed in the mildest of England's climates. It was sunny, as bright as summer almost, and when she looked across the wide expanse of parkland, she could see the jutting crags that rose above the sea.

"I think I should like to ride," she decided impulsively.

"Ye want as I should send down to Ned?" the maid asked.

"No. I think I'd like to go alone."

"Well, the air'd do ye good—no doubt about that—but his lordship ain't—"

"There are no smugglers out in the day."

"No, but—well, ground's rocky, ye know—ye could lose yer footing, and—"

"Just get a habit!" Elinor snapped. Contrite on the instant, she passed a hand over her face, apologizing, "Your pardon, Mary—I know not what ails me."

"Humph! It's the old man, if ye was ter ask me. Twenty and ye ain't—"

"I don't want to hear it! Do you think I like this life I lead? Well, I do not! But what am I supposed to do about it? Flirt with the likes of Bellamy Townsend? Poison Arthur? I am well and truly caught, Mary—well and truly caught!"

"Oh, madam—I did not mean—well, he ain't going ter last ferever, ye know."

"So my father told me—five years ago." Then, realizing what she'd said, Elinor sighed again. "Mary, I don't want him to die precisely. I—"

"Ye just wish he'd a-wed somebody else, don't ye?" the maid clucked sympathetically. "Aye, but then ye'd not be Lady Kingsley, would ye?"

One should not admit one's private thoughts to one's servants, but Elinor could not help it. "As if I ever cared for that, Mary—as if I ever cared for that. I should rather have been a—a *milliner* and had someone to love me!"

"Aye, I know. Me—I wish we was back in Lunnon. I got me eye on Jem."

"Jem?"

"Jeremy. Ye know—the one as was at St. James Market with ye. The day that Longford—"

"Yes," Elinor muttered, cutting her short. "I remember it."

"Well, he ain't no older'n me, ye understand, but we like each other well enough." The maid colored, then looked down at her feet. "Oh, ye don't have ter worry about no babes—I told him I was a-wanting to wed first, ye understand." As she spoke, she shook out a black riding habit trimmed with black braid. It was rather austere, but when one was in mourning, there was not a great deal of style. And for all Elinor cared, it could have been a black sack.

Once she had it on and Mary had fastened the frogs across her chest, she viewed herself in the cheval mirror. She looked more hagged now than when Longford had been so very ill. Longford. The man was everywhere within her thoughts. She sat, letting the maid brush her hair and twist it into a knot on her crown.

"Was ye wanting the hat with the turned-up brim?"

"It doesn't matter."

"Well, it becomes ye, I think—frames yer face, ye know, and the veil ties around it right nicely."

"I told you—it doesn't matter."

Mary placed the hat over her hair, taking care not to loosen it, then pulled the veil down and tied it at the back of her neck. "Aye—it becomes ye," she decided, satisfied.

"I look like a woman trying to hide."

"Nay, ye look real mysterious—like one o' them females in the novels."

"There are times when I feel like a Gothic heroine," Elinor admitted. "Sometimes I think there is nothing else as can go wrong in my life."

"Ye riding ter the sea?"

"No." Elinor took a deep breath, then exhaled fully. "I am going to see Charley."

For a moment, the maid's face betrayed her alarm. "But he's dead!"

"The cemetery. Why must you and Longford assume I mean to throw myself off a cliff?"

"Oh. Well, it don't seem like the place ter go, but—"

"It is quiet, and no one prattles there."

She ought not to have said that, she ought not to have said a lot of things, but she was out of reason cross. It was not until Ned, the stable boy, brought her smart little bay mare to her that her mood lightened. Air—she was going to breathe the air. And for a little while, she was going to forget Longford.

The path to the cemetery was rocky and narrow, cut deeply by centuries of use, and the small stone church stood as it had since there were Plantagenets on the throne. Mignon picked her way down the steep lane, then stopped at the gate.

Elinor dismounted, tied her horse to the iron grating, then let herself into the churchyard. Despite the sun, the spreading branches of a tree that had been used to hang cavaliers on during Cromwell's war cast shadows over the moss-covered stones. She walked slowly among the graves, taking the long way around to the brown, still-soft earth that covered Charles.

She stared down, trying to weep, trying to feel, but she was empty. Finally, she dropped to her knees and began to talk to him, speaking at length of things they'd shared, of dreams, of laughter, of a common defense against Arthur's coldness, until the words tumbled out, one over the other, so rapidly that she scarce made sense.

"I read the journal, Charley—every word. I read it over and over," she said finally. "And I thank you for it." She sucked in her breath, this time trying not to cry, and went on, "Thank you for loving me, Charley. Thank you for standing with me." The tears began to flow, trickling at first, then streaming freely down her cheeks. "I did love you—I did," she whispered, choking. "But not as you asked. You said—you said I didn't have to say it—that I didn't have to promise. You said it was enough if I cared. And I did—Charley, I did! And—and no matter what happens, you are forever in my heart."

The wind moved the leaves, rattling them softly, making the shadows dance over the spaded earth. "Maybe if you'd held me—maybe if you'd kissed me more—if I'd known sooner—" She stopped. She was doing it again—she was telling him what he'd always wished to hear. "No," she admitted sadly. "You are—you were—my friend, Charley. Always my friend.

"It's funny, isn't it? I guess there are different ways to love. If you'd come back, I'd have had to tell you, you know. But I know what you felt. I know what you felt, for I feel it now also. I—I think I love Longford, Charley—and I cannot. I cannot!"

"Here now, missy—it don't do no good talking to the dead." She looked up, startled by a man's voice. "The dead don't answer, 'cause they can't hear." It was one of the men who'd buried Charles. He tamped a lump of earth with a heavy, dirty boot. "Best go on—got another one to dig."

"Who?"

"The Barrett boy. Fell off his horse—banged his leg bad."

"His leg?" she asked incredulously. "I never heard of anyone dying from such a thing."

He nodded. "Turned bad—poisoned him." He walked closer, and she could smell sweat and smoke on his clothes. It was obvious that he did not recognize her. "Guess you heard about the earl, eh?"

Her heart nearly stopped. "The earl?"

"Longford."

"No—what?" she asked cautiously.

"Nearly died—guess they didn't get all the bullet."

"Oh." Relief flooded through her. For a moment, she thought something else might have happened to him. "Yes, I know, but he is recovering."

"Glad to hear of it."

He moved on, leaving her alone again at Charles Kingsley's grave. And it was as though she could hear Charley speak, she could hear his enthusiasm when he'd seen Longford at Hookham's. Charley'd idolized him.

She walked back to where she'd left her horse and mounted it, draping the skirt of her habit over her knee. Leaning forward slightly, she brushed the dirt and dead grass from the black cloth, then she nudged Mignon forward, wishing fervently that some long-distant queen had not brought the darned sidesaddle to England.

She couldn't say she felt good, but at least she felt better. She'd had the chance to say the goodbye that everyone had denied her.

The breeze blew through the black veil, drying her

tears. That part of her life was over. But not forgotten. Never forgotten.

She was probably a terrible fool, but when she'd told Charley that she thought she loved Longford, she'd meant it. Even now, she had but to think of him to remember everything about him—the way his black hair lay wetly against his forehead when his fever broke, the beautiful, nearly perfectly chiseled features, the strong, well-defined chin, the size of him. But most of all, she could feel his body against hers, she could remember the way he'd made her feel when he'd kissed her. And she wished fervently that Fate had been kinder, that somehow Longford had not been wed when her father had thrust her into that inn room those years ago.

She wanted what other women had—she wanted someone to love her in mind and body and spirit. She wanted someone to hold and someone to hold her—and she wanted that man to be Longford.

She looked up, seeing the road that divided between Langston Park and the village of Bude. And on impulse she took the side she knew she ought not to take. She was frightened, armed only in her fragile pride. It was not until she was within the gates of the Park itself that she wanted to turn back. But she was too late—he was standing on the wide portico with someone—and he'd seen her.

She raised her hand in salute, then reined in. It was George Maxwell—Leighton—who came to dismount her.

"Lady Kingsley—what a pleasure."

But the earl was watching her quizzically, his black eyes betraying nothing beyond curiosity. She wanted to run and had nowhere to go.

"I—uh—Mignon stepped on a rock—and I—I thought she might be going lame." It sounded stupid even to her own ears, for they'd seen her ride up. She looked to Longford. "I thought perhaps you might send me home in your carriage."

Leighton smiled, then offered gallantly, "Happy to take you up myself. First time I've had a decent conveyance since Bell came—took himself off this morning, by the by."

"No." Longford spoke curtly, his eyes still on Elinor. "I'd have somebody look at her horse."

"Send it home later," Leighton suggested.

She wiped damp palms on her skirt and shook her head. Her heart was pounding in her throat. "No—if she is all right, I suppose I ought to ride her. I just thought—"

"Yes, well—happy to, you know. Got to run—promised Wilmington I'd stop in. He couldn't abide Bell, I'm afraid, but I suspect it was more that he thought Lady Wilmington could." As he said it, he winked at Lucien, who did not respond at all.

Lucien waited until Leighton's carriage was halfway down the drive before he said anything to her. "You might as well come in and have a glass of punch." The familiar, faintly derisive smile that had haunted her for five years played at the corners of his mouth. "If the horse is not lame, I'm sure it needs a rest."

He held the door for her, and she walked past him, every fiber of her body seemingly aware of just how close and yet how far away he was. He stopped long enough to inform a footman to send to the stables for someone to look at "her ladyship's horse, which may be going lame," then he opened another door, this one to a comfortable saloon. He waited only until she was inside, then he closed it carefully.

As pale as she was, she was still the most beautiful creature of his memory. For a moment, he merely wanted to drink in the sight of her. His eyes met hers soberly. "I'm honored, Lady Kingsley."

And once again she thought he mocked her. She swallowed hard, trying to stifle the awful fear that threatened to overwhelm her. While he watched her, she reached to untie her veil and remove her hat, letting it drop to the floor.

"You must wonder why I have come," she began, scarce hearing her own voice for the pounding in her ears.

"Yes." His expression grew wary. "You cannot accuse me of anything I have not accused myself." He turned to ring for the punch.

"Please don't." She swallowed hard, her throat aching, and her chest seemed almost too tight for breath. She waited until he swung around to face her, then she dared to meet his eyes. "You see, I—I am here because I need someone to hold me. I—"

She got no further. He was there in the instant, and his arms closed around her with an eagerness that matched her own, and he buried his face in the knotted hair on her crown. "Nell, Nell—" he whispered, his voice sending a shiver down her spine, "I've scarce thought of anything else." He stood there, holding her closely, savoring the feel of her.

"I—I don't want you to let me go, Lucien," she choked, clinging to him as though he were life itself.

He could almost feel her pain, and he knew what it had cost her to come. While he still had resolution, he tore her arms away and pushed her back that he could look at her. "Do you know what you do?" he demanded harshly. "Do you know what you are wanting?"

She nodded. "More than anything in my life, Luce."

His hands were in her hair, tugging at the pins, hurting her, and she did not care. She raised her head, parting her lips for his kiss. And as his mouth crushed hers, possessing it, liquid fire coursed through her veins once more, and the wanting, the yearning was nearly unbearable. His hands were everywhere, twining in her half-undone hair, moving over her shoulders, holding her, pressing her, molding her against him, smoothing the skirt of her habit over her hips. Abruptly, he broke away, his dark eyes black with passion, his breath ragged, uneven.

"Are you sure?"

"Yes."

He caught her hand, pulling her toward the door, looking for servants. Seeing none, he hurried her up the back stairs and halfway down the carpeted hall.

Although his bedchamber had an elegance to match Arthur's, she would be hard-pressed later to remember any of it. He stopped only long enough to turn the key in the lock, then he faced her, his chest heaving, and she felt suddenly shy.

"Your—your wound," she managed through parched lips.

"If I did not take consumption last week, nothing will hurt it." He moved closer, his eyes on hers, and his hands reached for the frogs that closed the front of her habit. "I'd see you, Nell—all of you." When she stood there woodenly, he smiled crookedly. "What did you think—that it would be groping in the dark again?"

"No—no, but—"

"It is how it is meant to be, Nell," he said softly, unhooking the braided frogs.

As his hands moved down her chest, she thought she would shatter into pieces. He worked slowly, as though he did not know the urgency within her. As the jacket came open, he pulled the lawn waist up, baring the zona beneath. He bent his head deliberately to nuzzle pink-tipped breasts, and to her embarrassment, her nipples tautened.

"Please—"

But his fingers already worked the laces of the zona that pushed them up, and as his mouth returned to hers, the band slipped to the floor. This time when he kissed her, his urgency matched her own. He unfastened the skirt and untied the half-petticoat, pushing them down. She was standing there, her body bare except for her open jacket and her riding boots, and then he was holding her, his flesh warming hers through his clothes, his mouth moving hotly from her mouth to her ear.

With one arm still around her, he began removing his clothes, unbuttoning his breeches, freeing himself, and she felt the heat of him against her skin, and it no longer mattered what he saw of her. She clung to him eagerly, demanding more of him as he rubbed against her.

He'd meant to wait, to teach her how it could be, but the heat between them was consuming him. Abruptly, he lifted her and carried her to his bed, where she sank back into the deep feather mattress. His hands worked feverishly now, removing her boots and the rest of his clothes, then he followed her down, pressing her deeper with the weight of his body, and waited no longer.

She felt him slide between the wetness, this time with ease, and her legs closed around him as he ministered to the ache deep within her, stroking, driving as she moaned and panted beneath him, scarce able to stand the intensity of what he did to her. She lost all rational thought as she writhed and bucked, her whole body hot, sweaty, and demanding, every fiber of feeling centered where he stroked.

"Cannot wait," he panted, matching her rhythm. He groaned loudly, drove harder until he shuddered, and she felt the pulse of his seed, then it was over. He lay above her, his weight resting on his elbows, his head on the twisted lawn waist above her breasts. When she started to pull away, he drew one arm up to hold her there. "Don't," he murmured. "Not yet."

She could feel him shrink within her, she could feel the warm, sticky liquid oozing between them, and still he did not move. When she opened her eyes, all she could see was the ruffled black hair, and she felt a measure of contentment. For the moment, for now, he was hers.

Finally, as his breathing evened out, he eased off her and pulled the covers up over them. She swallowed hard and twisted her head away. "What you must think me," she whispered, stricken.

"Shhhhhh." His fingers moved over her mouth, silencing her. "Let us take what we can without regret."

"It's a sin."

"God loves the sinner as much as anyone," he countered, drawing her into the crook of his arm. "And God knows there is little enough happiness in this world for either of us."

"Do you think He cares?" she managed to ask, turning into his good shoulder.

"No." His hand stroked her tangled hair where it spilled over the covers. "He is too consumed with Bonaparte to spare a thought for this."

For a time, they were silent, and he lay there, savoring the feel of her against him. It was odd, for they all were possessed as Jack would have put it crudely, "of the same holes," but somehow he wanted this one to be different. He wanted this one to mean something. Maybe it was that he owed her his life, but he really believed he could care about her.

She stirred slightly, and he looked down. "I ought to—that is—" Her face reddened and she mumbled something about cleaning herself up. But he didn't want her to leave him.

"We're not done," he decided.

She couldn't meet his eyes. "I cannot be gone forever."

"What day is it?" he murmured.

"The seventeenth—my birthday."

"Your twentieth, as I recall."

"Yes."

He rolled over to brace himself on his good arm and faced her, grinning boyishly. "Then I'd say I owe it to you to make it worth remembering." His fingertip traced a circle around one bared nipple. "Though I take leave to warn you that the second time never goes quite as quickly as the first."

She squirmed as it hardened. "Surely you do not mean to—?"

He nodded. "By the time you are returned to Stoneleigh, madam, you will be quite sated." Before she could protest, he bent his head to hers, tasting again of her lips. "I don't mean to send you home until you have howled, Nell."

Her eyes widened. "Surely not."

"Howled," he repeated definitely, his hands moving to ease her jacket from her shoulders.

"Your wounds—"

"My wounds be damned. I'd rather be doing this than anything."

HER HAT COVERED the ineptness with which Longford had pinned her hair, and the veil hid her swollen lips. Nonetheless, when she dismounted at Stoneleigh and the groom led Mignon away, Elinor was afraid that any who saw her would know what she'd been doing. She slipped around to the back of the house, hoping to take the back stairs up, but Arthur was coming out of his bookroom and spied her.

"Enjoy your ride, my dear?" he inquired mildly.

She felt the blood rush to her face. "Yes."

"It was a pleasant day for it."

"Yes. Yes, it was." She had her hand on the stair post, ready to flee, hoping he'd ask no more.

"You must be careful—there have been smugglers afoot again," was all he said.

"I saw the royal revenuers," she lied, hoping that would satisfy him.

"Then I daresay you were in no danger."

"No." She started up the stairs. "I'd bathe before we sup, my lord."

"I hope you do not mind it, but I have invited guests. Nothing improper as we are in mourning, but I thought perhaps you would wish to share your birthday with the vicar and his wife."

She wanted to escape, to seek the solitude of her bedchamber, where she could relive every moment of lying in Longford's arms. "Yes," she said simply.

"And I have asked Leighton."

She stopped. "Leighton?"

"You have perhaps taken him in dislike?"

"No—of course not—not at all."

"We passed his carriage near Wilmington's."

She felt taut, as though somehow he *knew,* but that was absurd, she reassured herself. "Oh?"

"Now that Townsend is gone, he's about more."

"Yes."

"By the by, Mrs. Peake has your ribbons and laces for you. In fact, I believe she has given them to Mary."

"I thank you for getting them."

"It was nothing—the merest inconvenience, I assure you. Well, you run along up—best make yourself presentable before they come."

She climbed the stairs thankfully, glad to be away from him. She waited until she was safely in her bedchamber before untying her veil and removing the brimmed hat. One side of her hair came loose, falling over her shoulder, as she tossed the hat aside. Crossing the room, she peered anxiously into the mirror, trying to see if anyone could tell what she'd done, then she rang for Mary.

"I'd have a bath," she said quickly, turning away. "And I can undress myself."

Later, as she soaked in the scented water, she stared down at her breasts, feeling again the sensation of Longford's mouth, of his tongue and teeth teasing her nipples. She leaned back, remembering it all, thinking she did not believe there had been an inch of her body he'd not explored. And for the first time in her life, she felt utterly complete.

Tomorrow, he'd said. Meet him again tomorrow just past noon. As though she could somehow stay away. His hot breath against her ear seemed to whisper again, "If it rains, I will take you up in my carriage. If not, I'd meet you where the road goes to Bude." And now she wondered what she could tell Arthur, what excuse she could give him to be gone again.

Guilt washed over her. And yet she wanted what Longford did to her enough to lie, to dissemble, to do whatever she had to to be with him again. It was more than that she wanted it—it was that she needed it. The physical union, no matter how wrong, made her somehow whole.

Slowly, lethargically, she soaped the cloth and began to wash, to destroy any trace of the earl she'd carried back. Her whole body felt languorous, as sated as he'd promised. She dipped lower with the cloth, washing between her legs, recalling the feel of him there, and the newly familiar weakness made her want to know that again . . . and again . . . and again.

"His lordship will not like it that ye are lingering at yer bath," Mary reminded her, pulling her back to the present.

"I was woolgathering."

"Aye, but he said to remind ye of the company, that he'd have ye come down first."

She dressed quickly, and the maid braided her hair, twisting the plait into a copper crown. And when she went down the wide staircase, the black taffeta of her mourning gown swishing against her petticoat, Arthur awaited her in the hall. Apparently he viewed this birthday somewhat different from the others, for he'd gone to the formality of donning knee breeches, dressing much as he'd done for Almack's. He bowed over his cane, nodding approvingly.

"You are one of the few black becomes, my dear," he murmured.

"Thank you."

"A bit of madeira before dinner?" he offered, leading her into the formal front saloon.

"Yes." She felt stiff, awkward before him, as though he must surely tell what had happened by looking at her.

He handed her the glass. "To you, my dear."

And once again, the stab of guilt was nearly unbearable. She averted her eyes as she sipped. "To you also, my lord," she murmured over the rim.

He set his glass aside and reached into his coat pocket, drawing out a velvet pouch, from which he shook out a necklace of cut black beads. "Obsidian," he murmured. "It ought to be diamonds, but because of—"

"Yes," she said quickly. "It's lovely—and I have enough of the other for ten females."

"I'd put it on you."

She leaned over obediently, feeling his long, thin fingers on her neck, and she did not think she could stand his touch. Not after Longford. He fastened the clasp and stood back to admire the effect.

"Quite lovely, my dear—had I known it would show your skin to such advantage, I should have bought it sooner." The back of his hand brushed against her face.

"But you ought to pinch your cheeks, Elinor, for in your grief, you've grown pale."

He always seemed to hold her at a disadvantage, a sort of game he played. "In my haste, I forgot to have Mary apply the rouge pot," she explained. "If you would, I—"

"No, no. Mrs. Thurstan will no doubt like you better without it."

It was going to be a long evening, for the vicar's wife was a sad prattle, forever going on about people Elinor had never heard of. It was a wonder to her that Arthur had invited them, for she did not think he could abide Eliza either. She cast a quick sidewise glance at him, knowing he did nothing without a purpose.

"You surprise me, my lord."

"One never knows when one will need the service of a churchman," he observed obscurely.

"As I recall it, you once told me the only purpose to the clergy was to preside at the 'hatching, matching, and dispatching.' " Her eyes met his once more over her glass. "At the moment, I should not say we are in need of any of those services."

"One never knows."

"A month ago, I would have given you up, Arthur," she admitted, "but you seem to have recovered."

"As have you."

Once again she felt the stab of guilt. But it was not that she did not still mourn Charles—what she felt for Longford was vastly different from what she'd shared with Charley.

"I considered inviting Longford."

She nearly choked.

"But," he went on smoothly, "his health is such that I did not expect him to make the journey back so soon."

"I did not know you liked him."

His eyes seemed to pierce hers for a moment, sending a chill down her spine. "I like him quite well now that he is more received, Elinor. The point is—do you?"

Her fingers tightened on the stem of her glass, but she managed to answer casually, "One cannot struggle for a life and not care about it, I suppose. Yes, I like him well enough."

"More than Bellamy Townsend?"

"Definitely more than that," she answered.

"Good. Townsend has led more than one female to grief, I am told." He turned to pour himself more madeira. "What think you of George?"

"George?"

"Maxwell—Leighton."

"He seems quite kind."

"Kind men are rather boring, don't you think?"

Once again, she felt the chill and wondered where he led her. "Well, as I scarce know him, Arthur, I cannot tell."

"I was just wondering if perhaps you could find him worth knowing," he murmured. "The bloodline is good, you know—although it is Scots," he added, betraying a hint of prejudice.

"If you are asking if I could flirt with Leighton, my lord, you are wide of the mark," she declared. "He is the sort of man one ought to marry."

"Oh?"

"Kind, considerate, and mildly amusing."

"And rich."

"And rich. But I am scarce in the market for another husband—unless you are hiding some dread illness from me," she said lightly.

"No. In fact, I have never felt better, my dear."

"The Reverend and Mrs. Thurstan," Peake announced somberly.

That lady hurried to Elinor, clasping her familiarly, brushing a chaste kiss against her cheek. "Oh, my dear—twenty today! Tell me, Edwin," she murmured, turning to her husband, "but does she not appear quite—"

"Ravishing," he supplied for her, drawing her frown. "Under the circumstances," he added quickly.

The woman wore a purple dress, but out of respect for their mourning, she'd added black ribbons at the sleeves and a pair of black lace gloves. "I still cannot get over—so very young—so—"

"Harumph!" The vicar cleared his throat, cutting her off. "Twenty, eh? Cannot recall the age myself, but—"

"George, Viscount Leighton!" Peake reported from the doorway.

"Well, had I known you meant to come, my lord, I should have brought Clarissa," Mrs. Thurstan tittered.

''But then I should suppose not, for the girl is quite in awe of you.''

''Tongue-tied,'' her husband muttered.

''Of me?'' Leighton asked, lifting a brow. ''Are you quite certain it's not Longford?''

''Longford!'' the woman sniffed. ''Certainly not. He may be redeemed in some eyes, but not in mine.''

''Eliza—''

''Oh, I know he was here for an age, but I count that quite different, for under the circumstances, dear Lady Kingsley could not turn him away. But I quite felt for you, my dear—truly I did. It was a Christian thing you did, nursing a man of his stamp,'' she told Elinor. ''I am not at all sure I could have done it.''

''Dash it, the man was dying!'' Reverend Thurstan protested. ''Christian feeling—''

''Well, dear Lady Kingsley does not have a daughter to protect, Edwin. I should not wish him in the same house with Clarissa or Phoebe—or Cassandra even.''

''Cassandra is but five,'' he reminded her. ''I hardly think—''

''One never knows what a man like that will do,'' she retorted. ''And I cannot say but what I breathed more easily when he left Stoneleigh. Now if he would but take himself off to London where he belongs—''

''Dash it, Eliza, but he nearly died for this country!''

''I found him quite agreeable,'' Arthur murmured, taking Elinor's arm. ''Did you not also, my dear?''

''Charming,'' Elinor agreed. ''Or I should say as charming as he could be under the circumstances.''

''Got as much a right to be in Cornwall as any of us,'' George declared. ''Owns Langston Park.''

''But he was not *born* here,'' Mrs. Thurstan insisted, then recalling that Leighton was an exceptionally eligible bachelor who'd come from elsewhere also, she hastily tried to retrieve the situation. ''Of course that is not to say that one must be—there are circumstances where one is welcomed—yourself, for instance.''

Elinor had had enough. ''I collect the difference is that Lord Leighton is possessed of a considerable fortune?''

''Dash it, I haven't any more than Longford!'' he protested. ''Less, more likely.''

"Ah, but you have not had the misfortune of a scandal not of your making, have you, sir?" she countered.

"Got the truth of that. Fellow's paid for—"

"One cannot pay for a divorce," Mrs. Thurstan said stiffly. "And I understand there is a child."

"Eliza—"

Thinking to turn the subject to safer ground, George addressed Elinor. "I trust there was nothing serious wrong with the horse?"

"Uh—"

"What horse?" Mrs. Thurstan demanded curiously.

"Lady Kingsley's horse appeared to be going lame earlier today."

"Where was that, my dear?" Arthur wondered. "I thought you rode her in."

"Actually, she'd stepped on a rock, and I merely feared it," Elinor managed. Not daring to look at Lord Leighton, she added, "It was on the road between here and Bude."

The viscount betrayed nothing. "Offered to take her up, you understand, but she thought the animal could make it home."

"Oh, my dear, but you must take a groom with you!" Mrs. Thurstan declared. "Think of what you might have encountered! I declare that with the Earl of Longford about, I cannot think any female safe!"

"You forget she nursed him to health. I daresay he would not repay her with any impropriety," the vicar said. "Myself, I should rather have worried over Lord Townsend."

"Naught's wrong with Lord Townsend. Indeed, but Clarissa was quite taken with him"—she looked to Leighton before adding meaningfully—"also."

"Every female seems taken with Bell," Leighton murmured. "Save one."

"It seems to me," Elinor said evenly, "that there is something amiss when one man is forever punished for divorcing his errant wife, while the man who led her astray is received everywhere."

"Just so," Thurstan agreed, nodding. "Long thought so myself."

"What an innocent you are, my dear," Eliza said. "Lord Townsend—"

"Dinner, my lord," Peake announced.

The evening seemed interminable, a poor social mix, with Mrs. Thurstan having an opinion on nearly everything, taking off on a new tangent every time Leighton tried to divert her. Before the evening was done, there was not a doubt in the room as to where she stood on the Whigs, the Prince Regent's reprehensible behavior to his wife, the decadence of the London Season, the importance of cold baths for children, the latest cough remedy, the efficacy of lint as a chest warmer, the war, the cost of lace—until Elinor sat there, utterly irritated, wishing fervently that Reverend Thurstan could be brought to take his wife off early.

Finally, the last course had been served, a final toast offered for "many long years of health and happiness" to Elinor by Lord Leighton, and it was over. At the doorway, as he was leaving, the viscount possessed her hand, and for a moment Elinor considered thanking him for not betraying her. Instead, she merely thanked him for coming.

It was not until she was abed that she thought to pray that Arthur would not come up. But as she lay in the darkness, listening to the steady ticking of the ormolu clock she'd forgotten to stop, she heard the door open, and she did not think she could bear it, not this night.

But he was there. There was the rustle of his dressing gown as he removed it, then the bed creaked beside her. She lay very still, hoping he would think she was asleep. He rolled over against her, and to her horror, he moved his hand over her hip, gathering her gown, pulling it upward. She flinched.

"I'd feel you, Elinor," he said, his voice raspy.

She caught at his hand. "No," she whispered. "No."

But he shook free and his hand slid beneath the hem of her gown to the bare flesh underneath. "I'd just touch you—nothing more."

Not since her wedding night had he done this, and she felt the revulsion rise, nearly choking her. Willing herself to lie stiffly beneath his hand, she felt his fingers touch the softness between her legs, stroking the hair. She swallowed, hoping he meant to do no more, but he probed inside, violating the place where only Lucien had been. She was afraid she was going to vomit, but his finger explored, going deeper.

"Please, I'd not—"

Abruptly, he withdrew his hand and lay back, satisfied. He'd had his answer. She was still the vessel of his ambition. He'd give them a month, possibly two, but no more than that.

IT WAS AS THOUGH the weather conspired against her. She stared out the window, seeing the blowing rain scatter the last of the rose petals across the cobbled walk. She crossed her arms, holding herself, wondering what had become of her. Was she so wanton that she could think of naught else? What if he did not come because of the weather? And what if he did? She could scarce bring him up to her chamber, not beneath Mrs. Peake's and Arthur's very noses.

One day of lying in Longford's arms, and she was utterly, completely obsessed with him. One day and he'd opened a whole new world to her, showing her what pleasure her own body could give her beneath his touch. One day and she was prepared to tell whatever lie, practice whatever deception it took to spend another like it. It was as though after five years of lying beside Arthur, of being denied any physical or emotional satisfaction, she'd come alive beneath Longford.

Mary came up behind her and looked out the window. "Well, ye ain't going ter be riding terday," she observed practically.

"No."

"Look a bit hagged. Mayhap if ye was ter go back ter bed—"

"No. I did not sleep much last night, but I am awake now."

"It ain't right—a man his age a-worriting ye. If it was me, I'd a-given him the laudanum—fer his gout, don't ye see?"

"If he comes tonight, I mean to."

"More like it."

Elinor let the window hanging drop. "I have been thinking of sending for Jeremy," she mused finally.

"Eh?"

She turned around. "I don't think it at all fair that you have no one, Mary."

"Well, it ain't as though he don't write to me," the maid conceded. "Got a whole collection, I do."

Elinor shook her head. "Too many things happen. All we have left of Charles are his letters and the journal, you know." Her eyes met Mary's for a moment. "Life is too short to deny it, don't you think?"

"Me 'n' Jem ain't got the money—be years before—"

"No." Elinor went to her desk and took out the box where she kept the pin money Arthur allowed her. Most of it was still there from last quarter day. She took out a handful of bank notes and held them out. "Tell him you want him to come, Mary."

"Oh, mistress!"

"Fiddle. I'll have Mrs. Peake send to London for him."

The day wore on slowly, inching its way through a silent nuncheon shared with Arthur, who read the papers posted from London at his end of the table. It was as well. After what he'd done to her last night, she didn't even want to talk to him. Instead, she kept her head down, staring at her plate, pushing her food around without much enthusiasm.

"Lord Longford, sir!"

Her heart leapt, but Arthur merely looked up from his paper. "Tell him he is welcome to join us for nuncheon," he murmured. "Or he can wait in the front saloon." He peered over the top of the sheet at her. "Is that quite all right with you, my dear—if he should join us, I mean?"

"Of course."

He was still wiping the rain from his face when he came through the door, and it was as though his presence filled the cavernous room. When a footman hastened to lay another place, he shook his head.

"I've eaten. Deuced unpleasant out," he said to Arthur.

"Not precisely the best day for a drive," the old man acknowledged.

"Foolish of me, I know," the earl said, his eyes still

on the baron, "but I've new cattle just sent down from London, and I rather fancied taking them out."

"What sort of cattle?"

"A bang-up pair of grays—identical down to the speckles on their noses. I don't suppose you'd like to accompany me while I put them through their paces."

The old man appeared to consider it, and Elinor's heart was in her throat, but in the end, he declined. "Rain's bad for m'legs, I'm afraid."

Lucien turned to her. "Lady Kingsley?" he inquired casually.

"Well, I—"

Arthur looked up. "If you do not mind the rain, I've no objection. Better than being cooped up with me, I'd think. Besides, I am committed to a hand of piquet with Daggett." His eyes took in her still-filled plate. "Humph! If that is all you mean to eat, you might as well do something."

She felt like a child let out of school on holiday. "Well, I'd hoped to take Mignon out—to test the foot again—but as the weather does not appear as though it will clear—" She drew it out, hoping that Arthur would push her. Somehow that made it seem less furtive, less dishonorable.

"Told you—go on. If you want, you may take Mary, but there ain't much as I'd think you got to worry about in a carriage. Besides, Longford knows what he owes you—don't you?"

"Yes," Lucien answered tersely.

She rose, passing him on her way out, and she could almost feel the heat between them. Already her pulse pounded with the thought of being alone with him.

He watched her race up the steps, his expression sober. He felt guilty for what he was doing to her, for he'd already glimpsed her conscience. If he were an honorable man, a truly honorable man, he'd leave her alone. But it had come too far for that, and now he could not. He was as eager for her as a boy discovering his first calf love, as enthralled by her as by anyone from his salad days. At thirty, he was rediscovering his youth, rediscovering the life he'd nearly lost.

He paced the floor waiting, his impatience mounting,

not with her, but with time. It was taking her too long, and he'd not wait.

Arthur came into the hall behind him, startling him. "Best see that you have a carriage rug," the old man said mildly. "If the roads are too muddy, you may become stuck in the mire."

"I have one."

"Get another from Ned," Arthur advised. "Unless you are into bundling."

The old man knew, and he was letting her go, disgusting Lucien. But at the same time, it was as though he now had tacit permission to take her, as though Arthur Kingsley gave him the right to possess her, exonerating him. He wanted to lie to him, to deny it, but he could not.

"Ready, my dear?"

The old man looked up as she came down the stairs, seeing the simple black dress with the row of tiny buttons closing the high-waisted bodice. Over her arm, she carried her pelisse.

"You are better advised to take a cloak," he told her, then turned to Lucien. "What say you, my lord—is she not a woman to give a man pride?"

She looked almost regal despite the plainness of her gown, and just watching her, Lucien felt his mouth go dry with desire. "She is that—most definitely she is that." He took the pelisse from her and held it for her. As she stuck her arms into the sleeves, he pulled it close and fastened the frogs.

"It's all right—I am not cold," she murmured in understatement.

She waited until they were outside, then she admitted, "I thought you were not coming."

"As if I could stay away."

Even the low timbre of his voice was exciting. "Where do you mean to take me?" she managed to ask.

"That, my dear, depends on you. Now, if I were Bell, I should offer you Paradise, but you behold a merely mortal man." He opened the door and boosted her up, leaning closer to add, "Albeit a besotted one."

She sank into a seat and leaned back against blue velvet squabs. "Well," she admitted shamelessly, "I am ready to go anywhere."

He dropped onto the bench opposite and smiled crookedly, reminding her of a wild schoolboy. Tossing his hat onto the floor, he leaned back, watching her. "But in truth we are going nowhere."

"Nowhere!" For a moment, she betrayed her dismay. Then the coach began to move as the driver flicked the whip from the seat above them. "Oh, I collect you are funning."

"Not at all."

She turned to stare out the window, seeing the parkland passing by. "One of us must be going mad, my lord, for we seem to be traveling."

The smile twisted more, turning one corner of his mouth decidedly down. "Actually, I think we both are." His expression sobered abruptly. "You deserve better than this, you know."

She sucked in her breath, then let it out. "I am willing to take whatever I am allowed, Luce."

He said nothing for a time, but the air in the passenger compartment seemed to crackle with the tension between them. Finally, he spoke softly.

"Come here."

She slid across the seat into his arms, feeling once again the solid hardness of his man's body through the greatcoat he wore. He pulled her into the crook of his good arm, holding her, savoring the smell of the lavender in her hair. She slid her arms around his waist and laid her head against his shoulder. His hand massaged her arm, and had it not been for the terrible need, the desire that left her taut as a bowstring, she would have liked to have been held like that forever. But now . . . now . . . she wanted something more.

He twisted his head to look down at her. "I don't think I can get enough of you, you know."

She buried her face in his greatcoat that he could not see what even his words did to her. "You could try," she whispered.

"Oh, I mean to, Nell—I mean to. But first I've got to get out of this." He shifted her again and eased the greatcoat from one side, then from the other. It fell back against the seat behind him. "You know you've got too damned many clothes on, don't you?" As he spoke, he reached to slide the window cover closed behind her, plunging the tiny world into semidarkness. "Take off the pelisse."

Her hands shook as she unfastened the frogs, then eased out of the jacket. As she folded it and leaned to lay it across the seat opposite, he shut the other window cover. Her heart ticked as loudly as the ormolu clock in her bedchamber.

She could hear the rustle as he did something with his own clothes, then she felt his hands on the tiny buttons at her bosom. Despite the darkness, she closed her eyes and swallowed as her own desire nearly overwhelmed her. He fumbled and muttered until she began unbuttoning them for him. His hand slid beneath the cloth, finding her breast, and despite the fact that it was no longer totally new to her, she sucked in her breath, nearly sobbing as he rubbed her nipple.

He lay back against the side of the compartment, pulling her with him, lifting her until her head was above his, then his mouth was on her breast, pulling, teasing until she could scarce stand it. Her hands rubbed his hair, combing it restlessly, opening and closing in the thickness of it. But as the familiar ache welled deep inside of her, she knew this would be all she could get of him, that he would have to leave her wanting.

"Please," she whispered brokenly, "oh—please—" Her whole body was hot, and already she could feel the wetness below. "Oh," she moaned.

He pulled up her gown, baring her legs above her silk stockings, moving his hands lightly over her thighs until she quivered. And then he reached higher, slipping inside her with ease. She arched and tried to move against his hand, and then he was gone. And once again, she could hear his working with his clothes. He sat up, disappointing her.

"It's all right," he whispered against her ear. "Just kiss me. And put your knees on the seat."

She knelt awkwardly, nearly losing her balance from the motion of the carriage. He caught her. "You've got to sit facing me."

"I don't—"

To her shocked surprise, he lifted her, settling her onto his lap as his hand guided himself inside her. At first, she had no notion what to do, but as he rocked beneath her, she began to move, to gyrate, to grind her hips against him, feeling a certain power over him. She caught hold of the seat behind him and worked, savoring the freedom, the intensity of what she was feeling inside. His mouth moved hotly over her arched throat, finding the sensitive hollow, then he buried his head in her breasts, tasting them, rolling the nipples with his tongue, and finally sucking deeply.

She moved with abandon against him, sliding, slipping, holding, until she felt it, and wave after exquisite wave of ecstasy consumed her. It was so complete, so intense, that she did not even hear him cry out, nor did she feel the flood he released into her.

She collapsed, resting her head on his shoulder, gasping, panting for air. His arms held her tightly to him and his head was still buried in the softness of her breasts. She didn't want him to leave her, not now, not ever. She was still floating, savoring the peace that came after when she heard him murmur, "I knew I could make you howl."

"You didn't."

"Oh, but I did." He moved slightly and flinched. "Damn!"

"I hurt your shoulder, didn't I?"

"One of us did."

She pulled away reluctantly, then groped for the other seat. He opened the window cover slightly, then began buttoning his breeches. Keeping her eyes averted, she fastened the tiny jet buttons at the neck of her dress.

"You didn't wear the zona."

She reddened all the way to her toes. "I know." Turning away, she struggled to pull down her petticoat and her dress.

He leaned back, watching her lazily. "You're beautiful, Nell—the loveliest woman I've ever seen."

"And you have seen many."

"More than my share," he admitted. "But there is only one of you. Come here."

Her eyes widened. "Again? Oh, but I—"

"No. I'd just have you hold me." When she hesitated, his eyebrow went up slightly. "You did not think you were the only one who does not want to be alone, did you?"

"No, of course not." But as she slid across the seat and laid her head against his good shoulder, encircling his waist with her arms, she had to admit he'd surprised her. After Arthur, she could not imagine a man who wanted, who needed to be held.

He opened the window shades, and she roused slightly. "Where are we?"

"On our fourth or fifth turn about Langston Park, I think." His arm tightened around her shoulder. "I told him I should not be satisfied with less than twenty-five."

He was warm, he was secure, and she was sated. She leaned into him, hearing the beating of his heart beneath his shirt, and closed her eyes to enjoy these moments with him. And all the while the carriage swayed easily on its springs, lulling her.

When he looked down, she slept, and he felt a deep need to protect her, an unexpected tenderness, and for possibly the first time in his life, he wanted to take a woman home with him, he wanted to keep her. And the greatest, the most bitter irony of it all was that she was another man's wife.

SHE RODE EVERY DAY that it did not rain, meeting Longford at different prearranged places. But there was something less than satisfying, something degrading, about the furtiveness, the lies, the constant fear of discovery and disgrace. But she could not stop, and she knew it was because she loved him passionately, hopelessly, completely. It was as though for the first time in her life, she had a reason to live.

And it was more than the intensity of the physical relationship between them. There was a growing closeness beyond that. On the days when she had her courses shortly after they began seeing each other, he'd been content to hold her, to talk of nearly everything, to tell her some of the life he'd led. If she asked, he would tell her nearly everything, except when she'd wondered about Mad Jack. There was such a wellspring of bitterness there that it was like a boil, still too tender to touch despite the years that had passed.

She learned the real horror of the war, that which the papers did not tell, the stories of great heroism tempered by the ever-present terror of facing guns whose shells could cut a man in half, tales of those who had screamed until they died, and her heart went out to him as he relived the awful memories.

And they talked of Charles, of the hopes and promise of a boy who never got to be a man, of his idealism, of his very real love for her. That still haunted her—the notion that somehow she'd failed him. But it was not she, Longford reassured her, for she'd given Charley more than she knew—she'd allowed him to have his fantasies of her, she'd let him dream, and that alone had been worth everything to the boy. No, if there ought to be any recrimination, he told her, it was for his own sense of failure, that he could not save the boy from his youthful dreams of glory. And the irony of it all was that while Charley had died, he himself had come home a hero, that now there were those willing to receive him, not because he was any worthier, but because he'd taken two balls, both of which had nearly killed him. It made survival seem somehow more honorable than dying.

The more they talked, the more she knew of him, she finally dared to broach his nightmares to him, the tortured, fevered meanderings he'd shared when he was too sick to know. What *had* happened to his mother? He'd been silent then, until she thought he did not mean to answer, but in the end, he'd told her that he believed his mother had taken her own life, that she could no longer stand loving a man utterly, totally unworthy of her. And he remembered the awful anger he'd felt then, the anger of a boy left behind. There had been a time, he told her, when he'd hated his mother almost as much as he hated Mad Jack. Only now had he begun to pity her for the emptiness of her life. And Elinor forbore telling him that she thought there must have been madness on both sides, for what sort of woman would abandon a small boy to a husband she despised?

A fortnight after their own madness, their own illicit passion had begun, she rode to meet him, only to be taken to a small rock cottage overgrown with vines, a secluded place within the Park itself. To her surprise, he'd had it furnished, making it into a snug retreat where neither of them had to face the world, a place where they could play at being as any other man and woman besotted of each other, where they did not risk discovery. And she dubbed it "Haven," saying it provided her with a sense of home that Stoneleigh could not.

It had been a tenant's place, but the tenant had left to try something else, and it had apparently stood empty since before Lucien had bought Langston Park. But now it had a bed, a washstand, a newly installed stove, a settee, two chairs and a rug in front of the hearth—and a fresh coat of whitewash on the wall. The earl had told the curious that he was thinking of getting another tenant, and failing that, it could be used as a hunting box. Aside from a bit of local muttering about the wastefulness of the Quality, not much more had been thought about it.

She had loved it on sight. There she was no longer Baroness Kingsley, but rather just plain Nell, she'd told him happily, to which he had replied that she could not be just plain anything. And he was not the Earl of Longford, nor Lucien de Clare either, but instead answered only to Luce. He teased her that it was like Marie Antoinette playing the milkmaid at Petit Trianon, but that he hoped for better results.

That was the one area neither dared discuss. It was as though there was no past and no future, nothing beyond the present. Because he'd never said it to her, she could not bring herself to tell him she loved him. What she did not know and could not understand was that for whatever happiness she gave him now, he did not believe himself capable of loving or being really loved by anyone. When it ended, it would end, he told himself, trying to prepare for what he hoped never came. It was enough that she lay in his arms, that she laughed, that she teased, that she drove the devils within him away. There would come a time, he supposed, when she would leave him, but for now, he'd not think of that.

September faded into October and November and despite the mildness of the climate, the leaves turned, falling to the ground, adding an autumn mustiness to the smoke from Langston Park's many chimneys. And still the passion was as new as when it had begun.

Swathed in a blanket from the bed, she sat before the cottage fire, watching the flames dance, contented to be there with him. He carried a steaming cup of tea to her, then dropped to sit on the floor beside her, leaning his head against her knee. She could stay there forever. She sipped, wondering for a moment if she ought to tell him, afraid somehow that it would change things between them. It would be difficult enough telling Arthur. Later, she decided—later when it could not be hidden. Besides, it was early days yet, and she could be mistaken.

"You are rather quiet today," he chided her.

"Am I? I suppose I must be thinking."

"Blue-deviled?"

Her hand crept to his head, savoring the feel of the thick, nearly blue-black hair beneath her fingers. "No. I was wishing that I could spend the night. Just once I should like to be held then."

He shook his head. "We risk enough as it is."

"I know, but sometimes I do not care."

"You would. You cannot know what it is to have people pass you, to speak to those around you as though you are not there. Believe me, I know, Nell—I know."

She wondered what he would say if he knew her secret, if he'd offer to take her away, but she did not dare to put it to the touch, for what if he decided he did not want to acknowledge it, what if he did as Bell had apparently done to Diana? And that did not bear thinking.

Outside, the wind was coming up. He rose to look out the window, then turned back to her. "You'd better go before it storms."

"Not yet." She stood, letting the blanket fall, and watched the desire kindle in his eyes. "Not yet," she said softly.

As many times as he'd seen her, he thought he knew every inch, and yet there was that about her that never failed to draw him. "Nell, there's not time." Yet even as he said it, he moved toward her. "God, but you are beautiful," he breathed, reaching for her again.

* * *

It was already raining when she reached Stoneleigh, and she was soaked. Her teeth chattered as Ned took Mignon. In the foyer, she shook the water from her cloak and removed her hat. Her hair straggled wetly against her neck, dripping onto the jacket of her riding habit.

Peake favored her with a look of disapproval, then told her, "His lordship would have a word with you before you go up."

"Tell him I would change first."

But Arthur was already standing in his bookroom door. "Now," he said. "I have had a hot punch prepared. It will chase the chill from your bones, my dear."

She could scarce stand the sight of him anymore, but still she did not defy him openly. Reluctantly, she followed him inside and moved to warm herself at the fire.

"You are rather late," he murmured, carrying a cup to her.

"I got lost. It was the rain," she lied.

"Sit down."

"I'm wet."

"In more ways than one, no doubt."

She took the chair he indicated, wondering what he wanted. For a time, he merely watched her, saying nothing, and she felt exceedingly uncomfortable. She tried to concentrate on the punch. It was hot, fruity, and laced with spices and something she could not identify, perhaps rum. She waited, hearing the crackling of the fire, and still he was silent. Unable to stand it, she drained her glass and held it out for a refill.

"It's good," she said.

He ladled more into the cup and handed it back. The air was heavy, almost pregnant, and she felt a sudden dread. "You wished to talk with me," she prompted finally.

He leaned back, his fingertips together, considering her. For two months he'd waited and watched benignly, pretending to believe her lies, letting her think she had misled him. But there was no mistaking that which he'd not counted on. He'd expected the affair to be brief, intense, and over by now, with Longford moving on as Mad Jack had so often done. Instead, he had witnessed his wife falling madly, passionately in love with the other man, and he was ready to put an end to it.

"It's not all that far from Langston Park, my dear," he said finally.

She knew she ought to deny it, but she was sick of compounding one lie with another. For a brief moment, her world seemed to stand quite still, as though even her heart stopped, then she managed to ask, "How long have you known?"

"From the beginning—and even before."

She almost felt relieved. The thought crossed her mind that perhaps she could leave him, perhaps she could go to Longford. But if she did, she'd brand her babe a bastard.

He nodded. "Just so." He reached into his coat and drew out the leather folder. Opening it, he retrieved the bank draft and handed it to her. She looked down, reading "Pay to the order of Lucien, Earl of Longford." It was for ten thousand pounds.

"My heir comes dear, don't you think? The stud fee was steep."

The room seemed to spin around her. "Your heir?" she said hollowly.

"You did not think I made my money for naught, did you?" he countered mildly. "And Longford was happy enough to oblige."

Her chest tightened until she could scarce breathe. "I don't believe you—I don't believe you!" She started to rise, but the dizziness overwhelmed her. "He is not that sort of man!"

"I'm afraid men view this sort of thing rather differently, Elinor. I offered, and he took." He smiled faintly, then leaned forward. "And Agnes tells me you have not needed any rags," he added meaningfully.

"I don't believe you!" she cried. "He loves me!" But even as she said it, she knew Lucien had never used the words.

"Love!" Arthur snorted. "Ah, my dear, but what an innocent you are. Longford does not care about anything beyond his own pleasure."

And it was as though she could hear Sally Jersey's warning, that Longford was a dangerous man for he could not be brought to care. But she could not give up easily. "I'd see him—I'd hear it—" she said, her voice desperate.

"I don't think that would be wise, my dear. There is enough talk already." Again he favored her with a thin smile. "No, we are for Ireland—I own property there, you know."

"Ireland!" Her voice rose almost hysterically. "Arthur, you cannot! I must see—I must hear—"

"There is no time. Mary has already packed what you will need, and I expect to depart in the morning."

"I won't go! I won't!" The room was spinning even faster now, until she could scarce think. Her eyes moved wildly about the room as though somehow she could still escape. "I hate you, Arthur—I hate you! I despise what you are!"

"You are overset merely."

"Overset! Overset?" She tried again to rise, and this time she stumbled, nearly falling. "Arthur, you have drugged me!" She collapsed then in a heap at his feet, her head against the leg of his chair, and she wept uncontrollably.

"I think I shall name the child after myself," he decided. "It will cause less comment. Arthur Charles Philip Kingsley—actually, I rather like the sound of it."

"I should rather die."

His hand smoothed her hair. "It's to be hoped he favors you rather than Longford."

Her world was spinning out of control, like a child's top on the brink of an abyss. She clung to the chair leg, trying to keep from descending into the blackness, but she could not.

He waited until she was unconscious, then he reached for the bellpull. "Peake, Lady Kingsley has fainted, I'm afraid, and must be helped to bed."

* * *

The drug had not set well on her stomach, and she had awakened vomiting violently in the night. And Mary had held her, listening to her weeping, her tortured confession, soothing her as best she could. Come morning, the maid had reported to Lord Kingsley that "her ladyship is beyond going anywheres t'day." And when he'd refused to listen, she'd clinched the matter by declaring, "Well, I'd not want ter ride in a closed carriage with her a-casting up her accounts, ye know." In the end, the departure had been postponed until the morrow.

As Elinor lay abed with Mary pressing cold compresses on her swollen eyes, she asked dully, "What time is it?"

"Nigh ter two."

Two o'clock. Longford would be waiting for her. And then she remembered and began weeping all over again. If Arthur could be believed, she was the greatest fool on earth. *If Arthur could be believed.* As miserable as she was, as sick as she felt, she had to *know,* she had to hear it from Lucien himself.

"I think I might be able to take some digestive biscuits," she managed.

"I'll get ye some," the maid promised. "Aye, and a bit of tea ter ease ye."

As soon as Mary was gone, Elinor rose, throwing her

cloak over her nightgown, and slipped down the stairs. And when Ned protested, "Here now, yer ladyship, ye cannot be out, fer it's rainin,' " she ordered him to saddle Mignon anyway, threatening him with dismissal if he did not.

She rode recklessly, crossing the fields rather than following the roads, lest Arthur should send someone after her. It was not until she was nearly there that it occurred to her that Lucien might not be there, that because of the rain he would think she did not come. But a curl of smoke swirled valiantly into the heavy sky.

He heard her, for she shouted for him as she rode up, and he came to the door, totally unprepared for what he saw. She was pale, disheveled, her wet hair dripping, her eyes wild.

"What the—?" He stepped forward to dismount her, but she pulled Mignon back.

"I have to know, Luce!" she cried hysterically. "Did Arthur ask you to do this? Did Arthur ask you to get a babe of me?"

"It isn't what you think, Nell!" Again he moved toward her, and again Mignon backed away.

"Tell me, Luce!"

"Yes, but—"

He lunged for her, catching her reins, but before he could stop her, she'd raised her whip. She brought it down with all the force she could muster, cutting open his nose, striking him again and again, marking his cheek, screaming at him that he'd used her and that she hated him for it. He had to close his eyes and duck. Grabbing blindly, he managed to wrest the whip from her hand, nearly unseating her. But she kicked at him, then kicked Mignon hard. The horse, unused to the violence, bolted.

He was on foot, but he ran after her, shouting for her to stop, shouting that she didn't know the whole, but the wind and rain seemed to carry his words away. Blood dripped from his nose and cheek, and when he ran his hand over them, he could see his red, wet palm.

She rode as though hell pursued her, this time taking the road, and there was no way to catch her, no way to explain. So the old man had told her, casting him in the worst possible role. He felt sick, as though his stomach had knotted and lay like lead within. His mind working feverishly, he knew he had to see her before something terrible happened. He did not think she could stand Charley and this.

He turned and walked back to Langston Park to get his horse. If he had to kill Kingsley, he was going to see her.

"Yer lordship'll take yer death," a stable boy told him, but he didn't care. Rather than waiting for someone to do it, he saddled his big bay himself. And as he turned down the road toward Stoneleigh, he was afraid. Not a praying man, he nonetheless begged the Almighty not to let her do anything rash.

Two mounted men were waiting for her, and between them, they boxed her horse. One leaned to take her reins, the other steadied her. Neither knew what to expect for Lord Kingsley had told them that her mind had snapped, that her grief for Charles had finally taken its toll. But she did not resist, and when they reached the yard, she slid numbly to the ground.

Under Mrs. Peake's cold stare, she was carried upstairs, where Mary chafed her cold hands, stripped her wet clothes, and put her to bed. She did not even protest when Agnes brought her toddy. She wanted to be insensate now, she wanted to forget what a fool she had been. Her gorge rose, and she was afraid she was going to be sick again, but somehow she managed to swallow and keep it down.

Too miserable for speech, she drew up her knees and rolled into a ball, kneeling beneath the covers. She wanted to cry, to rid herself of the wellspring of bitterness inside, but she could not. She felt used, betrayed, and worthless, an empty shell. Her love for Longford had been cheapened by the knowledge that Arthur had had him breed her like a mare.

"Is she all right?" she heard Arthur ask somewhere in the distance.

"Aye," Mary muttered.

"I have decided to leave anyway. The change will do her good." He looked down at Elinor, her shivering body crouched beneath the heavy coverlet. "Bundle her, and Jeremy and one of the others will carry her down."

"She ain't in no case fer a journey," the maid protested. "Be a wonder if she ain't taken her death as it is."

"I've ordered hot bricks," was all he said.

When Lucien rode up, he carried his dragoon pistol, ready to force his way inside. Instead he was greeted by Peake, who informed him stiffly that "Lord and Lady Kingsley have but left, I'm afraid. You missed them by a scant quarter hour."

"Where? Out with it, man! Where?" His hand snaked out, lifting the butler by his coat "Damn it—where?"

"He did not tell me, my lord."

"I could choke it out of you!"

"It would do no good, for I do not know."

He released the man and stepped back. Water ran in rivulets from his face, his hair, his cloak, dripping onto the polished foyer floor. "Is it London?" he demanded, wiping his wet face.

"I told you—I was not made privy to his lordship's plans." Straightening his coat and his dignity, the butler turned to the silver tray on a small table. "But he said if you were to come, I should give you this."

Lucien's fingers tore at the envelope's seal, opening it to reveal the bank draft and a single sheet of paper where the old man had written in his own spidery hand, "For services rendered." And he knew why Nell had turned her whip on him. Not even in battle had he ever wanted to kill anyone as much as he wanted to kill Kingsley now.

"Her ladyship—how is her ladyship?" His voice was harsh. "I've got to know—damn it, but I've got to know!"

Before the man could answer, his wife stepped from the saloon door. And there was no mistaking the contempt in her face as she told him, "Her ladyship has lost her mind."

The image of Elinor being put away in some asylum to languish as punishment for what they'd done came to mind, but then reason reasserted itself. He looked down at the bank draft, seeing the sheet of paper, and he cursed Kingsley. *For services rendered.* It could only mean that she was with child, and Arthur had taken her away from him.

Very deliberately, he put the draft back in the envelope with the note, then tore the whole in half. Handing both pieces to the bemused butler, he turned to leave.

Passing a curious footman, he declared, "I'll match

the amount to any who will tell me where Lady Kingsley has gone."

The fellow waited until he was gone, then looked to Peake. "How much is it?"

"Ten thousand pounds."

"Gor! It's a bloomin' fortune, the likes o'which ain't neither o' us like ter see!"

"Well, his lordship did not tell me!" Peake snapped.

As Lucien rode back to Langston Park, he felt utterly, completely defeated. The idyll was over—she was gone.

FOR A TIME, Elinor did not care if she lived or died. She was despondent, bitter, and utterly disinterested in the Irish countryside. But most of all, she was *bitter,* for she'd finally come to realize that despite years of dreams, there was in truth no love in this world for her. And the hardest death for her mind to take was the death of dreams. It was even worse than the loss of Charles, because now she no longer believed in hope.

With Longford gone, Arthur treated her solicitously, taking great care to see that she ate properly, took the Irish air, walked the paths through the picturesque valley that ran through his Irish estate, but she did not care as one day faded into another . . . and another . . . and another. Indeed, but it was as though he were devoted to her, that his purpose in life was now to amuse her, to tend to her. And not since that night at Stoneleigh had he ever mentioned the earl's name. It was as though he studiously sought to dispel the notion that anything had ever happened.

Outwardly, she maintained a semblance of calm, perfunctorily going through the motions of living, but inwardly she hated as she'd never hated before. She hated Arthur and everything he did for her, but most of all, she hated Longford, for he'd allowed her to dream, then betrayed her.

At first, her pregnancy had not set well with her, and she'd been too sick to eat the delicacies that Arthur had sent for, but finally that had passed. But still she resented—no, that was not nearly a strong enough word for what she felt—she *hated* being a brood mare for Kingsley's ambitions. But one day, while unenthusiastically enduring yet another dogcart ride with her elderly husband, she felt the babe within her move. She sat very still, thinking she'd imagined it, and then it happened again.

That night, she'd lain awake, hoping to feel it, pressing against her slightly rounding stomach. And there it was. There was life within her, and it no longer mattered that it had been put there by Longford. It was hers.

Arthur no longer slept with her at all, saying she needed her rest, so for a time she did not even have to share the wonder of her discovery. It was hers. Not his. Not Longford's. Hers. And now, finally, she had something to live for.

Arthur was pleased by the change in her spirits, and with characteristic self-centeredness took credit for it. When spring came, and with it the news that Longford had returned to London, he determined it was time to go home, for his son should be born at Stoneleigh. It was as though he went home in triumph, his young wife's body swollen now with child, a condition he was also determined to take credit for. He even told her he considered her rounded belly quite pleasing.

What she could not stand as her pregnancy progressed was his habit of laying his hand upon her stomach to feel the movement of "my son" within. In company, despite the fact that females in interesting conditions were usually rather discreetly absent, Arthur showed her off. She was, much to her chagrin, proof of his supposed virility. Privately, she imagined there were any number of people who laughed behind his back about his "miracle."

"You know," he told her one day, "I do not believe you are eating sufficiently to sustain the babe."

"I am as fat as a pig," she protested. "Mary must put on my stockings and roll them for me."

"Yes, well, I am told that calves' brains are conducive to intelligence, so I have ordered—"

He got no further. "I have not the least intention of partaking of any brains," she declared flatly. "Nor do I wish for any more pork jelly. Both of us are quite well, thank you."

"Still, one cannot be too careful, and—"

"Arthur," she snapped with asperity, "I am growing a babe, not a cabbage in need of fertilizer. I daresay that whatever looks it possesses, whatever intelligence, has already been determined."

"Not 'it,' my dear—*he.*"

She considered suggesting that she might carry a daughter, but she knew he would not hear of it. And the London physician he'd had travel to examine her had declared that "given the babe's position, it's most certainly a boy." Indeed, even Mary was positive of it, saying that the intensity of her earlier illness was proof of a son. And Mrs. Peake, attempting to please her employer, had remembered that a midwife had once told her that a babe carried high was always male. And Elinor carried her child high, so much so that she could scarce breathe when she sat down.

"Your lordship, the workmen are here," Peake announced as they sat in the front saloon, Arthur with his paper, she with the latest novel from London.

She looked up. "Workmen, Arthur?"

"I thought perhaps to refurbish the chamber next to mine for a nursery," he responded.

"Babes cry," she reminded him coldly. "I cannot think you would wish to be disturbed."

"Nonsense. I mean to see he is precisely what I would have him."

She felt a chill, for those had been the very words he'd used when he'd offered for her. It was as though he were telling her that he meant to take over her child also. And his next words confirmed it.

"Tomorrow I have arranged for you to interview wet nurses," he continued mildly. "The London agency I have contacted assures me that each girl is of the highest quality—and possessed of excellent morals."

"If they are moral, how is it that they are able to nurse?" she inquired acidly.

He shrugged. "Among the lower classes, babes are more inclined to die, my dear."

"Thank you, but I should prefer to do it myself."

"I would not ruin your looks, my dear."

She knew he meant to have it all—a wife to be envied for, a son to carry on the Kingsley name. Only now instead of having merely one to manipulate, he meant to have two. And it did no good to think he might not live to do it, for if anything, his health seemed better than ever. Ireland, for all that she had hated it, had suited him. No, she would not be surprised if he lived well into his seventies.

When she said nothing, he changed the subject slightly. "Did you see the cradle I commissioned?"

"Yes."

She disappointed him by not praising it, for he had gone to great lengths to have a replica of Princess Charlotte's made for his heir. Even the linens had been ordered of finest lawn hand-embroidered in Switzerland, as had the babe's christening gown, eliciting her tart observation that it must surely appear that he awaited not the birth of a Kingsley, but rather of a king. To which he had replied as though she'd not said it that he would have preferred to have acquired the babe's linens from Flanders but the Flemish were still prohibited from trading with England, so the Swiss workmanship would have to do.

"I thought perhaps an Aubusson carpet," he mused, "for there are yet some to be had for a price in London."

"For a babe?" she said incredulously.

"For my son."

It was as though Longford had never existed. "Arthur—"

"He must not smell of the shop, Elinor. He must have all that I can give him—the finest of everything. I'd not have him suffer as I have done, my dear. I'd have none remember whence came his fortune."

She bit back saying that more were likely to wonder at his blood, but then she knew that no longer mattered. As long as Arthur acknowledged the babe, as long as there was no scandal, for all that everyone would know that she'd lain with someone else, her reputation was intact. To them, unaware of what she had suffered, she'd played the game by society's rules, and given the age of her husband, she was not to be blamed for presenting him an heir of questionable parentage.

The more he talked, the more he planned, the more loath she was to have the child come out. For now, it was hers, wholly hers. But once it came into the world, it would be Arthur's.

"I think I should like to have my mother," she admitted.

In the ordinary way of things, he did not care much

for her family. Despite the fact that her blood was better than his, he considered Thomas Ashton and the rest of her family beneath him. But just now he meant to humor her, for he'd have nothing go wrong.

"By all means—if it pleases you, send for her. You may even offer her the carriage as a means of conveyance." He could not resist one small barb. "It's a pity Ashton had to lose his."

"Yes."

"A man ought not to drink and game, particularly not an unlucky one. And when you write to her, you may add that I have not the least intention of increasing his allowance. It's like pouring money off a bridge into the Thames."

"Do you have no vices?" she snapped, irritated by his superior tone.

He appeared to consider for a moment, then nodded. "Vanity, my dear—it's the only one." He leaned across the table to lift her chin with a long, thin finger. "And for all that you behave as a petulant child, you feed it."

* * *

"I am told she is back, and those who see her say she appears well," Leighton had written him, drawing Lucien home to Langston Park. What he had not said, but what nearly everyone in the neighborhood had speculated, was whether Lady Kingsley's interesting condition could be blamed on Viscount Townsend or the Earl of Longford.

In the five months since last he'd seen her, he'd thought he'd driven her from his mind. God knew he'd tried, throwing himself into a number of brief, unsatisfying liaisons with exquisite, willing opera dancers and demireps. He'd gambled recklessly, winning shamelessly, and he'd drank enough port, madeira, and brandy to fill a river, Leighton told him. But none of those things had done anything for the void in his soul.

At first, as his face healed, he'd thought he'd go mad, but gradually, in order to save his sanity, he'd progressed from despair to a semblance of indifference. Finally, he'd nearly convinced himself that he hated her for doing this to him, for not letting him explain, for running away. Until Leighton's letter had come.

He knew his return had occasioned more comment than he wanted, but he could not help it. In the beginning, he told himself he had but to see her from afar, to know she was all right, but after a few distant glimpses of her at church, glimpses that he dared not publicly pursue, he knew she was as much an obsession with him as ever. And it did not make it any easier when he saw her swollen body, bringing home to him that she did in fact carry a child he could not claim.

It had been a mistake to come back, and he knew it, for now he knew even less peace, and once again she haunted both his dreams and his waking thoughts. He was torn between wanting to see her again and by knowing that for both their sakes, he ought to leave well enough alone. Finally, he sent Leighton as an emissary.

She sat wrapped in a large shawl, her legs drawn up into the chair, absorbed in Jane Austen's latest, when the viscount was announced.

"No—no, no need to rise," he assured her. "I quite understand."

"How kind of you," she murmured, unfolding her legs and covering them with the shawl. "I am a bit awkward, I'm afraid."

"But lovely," he offered gallantly.

"Spanish coin, my lord." Nonetheless, she smiled. "I shall however accept it." She looked up at him. "Do sit down, sir. Arthur—"

"Actually, it's you I am come to see, Lady Kingsley." He dropped into a chair, then leaned forward. "Lucien would know how you fare."

For a moment, she gripped the arms of her chair, then it was as though she had turned to stone and even her face hardened. Finally, she said coldly, "I hardly think it matters."

"He is returned to Langston Park."

"Has he now?" Despite the question, her eyes betrayed not the least interest. "I should rather think he ought to have remained in London, for I am quite certain there is more sport to be had there." Laying aside her book, she reached for the bellpull that Jeremy had attached to her chair. And when the footman appeared, she inquired coolly of Leighton, "Do you stay to tea, my lord? Or perhaps a glass of brandy before you go?"

He was failing miserably, and he knew it. "Brandy would be fine," he murmured. "And you?"

"Oh, I shall take nothing. Arthur would have nothing pollute his son." For the briefest moment, her bitterness showed, then her amber eyes were once again distant, impersonal.

He waited for his brandy, took a sip to fortify himself, then inquired casually, "And when is the interesting event to occur, dear lady?"

"In early July—or so Dr. Moreston believes."

He was surprised to learn she'd chosen a prominent London physician. "So you will travel to the city, then?"

"No. Arthur has arranged that Dr. Moreston will come to me. Foolish, isn't it? Particularly when one considers that females have been doing this for centuries without much assistance."

"I understand Moreston is the best. Arthur must be quite concerned for you."

There was almost a glimmer of the old Elinor Kingsley as a faint smile played at the corners of her mouth. "My dear Leighton, you are unfortunately mistaken—it is rather that nothing is too good for his heir. I am merely the means of the arrival, you see. If babes came by carriage, I should be decidedly *de trop*."

"You undervalue yourself, Lady Kingsley."

"Do I?" The smile broadened ruefully. "My lord, if you knew but half the preparations my husband has made for one small babe, you should be astounded."

George heard Kingsley's voice as he spoke with someone outside, and he realized he had to speak up for Longford then or not at all. Manfully, he leaned forward again, this time possessing her hands.

"What can I tell Lucien to reassure him you are quite well? That you—" He got no further. She pulled her hands away and rose awkwardly, standing above him.

"You can tell him I shall see him in hell."

"Lady Kingsley, I assure you he—"

"And if he would know, let him ask for himself." She started to leave him sitting there, but she was too late. Her husband stood in the door.

But if he'd heard, he gave no sign. Instead, he walked

in, crossing the room to her. Bending slightly, he brushed a cold kiss against her cheek. "You look a trifle peaked, my dear," he chided her. "Perhaps you ought to be abed."

"I am fine, my lord." She turned back to Leighton. "Now that Arthur is here, I really must see to supper. Good day, sir."

He watched her go, thinking that Longford had been a fool. Had it been he, he would have fled with her, and he was not even a particularly romantic sort. As it was, they were both condemned to misery. He set aside his empty glass and rose also, murmuring apologetically, "Got to run myself, I'm afraid. Merely promised Mrs. Thurstan to convey her regards to Lady Kingsley."

Arthur waited until he'd retrieved his beaver hat from Peake at the door, then he spoke up, his voice quite cold. "Do not think I mean to make the same mistake twice, George."

Leighton turned around. "You know, Arthur, there are times when you remind me of one of the French Louis."

"The Fourteenth?" the old man inquired, somewhat pleased.

"No—the Eleventh."

For a moment, Kingsley's brow furrowed.

"The Spider King," George said. "Good day, my lord."

* * *

Lucien sat alone, brooding with naught but a bottle of brandy for company, in the cottage where he'd spent so many hours with her. Damn her! Why had she not listened to him? Leighton's report of her words rang in his ears. *You can tell him I will see him in hell . . . in hell . . . in hell . . .* As if he were not there already. *And if he would know, let him ask for himself . . . let him ask for himself . . .* What the devil had she meant by that? Was that some sort of invitation?

He lurched to his feet, beyond caring for appearances anymore. Whether she wanted to hear it or not, he wanted her to know that Arthur had lied. He wanted to tell her that if she would go with him, he'd take her anywhere, that he would wed her when the old man died. He wanted to tell her that she'd given him the only happiness in his life, and that he wanted her back, whatever the cost. For her, he'd even face another scandal.

It was not until he was nearly to Stoneleigh that he sobered slightly, that he began to realize he rode on a fool's errand, for even if she would go, could she do that to the child? He reined in, torn between want and right, and sat there, staring at the huge country house in the distance. And want won.

He nudged the bay forward, telling himself he might never have another chance to put it to the touch, to ever see her again. It would be like Arthur to take her somewhere else if he even thought she might come to Lucien again.

He rode straight for the portico and dismounted, tossing his reins to a silent ostler, then mounted the steps unsteadily to pound the heavy brass knocker. The door opened, but the butler blocked the entrance, inquiring stiffly if he could be of any assistance to his lordship.

"I am come to see Lady Kingsley."

"She is not receiving, I'm afraid."

"But she is at home?"

"As to that, I'm sure I cannot say, my lord."

Lucien pushed past him into the foyer, and started up the stairs. Two footmen caught him from behind, holding his arms, and as he tried to shake them off, he nearly lost his balance.

"Got to tell her—I've got to tell her! Damn you—let me go!"

"Here now—ye got ter leave," one of them insisted, pulling him back. "Jem—bring up his lordship's horse!" he shouted, trying to turn the earl around.

"Nell! I know damned well you are up there! Nell! Cannot go until—" He swung around, breaking one footman's hold, and started dragging the other up the stairs. "Nell!"

She'd heard him when he confronted Peake, and for a moment, it was as though her heart stood still, as though her blood had turned to ice. And yet there was that within her traitorous mind that wanted to see him again, as though that somehow might end it once and for all. She forced herself to open her bedchamber door and step into the hall.

"Come out, Nell!" he shouted. "Want to tell you—"

"You want to tell me what?" she asked coldly, standing at the top of the stairs. "That you are too sotted to stand?"

"Got to listen! I want the babe—d'you hear me? I want it, Nell! Take you—" He took another step up, then stopped, swaying.

Jeremy lunged for him, and this time he and the other footman managed to pull both of the earl's arms behind him. "Come on, my lord—you are in no case—"

Lucien looked up, seeing her face for the first time since the day Arthur had taken her away. His gaze dropped to her swollen body. "Still beautiful, Nell—even with the babe."

His black hair was rumpled as though it had not been combed, and his black eyes were bleary as though he'd not slept. And despite the scar that crossed his nose and cheek, he was still the handsomest man of her memory. Others could admire Lord Ponsonby, but he would pale against Longford. She had to hold the banister and draw from the well of pain within her to keep from going down. She had to remember how much she hated him.

"You are disgustingly disguised, Luce," she told him.

"Want you—never wanted—"

"Get out of my house, Longford, else I shall fire." Arthur had come into the hall behind the earl, and he held a pistol leveled at the center of Lucien's back. He looked up at Elinor. "Well, my dear?"

"Come on, Nell—tell him which of us you want," Lucien mumbled. "Tell him—"

If she went down, she had not the least doubt that Arthur would shoot him. She closed her eyes, remembering how Longford had betrayed her, and she shook her head.

"Perhaps you'd best answer him, Elinor," Arthur prompted, cocking the piece.

"I don't care if you kill him." As she turned back to her bedchamber, she could feel her babe kick beneath her ribs, convincing her she did the right thing. Even if she had still loved Longford, which she did not, she owed her child Arthur's name. Even if later she had to fight for its soul.

"Nell!" Longford shouted as they dragged him away.

She closed the door and stood with her head against the wall for a moment, then she went to the window to look as it took three men to force Lucien outside. Had he not been drunk, he'd not have come at all, she told herself, and yet she could not help staring down as he somehow managed to swing up into his saddle, nor could she help watching him until he was out of sight.

Utterly dispirited, she sat down at her small writing desk and began a letter to her mother, begging her to come, telling her that she'd try to intervene with Arthur on her father's behalf if only she could be supported through the last of her pregnancy. "Please, Mama," she wrote, "I have greater need of you now than in any time since my own birth."

Stoneleigh: July 6, 1813

THE PAIN CAME IN WAVES, tightening her distended abdomen, gaining in intensity until Elinor thought she was being ripped apart, and still the babe did not present itself. She was tired, so tired that all she wanted was for it to be over, and her lips were bloodied from being bitten. Her mother sat beside her, wiping her sweaty brow with a cool, wet cloth, while Dr. Moreston prepared yet another dose of laudanum. Somewhere below Arthur waited, ready to toast the birth of the Kingsley heir.

Through the mist of pain and drug, Elinor could hear the physician tell her mother, "The position is wrong, I am afraid."

"Is it breech?"

"No—it's on its side and will have to be turned."

"She's bleeding."

She was dying, and she knew it. Elinor strained still, trying to relieve herself of her burden before she took the babe with her, dimly wondering if she did it any service at all in leaving it to Arthur. Mary lifted her head, forcing her to drink more of the hated laudanum. She gagged, then managed to swallow. The voices around her grew more distant, and her mother's hand left her forehead to clasp her fingers.

Something was pushing upward at the same time an intense cramp pushed downward, and somewhere in the distance she could hear herself scream. She couldn't be dying—she could still feel it. Pain after pain after pain.

"Luce! Luce! *Lucien*!" she cried, wanting him to hear her.

Someone thrust something between her teeth, and she bit down hard as there was one last searing tear, then a brief respite before it began again, this time with far less intensity. She could feel the kneading on her stomach, the wet mass coming forth, and then it was over. She floated, hearing nothing.

Leaning over her, her mother soothed her wet hair, murmuring soothingly that it was done. Finally, there was the thin, thready cry of an infant, and then a more insistent squalling. She tried to open her eyes to see her son and could not.

"Is he—is he all right?" she whispered through swollen, cracked lips.

There was an awkward, momentary silence, then her mother told her, "It's a girl, Nell—you have a beautiful black-haired daughter."

"I don't know how to tell him," she heard Moreston say.

It came home to her then. She had a daughter. A *daughter.* As Mary swaddled the babe and brought it to lay in the crook of her arm, she managed to look down, and then she began to laugh hysterically. The jest was on Arthur—*she had a daughter*!

Thinking the laudanum had affected her mind, the physician tried to calm her, reassuring her that she could have a son the next time. She shook her head, unable to control the high-pitched laughter.

"There cannot be a next time!" she gasped finally.

There was another silence, and it was obvious that none wished to go below to tell Lord Kingsley the babe was a girl, that everyone had been mistaken. Finally, after downing a large glass of medicinal brandy from his bag, Moreston faced the task with great reluctance, saying that he hoped the unfortunate circumstances would not affect his lordship's willingness to pay the agreed-upon sum.

"Nell, you must get hold of yourself," her mother told her severely. "What was Moreston to think?"

To which her daughter dissolved into whoops once more. "Don't—don't you see, Mama? I have finally done it!"

"Dearest, if you do not stop this, it will be said you have lost your mind."

"No—no—he will not wish to rule her! It's a girl, Mama!"

Her mother moved the cover from the infant's head and peered more closely at it. "Well, under the circumstances, it would have been ever so much better were she possessed of your hair. There is bound to be talk—''

''No.'' Elinor caught her breath finally, then exhaled to calm the elation she felt. ''He has made so much over preparing for the babe, he cannot deny it.''

Arthur did not come up, nor did the physician return, and the whole household seemed to be plunged into silence as the whispered word spread that Lady Kingsley had borne a daughter. For a time, Elinor slept, content to feel the small bundle against her, and when she wakened to its wail, she marveled at the tiny, screwed-up face, the little rounded mouth, the red, shaking fists.

Her mother uncovered one of her breasts, set the child to it, then tickled the babe's cheek until it tried to suck. ''There's no milk yet, but it will come,'' she reassured her.

That too gave her a measure of satisfaction. No doubt now Arthur would not care whether she had a wet nurse or not. Indeed, but he was probably too angered with her to look at the babe he would have to claim.

When it calmed, Mary laid the babe in the expensive cradle, and began rocking her. Elinor slept again, this time the sleep of the exhausted, and did not hear her husband come into the room, nor did she see the fury in his face as he raised his cane. She came awake screaming as he beat her unmercifully, striking her head and shoulders again and again, calling her a whore, shouting that she'd cheated him. Her mother, roused from her bed, tried to intervene, only to be struck also.

The footman Jeremy, wakened by the shouting, ran half-clothed into the bedchamber to stop Kingsley, at first trying to calm him, then wresting his cane from him. Even Peake and Mrs. Peake came to stare. Convinced that the old man was better, Jeremy made the mistake of releasing him, and Kingsley turned his anger to the cradle. Screaming that he'd be hanged before he acknowledged Longford's bastard, he turned it over, dumping the babe onto the floor, startling it, and it squalled loudly.

''My lord,'' Peake remonstrated with him, ''it's but an infant!''

''I'll kill it—I swear I'll kill it!'' With that, the old man limped painfully from the room, leaving a stunned staff to stare at each other.

Bruises were already visible and one eye was closing as Elinor took her daughter from Mary's arms and began crooning softly to stop her crying. Downstairs, there was the sound of crashing as though in his fury Arthur was bent on destroying everything.

It was the young footman who dared to speak first. "Her ladyship's got to get out of here."

"Where—?" Elinor's mother hesitated. "It's the middle of the night, and she cannot simply—"

"Got ter go ter Longford," Mary declared.

"Longford! The scandal—" Lady Ashton caught herself and shut her mouth quickly, thinking perhaps they did not know.

"I daresay it will be a scandal anyway," Peake pointed out reasonably. There was another crash from below, then an outraged bellow. "Under the circumstances—"

"No," Elinor said hollowly, "I could not."

They heard a pistol report, and there was a sudden silence as each thought the worst. Then Arthur shouted again, his voice carrying up the stairs, "I'll kill the little bastard before I acknowledge it!"

"My lady, you've got to go," Mrs. Peake insisted. *"Now."*

"An inn—perhaps an inn."

The butler shook his head. "It will be a more public scandal than Longford. At least the earl might hold his tongue, which is more than I can say for—"

"No."

There was another pistol shot, indicating that Arthur had reloaded. Not waiting to argue, Mary threw a clean blanket over her mistress, then took the babe from her. "The back stairs—he don't come up 'em," she whispered urgently.

For once, neither the butler nor his wife appeared stiff and unconcerned. The housekeeper grasped Elinor's arm and pushed her into the hall, while Peake directed Lady Ashton behind them. Outside, at the back of the house, the lantern was nearly obscured by fog.

"We cannot go," Elinor protested.

"Ye got to. Fer the babe's sake, if not fer yer own," Mary insisted.

Convinced now that her elderly son-in-law was indeed a madman, Lady Ashton pulled her wrapper closer and demanded that someone procure the carriage. From time to time, as they stood in the swirling, cloudy darkness, another shot could be heard coming from within the house. Finally, the Kingsley coach rolled out of the carriage house, with the sleepy driver complaining of the hour, only to be told that the old man meant to kill them all.

It was not until Elinor, the infant, Lady Ashton, and Mary were safely bundled into the carriage, that Jeremy turned back to the house.

"Ain't ye going?" Mary called out in alarm.

"Got to disarm him before he hurts himself!" he shouted back.

"Nay—ye cannot!" Then, "I pray ye be careful!"

Peake and his wife hesitated, then decided not to go, saying that they would hide until it was safe to return, that they thought once Elinor and her babe were removed, his lordship could be soothed.

As the driver's whip cracked and the coach began to move, Elinor swallowed hard. "Mama, I cannot go to Longford—I cannot—I cannot."

"Ye got to," Mary pointed out practically. "He ain't like ter turn his own flesh and blood away." As she spoke, she settled the babe into Elinor's arms.

"Well, I cannot like it, of course," Lady Ashton murmured, "but I cannot see as there is a great deal of choice, Nell."

Elinor turned her face to the carriage wall and whispered low, "You don't understand—I'd not face him."

"It would have been very much better for us all had you decided that last year," her mother retorted, then relented enough to clasp her hand. "But we shall contrive, dearest—we shall contrive."

Elinor huddled miserably against the side and pulled the blanket around her infant daughter and herself. They did not understand that she hated him, that she'd almost rather die than ask him for anything.

* * *

It had taken the driver's persistent knocking to rouse the house, and even then the lights within were slow to come on. Mary held one of Elinor's elbows, her mother the other, while she herself warmed her babe within the blanket.

The bleary-eyed butler stared for a moment, as though he could scarce believe what he saw, then he managed to utter, " 'Pon my word—get his lordship, will you, Will?" He stepped back, allowing them to enter. "Has there been some sort of accident?"

Wakened by the noise, Lucien himself came out upstairs and looked over the polished rail, seeing the three women, all in their nightgowns. "Good God—what happened?" he demanded, coming down, taking the steps two or more at a time. He stopped when he got closer, stunned by the sight of Elinor's battered face, and his jaw worked as he fought rising anger.

"Did Kingsley do this?" he demanded.

Before her mistress could refuse his assistance, Mary burst out with, "Oh, yer lordship—it was terrible! And my lady was but delivered of the babe! Why, it was a hard birthin', and she can scarce stand, and he—"

Elinor closed her eyes and swayed between her maid and her mother. "I did not want to come," she whispered. "I did not want to come."

It was then that he saw the blood on her nightgown and on his foyer floor, and he thought she was going to faint. He reached for her, but she kept her arms clasped around her babe. The blanket fell open, revealing the red, wrinkled little face—and the shock of black hair.

"It's a daughter," Lady Ashton said simply.

With an effort, Elinor forced herself to look up at him. "Please, Luce—perhaps the cottage rather than here."

"No."

"Lord Kingsley's gone mad," Mary reported. "He was shootin' his pistol when we left."

"Then you are safer here," he muttered tersely. "Here—"

He would have lifted her, but Elinor twisted her body, struggling. "Don't touch me!" she cried. "Don't touch me!"

"Don't be a fool, Nell!" he snapped. "You are bleeding like a stuck pig—you've got to have a doctor." This time, instead of picking her up, he caught her beneath her shoulder, telling Mary, "I've got her—you get the babe." She was shivering, and he could not tell whether it was from cold or his touch. "Come on. Between your mother and me, we'll get you to bed."

She felt weak, dizzy, and as they took her up the stairs, she stumbled several times, but each time when he would have picked her up, she shook her head, mumbling, "I am all right."

"Get Beatty," he ordered over his shoulder. *"Now."*

Her hands were like ice and her teeth were chattering by the time they got her to a bedchamber. "It's the loss of blood," he muttered, "I've seen it before."

"She'll ruin the bed," Mary said. By now, the babe had wakened and was squalling indignantly. To still her, the maid stuck her little finger in its mouth. "And her ladyship's in no case ter nurse."

It was as though the entire household had come to life. Lucien's housekeeper rolled sheets to place beneath Elinor, while his valet produced one of his nightshirts, apologizing to Lady Ashton that "As there are no females in residence, it's all we have." One of the chambermaids came forward, remembering that "Molly Fairchild's boy is near to weanin,' " whereupon a footman was dispatched to fetch the woman and urged to make haste.

As the women cleaned Elinor and changed her gown, Lucien made his way down to await Beatty. It was not until he sank into a chair in his saloon that it came home to him that he had a daughter, that he and Elinor had a daughter—a red, screaming, black-haired daughter.

As tired as he was—he'd been asleep but a quarter hour before—there was a certain exhilaration that accompanied the realization. But it was tempered by fear. And anger. If anything happened to Elinor, he would take Arthur Kingsley's cane from him and beat him senseless—before he killed him.

Beatty came and went upstairs for what seemed an age. The floor above creaked with the footsteps of people moving about in the bedchamber. The Fairchild woman arrived and was promptly dispatched up also, and then there was a respite of silence. Lucien sat slumped in his chair before the empty fireplace, waiting and listening to the steady ticking of a mantel clock. Finally, when he could stand it no longer, he reached for a decanter and poured himself a glass of port, then stared into the dark red liquid for a time.

She'd not wanted to come. If she'd had anywhere else to run, she'd have gone there. She could not even stand for him to touch her anywhere. His hand brushed over his face wearily, and he felt the thin, fine scars on his cheek and nose. She'd damned near cut his face open, and the whip marks had taken a long time to heal.

What he'd not wanted to admit, what stung his pride, was that he'd been unable to heal inside. Despite all the pain, he still wanted her.

"Ahem."

It was Beatty. Lucien straightened up and gestured to the port, but the doctor shook his head. For a moment, the earl was afraid to ask, and yet he had to.

"How is she? You were up there a long time."

"You want it delicately—or would you have the truth?" Beatty asked, dropping tiredly into a chair.

"The truth."

"For all his reputation, Moreston's a butcher."

For a moment, Lucien's blood ran cold. "What do you mean?"

"Woman's all torn up—the babe was coming wrong, and he had to turn it. Damned near let her bleed to death."

But she will recover?"

He nodded. "Had to stitch a bit—daresay it'll be awhile before she wants to have another. Weak," he added, "damned weak—and the beating did not help matters." His eyes met Lucien's. "Healthy babe, though."

"She's mine," Lucien admitted baldly.

"Not hard to tell it."

"No."

"Thing is, don't see why he had to beat her—must've known long before now."

"He didn't want a daughter."

"A man as would beat a female in her condition ought not to live," the doctor declared, rising. "Best go before Mrs. Beatty calls out the constable to look for me—didn't have time to tell her where I was going." Momentarily, he clasped Lucien's shoulder, then released it. "Aye—she'll recover."

A long time after the physician left, Lucien sat there, wanting to go up, to see for himself. His drink sat untouched on the table beside him. Finally, he heaved himself up from the chair and went up, not to see her, but to dress. And when he came down, he was ready to ride, armed with his dragoon pistols and his rifle. Beatty was right—even if Elinor survived, Kingsley did not deserve to live.

DAWN WAS BREAKING through the fog, making the morning mist almost rose. Beads of water condensed on his face like perspiration, and even his cloak, his breeches, and his boots were damp. He spread his cloak, exposing his coat to cover his saddle holsters, to keep his pistols dry. In front of him, slung over his military saddle, lay his rifle, its bayonet gleaming wetly in the early light.

Not even the coolness of the mist on his brow could ease the heat of his anger as he thought of Kingsley. And it did not matter that he would probably swing on the Nubbing Cheat for what he meant to do. He should have done it long ago—he should have done it when the old man had first offered Nell to him. For he'd known then that her life was little better than a hell. But instead, no matter how it happened, he'd done what Kingsley asked, and he and Nell had paid bitterly for it.

The house loomed ahead, rising out of the mists, a monolith of stone like something in a Gothic novel. There was almost an eerie silence to it, as though it awaited him.

He dismounted some distance from the house, drew his pistols, checked his load, the single ball and powder cap in each of them, then walked purposefully to the door to bang the knocker. When no one answered, he tried the door, surprised when it swung inward. It was as though the place were deserted, empty of all but the trappings of the old man's wealth. His bootsteps echoed as he crossed the marble floor of the foyer, and still no one came to stop him.

With his elbow, he pushed open the door to the front saloon, unprepared for the devastation that greeted him. There was glass everywhere, from shattered windows to the shards of stemware, the elegant window hangings had been pulled from their tilted fixtures, and the walls bore holes as though there had been a siege of sorts. Then he saw Kingsley.

His first thought was that he'd been cheated, that the old man had committed suicide. The baron lay facedown, his arm outstretched, his own pistol a few inches from his hand. And a dark red stain had spread across the thick, expensive carpet, seemingly coming from beneath him. An ammunition box and an old-fashioned powder horn lay empty beside him.

Lucien walked closer to stand over him, then turned him over contemptuously with the toe of his boot. There was no hole, and pieces of a crystal decanter betrayed that it was port rather than blood on the rug. Although his eyes were closed, Kingsley's chest rose and fell.

"Get up—damn you—get up!" Lucien shouted at him. "Get up! I'd have you know when I put a ball into you!"

"I'm afraid he cannot."

He swung around, seeing Peake, who shrank at the sight of his pistols. "Get him up," he ordered. "I want him sobered."

The butler, who considered that he had perhaps passed the worst night of his life, did not move. "I cannot—we have tried to rouse him to no avail." His gaze went from the pistols to Lucien's face. "It would appear he has suffered a fit of apoplexy, my lord. Indeed, but Dr. Beatty has been sent for."

"I don't believe you!"

Peake shrugged. "Well, he can see, but he is unable to speak." His eyes dropped to Kingsley. "One of the footmen discovered him thus less than an hour ago." He walked past Lucien and bent to retrieve his employer's flintlock pistol, then held it out. "We've had rather a bad time of it, I'm afraid. We had to wait until it was thought he'd exhausted his powder, and thus he had spent the better part of the night shooting up the place. Twice Jeremy attempted to disarm him, but was fired upon."

"He's drunk," Lucien muttered.

But even as he said it, he knew better. The old man's eyes had opened and there was a terror in them, and it had nothing to do with him. It was as though Kingsley's face were frozen, as all that moved were the eyes. Spit drooled from the corner of his mouth.

"I'm afraid you have come to kill a dying man," Peake said tiredly, sitting down. "But you are welcome to await Dr. Beatty that it can be confirmed." He looked up at Lucien. "How fares Lady Kingsley?"

"I don't know—Beatty says she will live."

"Dreadful business—I am sorry for it."

Lucien walked to a broken window and peered out from a drapery that hung askew. "Beatty's been up all night."

"So have we all. Poor Mrs. Peake is in a taking, for we had to seek shelter in the stable. And the maid Agnes is engaging in a fit of hysteria. Dreadful night, sir—dreadful." The butler shuddered visibly. "At least we were more fortunate than the others, who were forced to hide in the cellar with the rats. It's apparently what ails Agnes—I am told she was bitten as she tried to sleep against a sack of flour."

He rambled on, trying to describe the horrors of the night, but Lucien was beyond listening. He had to wait for Beatty. He had to know if Kingsley would survive.

It was a long wait, for the doctor had grumbled over being rousted from his bed twice, but in the end he'd come. As the household came to life, many gathered outside in the hall to hear. Beatty knelt beside the old man, moving a candle above his eyes, then attempted to flex Kingsley's limbs. "No doubt about it," he declared when he rose, "the brain is involved." He looked to Peake. "You can move him upstairs."

"How long will he live?" Lucien asked grimly.

"Well"—Beatty attempted to wipe wine stains from his breeches before he answered—"as to that, I cannot say, my lord. If he has another equally severe episode, I'd say that would end it. But I have seen cases where the patient regains a portion of his powers and continues on for years. Given his age, I'd not like to make a prognosis yet." His eyes met Lucien's. "In any event, he is not likely to offer violence to anyone again. You may reassure Lady Kingsley on that head."

Lucien gestured to the pistols. "I came to kill him."

"You won't have to. How old is he—sixty-six? I should

think it highly unlikely he will survive overlong. Perhaps not the night, perhaps not the year."

"It's not good enough. He ought to be dead for what he has done to her."

Beatty shrugged, then shook his head. "Sometimes, my lord, this is worse than death."

As Daggett directed footmen in carrying the baron upstairs, Peake recalled his duties. "A glass of sherry, sirs? I am afraid we are out of port at the moment. Unless, of course, you would wish me to send to the cellars—"

The doctor nodded. "After the night I have passed, I could use it. My lord?"

Lucien shook his head. "No. I am for home."

As Peake discreetly withdrew to search for a whole glass, Beatty stopped Lucien. "Were I you," he advised, "I should bring her back as soon as she can travel."

"No."

"Scandal can be a dreadful thing, my lord—and there is a child to consider."

"After what he has done—" Lucien choked, unable to finish for his anger. Exhaling to control it, he said, "You saw her—how the devil—?"

"He is in no case to harm her," Beatty repeated. "But you of all people have witnessed what wagging tongues can do, have you not?"

"I won't even be at the Park—I have orders to leave day after tomorrow. With Cotton still ill, I have to go."

Beatty's eyebrows lifted. "Back to the Peninsula? My dear Longford—"

"We are invading France."

For a moment, the doctor appeared startled by the news, then his mouth formed a silent "Oh."

"Yes. Do you think I could go and leave her at his mercy? What if he should recover enough to do this again?"

"I hardly think it likely, my lord."

"I don't want to deal with 'likely,' sir!" Lucien snapped. "I want to know she is safe!"

"If you leave her at the Park, you brand her—aye, and you tell the world your daughter is a bastard. Perhaps if her father were to come—"

"Her father!" Lucien snorted contemptuously. "You've seen him, and you would suggest it?"

"Then perhaps Lord Leighton? I collect he knows. Let him deal with Kingsley for you," Beatty suggested reasonably. "Surely she could flee to him if—"

"And compound the scandal?"

"No. No, you mistake my meaning. Should Kingsley recover sufficiently to understand it, perhaps Leighton could negotiate the terms for her remaining here. Kingsley is, after all is said, a proud man. When his disappointment is over, he will wish to acknowledge the child, I'd think."

"Still—"

"For him it must surely be better than having the world know he has been cuckolded, than having it said he's naught but an old fool," Beatty argued reasonably.

"And until then—until he comes to see the sanity of that?" Lucien demanded harshly.

"You've got to send her back—for her sake and for the child's."

"No. Look around you—you have seen what he has done."

"My lord, he cannot even hold the pistol."

* * *

As he rode back to Langston Park, Lucien felt as though his cup of gall overflowed. It seemed as though all his life he had been embittered by one thing or another—his mother, Mad Jack, Diana. The only respite had been Elinor, and it had been a brief one. And now, when he might have the chance to redeem himself with her, to win her love, he was going back to Spain, perhaps never to come home again.

Cold reason told him Beatty was right—he'd have to send her back to Stoneleigh. And Arthur still lived. Damn him—he still lived.

He struggled within himself, arguing that he could resign his commission and take her away—but where? Although Wellington had won at Vittoria, the war still raged on. And it was laughable to think they'd be welcomed in America. And even if there was some place, even if she would go, which he doubted, she would be branded before society as his mistress.

If Kingsley recovered at all, he would be within his

rights to repudiate the child. The world would know her for a bastard. The irony of it was not lost on him—as long as Kingsley could be made complacent in the matter, everything was all right, and Elinor's behavior was if not entirely condoned, certainly not condemned. As long as Kingsley did not kick up a dust, Elinor would be considered no worse than Sally Jersey or Lady Holland, both of whom were received everywhere.

By the time he reached home, he was not only bone-weary but heartsick. And as bitter as he'd ever been. Never in his life had he been given a decent choice. He still had no hope of happiness.

Putting his pistols and rifle away, he trudged the stairs like a man going to the gallows. He hesitated outside her bedchamber door, then pushed it open. Mary rose when she saw him and placed a finger over her lips, indicating the sleeping figures on the bed. "Beatty gave her ladyship opium," she whispered, "but it's just now as we got the babe ter sleep." Nodding, he gestured silently for her to leave.

He waited until the maid was gone, then he pulled a chair close to the bed. Sitting, he leaned forward to brush the tangled copper hair back from Elinor's swollen, bruised face. In contrast, her hand, where it clutched the covers, was white and bloodless. Despite all the bitter, angry words she'd flung at him, he felt a great tenderness for her. And he cursed himself for failing her.

His gaze rested on the tiny babe that lay sleeping in the crook of her arm, its black-thatched head barely visible above its swaddlings. His daughter. He had a daughter born of the greatest passion of his life. He wanted to touch the dark hair, to look into his child's face, but he dared not waken her. He dared not even claim her. She'd been born a Kingsley, and if he loved either of them, he'd have to leave it at that.

Still, he could not help the acute longing that tore at his soul when he looked on them. If anything were right in this world, Elinor would have been his wife, the babe the firstborn of his name. Instead, he would have to send them back to Kingsley.

His eyes returned to Elinor, remembering how she'd scarce let him help her up the stairs. God, how she must hate him, what it must have cost her pride to come to

Langston Park. For a moment, he allowed himself the luxury of touching her again, of tracing the fine profile, of feeling the softness of her breath against his hand. There had been a time when that breath had come in great gasps, when those amber eyes of hers had been almost dark with an answering passion, when she'd drawn him to her, when she'd wanted him as much as he'd wanted her. When she'd conceived his daughter.

The aching loneliness inside him was almost too great to bear. For a long time, he sat there, staring at the copper-framed marble face, wanting to waken her, to tell her that Arthur had lied, that it had been love as much as desire that made their child. But he was going away, and she was going back to Arthur. And even if she believed him, even if by some miracle she could love him also, he could not do it. He'd seen her agony when Charles Kingsley had died, and if he did not come back—no, he could not do that to her again. If he perished, it was better that she thought she hated him.

Finally, he leaned down to steal a kiss from Nell's cold lips, then brushed his daughter's black hair with his hand, marveling at how small she was. If—when he came back, she would not look like this, and he knew it.

He looked again at Elinor and whispered softly, "I tried to kill him for you, Nell, but I was too late. I tried to free you from his prison, but I couldn't shoot a helpless man. I was willing to hang for you, Nell."

He rose wearily and passed his hand over his eyes. She couldn't hear him, and even if she could, there were no words he could give her now, not while she still belonged to Arthur, not while he was going back to battle. Someday—if he lived—he'd tell her Kingsley lied, that what had been between them had nothing to do with Arthur. That he'd wanted her for a long time before he'd gone to Stoneleigh.

Resolutely, he straightened aching shoulders and went to the door. His hand on the knob, he turned back for one last look, then he wrenched the door open. Today he was going to bed. Later, he'd see Leighton. And tomorrow he would leave again for hell.

FOR TWO DAYS, she lay in a near stupor, drugged while her body began to heal. And when she'd finally wakened, her mother had told her that Lucien had gone, that England was finally going to invade France. And she had turned her face to the wall to hide her tears. For all that she was bitter, for all that she had tried to hate him, she could not help feeling abandoned all over again. She listened dully as her mother explained that Longford had settled it with Leighton, that the viscount was going to broker her return to Stoneleigh. That Arthur had suffered a fearful stroke and was no longer a threat to harm anyone.

Her father, who'd journeyed posthaste on the mails, afraid that she might jeopardize her widow's portion, added his own assurances. Her mother would stay with her as long as needed, and Lord Leighton stood ready to receive her if anything went awry. It was better for everyone, he argued, for at Stoneleigh, the babe could be properly christened, averting further scandal.

Leighton himself came to call, saying that he'd been to see Arthur, and that the old man was in sad case. He was beginning to regain his speech, but Beatty doubted he would ever have much use of his limbs. The prognosis was that Arthur Kingsley would be abed the rest of his life. But he'd understood, or so Leighton thought, and he'd managed to nod his head as the viscount had outlined Longford's terms: Elinor would return, saving him the pity of his neighbors, and he would acknowledge the child. Beyond living in his house, she was not expected to have any further discourse with him.

"And he agreed to it?" she asked incredulously.

"Yes," Leighton declared simply. "Longford was right—as ill as he is, Kingsley still has his pride."

"I see." She looked up at her father, who nodded approvingly. "Very well—it would not seem as though there is much choice, is there?"

"Well, you could remain here, of course. Longford said if you decided to, he would make provision for you and the child." Leighton's blue eyes regarded her soberly. "But I should not advise it. For the babe's sake, if not for your own, I think you ought to go home."

"Make the babe an heiress," her father insisted. "Can't deny her his fortune, can you? Besides, you got your widow's portion to consider."

Leighton flashed him a look of considerable dislike, then turned again to Elinor, his face a mirror of sympathy. "You have but to send to me, and I will come," he promised. "I gave Lucien my word I would see to your safety."

For public consumption, it would be given out that Lady Kingsley's lying in had been an exceedingly difficult one, and that she had curtailed all activities while she recovered. Then Arthur's own illness had further complicated matters, explaining why no one, not even the vicar and his wife, had been invited to view the babe. And as she had the sympathy of the entire household staff, including Daggett, it was unlikely any gossip would escape from Stoneleigh.

It was done. There but remained the matter of taking her home, which Leighton did within the week, providing a closed carriage for her, the babe, her mother, and her father. Already rumors floated about the infant, with many going so far as to speculate that if it were indeed Kingsley's, perhaps because of his age, it was either an imbecile or deformed. It was time to show the child before the talk got worse, Lord Ashton insisted. Despite Arthur's condition, plans must be made for a public christening.

Her first two days home, she kept to her chamber, nursing and tending her babe, trying to reconcile in her mind once again that Lucien had never loved her, that it had been as Arthur had told her. Finally, she came out, dry-eyed and composed. She was a woman grown now, not a child, and she would do what she must to protect her still-unnamed daughter.

That afternoon, to take her mind from what her papa

called her "unreasoning fear" of him, she visited Arthur, totally unprepared for what he had become. He seemed shrunken, smallish like a curled spider, and he was as helpless as Leighton had painted him. His eyes followed her as she came into the room, and there was no mistaking that he was glad enough to see her. He lifted a frail hand as though he would beckon her closer, then he let it fall limply to the covers.

"You—came—home."

"I had nowhere else to go," she said simply.

Tears formed in the rheumy eyes and spilled over onto his sunken cheeks, and he had not the coordination to brush them away. "Sorry—for—it," he whispered.

"For what?" she asked coldly.

"Ever—Every—thing."

As much as she hated him, she felt a certain pity for him. To a man of his pride, how it must gall him to have to lie there like that. She pulled up a chair and sat down. "Do you hurt, my lord?" she managed to ask him.

"No—cannot feel—beyond"—he gave up for a moment, marshaling his breath before going on—"beyond my—arms."

She sat there, not knowing what to say, trying to separate the pitiful creature before her from the husband who'd cost her so much. Finally, she started to rise.

"Don't—go—yet. The—the babe?"

"She looks like Lucien," she told him brutally, "so we are both cheated, aren't we?"

"Sorry for—that—also." His voice was thin, breathless, and so faint she could scarce hear him. "Misjudged him." Then, sucking in air again, he managed to ask, "What name—do—you—give her?"

"I don't know. I'd thought perhaps Elizabeth—it's my second name."

He nodded weakly and closed his eyes. Once again, she started to leave, only to have him stop her. "Not yet," he gasped. "Stay—read—anything."

She would have denied him, but she could not deny a certain pity for him. Reluctantly, she reached for the book that lay on the small stand beside his bed. To her surprise, it was *The Iliad,* the book Lucien had teased Bell with in what seemed another lifetime. She opened it to a folded-down page and began to read, losing herself in the epic tale of fabled heroes. After an hour or so, when she laid it aside, she heard him whisper, "My thanks."

Later, early in the evening, word came that he wanted to see "his daughter," as Daggett reported it. Taking her mother for support, Elinor carried the infant into his chamber that he might see her. Yet, as helpless as he was, she kept her daughter beyond his reach. But he held out his hand, trying to touch her, and finally she drew close enough that his wasted fingers found the babe's arm.

"Pretty—like you."

"Thank you."

"Elizabeth—Louise—Char—Charlotte—Kingsley."

The next day, when the vicar and his wife made a late afternoon call to finalize preparation for the babe's christening, Eliza Thurstan made over Elizabeth, saying that she was honored to have the child named for her. And she remarked with a completely straight face how much the infant looked like Arthur.

She took them up to see him, thinking perhaps it would lighten his spirits. Eliza gushed over "little Elizabeth," to which he replied, "Named her—for—my mother—also. Pretty little—thing." After they left, Elinor started to thank him for carrying on the sham, but he shook his head. "Got to—keep—my bargain." He gestured to the laudanum bottle on his bedside table. "Might—as well—give me—some. Cannot do—aught—but sleep."

"Are you hurting?"

"No."

Once again, she felt sorry for him. A man who had striven so hard, sacrificed so much for the emptiness of money and station, and he had nothing worthwhile left to him.

"I could read to you again," she offered.

"No. Go on—got better—things—to do."

But she didn't. She picked up the book and read aloud again, until Mary came to tell her that Elizabeth was rather insistently hungry. As she laid aside *The Iliad,* she saw that Arthur slept. Without the laudanum.

After that, as much to pass her time as his, she took to reading to him twice each day, and when she was informed that he'd quit eating, she began feeding him also, ordering that instead of gruel and jellies, he ought to have what the rest of the household ate minced for him.

Still, he did not seem to want to eat. After a few bites, he pushed feebly at her hand.

"Don't know what your lay is, Nell," her father complained. "He ain't like to push off if you keep it up."

It seemed odd—after nearly six years of waiting for him to die, she was prepared to see her elderly husband live, and until he was gone, she'd do her duty to him. After all, despite everything else that had passed between them, he had given Elizabeth his name.

* * *

When the christening came, it drew the curious, but she managed to hold her head high as she watched the vicar dribble the baptismal water over her child's head. At her side, Lord Leighton stood godfather in the absence of any other. And it was duly recorded in the parish register. *Elizabeth Charlotte Louise Kingsley, b. 6 July, 1813, d. of Arthur, Baron Kingsley, and his wife, Elinor.* She was officially now and forever legitimate, despite Elinor's rearrangement of the names Arthur had wanted. Somehow they sounded better in that order.

Afterward, she took the babe, still in the exquisite christening gown he'd ordered from Switzerland, to show Arthur. And once again, he pronounced Elizabeth pretty. She and the infant stayed for a while, until he said he was tired. He appeared despondent, and despite her offer to come back to read, he shook his head.

Even a suggestion that perhaps on the morrow Jeremy and Daggett might take him down to sit in a chair on the porch did not seem to improve his spirits. She quarreled with her father over that, sending him home in a huff, muttering if she continued, Arthur was going to outlive him. But as agreed, he left her mother, advising her privately to keep an eye on his expectations. His departure suited both of them.

Two days later, Arthur spent perhaps an hour with the solicitor he'd demanded. And later he surprised everyone by asking to be carried downstairs. He lay upon a settee, watching as Elinor sat stitching, her bright hair falling forward as she leaned toward the light from the window. Aye, she was as beautiful as ever, a woman to do a man credit, and for all that she'd betrayed him with Longford, he did not blame her for it. It had been his idea from the beginning, and it had not taken much suggestion for the earl to act upon it.

If he regretted anything, it was Charles. He lay there, propped against pillows, remembering reading the boy's journal, thinking how little he'd known him. And a man ought to know his own flesh and blood, for in the end, money had no memory, money did not grieve. Now he had no one to cry for him, and even if he chose to live, it was unlikely that little Elizabeth would remember him as anything beyond a sick old man. What Elinor and the infant needed was a strong man like Longford, someone who could take care of them with more than money.

He looked again to Elinor, thinking that her real worth lay not in her beauty, but rather in her capacity to forgive, to live and survive in adversity. If anything, her beauty had been enhanced by it, for it gave her a certain character that so many lovely women lacked.

If he'd made mistakes in assessing her, his worst he supposed was in assuming she was as fickle, as empty as the rest of them. Despite her professed hatred of Longford, he did not doubt that there was still a bit of a spark there, something that could be rekindled when he was gone. And the realization brought with it a pang of regret that he'd not been younger when he'd wed her.

He could still remember the triumph she'd given him in London. He had made it to Almack's. He had hobnobbed with the *ton,* speaking with the likes of the Jerseys, the Seftons, the Melbournes. She'd gained him the entrée he'd asked for. And had it not been for poor Charles, she'd be the reigning Incomparable still.

She looked up, aware of his scrutiny. "You look a trifle hagged, my lord. Perhaps you have been down too long."

"Aye."

She rang for the footman, ordering that his lordship be carried back to bed. As they bundled his blanket about him, he asked for a bottle of port, surprising her. He still had difficulty swallowing. But if Daggett were there . . . She nodded.

It was not even his household anymore. He was so helpless he had to ask for everything. And to him it was as though he'd lost all consequence, as though he were merely *de trop*, as though the world had already left him, and there was nothing left for him to do—except one last thing.

She laid aside her sewing and followed them up to see that he got his port. She reminded Daggett that someone ought to stay with him lest he choke, then she left to feed Elizabeth, who could be heard wailing down the hall. To him, it was almost obscene that she'd chosen to nurse the infant herself, but he supposed that was another thing that had passed him by. In his day, his first wife had nursed his son because he'd not had enough money to engage a wet nurse. And he'd always felt sorry about that.

He let her go, then stared for a time at the ceiling, seeing the gold-leaf rosettes he'd had copied from Marie Antoinette's bedroom. He'd managed to get it all—more money than he'd ever dreamed existed when he was a boy. But a man had to be ruthless to get what he wanted, and he wondered briefly if he'd see any of his enemies again.

He took the glass Daggett poured him, then waved him away, muttering that he was not a child. The faithful valet hesitated as though uncertain as to whether to obey him or Lady Kingsley. In the end, habit triumphed, and he left also.

Arthur lay there for some time, sipping slowly, thinking of his life, wondering if much of it had been worth the price. Finally, he poured himself some more of the port, spilling a great deal of it on his covers. Then he reached for the bottle of laudanum he'd been hoarding beneath some papers in a bedside table drawer. His hand trembled so much he was afraid he'd drop it, that he'd spill some of it, but he managed to get it. "Daggett—"

"Aye, my lord?" As always, the valet hastened when the bell was pulled.

"Get—the—stopper out, will—you?"

"Aye."

"And do not—set it—tightly, for I may—have need—of more later."

"Would you have a dose now? Should I inform Lady Kingsley you are in pain?"

"Not yet."

He waited only until Daggett was out the door, then

he emptied the bottle into his cup. At first taste, he thought he would vomit, then he drank enough to add more port. Finally, he had it all down. His stomach churned, but he lay quite still, hoping it would settle. Then he waited until he began to feel drowsy, until he knew it would be too late. Slipping the empty laudanum bottle beneath his pillow, he rang again for the valet.

"Fetch—Lady Kingsley," he gasped. "So—little—time."

Mystified by the message, Elinor came back to sit with him. "What do you need?" she asked him.

"Hold—my—my—hand."

She was used to his sometimes childish behavior, but just now he surprised her. Nonetheless, she took his hand between both hers.

His speech sounded even more slurred and she began to wonder if he were having another stroke. "Arthur—?"

He blinked, then roused. "Tired—so tired."

She leaned over him to pull him up onto his pillow, and saw the empty bottle. "What on earth—? Arthur, what is this?"

"Too—late," he mumbled.

"Daggett! Daggett!" Her voice rose. "Daggett—now!"

"Aye, my lady?"

"Send someone to fetch Dr. Beatty on the instant—and have him take a good horse! *Now,* Mr. Daggett!"

"Is aught amiss?"

She held up the bottle. "I think he drank it."

"It was full."

Arthur roused again, and his eyes blinked as they sought Daggett's. "Aye."

"But why, Arthur—*why*?" Her eyes were hot with unshed tears.

"Too—old," he mumbled.

"Arthur!" She half-crawled onto the bed with him and shook him hard, trying to keep him awake. "Arthur, you cannot—it's a sin!"

"Cannot—"

Mrs. Peake, Lady Ashton, Mary, Peake—full half the household came as she began screaming. But they were all too late. Arthur Kingsley slipped deeper, drawing away from the world that no longer pleased him.

By the time Beatty arrived, he shook his head. "Nothing to do but wait, I'm afraid. By the sound of his breathing, it would do no good to make him vomit. Besides, he cannot swallow now—it would go into his lungs."

She sat there, perhaps another hour, until the physician announced it was over. When she looked up, she managed a twisted smile. "It was Arthur, was it not? He was still determined to control what he could."

"Sometimes, Lady Kingsley," Beatty murmured, "it's easier to die than to live."

* * *

Two weeks after Arthur Kingsley was interred beside Charles, Eleanor, her parents, and Lord Leighton sat in the bookroom at Stoneleigh for the reading of his will. And the provisions of it shocked nearly everyone. The title he could not keep from his distant Cit relation was duly mentioned, but with it went nothing but one thousand pounds in total for its maintenance. No house, nothing else, as all of his possessions were acquired and therefore not entailed.

To Elinor, there was the customary one-third widow's portion, enough to make her incredibly wealthy for life—"on condition that she spend none of it beyond what I have mentioned on her relations," which amounted to five thousand pounds each to her sisters "for their marriage portions," and one last ten thousand pounds to "Baron Ashton," for a final settling of his debts, beyond which he must not apply to Elinor. And the jewelry, of course, was to be kept for her use "so long as she shall live, whereupon it shall be passed on to Elizabeth, my daughter." Stoneleigh was to go to her "during the child's minority," and then it would belong to Elizabeth, as would the remaining two-thirds of his estate.

In that one document, Elizabeth Charlotte Louise Kingsley had become a great heiress. His only request was an odd one—he'd have Elinor and the child visit his grave annually in remembrance of him. It was, Lord Ashton whispered, "a small price to pay for the enormous fortune he's left the both of you."

But perhaps the most startling portion was that which named "Lucien, Earl of Longford, my daughter's guardian during her minority, which shall for these purposes be determined to be the age of twenty-five. In the event of his absence from the country, I should ask George, Viscount Leighton to act in his stead."

It was at that point that her father started from his chair. "No! By God, it's a miscarriage! The guardianship ought to go to me—as the babe's grandfather, it's my right!"

The solicitor looked up over the rims of half-spectacles. "Lord Ashton, I am afraid Lord Kingsley was most specific in his preference. Thrice I asked him, and thrice he said it was to be the Earl of Longford. I'm sorry, my lord."

"Sorry! Sorry?" Ashton's voice rose. "I had quite counted—" He stopped, and it was as though he could hear Arthur speaking from those years before, saying it was never wise to count another man's money. "I don't suppose the provisions can be broken?" he inquired hollowly.

"Only if Lady Kingsley and all other heirs can be brought to agree."

He turned to Leighton, appealing, "You've no wish for the duty, have you? And Longford—Longford—" He fairly choked on the name. "Well, I'll not abide it, sir! Not after what he has done!"

Leighton shrugged. "I shall, of course, do as Lady Kingsley asks me. I quite count myself a friend to both her and Lucien."

"Puss—tell him—"

She sat there, her hands gripping the arms of her chair until her knuckles were white. Arthur had named Lucien Elizabeth's guardian. Why? There could be only one answer—only one. For a moment, it was as though her heart stood still, then relief flooded over her, bringing tears. And she could scarce contain what she felt in that instant. *Arthur had lied.*

"Lady Kingsley, are you all right?" Leighton asked gently.

"Yes. Yes." She bit her lip to maintain what composure she could. Looking up at her father, she managed to shake her head. "I am satisfied with the terms, Papa," she whispered.

"It's a disgrace! You shall be a laughingstock—or

worse! When the world gets a look at Elizabeth and makes the connection—''

Lady Ashton rose. ''That will be quite enough, Thomas,'' she told him sharply.

''Enough!'' he howled. ''It'll be a scandal! She cannot recover! The child—''

''The child will be so wealthy I doubt any will cavil over an old scandal,'' Leighton cut in coldly.

Elinor's father turned on him. ''You did this!'' he accused.

''Papa, stop it!'' She looked across to Leighton. ''If you do not mind it, George, I would that you wrote Longford of this. And tell him that I do not object.''

''Puss, you cannot!''

She stood to face her father. ''Papa, do you not understand? I am rich enough to do as I please—you saw to that when you sold me.'' She nodded to the solicitor, then to Leighton and her mother. ''If I may be excused, I should like to tend to my daughter.''

The black silk skirt of her gown swished against the petticoat beneath it as she passed her father. He started to reach out to stop her, then dropped his hand. He stared at her in bewilderment before looking at his wife.

''Why?'' he asked.

''When you sold her to Kingsley, you gave up any claim to her, Thomas.''

''I did it for her!''

Lady Ashton met his eyes for a long moment. ''Did you, Thomas? I don't think so.'' Moving around him so that she did not even touch him, she left the room also.

Behind her, she could hear him insist to Leighton and the solicitor, ''I did it for her own good—tell them—''

''Yes, well—'' Leighton reached for his hat. ''If there's naught else to be attended to, I shall go home and write Longford.''

''Tell them!''

But the solicitor ignored him. ''There's naught else for now, my lord,'' he told Leighton. ''You may write the earl that I shall await his instructions.''

August 30, 1813: Outside St. Sebastian, Spain

IT HAD BEEN A grueling month since he'd arrived, one that had seen appalling losses among Britain's ill-fed Spanish allies, so many that after their victory at Sorauren, they'd been unable to pursue the French back over the Maya Pass. And now they were poised for another assault on St. Sebastian, which still held out. Rumor had it that Marshal Soult was preparing a force to relieve the British siege from across the Bidassoa, so time was short.

Lucien, who'd spent much of the day in his saddle, riding up and down the assault lines, returned to his tent to discover Leighton's letter. Bone-weary, he ordered his aide to pour him a cup of port, and he sank to his cot to read.

> My dear Luce,
>
> It is my not altogether sad duty to apprise you that Arthur Kingsley has died by his own hand, which may or may not surprise you. The poor fellow was confined to his bed, and I suppose ultimately it affected his mind.
>
> In any event, in his final disposition, he proved more than fair, leaving Elinor her widow's portion as well as a fortune in her jewelry. Most of the rest goes to the child, Elizabeth, with yourself chosen to act as guardian and conservator until her majority. Under the terms stated, in your absence, I am to carry out your directions and act in your behalf, until such time as you are come home to deal with matters more directly. So I suppose I must ask what you would that I did, although I cannot think it much, for the infant is too young to require more than her mother provides for her.

Lady Kingsley herself is well, having routed Ashton from Stoneleigh, and her mother remains with her. Whenever I can, I intend to ride over to guard your interests there. One disquieting bit of news has come my way, however—Sally Jersey writes that Bell is seeking to purchase a place in Cornwall. Shall I give him the heave-ho for you?

I remain, as ever, your friend. George.

For a moment, Lucien was too stunned to think, then he reread the letter. Kingsley was dead. Elinor was free. He looked at the date at the top of the page and realized that Arthur had not waited very long after he'd left to do it. And now he sat in a stinking tent waiting to strike another blow against the French.

He read the words again, feeling a sense of unease over the bit about Bell, thinking perhaps he ought to have told Elinor he loved her, after all. But then there was the question of his own mortality. If she'd believed him, if she'd loved him in return, he'd not have her grieve twice. No, it was better to wait. Still, Arthur's will gave him a reason to write to her.

Ordering his paper and pen, he sat there, trying to compose something to encourage her. What he wanted to say, he could not—it had to be small, this opening, like the first breech in her defenses. Otherwise, she might consign his words to the flame. She might anyway. Finally, he sucked in his breath, exhaled fully, and began to write.

"My dear Lady Kingsley," he began, then stopped. Too formal, considering what they'd once been to each other. He crumpled the paper and tried again, this time addressing her as "Elinor, Lady Kingsley." That too landed in a wad at his feet. Perhaps just Elinor. But even that did not satisfy him. Telling himself he'd soon run out of the precious paper, he started over the last time.

My dear Nell,

I am in receipt of George's letter, and had I liked Arthur better, I should offer my condolences. Suffice it to say that I leave it to God to judge him. George

> tells me that you and Elizabeth are both well, and for that I am thankful.
>
> It's odd that you should have chosen to call her Elizabeth, for that was my mother's name. May she have a happier life than that namesake.

He stopped. There was so much that he yearned to tell her, but none of it was suited to a letter. If he wrote his thoughts, he should sound as moonstruck as Charley. No, this was his opening, nothing more. He went on.

> If you should find Arthur's instructions onerous, if you would rather have another guardian for the child, I can recommend none finer than George. However, lest you think I want out of it, let me say I will count myself honored if you will but let me be a part of Elizabeth's life.
>
> I saw her, you know, while you slept. And were it not for that black hair, I should count her a beauty like her mother. Myself, I rather preferred your red hair.

He stopped again. If he ran on like that, he'd be declaring himself before the end. The child. He had to focus on his daughter.

> I do not suppose there is much a guardian does for an infant, but if she has need of anything, I shall direct George to provide it. It will not be until later, when she is possessed of your looks and Kingsley's fortune, that we shall have to guard her against the rakes and rogues like Bell and myself. In between, we have but to look forward to governesses, schools, dancing and music masters, all the while taking care that she does not become merely another insipid cipher for some self-centered fellow. If we are fortunate, perhaps she will be like you—possessed of everything from wit to kindness.

He'd said enough. Every sentence tried to turn to that of a lover rather than a guardian. He quickly penned a closing of "Until I may see the both of you again, Lucien, Longford."

But long after his aide had taken it out to add to the dispatch bag, he sat upon his cot, thinking of her. Despite the discomfort, despite the flies, he could close his eyes and smell the lavender in her hair, and he could remember the feel of her beneath him, the yielding of her body to his, and the answering urgency of her passion. His mouth was dry, and his whole body ached with the memory of how it had been. Mad Jack had been wrong—there were more than the right holes to a woman. There was tenderness, there was giving—even where it was undeserved.

When he got home, he was going to win her again, even if it took every power of persuasion he possessed. And God willing, he could make her remember the good times, the times before she'd come to hate him.

"My lord—?"

"Huh?" He looked up. It was Barry, come to drag him back to the present, to the war, to the terrible, awful onslaught that was coming. He wasn't going home to Elinor. He was going to France over the Pyrenees, and he was going to fight until the last Frenchman laid down his arms. And then if he survived, he was going home.

"Are you quite all right?"

"Yes." It was then that it came home to him, that Arthur Kingsley had made him guardian to his own daughter. And he knew why—he knew that Lucien would keep that enormous fortune intact for the child. "Yes," he repeated.

"Soult's coming. If St. Sebastian falls, it will have to be tomorrow. Old Douro means to attempt a daylight assault."

"Daylight?"

"Got to, he says—for the artillery to be effective. Cannot afford to fire on our own men. Going to start firing in the morning." Barry looked away. "A lot of us are going to die."

"Probably one in three," Lucien agreed grimly.

"He wants a staff meeting over supper."

"I'll be there."

After Barry left, Lucien drained the last of his cup of port. It was as well that he'd not written anything else to Elinor. He'd be damned lucky if he saw the sun go down tomorrow. And if he survived that, there were dozens, perhaps a hundred such battles to be fought between St. Sebastian and Paris.

* * *

There was smoke and fire everywhere—from the belching guns to the flames that licked along the walls of the little fortress town. And the roar of the cannon was deafening, so much so that Lucien had stuffed lint into his ears against the sound. With a handkerchief tied over his nose to allow for breath, Lucien rode along the wall of men, urging them on, watching helplessly as they fell back. The hills were covered with red-coated bodies, some still quivering and jerking, while others heroically braved the fire to carry those that lived back down. And through it all, he told himself that he had to survive—that he had to go home this time.

Later, it was calm save for the cries and the moaning. Above, St. Sebastian was naught but a smoldering ruin, over which flew the British flag. It had been another costly victory—some regiments reported casualties of more than half, some more than one-third, and nearly every one had lost at least a quarter. Outside the fortress itself, four thousand French, those who'd come in vain to raise the siege, lay dead. In the twilight, a French flag, its standard still clutched in a stiff hand, fluttered alone.

This time he'd been lucky. Aside from soot and blood that smeared his face and uniform, he'd been untouched by it all. He sat on the grass alone, wiping the bloody blade of his bayonet with the dirty handkerchief that had covered his face.

"One down—God knows how many more to go," Barry murmured, dropping down beside him.

"It's a long way to Paris."

"Aye—but that's how it's done—one victory at a time."

"I know."

"Mad Jack would have savored this."

Lucien threw his handkerchief away, then rose. "I'm not Mad Jack. I've got someone to go home to." He looked down at Barry. "Jack didn't have anyone. Fool that he was, he didn't know he needed somebody." Then, feeling somehow ungracious to the older man, he clapped his shoulder. "Your pardon, but I've got a letter to write."

* * *

On September 3, a semaphored message was received from offshore, telling that Austria and Prussia had joined Russia against France. It was what Wellington had been waiting for. But first the British army had to break through Soult's mountain defenses. They were going to have to fight their way through the heights and passes, pushing the French back mile by bloody mile.

All manner of alien places came into Lucien's vocabulary, rolling off his tongue as though he'd been born to speak them—Hendaye, the Bidassoa, the Nivelle, St. Jean de Luz. They had to close off any means of restricting supplies from the sea.

On October 7, the light companies of the 5th Division waded armpit deep across the Bidassoa River to surprise the French on their frontier. Another bloody battle, and then the Pyrenean heights, from whence they looked down into France itself. And still Lucien lived as the lists of casualties sent home mounted, some of them taking a full dispatch pouch crammed to the buckle.

By November, they'd broken through Soult's lines along the Nivelle. It was rough country—hard, high, craggy—in some ways as barren and rocky as parts of Cornwall. But they took it and moved on. And again Lucien wrote to Elinor, not as a lover, but as Elizabeth's concerned guardian. But with each subsequent battle, he began to feel as though he would eventually go home alive.

Now as they pushed into France, there were half-buried, half-decayed corpses of Napoleon's *Grand Armee* everywhere, but the Little Corporal would not yield, preferring to live with the fantasy that he could somehow survive. It was going to be a fight to the death between the French and the world, for little countries once subjugated, fell into the fray on the allies' side now. And Wellington, fearful of an early peace, one that would not leave Napoleon beaten, pushed harder and harder.

To Lucien, it began to seem as though the war would never end. Christmas, the new year of 1814, a winter of battle after battle, of heavy casualties offset by heavier ones on the other side, of massive French desertions, of surrenders that strained the supplies. Still, he wrote Elinor, sending perhaps a letter a week, telling of where he was, what he did.

And to his surprise, she finally answered. It was old news, having followed him for two months, but it was from her nonetheless. But he read it and reread it, seeking something not said, and found nothing. She talked of the child, of its first tooth, of how much the little girl grew—but nothing beyond "as for me, I am quite well." Not much to pin great hope on.

By now, he knew he loved her desperately, that if he could have honorably done so, he would have gone home to put it to the touch. He no longer even worried about Mad Jack—he'd proven to himself he was different. Yet still he could not bring himself to write it. When he poured out his soul, he wanted to be home.

ELINOR READ AND REREAD every letter over and over again. As his letters were more news-filled than lover-like, she took to sharing them with Leighton. And she prayed silently. And prayed. And prayed.

And she followed the war through the posts. Every paper that came from London was filled with the glory of great victories. December brought not only Christmas, but also the chilling news that while the British had taken Bayonne, the cost had been horrifying, a "slaughter" of the victors, the papers called it, and the lists of the dead went on for page after page after page, on and on, and Elinor read every one with dread. They would not notify her, after all, for she had no legal claim on Longford.

In January, when a packet of his letters arrived, some bearing dates beyond the battle, she literally wept with relief. Had it not been for Leighton and her daughter, Elinor thought she would have gone mad. But by now Elizabeth had discovered she could propel herself about by scooting, something that Elinor promptly wrote of to Lucien.

But sometimes in the night, sometimes when the house was silent and dark, she lay awake thinking of him, wondering if he cared anymore. If he did, he never spoke of it in his letters. If he did, he gave her little to believe so. And still she lay there, her body aching with remembered passion, her mind longing for him to hold her again, to tell her he loved her.

In March came letters from Longford, describing Britain's new weapon, the Congreve rocket, which was "extraordinary inaccurate but nonetheless useful, for it sets whatever it hits on fire. We shoot them into the air, and regardless of where they come down, something French burns.'' And the Russians, Prussians, and Austrians crossed into France over the Rhine.

There also was word of another terrible, costly battle, this one costing more than two thousand British lives. And again, Elinor and Leighton scanned the papers looking for Longford's name. But still Britain rejoiced—the Allies were advancing on Paris. At the end of the month, Lucien's letter mentioned sleeping in a ''real bed for the first time in months.''

Days after, April 5, two things happened—Bell Townsend returned to Cornwall, and the papers finally printed the news everyone had been waiting for—Paris had been taken, and thirteen thousand French defenders had died. Elinor prayed for them also, and Bell chided her that it was silly to pray for the enemy.

By Easter, Napoleon was facing abdication, but the British still fought in southern France, and then word came that Toulouse had fallen. The war was over. Even in the relative isolation of the Cornish countryside, church bells rang and there were as many fireworks and bonfires as on Guy Fawkes Day in November. As Elinor breathed her relief, Bellamy Townsend decided he'd wait no longer. He was going to offer for her.

Leighton had come over, played dutifully with his goddaughter, and shared hugs with her that it was over, then he had gone home, leaving Townsend to sup at Stoneleigh. Although it was chilly, Bell suggested after dinner that she wrap herself in a warm shawl so that they could go out and watch the fires sparkle against an unusually clear night sky.

As they walked up a rocky path to the crest of a hill, he caught her elbow, and she knew she ought to go back. But the night was crisp, the smoky air exhilarating, reminding her of the autumn, of another year when she'd been so terribly besotted of Longford. But this was different. As she stole a sidewise glimpse of Townsend's extraordinarily handsome face, she felt nearly nothing.

He knew he ought to wait, that the year was not yet over, that Arthur had died in August, not April, but the news that the war was over, that Longford would surely be coming home soon, pushed him. Finally, he chose a place where a fallen log provided a seat.

''We can see the fires from here.''

She didn't know why she'd come, loneliness perhaps, but she knew she ought to go back. For all that she ached with longing, for all that she wanted to be held, she had no right to let Bell think she could care for him. But his hand tugged insistently, pulling her down beside him, and when she dared to look at him, there was no mistaking the almost lazy desire in his eyes. His fingers traveled lightly up her arm.

"Lady Kingsley," he murmured huskily, "I've waited a long time for this."

"No."

"I'd not ask you to do anything you do not want," he whispered, brushing strands of hair back from her face.

"I'd best go back, my lord. It was wrong of me to come. Elizabeth—"

"It does not bother me that she is Longford's, Elinor," he said softly, drawing her stiff body into his arms. "Come on—" His breath rushed against her ear, sending a shiver down her spine. "It's been far too long for you, hasn't it? You haven't been held by a man in a long time." As he spoke, he turned her head with his hand, and bent to kiss her. For a moment, she yielded to the feel of his body against hers, of his lips on hers, and then she pulled away.

"It's wrong, Bell."

"You want it—admit it."

"Yes—but I owe both of us more than this."

"I can see it in your eyes every day, Elinor."

"That does not make it right."

"Forget Longford," he murmured, tracing the flesh along the edge of her shawl. "I'll marry you. Tomorrow, if you'd like. Take you anywhere—anywhere."

"Bell—"

His lips moved lightly along her jaw, then played with the lobe of her ear. "Want you more than anything, Elinor."

She held herself very still, trying not to respond. "I—I cannot, Bell."

"Yes, you can." He nibbled at her ear, and the warmth of his breath was enticing, tautening every nerve. "Waited through the boy, Longford, Kingsley—don't mean to wait any longer."

She closed her eyes and shook her head. "Please—"

He tipped her over onto the grass and lay beside her. His gray eyes were like silver in the moonlight. A slow, sensuous smile curved his mouth as he watched her. "I know how to please you—I'll make it good."

She turned her head, torn between physical wanting and the certainty that she did not, could not love him. It would be so easy to let him slake her desire, to feed the need within her, to close her eyes and pretend that once again it was Luce that held her, but she knew she couldn't, that it had to be Longford or none.

"No."

"I'm as good as Longford, Elinor—and I want to wed with you."

His hands were warm where they touched her cold flesh, and for a moment, she was still torn. But as his mouth possessed hers, she began shaking uncontrollably.

He did not doubt his ultimate ability to persuade her, but he wanted more than that. As long as he'd waited for her, he wanted it all—he wanted her to love him body, heart, and soul. Reluctantly, he stopped trying to kiss her, and just held her. "It's all right. I love you, you know." When she did not stop shivering, he rolled to sit. "I don't guess it has to be tonight. I can wait a bit longer."

And it was as though something inside her broke. Tears welled in her eyes and her chin quivered. "Bell, I cannot," she whispered desperately. "If I did, it would be because I am lonely—because I would be held—not because I loved you."

"You think me a frippery fellow, don't you?" he said finally.

"No. It's that—"

"I'm not old like Kingsley—nor faithless like Longford, Elinor. I won't look at another." He lifted her chin, forcing her to look at him. "My salad days were good ones, but they are over."

"I—I'm sorry."

"Here—I didn't mean to make you cry." This time, when he drew her into his arms, he felt an aching emptiness rather than passion. "I guess what you would tell me is that it's still Longford, isn't it?"

"Yes. Always."

"Did I ever have a chance?" he asked bleakly.

She shook her head against him. "I have dreamed of him since I was fifteen, Bell."

Her words hurt, but he supposed it was a bitter sort of justice. And while he could not be happy with it, he supposed he deserved it. His arms tightened around her as he let her weep against his shoulder.

"And if he does not come home, I shall die!" she wailed.

"He'll come home," he murmured, smoothing the satin of her hair. "He'd be a fool not to."

She pulled away and sat back, wiping her eyes sheepishly. "I am not usually a watering pot," she apologized.

"And I am not usually a loser—not with a lady, anyway."

"I'm truly sorry."

"It's all right. I wouldn't want a woman who wanted someone else, who had to pretend she wanted me." He rose, pulling her up. "You won't have any difficulty making Luce come up to scratch when he gets home, Elinor. You are not the sort of female a man can easily forget."

"He doesn't love me. But I—I cannot help it—I'd still have him, Bell."

He caught her hand and started back down the path. "You know," he told her, "you're the first woman I ever brought back in tears. Usually we're both a great deal happier than this."

"You'll find someone." She forced a watery smile. "You are far too handsome and far too accomplished not to."

"No. You behold a fellow who will go on as I have always done—until duty makes me settle for someone who can pass on my name." He looked down at her and his mouth twisted. "Grand passions can be deuced painful, you know. I'm not sure I should wish to try this again."

September 17, 1814

ALL SUMMER SHE HAD WAITED, and then she knew. He wasn't coming home. He didn't care about her. Every letter he'd written had been about Elizabeth, not her, and the last one had said that his company would be staying in France as part of the occupation, that he did not know when he'd be home. And that had been more than a month before.

Now as autumn was upon them again, as her birthday had come again, her loneliness was almost desperate. Never again was anyone going to hold her, never again was anyone going to love her. It was almost enough to make her wish she had taken Bellamy Townsend. But not quite.

Every day that she looked in her child's face, she saw Lucien, for it was as though her daughter had gotten nothing of her. The child, now weaned, was already beautiful, a curse Elinor could not wish on her. But as the babe squealed and toddled unsteadily about Stoneleigh, everyone—the lowest footman, the kitchen maids, the tweenies—even Daggett and the Peakes—adored her. It was a wonder she walked at all, for there was always someone eager to carry her.

This day, it looked as though it could rain, making Elinor even more restless, so much so that even the child could not divert her. Finally, as Mary laid Elizabeth down for her nap, Elinor decided to ride. Perhaps the wildness of the wind in her face, of the sea air blowing in across the cliffs would exhilarate her, would make her care that she turned twenty-two, that she still had a long life ahead of her.

Mary looked up, seeing her mistress take out her new green habit. Now that nearly two years of mourning, first for Charles Kingsley, then for his grandfather, were over, she could wear anything she liked. But poor Lady Kingsley, for all that Arthur had left her, was lonely for the company of a man, she told Jeremy. And now that Lord Townsend had left Cornwall—Mary'd heard from one of the grooms that his groom had said they were going to India, of all places—there was only Lord Leighton. And for all that he had was reasonably handsome and exceedingly kind, Mary did not think he was suited to Lady Kingsley.

"It's going ter rain."

"I don't care."

"Ye will if ye catch yer death."

"I won't. I'm never ill."

"Ye going ter take a groom wi'ye?"

"No. The neighbors are used to my peculiar ways. 'The eccentric Lady Kingsley,' " she murmured, mimicking Eliza Thurstan. "It's almost amusing—while an unmarried female or a wife is quite constrained, no one seems to give a fig about the behavior of widows."

"Well, if any was ter inquire, where might I say ye've gone?"

"I thought perhaps I might ride over and ask George if he would come to sup tomorrow night. We've postponed my birthday dinner, anyway."

"Humph! One o' these days, there's going ter be talk," Mary predicted direly. "Even widows oughter not call on bachelor gentlemen unattended."

"George?" Elinor laughed. "Nonsense. He is kind—nothing more."

As she rode over to Leighton's, she could not help thinking that it was exactly two years to the day since she'd gone so shamelessly to Longford's. Two years to the day since she'd thoroughly, completely discovered the pleasures of passion—before she discovered the price.

But now that passion was but a haunting memory. After more than a year of waiting and hoping, she had finally come to realize that he did not mean to come home to her. The dreams that once sustained her, that heated her body at night, were forcefully buried by the realization that if he ever did come back, it would be to see Elizabeth, not her. It was the blood, Mary had said. He couldn't be blamed for being like Mad Jack.

George seemed surprised to see her. "My dear Lady Kingsley, I had expected you to be home today."

"Why? Because it's going to rain?"

"No." He took both her hands and kissed them gallantly. "Did you not hear from Lucien?"

Her breath caught, and she could scarce breathe. Somehow she managed to recover, to respond casually, "No, but I collect he is still in France." But it hurt to think that he'd written to George since his last letter to her. "Did he have any news for you?"

He recovered also. "No—nothing of import."

"Then let us not think of Luce." She flashed him her most dazzling smile. "In fact, I have come to invite you to sup with us tomorrow."

"Tomorrow?"

"Well, today is my birthday, but the apricots did not arrive, so the cook promises the tarts for tomorrow," she explained.

"Your birthday? Never say it has been another year?"

"I am two and twenty, George, so there is no need to make it sound as though I am in my dotage."

"Ah. The sharp tongue," he teased. "And just when I thought you'd come to cast out lures to me."

"Stuff. You are the only friend left to me, and you know it. I should not want to ruin that with a romantical attachment."

"I'll drink to that one. Ratafia?" But even as he said it she made a face.

"For my birthday?"

"Madeira? Port? Hock? Brandy?"

"A small bit of madeira, then I'll have to go before the sky pours." She followed him inside, and her gaze traveled up the portraits that lined the wide staircase. "Distinguished ancestors," she murmured, "particularly the one in the Elizabethan ruff."

"Oh, they're not mine." He grinned apologetically. "Belonged to the last fellow before he lost the place, but they looked better than a bunch of fierce, half-savage Maxwell Scots, so I left them up there."

"Half-savage? Looking at you, I'd not believe it."

"You have not seen me angered, have you?"

"No," she admitted. Then, "Do you never miss Scotland?"

He considered for a moment before nodding. "Yes, but not in the fall or winter."

He opened the front saloon door for her, then walked to pour two glasses from the madeira decanter. Holding one out to her, he offered, "To friends. Or as Luce would have said, 'May there always be truth between friends.' "

Once Longford had used those very same words to her. Her hand shook, nearly spilling the wine. "I—I cannot."

"Sorry. To a brighter day than this one, then."

She sighed. "As the clouds are everywhere, it's not difficult to drink to that." She sipped from the glass, then set it down. "And by the looks of them, I'd best go."

"It's odd—I'd thought you would have been the first he'd written," he murmured. "Perhaps it got lost."

"What?"

"Nothing."

"Then I would you did not say it." She looked out the window, seeing that the wind blew harder. "You know, it might be better if I waited it out."

"You've got time," he assured her.

"One would think you wished to be rid of me," she observed.

"Not at all—just think you ought to go home, that's all. Always glad to have you, but if the storm worsened, if you had to spend the night—"

"My rep's in shreds, anyway," she reminded him. "It would merely be said I am a lonely widow."

"Are you?"

"Yes."

"If I thought I could make you forget Luce, I should be tempted, my dear. But I am not the fool that Bell was."

She stood on tiptoe and brushed a light kiss against his cheek. "Sometimes, George, I wish you were. You are the most comfortable man I know. But you are quite right, as always."

He watched from the window as one of his ostlers mounted her, then he smiled. She was going to be mad as fire when she got home soaked and found Lucien there. Perhaps he ought to have told her, but he didn't think it was his place.

He let the drapery drop, and sighed regretfully. She was a lovely creature, and there was not a man in the neighborhood who did not envy him for her friendship—nor a woman who did not suspect it. And the only difference between him and Bell was that he'd always known he could not beat out Longford. Besides, he was not at all certain he wanted to be merely a "comfortable fellow."

* * *

The clouds rolled in from the sea more quickly than she'd expected, and before long the sky would pour. Already the lightning along the horizon was making Mignon skittish, and in a sidesaddle that could be hazardous. She'd reached the road between Bude and Langston Park, much the same place as that fateful day two years before. A low rumble of thunder decided her. Reluctantly, she turned toward the Park.

The cottage was still there. But she did not know why that surprised her, for it had stood long before she'd been born and no doubt would be there long after she was gone. The first spray of rain came through the autumn leaves, rattling them. Drawn, she dismounted, tied her mare to the post, and tried the door. It swung inward, creaking on its hinges, as she went inside.

It was musty, as though no one had been there in years. For a long time, she stood in the center of the room, her eyes moving to the bed where she'd probably conceived Elizabeth, and the memories that flooded over her made her throat ache until she could scarce swallow. And there was her chair—the rough rug before the empty fireplace. As she looked around, it seemed as though everything was in its place, reminding her that they'd lain together nearly everywhere—in the bed, before the fire, in the big chair . . . And suddenly she was stifled by all of it, choked, and she had to get out.

But when she opened the door again, the rain came down in a solid sheet. Now she wished devoutly she'd not come. Moving back to the empty fireplace, she picked up several hands full of kindling and a ball of lint from the box. The wood ought to be dry after having been there so long. She unfastened her Hussar shako and removed it from her head that it would not fall into the fire, then loosened the braided frogs that closed her jacket, and removed it, exposing the pleated lawn waist. Bending over, she piled wood loosely over the lint and kindling, then searched for the sparker. The flint was still good in it. She squeezed it, striking the flint several times, until the lint finally caught.

It seemed like it took forever to coax the rest of it to catch and she had to keep adding lint. She was so absorbed in the task that she heard nothing until the chill, wet wind swept in the door, and then she supposed she'd not closed it properly. She rose and half-turned, thinking to shut it, and it was as though her heart paused, as though time itself stood silent.

He stepped in and closed the door behind him, throwing the bar, filling the room. Beads of water clung to his scarlet coat. Her gaze traveled upward from the bright brass buttons to the shiny gorget at his neck and then to his face. The faint scar she'd given him was still there, crossing his nose and cheek, but otherwise he appeared whole—and every bit as handsome as she remembered him. She swallowed hard and waited for him to say something.

He drank in the sight of her. Nothing in his memory could compare with her in the flesh, with that copper hair, the amber eyes, the perfect skin. Finally, his mouth curved into the familiar crooked smile.

"I collect you did not get my letter?"

Her whole body shook, as though she'd taken a chill. "No. I thought you still in Paris."

"Until Monday, I was."

"You missed the grand celebration here," she said foolishly, thinking he'd come home a stranger.

He made a face at that. "I heard Prinny made a fool of himself and that the day was Alexander's."

"I did not go." She dared to briefly meet his eyes. "I collect you have come to see Elizabeth."

"I've seen her—I just came from Stoneleigh, then from George's. I'd begun to despair of finding you until I saw the smoke. But you were right in your letters, Nell—she is definitely a beauty."

"I cannot take credit for that, Luce. She looks like you."

It was as though an abyss separated them. For the first time in his life, it seemed as though he had to struggle for the right words. The speech he'd memorized between the Park and Stoneleigh had fled, leaving him to try it from the heart.

"I've a fair notion now of what Arthur told you," he began finally.

"It doesn't matter anymore, Luce. You don't have to explain. That was a long time ago." But as she spoke, she wiped damp palms against her skirt, for she really did want him to say it. Even though she knew, she wanted to hear it.

"Yes, it does. I promised you the truth, always the truth, and you shall have it. After that, the choice is yours." He sucked in his breath, and let it out slowly. "All he ever did, Nell, was plant the seed in my mind, and I let it grow until I could think of nothing else. But it wasn't Arthur in the beginning—I wanted you before that. It was that he gave me *permission*, that somehow it did not seem quite so wrong. But the fault was mine, Nell, for I did not count the cost to you."

She held her breath and said nothing, letting him go on.

His mouth twisted again. "You know you've given me my soul, Nell—you've proven I'm not like Mad Jack. I don't want anybody but you." He moved closer, closing the gap between them. "I love you, Nell—more than anybody, more than anything, and all I could think of as we fought our way up and down the Pyrenees was that I had to live, that I had to come home to you and our daughter." He reached a hand to cup her chin and looked into her eyes. "I want to wed with you, Nell—and if you'd have me, I'd wait no longer." Her eyes sparkled with unshed tears as his other arm encircled her, drawing her close. "There's no one else but you for me, Nell."

"Oh—Luce!" She turned her head into his shoulder, smelling the rain and the wet wool, thinking that surely her heart would burst from what she felt for him. "There's never been anyone but you," she whispered.

His arms closed around her, and he buried his face in the crown of her bright hair, smelling the scent of lavender. "God, Nell, but I've waited too long for this," he whispered.

For answer, she lifted parted lips to his, and he forgot all else. His mouth came down on hers eagerly, hungrily, sending the heat coursing through her, leaving her breathless as she clung to him like life itself. He was there, he was hers, and he was going to love her. His hands left her hair to move possessively over her body, eliciting a desire that was as intense as anything of her memory. She was hot, wanting, and she did not care about anything beyond what he would do to her. Finally, she broke away.

Slowly, while he watched her, his breath catching in his throat, she bent to remove her boots, then stood again to undo the waist and the zona beneath, baring fuller breasts than he remembered. Then she unhooked her skirt and pushed it and her petticoat down, letting them fall to the floor beside the boots. She stood before him naked and beautiful.

"You don't need to wait any longer, Luce," she said softly, daring to meet his eyes.

Wordlessly, he stripped, nearly tearing the metal gorget from his neck, then he walked to her. This time, when he kissed her, her hands stroked the bare skin of his back and hips eagerly, urging him to take her. Holding her, he backed to the bed, then carried her down with him, falling into the depths of the feather mattress. He rolled her onto her back, then lay there for a moment looking at her as her arms reached to encircle his neck.

He bent his head to her breast, touching the nipple with his tongue. Her hands twined eagerly in his hair, tugging at it, opening and closing restlessly, as she squirmed beneath him. As his lips moved upward and his breath caressed her flesh, she arched her neck, giving him access to the sensitive hollow of her throat. Her skin was hot, feverish almost, and still he wanted to prolong the moment, to look into amber eyes made dark with desire. This time, she did not hide from him.

"Make me whole, Luce," she whispered. "Make me whole again."

She moaned and her whole body quivered when he entered her, and then she began to move beneath him, and he forgot everything but the feel of her. He gave himself over to the rhythm, moving, riding, losing himself in what he did to her, until he could wait no longer, and he had to let himself go. Her nails dug into his back, her breath came in great gasps, and her animal cries ended in one long, ecstatic, primordial moan.

"I love you, Nell—I always have," he gasped, collapsing over her.

She lay there, her arms wrapped around him, savoring the completeness of the union between them. Unlike so many things, it had been even better than the memory. Finally, he rolled off her and reached over the side of the bed to fumble among his discarded clothes. When he turned back, he laid a folded paper over her breast.

"Whatever—?"

"Read it," he urged, smiling.

She opened it carefully and saw the archbishop's seal and signature. Her eyes widened. "It's a Special License."

He nodded. "I want the right to lie with you tonight and every night after, Nell. I want the next babe—and all the rest of them to have my name." His dark eyes met hers and he sobered. "But I'm not like Kingsley. I don't want to make you do anything that you don't wish." When she looked as though she might cry, he hastened to add, "I cannot give you Almack's—or promise you social success. But I do love you—and I've got my own fortune."

"As if any of that mattered," she whispered, her throat constricting. "I should be proud to be your wife, Luce."

He leaned over to kiss her, this time quite gently, then rolled to sit. "Come on—you'd best get dressed. I told Thurstan to wait for us until five o'clock. I told him if we weren't there then, you wouldn't have me."

"Luce, all I have is my riding habit," she protested. "I ought—besides, it's raining."

"It doesn't matter to me. You are quite beautiful in anything. And I have brought the carriage." He grinned almost boyishly and reached for her hand, drawing her up from the bed. "Tonight I'd sleep with you at Stoneleigh, then tomorrow I'd take you and Elizabeth to Italy. And when we come back, you can move everything to the Park." He began dressing hurriedly, then stopped to reach again into his coat. "I almost forgot—I hope this fits." He took her hand again, this time to slip a band of emeralds onto her finger. "Do you like it, Nell?"

"It's beautiful, Luce." She hesitated, then blurted out, "But does it have to be Italy?"

"Nell, we'll go anywhere you wish—India even, if you fancy it."

She looked about the small room, then smiled up at him. "No," she said softly, "I should like to come back here, I think."

"Anything you want, Lady Longford—anything you want," he promised her.

Lady Longford. After seven years of longing, she was going to have everything she'd ever wished for. Even his name.